S0-BBJ-241

Praise for *Tenth House*

"Tomasso gives us a ghost story, a love story, a murder mystery and a good detective novel all rolled into one . . . It's riveting from start to finish . . . This guy is GOOD! . . . The characters are terrific and I can't think of anything better on a cold winter's night than another Phillip Tomasso novel as my cat and I curl up in front of the fireplace. Well done!"

—Thom Racina, best selling author of *Hidden Agenda*, *Secret Weekend* and *The Madman's Diary*

"Phillip Tomasso III weaves a tale of mystery and suspense with dark threads of the supernatural. The protagonist, Nick Tartaglia, carries the reader's own sense of incredulity in a way that allows you to suspend your own. TENTH HOUSE is a well-written novel with wonderful characters that come alive on the page . . . I'll be waiting for Mr. Tomasso's next novel."

—Nancy Mehl, *The Charlotte Austin Review*

" . . . A highly original idea for a mystery series . . . "

—Pamela G. Ahearn, *The Ahearn Agency*

"Tenth House is meticulously detailed in both setting and character depth. The story will pull you in, shake you about, disturb you, keep you guessing and always wanting more. It delivers!"

— Keith Rommel, *BookReview*

Praise for *Mind Play*

"*Mind Play*, Phillip Tomasso III's first novel, is a brisk thriller in which TV News reporter, Randy Cook, attempts to defuse a complex network of mental controls that were planted when he volunteered as a college student for an experiment in hypnotic behavior. Ten years after the experiment, he runs a deadly race against himself to unravel the mesh of mystery that obscures his memory and dictates his actions."

—Owen Duke, *Edington Literary Agency*

"Phillip Tomasso III crafts an engrossing and 'edge of your seat' tale of deceit, betrayal and murder . . . The characters are three dimensional . . . This book is almost impossible to put down. The story line and Mr. Tomasso's writing held my interest until the very end."

—Nancy Mehl, *The Charlotte Austin Review*

"Fast-paced and deftly told—Tomasso knows his craft."

—Olivia Boler, author of *Year of the Smoke Girl*

"... A chilling psychological thriller ... a suspenseful page-turner ... a gripping tale ... a beautifully paced roller coaster ride, laced with mystery, greed, murder, and tragedy. As interesting as the major plot of the book is, the meandering sub-plots surrounding the relationships ... are even richer. Rarely are characters so three dimensionally drawn ... Had I not already known that this was Tomasso's first work, I would have thought him to be a well-seasoned novelist. His prose is adept and visually evocative. Like a sculptor, Tomasso deftly handles the psychological thriller genre, hewing out a mystery rolling with suspense and empathy. Mind Play is also a refreshing character piece, blossoming with a blend of humor, insight and realism. This is just the first of what will be a great contribution to the mystery and thriller literary tradition."

—Matthew Butler, *Table Hopping*

"Tomasso has a talent for building consistent characters and bringing them through some fast paced scenes."
—Judi Clark, *Mostly Fiction Review*

"A frightening premise made real; absorbing and scary . . . The reader is gripped and titillated by the brilliantly effective use of plotting and relationships between the affected parties that brings truth to light."
—Robert Tolins, author of
Unhealthy Boundaries

"Tomasso stands as a master conductor, bringing in one exciting movement after another . . . This might be your first time hearing Phillip Tomasso's name. Be assured, however, it definitely won't be your last."
—Jack Pantaleo, author of *Mother Julian and the
Gentle Vampire*

" . . . Every minute of this fast-paced novel is filled with intrigue and emotion. Tomasso is a talented writer who cleverly weaves an intriguing web around the reader's imagination . . . "
—*Patricia C. Behnke,* A Victorian Justice

Also by Phillip Tomasso III

MIND PLAY

Dry BonesAnthology 2000
(Editor)

To my Aunt Gemma,

PHILLIP TOMASSO III

TENTH HOUSE

Thanks for coming out to Eastview!

Phillip Tomasso
3/2001

Dry Bones Press, Inc.
Roseville, CA 95678

The Tenth House
by Phillip Tomasso III

This is a work of fiction. Names, characters, places, and incidents are either the product of the author's imagination, or used fictitiously, and any resemblance to actual persons, living or dead, business establishments, events or locals is entirely coincidental.

All Rights Reserved.
Copyright © 2001 by Phillip Tomasso III
Author Photograph, Copyright © 2000 by Jill A. Tomasso

Library of Congress Card Catalog Number 00–111014

This book may not be reproduced in whole or in part, by mimeograph or any other means without permission. For information Address: Dry Bones Press, Inc., P.O. Box 1437, Roseville, CA 95678 (415) 707–2129

The Dry Bones Press, Inc., World Wide Web address site is:
http://www.drybones.com/

Publisher's Cataloging-in-Publication Data
    FICTION
    Tomasso, Phillip III
    Tenth House / by Phillip Tomasso III
    P   cm.
    ISBN 1-883938-95-3
    1. Thriller 2. Private Investigator 3. Mystery
    I. Author II. Title

First Edition, 2001

Special Thanks

Though I need to thank every one, I would like to give special thanks to the following family and friends: Christine Wrzos-Lucacci, Linda DeCarlis, Stan Zon, Stan Thomas, Cindy Bamford, Michael Keenan, Valerie Richardson, Greg Palmer and Corrine Chorney; to my wife for her continued support— and for the photograph she took on the back cover of the book; to the magic pen that lets me write my own ticket; to God—and finally to my friend and publisher, Jim Rankin, for this wonderful opportunity.

To my wife:
You inspire me . . .

"It is one of the most subtle tricks of the devil to have incited those which he tormented to doubt his existence."

—Charles Baudelaire

Prologue

Six priests clad in black robes, faces hidden under drooping hoods, held hands and encircled the altar. Disciples of the church stood around the holy figures. They sang softly, a Latin hymn. From the priests came a chant, which blended with the rhythms of the song. Orange-red flames danced on the ends of black and white candles set around the room. There were two black candles at diagonal ends of the altar, two white in the opposite corners. Shadows danced on the walls, darkness filled the corners.

A door in the back of the church opened. The singing and chanting died. All heads bowed as a figure in a blood red satin robe entered the room. His face, like the priests, was hidden under a hood. He walked with his hands clasped together in front of him, as if in prayer. The people and the priests cleared a path for him as he walked up to the altar.

The silence lingered. The high priest held his hands in the air, palms up. He began to voice his prayer. The hiss of his words resounded softly, as if being spoken by a room full of snakes.

As the high priest spoke, the people in the room began to softly chant once again. They all held hands and began to sway. The high priest began to speak with vigor and enthusiasm.

The women in the room broke the chain of hands and stepped forward.

"Come on to me," the high priest said, feeling the excitement around him and swelling within himself. "Come on to me!"

The chanting in the room grew more intense. The flames flickered, but did not go out. The smell of fire and burning incense filled the room.

The high priest came down from the altar and walked around the beautiful women standing before him. He smiled, knowing his face was hidden under the hood of his robe. He held his arms out, the tips of his fingers extended and came close to touching the women while he walked around them. "And Satan smiled and he laughed and he devoured," the high priest said. "He devoured, *people*. And the sound of gnashing teeth filled the world as beasts devoured the weak, the undecided and the unfaithful."

The sound of the chant grew louder, became stronger. The flames danced

11

on wicks' end with pandemonium, threatened to go out, but continued to burn. The high priest stood an arm's length away from one young woman. He reached out his hand.

The choice, his choice, had been made. Around him, he heard the chants pick up speed, then fall to whispers. He imaged millions of snakes slithering and hissing around him.

The young woman swallowed, an expression of fear engulfed her previously vacant eyes. She tentatively took a hold of his hand. He smiled, licked his lips.

He squeezed her hand and pulled her in close, wrapped his arms around her, kissed her between her breasts, on the forehead and shoulders. His heart throbbed loudly in his chest, the vibration filled his ears.

The high priest led the young woman to the altar. He ignored the fact that she was crying and trembling. He ordered her to take off her clothes. She refused him silently, shaking her head. The high priest nodded. Two priests in black robes came forward. One grabbed her from behind, his arms wrapped around her chest and restrained her arms. She didn't struggle. The other bent down, pulled off her socks. He unbuttoned and unzipped her jeans and pulled them off her waist and legs. They took off her panties, top and bra then left her standing by the altar in front of the high priest.

She was crying. She had been violated. Assaulted. "No!" She said, crossed one arm over her breasts, placed a hand over her crotch. "No—this isn't right! I don't want to be a part of this. " She screamed. This amused him, aroused him.

The chant began to grow in volume once again, excited by the girl's emotional outburst. The words more clear, fierce. He watched as the young woman twitched as if being sliced by the words in the prayer.

"God, please no. Oh, God!"

The high priest came in close, grabbed her tight above the elbow. He stared intently into her eyes, saw them silently pleading with him to let her go, to chose another. He wanted to laugh in her face, to bite off the tip of her nose. "Quiet, blasphemer! Your soul is already burning in Hell and soon the rest of you shall be, too."

"Let go of me!" She shook her arm free. Her eyes darted around the room. He knew there was no where for her to run. She let out a scream. The two priests stepped forward, again, took her by the arms, held her tightly.

The high priest turned to his altar, mixed liquids in small goblets, poured the potion into a large golden chalice. He mumbled a prayer, eyes closed, swirled the chalice holding it low to the ground. He bowed his head. "Satan, hear our prayer."

"Hear our prayer," the disciples replied.

The high priest took the chalice and, despite her arms being restrained, tried to hand it to the naked girl.

She turned her head away. "Go to Hell!"

"All in good time, my child. All in good time."

The two priests holding her must have tightened their grip. She squirmed, tried to get free. They held tight, controlled her wriggling by wrapping arms around her waist.

"Drink. This is the blood of Satan. It is the blood of the new and ever-lasting. It has been shed for you." The high priest raised the brim of the chalice to her lips.

She moved her head back, then rocked it forward, banging her forehead against the chalice. The contents sloshed around, some splashed out.

"Lay her down," the high priest said. He was annoyed with her and her game. The priests lifted her into the air, placed her on a slab of marble beside the altar. She continued to struggle. Leather straps bound her ankles and wrists.

"Please let me go," she begged. Her last option. Her only hope was to beg, he mused. "Please don't do this. I don't *believe*. I don't want to die. I don't belong here!"

The high priest ignored her pleas. He grabbed her by the back of the head, clenched her hair in his fist and lifted her face to the chalice. He spoke through clenched teeth. "Drink. This is the blood of Satan. It is the blood of the new and everlasting. It has been shed, just for you."

She closed her eyes. She did not like looking into the dark hood of his robe. That she could not see a face, or even eyes, unnerved her. There was little use in fighting. She would ultimately lose. Her head felt weak and felt as if it were spinning. *This can't be happening*, was all that she could keep thinking. *This can't be happening.*

She felt the cold brim of the cup being pressed hard against her lips. Whatever was in the cup smelled badly, spoiled milk and dog food. She refused to willingly open her mouth. A hand grabbed her jaw.

She tried to struggle some more, felt the fight grow within her knowing this could very well be her last chance to get out of this nightmare alive.

Her mouth was forced open, she tried to bite the hand she felt on her teeth, but couldn't close her mouth. She couldn't stand the darkness any longer and opened her eyes. Faces crowded together, poised expectantly over her. She wanted to scream, but the sound was trapped in her thoughts, echoing in the halls of her mind never to be heard.

The high priest poured the liquid into her mouth and then her jaw was snapped and held closed. Another hand grabbed her nose, pinched the nostrils together.

She couldn't breathe. She squirmed on the table, felt pain in her strapped wrists and ankles as she fought for air.

"Just swallow." A whisper by her ear mixed with hot breath and spittle. "Swallow."

The fight was over. She thought she might pass out. Her ears reverberated the pounding of her heart into her skull. She needed air. She swallowed.

The cold fluid burned her throat; it tasted worse than she could have imagined. It was like sucking on pennies dipped in vinegar and feces soaked in blood.

The hands on her face released her. She began to gag. Gasping, she screamed: "Untie me. Untie me right now!" She'd had enough. She wanted to go home. She wanted to get out of this place, away from the sadistic man she knew was staring at her and smiling maliciously from under the shadows and safety of his hood.

Suddenly, he spun around and led the group in prayer.

I'm going to die, she thought lying there alone, listening to the prayers but not wanting to hear the words being said. *I don't want to die!* Her vision blurred, doubled. She felt nauseous, dizzy. Everything around her spun in slow motion at first, then began to spin a little faster. *Is this . . . this table spinning, or is it all in my head?*

She raised her head, it wobbled, and rested her chin on her chest. Her eyes were heavy, wanted to close. She fought to keep them open. The other people in the room began to walk toward her, surrounded her. They all prayed over her, chanted. Their hands raked across her naked body, blessing her. *Get away from me,* she wanted to yell. Her tongue felt swollen in her mouth. Her lips trembled, tears slid down the sides of her face and wet her ears. Sound was muffled. Her ears began to itch. She couldn't scratch them. She ground her teeth, hoping to relieve the discomfort of the itch. She clenched her hands into fists, her fingernails dug into her palms.

The straps restraining her were unfastened. A cramping pain flashed in her belly. She drew her knees up to her chest, wrapped her arms around her legs, hoping to comfort the pain and to cover her naked body. She opened her fists and scratched the itch in her ears. The sensation would not subside. It felt like bugs crawling around inside her ear canal. The tingling itch began to drive her crazy. The pain in her belly came again, only worse this time. She wondered if the odd cramps felt at all like being stabbed; sharp, hot.

I don't want to die, she thought again. *I'm going to die.*

The people came closer to her. Their faces loomed directly over her own. She closed her eyes, felt them touching her, again, rubbing her.

Bile made its way to her throat, sat there, burned. She thought she might vomit, wished she could, but couldn't.

"No," she managed to moan. "Help me." Fleeting thoughts of her mother raced through her mind, filled her memory. *What will mom think? Oh my God, what am I going to tell mom? She's going to hate me. I'll never get to talk to her. I'll be dead.*

She rolled off the table and fell hard on the cement floor. No one tried to help her to her feet. They stood around her, stared at her. She pulled herself up onto her knees and hands, felt like a dog down on all fours. Her head lazily roamed from side to side, up and down. She found it hard to focus, knew that whatever she'd been forced to drink was causing this and was ultimately killing her. A deadly hallucinogen.

They Chanted. Sang.

I hate this song, she thought bitterly, *never liked it.* She did not have the strength to stand, lost the strength or the will to stay on all fours and flattened her body on the cold floor. She rolled onto her side, hands reached out for nothing, anything, something.

Mom, she thought. *Oh God, Mom, I'm so sorry. Please, don't hate me.*

She coughed, choked. Someone whispered, "Look at the blood."

She smelled the blood then, tasted it in her mouth. *Tired*, she thought. *I'm so tired.* Her eyes closed. She fought to open them, strained to use every bit of energy in each eye muscle. Her eyelids fluttered, but stayed closed.

Someone held her legs while others dressed her.

She was lifted off the floor. She felt a coughing spasm coming on, tried to swallow it. She just wanted to throw-up. It felt good to vomit, usually took away some of the nausea. She did not want to cough up blood, though, which would confirm her impending death.

Her head rolled from side to side, no strength to hold it up. She was suddenly outside. She knew because she could no longer smell the musty, moldy scents of the Tenth House church, but smelled instead the fresh air. She was being carried somewhere, her toes dragged on the ground.

15

"God, man," she heard someone say. "How far do we have to carry her?"

"Shut up. He'll hear us talking. We ain't supposed to be talking," she heard someone else say. Men carried her. Their voices were twisted, slow, deep, slurred, like monsters in a horror movie. It was her head messing with her ears, she knew.

"Hey man, he can't hear us."

"He can. We've just got to drop her in the water, like we were told."

She felt cold, did not know if it was cold outside, or if it was her. "Please," she managed to whisper. "Please, help me."

"Shut up, Darla. Okay? Shut up. I can't believe the way you acted back there—"

"Shh! I'm telling you, he'll know we've been talking. He'll hear us!"

Silence. Darla struggled, chewed on her tongue, felt pain, tasted more blood. "Don't let me die, please. Help me. Take me to a hospital. I need my stomach pumped."

"What the hell did you think you were doing back there? You've been chosen. You should be thrilled, ecstatic. You're about to meet a god . . . and how do you show your appreciation, your gratitude? Huh? You struggle and cry and beg like a baby, a coward. I would have expected more from you."

"Shh—"

"No. You shh! You shut up. He can't hear us, not all the way out here. Darla, I want to know, how does it feel to know you're about to die?" one asked as though he admired Darla's situation.

Darla thought about it. One word came to mind. "Scary."

"Huh? Isn't it exciting? Don't you feel like you're about to board a plane and head toward some unknown, all inclusive, vacation resort . . . who knows where?"

"I don't want to die," Darla whispered.

"Sure you do. You just don't know it."

"Help me."

"Security," the other said, demanding silence.

The men fell to their knees and dropped Darla to her belly on the grass. Behind closed eyelids she saw shades of white, perhaps they were headlights, pass by. "Help—"

"Was that a cry for help? It was pathetic Darla. I could barely hear you and I'm not an inch away from your blood covered lips." He laughed.

She was lifted to her feet again.

"Should we leave her right here while we run and get the car? I don't think I want to drag her out to the parking lot. Someone will see us for sure, man. They'll stop us and wonder what the hell we're doing carrying around a comatose girl."

"Yeah. I don't want to cross the yard dragging her body. We'll get caught."

"The parking lot's right there! Leave us here, you run and get the car. Once we drop her into the canal, we can forget about this whole thing. All right? It never happened."

"You feeling freaked out a little?"

"Very. Now hurry up, man. I want to finish this thing up." He dropped Darla down into the grass, sat next to her and held her wrist. She felt an urge to bite him. The itch came back in her ears. Like an animal she began slapping at her head. "Hurry, man. She's flipping!"

Darla could hear the sound of distorted footsteps running away from her. She wished she could focus clearly. Her head was spinning too fast. "Help," she whispered. "Help me."

The one with her lifted her into a sitting position, held his arm around her shoulders, as if they might be a romantic couple getting frisky on the lawn. "Shut up," he told her. "Please, just shut up."

A sudden churning sensation began to rumble in her stomach. She tried to comfort herself by holding her belly. She knew she was about to vomit this time and welcomed it. She felt it brewing, boiling. She feared throwing up, knew it would be the end of her life. Like a rocket being launched from the pit of her stomach, blood and bile sprayed from her mouth and nose.

"Jesus, man," the one who held her said and pushed her away as he stood up.

Darla gagged on the blood, couldn't get it out of her mouth fast enough. She started to choke. Her hands grabbed at her throat. She couldn't breathe.

Mom . . . someone, Darla thought, *help me, help me!*

Spasms overtook Darla's body. She flopped around on the grass. Her eyes opened. The grip she had on her throat tightened, her fingernails dug into her flesh. The spasms stopped. Her eyes stayed open and her hands remained wrapped around her throat.

Chapter 1

The coffee mug sat nestled between my thighs. It was a ritual; waking up late, grabbing a cup of coffee, no time to drink it, hop in the car and put the cup between my legs on the way to work. The most difficult thing is trying to remember to bring the cups back into the house at the end of each day. I don't mean to be a slob, I just always have been.

The car radio was tuned in to a song I loved, but didn't know the words to, which forced me to mumble my way through the chorus. This was all right with me. I am, after all, my own best audience.

I made a right turn onto Long Pond Road. There she was. The jogger.

The best I could tell, she jogged every morning. The only times I didn't see her was when I was running later than usual; we seemed to be on similar schedules.

She exercised with dedication and determination. It was obvious—the outstanding figure—she was the beneficiary of practiced discipline.

She wore her mid-back length, straight blond hair in a ponytail. It bounced across her back while she ran; swinging like a pendulum and keeping in time with the rhythm of her run.

On this hot September morning, she looked wonderful in a white tank top. Her back was tanned, sweaty. Long legs, tightly wrapped in black running pants, moved her gracefully and with speed up the bridge over the Erie Canal.

I drove past her, eyes reverting to the rearview mirror. One last glimpse. Eyes back on the road.

A young man jogged in the opposite direction. He was tall, dressed in a navy blue sweatshirt, red shorts with white stripes down the sides, white tube socks with three red rings and black Nike running shoes.

Looking back to the rearview, I saw her jog down the side of the bridge, her stride never breaking. The male jogger was about to run past her, in the opposite direction. I shook my head. He's got it all wrong. Stop. Turn around. Run with her. Ah, if only I had the energy to jog.

Suddenly, the male jogger tackled the woman, knocked her off the side-

18

walk into the tall grass.

When I slammed on the brakes, the coffee spilled onto my legs. I tensed, waiting to get burned. It was cold. I put the car in reverse. At the spot where the woman was tackled, I stopped and jumped out of the car, leaving it parked across my lane, one tire up on the curb. My gun—a Glock Model 20—was in its shoulder holster, tucked safely under my seat. I reached for it, my fingers searching, but found nothing. I could not waste anymore time, so I left it.

Where had he taken her? Under the bridge?

I ran through waist-high weeds, heard the sound of my heart beating in my ears and grass being trampled on. My body responded to the humidity and started perspiring immediately.

The bridge grew like a dark mass along side of me. The streetlights did nothing to penetrate the blackness as I swerved around the trunks of maple trees, ducked under branches thick with leaves.

I heard the sound of struggling; muffled cries, grunts.

"Hey! Hey," I started to shout before I could see anyone. "Let the girl go!"

Coming out of the trees, the street lamp at the arch of the bridge provided enough light to see the canal. I stopped running just before plunging into the water. Spun around.

She was on the ground, still dressed. The male jogger was on top of her, knees pinned her shoulders, and hands tried to cover her mouth. "I said, let the girl go!" I hoped I sounded fierce.

If we fought, it could go either way. He might be in better shape, but as a trained private investigator, I've run into worse scum than the likes of him—and walked away the winner. This man seemed a coward who thrived on hurting women. I was pretty sure I could take him.

"Take care of this dope, huh, guys?" the male jogger asked. He ignored me, went back to attacking the woman.

"Guys?" I asked, baffled.

"Yeah, guys. Is there some problem with our buddy asking us to break in your face for him?"

I turned around. Two men stood behind me. "Problem," I said. "No. There's no problem." Great. This is just great. I should have looked for the Glock a little longer! I smiled, took a step back.

"And just where do you think you're going?" the larger of the two asked. He was built like me, five-ten one-hundred and eighty pounds.

"To stop your *buddy* from hurting the girl," I said.

"Help me! Help me, please," the girl begged. She screamed.

19

"Oh, you think that's what you're going to do, huh?" the smaller guy asked. He had hair like mine. Shoulder length, wavy, brown.

"No," I said. "I know that's what I'm going to do." I kicked the bigger guy in the testicles with all my strength. He doubled over. I grabbed a fist full of his hair, raised his head a few inches, brought it down and brought my knee up. When the two collided, something audibly crunched. My knee was fine, I assumed his nose is what broke. I let go of his hair and he fell to the ground. His hands cupped his face. Even in the dark, I could see the blood seep from between his fingers.

Staying on the ground, he cried. "My nose. You broke my nose!"

The smaller guy came forward, leery.

"Watch out," the girl screamed.

I spun around and sidestepped to the right. The male jogger was nearly on me. A quick punch to his stomach stopped his run, bent him forward. I slammed my elbow down on his spine, up near the base of his neck. He fell next to his buddy. Both groaned, looking to be in a lot of pain.

The smaller guy moved around the others. He took a step at me. "Get lost," I told him. "Go on, get out of here!"

He wanted to run. I could see it in his face.

I heard the quick burst of a siren coming from above. A bright light suddenly shown in my face, enlightening the area. "This is the police. No one move," a voice boomed from a bullhorn.

"I told you to get. Now it's too late," I teased. "Sorry pal. Looks like you're about to get arrested." I smiled.

While the two on the ground tried to get up, the smaller guy ran for the trees. I chased him, dove at his heels, caught his foot and sent him tumbling into the brush. He kicked at me, squirmed. I punched the back of his thigh, got to my feet and jumped onto his back.

"Freeze! Freeze right now," I heard someone saying. Hopefully the police had caught the other two thugs.

I grabbed the small guy by the back of his shirt and lifted him onto his feet. He squirmed some more, trying to punch and kick me. I gave him a right hook into the kidneys. He grunted. I hit him again—for good measure.

The girl and I stood by my car. The two police officers were cuffing and locking the men in the back of the squad car. In the east, the sky was changing from black to midnight blue with swirls of scarlet and lilac. I took a deep breath, tasting the humidity, thick, wet.

"Are you okay?" I asked Judy Swanson. I stood in front of her, my hands safely in my pockets. I did not want her to see me as a threat. Even though I'd helped her, right now I wouldn't blame her if she didn't trust any man.

"I'm okay. They didn't hurt me. God, you showed up at the right time," Judy said, quickly. Her bottom lip began to tremble. She tried to keep it still with her teeth, but started to cry. "They were going to hurt me. I've never been so scared in my whole life."

"It's over now," I said, softly. "They can't get near you."

"But if you hadn't of come—"

"I did come. Just forget the 'what ifs'. The police have the scum. It was a close call, but, well, you didn't get hurt, right? Scared real good, but for the most part, you're okay?" I asked.

"Yeah," she said, sniffling. "I'll be okay. Thank you."

"It'll work out. After you file a report with the police—"

"A report?" she asked.

Her eyes were blue-gray. I could not help but stare into them. "Yeah. You file a report against the three of them, they get prosecuted and they go to jail. It sounds complicated and it is a little, but not—"

"But they know what I look like. What if I file a report and they don't go to jail?"

"They'll go to jail."

"How can you promise me that? I read about things like this all the time. Women get raped, report it and they're the ones made to look like the criminals. The rapist ends up becoming the victim, gets more rights. Uh-uh. There's no way I'm going to let myself get humiliated," she said.

"Judy, you won't be alone. Unfortunately when a woman is raped, she's alone, there are rarely any witnesses. The whole court scene becomes her word against his. You have a witness. Me. I'll be with you," I said, smiling.

Judy looked over her shoulders, folded her arms. "Yeah?"

"Yeah," I said. I didn't want her to walk away from this. She had a certain responsibility to try and put these guys away. If she didn't go with the police, then the thugs could potentially be set free with little more than a slap on the wrist. This could not be their first time hurting a woman. The scene was too planned. If they walked, there was a good chance they'd just find a new victim. "What do you say?"

Before she could answer the police officer who had shown the light and arrested the three assailants walked over. He kept one hand on the butt of his nightstick, the other on the butt of his service revolver. He stood roughly five-ten, two hundred and thirty pounds, most of it fat. He had a horseshoe

21

head of hair and his scalp glistened with sweat under the streetlights.

"I know you," he said. "You're an investigator with Safehouse?"

"Nicholas Tartaglia. Nick. That's me," I said, casually. I saw Judy's eyebrows arch some as I shook hands with the police officer. Was she impressed?

"Yeah, well, I'm Mike Callister. I'm glad I happened upon your car there, parked half on the curb the way it was. I called in your plates, got out to take a look and heard someone scream. It sounded like it came from under the bridge. You done good Mr. Tartaglia. Miss, are you okay?"

"I think so. Yes," Judy said. She rubbed her hands up and down her folded arms.

"We're going to need to fill out a detailed report, okay? Mr. Tartaglia—"

"Nick, really."

"Nick, you told me quickly what happened, but let's go over it again slowly. All right? We can do it here, or if you want to get more comfortable and out of the heat, you can follow my partner and I down to the station. Which would you prefer?"

"Well," I said, hesitantly.

"My car's full," Callister said, "and besides, it don't have any AC. Without any breeze, sitting in that hot box even with all the windows down still makes you feel like you're baking in an oven. Know what I mean?"

"I guess we could go to the station," Judy said. She bit her lower lip, looked at me.

"I was on my way into work," I said. Judy frowned. "But there shouldn't be a problem," I finished. Judy smiled as I remembered my cell phone was in the car with my gun. I could call and tell them I'd be late, after all, I did tell her I'd help her every step of the way. How could I let her down?

"You want to follow me, the two of you? Ms. Swanson you can ride with me," Officer Callister said, as he looked at his squad car and sneered at the men locked in his back seat. "Or if Mister—Nick here wants to give you a ride?"

"I can give her a ride," I said. "That wouldn't be a problem."

Judy bounced on her toes. "That's fine," she said. "I'll ride with you, Nick."

"Great," Callister said, as he turned and waved to his partner who hopped in behind the steering wheel of the squad car. "Just follow us. We'll try to get this done as quickly and as painlessly as possible and have the both of you on your way. Okay?"

Judy tried to smile. Pursing her lips tightly together, she managed a grimace.

I watched Callister walk back to his car. "You have anyone to call?" I asked. I opened the passenger door.

Judy hopped in. "No," she said while reaching for the seat belt.

I closed the door, went around the front of the car and hopped in. I started the engine. "Hang tight," I said, for lack of anything better to say. "We'll get this over with. Put the whole thing behind us in no time." It was an empty, though sincere, promise. It served its purpose. It gave me comfort, anyway.

Chapter 2

Safehouse Investigations was located in Brighton, housed on the sixth floor of a plain red brick-faced building, with parking in the rear. Once on the right floor, I walked down the hall, stepped through the clear glass doors and smiled at the receptionist.

Betty looked to be in her late forties with thick, curly brown hair and large brown eyes. Tiny wrinkles, like arrows without heads, pointed from all directions at a mouth hidden under several coats of maroon shaded lipstick.

Neglected were her computer, a phone with a single line and an open calendar book all precisely arranged on the face of a large cherry wood desk. There was also an "in" and "out" tray, both empty. A well cared for plant sat in a corner of the desk. The leaves reached out of the small pot, beginning to stretch across the desk.

Betty returned my smile. "Where've you been? Everyone else is out to lunch. "

"I tried calling twice. The line was busy. What's up with voice mail?" I asked, smiling. I was annoyed.

"I wasn't aware that there was a problem. I'll look into it," Betty said. "You look terrible."

"I had a rough morning," I said flatly and quickly told Betty about Judy's run-in and how I had played the role of the gallant hero. There was no need to embellish on the story. The scenes I'd described told it all.

"Poor thing," Betty said. She rested her elbows on the desk and folded her hands. What happened to Judy obviously upset Betty. I was still upset myself.

"I know, it's awful," I said. "Oh, if an Officer Mike Callister calls or the girl, put them right through. I gave her one of my cards so she could get in touch with me if she needed to. Okay? "

Callister had taken forever filling out the police report; between bites on his bagel and his hunt-and-peck typing method, I thought for sure we'd never get out of there. Callister's office could be no better than his car. It was

24

small, cluttered and felt like something needed to be done to cool the place down. I felt worse for Judy. She looked embarrassed and tired. I could tell she mostly wanted to get home out of her running clothes and maybe take a shower. After a while Callister moved us to a conference room. The conditions were a little better. Judy and I felt less like we were being interrogated. There was more room and a large table instead of the desk. Things went smoother. Though I begged Callister, he wouldn't let me do the typing.

"No problem," Betty said. "Ned asked about you. "

Ned Baxter was the owner-slash-head detective. He'd served over ten years with Vice in Florida; took a bullet near the heart five years back on a drug bust gone awry. When he realized how close to death he'd come he retired and moved to New York. He worked with a detective agency for one year, which is where we met, but he hated having a boss. So, he decided to open Safehouse. I've been with him from the get-go. "He in his office? "

"Out to lunch with some of the others."

"Let me know when he gets in. Anything new?" Business was slow. Besides Ned and myself there was one other private investigator, two assistants and Betty, our fearless receptionist-slash-secretary.

"Not this morning. I billed the Cappelli's and the Smyth's," Betty said.

They were the two cases I'd just resolved. "Great. It's been so busy the past few months I just can't get used to things being this slow," I said. I had been working at least two cases at a time since May. Fourteen hour days, five—mostly six—days a week. Then, all at once, things died. I was the kind of man who needed to keep busy. I didn't have any kids and wasn't married. There was no girlfriend, or boyfriend for that matter. I enjoyed working and loved my job. In that sense, I was lucky because my job was all I had. Little else mattered.

"Relax a little Nick. Enjoy these quiet times, too. Business will pick up, always does."

Betty was right. Business always had its waves. Most of the time you were on top, zipping along, trying to keep your balance. But then the times did come when you sat back and waited for the calm to end. "Yeah. Sure, I know. Okay, listen, I'll be in my office. Anything comes over the wire—"

"I know, give you a buzz. Go and relax." She dismissed me with a wave of her hand and a sigh.

"Gotcha," I said. I sauntered away, both hands in my pockets. The entire foyer, covered in plush beige carpeting, reminded me of a foyer you might find in a large and wealthy law firm. My office was to the right, Ned's to the left. Just the two of us had private offices. Without the title, I was like

25

Ned's partner.

The blinds were drawn open over the windows along the back wall over three office cubicles. The sun showed through brightly. It looked like one hell of an afternoon. Too bad I felt as if my day had been spoiled.

Glancing at my watch, I couldn't believe it was nearly one o'clock already.

In my office, sitting in the black leather chair in front of my desk was a young woman. I snorted. "Can I help you? Does Betty know you're in here?" I asked. "Betty?" I called out the door.

"Yeah Nick," Betty called back.

"I thought you said there was nothing new?" I asked, flashing a smile at the young woman.

"There isn't," I heard Betty holler back.

I smiled again at the silent woman. She smiled in return. "Can you excuse me for a moment, Missus . . ?"

"You can call me Darla."

"Okay Darla, let me just check something out with our secretary," I said.

"She doesn't know I'm here, Mr. Tartaglia."

"Obviously." I held up a finger. "Just give me a minute." This was embarrassing. How could Safehouse project a professional image, and a sense of security, if people could come in, sit down and have no one in the office know they're here? Aren't we supposed to be extra alert and observant?

Darla's smile lingered.

I went back to the reception area. "Betty, there's a girl in my office. Her first name is Darla. I didn't get a last name. Didn't you see her?"

"That's impossible, Nick. I haven't been away from my desk all morning. Not even to use the bathroom. If someone were in your office I would have seen her come in," Betty argued. She looked angry. I wasn't calling her a liar. She seemed to think I might be.

"Well," I smiled, "just the same, there is a young woman in my office. Can you give me a company application? I can have her fill it out while I talk with her." I clapped my hands together. Back in the saddle. Dry spell's over.

Betty opened a file cabinet drawer, removed a stapled form, slipped it under the clasp of a clipboard and stood up. She took a pen out of a jar on top of her filing cabinet. "If you don't mind, I'd like to give this to Darla and while I'm at it, ask her how in the hell she got into your office without me seeing her?"

I stepped aside. "Be my guest, but be kind. We don't want to frighten anyone away."

Betty smiled brightly.

"Try not to show so many teeth, it's rather intimidating," I teased.

She scowled. "You think?"

Betty walked into my office, came back out. "Are you pulling my leg here, or what?"

I gave her a look that said, *what in tarnation could you possibly be talking about you crazy-lady, you.*

"There's no one in your office and despite having time for games, I don't feel like playing any, Nick." She walked briskly at me, handed off the clipboard and strode on by. "Hang on to it in case your imaginary client returns. Now if you don't mind, since everything is quiet, I'm going to use the little girls' room. You can man the phone, right?"

"When it rings, I answer it. Sounds simple enough. You go on and enjoy yourself. I should be able to hold the fort," I said, laughing.

Was Betty pulling my leg? There had been a girl in my office. I saw her. Young, pretty, quiet. Stepping into my office, I laughed again. Darla still sat, smiling in the leather chair. "Is this a joke?" I asked. "Betty," I yelled. "Is this a joke?"

A door slammed closed from across the way. Betty didn't answer me. "It's Darla, right?" I set the clipboard down on my desk.

"That's right," Darla said.

She sat with her hands folded in her lap. She had pretty, auburn hair, was dressed in a white turtleneck, white jeans and white sneakers. Her eyes looked unnaturally large and round. They were beer bottle brown. She looked familiar but I couldn't place the face. "The joke's over Darla. Ha-ha, it was funny and everything, I'm just too tired to laugh in hysteria, I guess. Tell Ned—"

"This is no joke, Mr. Tartaglia. I need help, your help." She stared at me intensely. Then the look softened. Her expression said she was sad, but scared. I'd seen the look before but seeing it on Darla was different. There was something odd about her. It was, I'll admit, intriguing.

Smoothing my tie against my chest, I walked around the desk and sat in a chair identical to the one Darla sat in. "My help? So the joke must go on, huh? Okay, I'll bite. What's troubling you?" Picking a pencil up and rolling it in my fingers, I leaned back in the chair. I continued to study her, searching my memory for a place where I might have seen her before, knowing for certain that I had. Ned liked to test me. Usually he'd verbally assault me with a situation, giving me minutes to solve the case. I'll have to admit, he was becoming more and more creative. I liked tests, they kept the mind sharp, kept me on my toes.

"When I was murdered last year I—"

"Whoa, whoa. Hold on there. Maybe you'd like to rephrase that opening statement because from where I'm sitting you don't look like you're dead," I said, leaning toward the desk, holding the lead tip in one set of fingers and the eraser in the other. I glanced at the clock. It was getting late. I was starving. I'd missed lunch. My stomach rumbled.

"No," Darla said.

"'No', what?" I asked.

"No, I would not care to rephrase my opening statement. I was murdered last year, in October. I—"

"Okay." I stood up, dropped the pencil and straightened my tie. "I've had enough. I'm going to grab a little something to eat. It's been a really long, really weird, completely trying morning. I haven't even had a cup of coffee yet." I thought of the cup that spilled on my lap. Luckily my pants were dark. The stain did not show.

"I need to tell you my story," Darla begged. So pretty, so young. I felt bad for her, delusions and all. I wondered if she might be homeless. The homeless often suffered from mental problems. The way she was dressed, I realized she could not be homeless. Another reason for coming to this conclusion? She didn't reek of body odor. Nice clothes, no body odor. Deciding factors in my book.

"Do you have any idea how expensive my time is?" I wanted to sound big, important, more expensive than I was.

"No. How expensive is your time?" Darla asked.

"I charge two hundred dollars a day and that doesn't include expenses," I said smugly. There was no way this kid could come up with that kind of money and we both knew it. Hopefully this realization would put an end to the little prank. "Well, I'm going to lunch, but my spirit will stay behind and take notes," I said, pointing to my empty chair. "He only charges half of what I charge. Spirit," I mocked, "take down everything she says. What she has to say is very important and I don't want you to miss a word. Got it?" Darla looked hurt. I couldn't help myself. "Don't worry. The spirit will get it all. His spelling's not the best but he's reliable." I headed for the door.

"Mr. Tartaglia?"

The sound of her voice stopped me, it sounded like she was going to cry. I'm not mean, a hard ass maybe, but mostly I was just hungry. "What?" I said, turning around.

She was gone.

"What the hell's going on, Betty? I just tore my office apart. How was it done, with mirrors? It's good. It's a great trick . . . I'll give you that. I mean, you had me," I said. I leaned in close to Betty's desk. "Hilarious, brilliantly executed. I give the illusion two thumbs up!"

Betty just stared at me. I snorted, shook my head. "Come on, where's everybody hiding?"

"Unless they all came back from lunch while I was in the little girl's room, I'm going to guess they're still stuffing their faces," Betty said. She looked at me oddly for a second, tilting her head to one side. Then, dismissing me, removed a mystery novel from a desk drawer. She read book after book with enthusiasm, consuming them as if they were filled with valuable information. Maybe they were her college textbooks on how to become a private investigator? Every year for Christmas and for her birthday, I knew exactly what to get her. A gift certificate from *Barnes and Noble*. "So what? I'm supposed to believe you did this whole stunt on your own?" I asked, head bobbing up and down, hands on hips, toe tapping

"Are you suggesting that because I'm a female and a secretary that I wouldn't be capable of pulling off a stunt?" She asked nonchalant-like. Her eyes never came off the pages. Long slender fingers held the book open. She chewed her upper lip while she read.

"So you did this all by yourself?"

She closed the book, using her index finger as the bookmarker. "You know what Nick? I haven't got a clue as to what in the hell you're talking about. I know you had a rough morning and everything, but try to relax. Go home and take a nap. You could use the break." Betty opened the novel back up and leaned back in her chair. Her eyes moved across the page, but this time I could tell she was watching me, perhaps waiting for me to walk away. I was watching her watching me, and I wondered how long she could keep up the act.

"You're good Betty. I've underestimated you." I wasn't going anywhere. "You're not going to tell me then?"

"Tell you what, Nick?" She closed her book, using her finger again to mark the page.

"How you made the girl appear and disappear in my office," I said. This was getting old. I'd had enough.

"What girl, Nick?"

"Darla."

Betty stared at me for nearly a full minute. "You're serious, aren't you?"

"Dead serious," I said.

"You really think someone was in your office? That's not possible. I already told you that. Nick, I went in your office, no one was there. I didn't see anyone." Betty smiled at me, sympathy on her face. "You look tired—"

"I am tired, but that's not what I'm talking about here," I said. I stuffed my hands into my pockets. "So you're saying it wasn't a trick?" I felt hot, thought a headache might be coming. I started to grind my teeth. I know what I saw and this was pissing me off.

"No. I honestly, honestly have no idea what, or who, you think you saw in your office," Betty said.

"You don't?"

"I don't. But if it'll make you feel better, I'll go and take another look?"

"No," I said, remembering my mother checking my bedroom at night before going to sleep. She'd look under the bed and in the closet. Some nights I would tell her to check twice. Feeling humiliated thinking about this, I said, "She's gone now." It came out in a whisper.

"She's gone now?"

"Vanished," I said, regretting the words the second after they were spoken.

"Vanished? Okay. Nick, I'm not asking you to go home and rest, I'm telling you to go home and rest," Betty said, setting her book aside.

Now what? What the hell was going on? I didn't want to sound *loony*, although the way Betty was staring at me, I had no doubt she was thinking I'd lost it. "I'm just tired, like you said. I'm not ready to go home, though. I'll be in my office."

"You sure you don't want to just go home, Nick?"

"Thanks Betty. I'll be fine. I'm okay." I turned to go, but turned back. "Hey, when Ned gets in, can you not—"

"Not a word, Nick. You just freaked out. I do it all the time. Never at work, but I *do* do it all the time." Her smile relaxed me some. More now, than ever before, I noticed how motherly Betty looked.

Thanking her was all I could do. I went back toward my office, stood outside the closed door. I grabbed the knob and turned it slowly pushing the door open. The room was empty. I sighed, shook my head, hopefully clearing away the cobwebs restricting rational thought waves.

I sat in my chair, threw my feet up onto the desk, crossed my legs at the ankles, laced my fingers, arms behind my head, leaned back and sighed. "What is wrong with you, Nick," I said out loud.

"Mr. Tartaglia?" said the voice of Darla.

She was in the chair again. Quickly, I slid my legs off the desk and leaned forward, staring intently. "Who the hell put you up to this? I don't find it funny and I'm not in the mood. I had a rough morning—"

"I need your help."

I stood up. A joke is a joke, but this was not amusing.

"I was murdered last year," Darla continued.

I walked around the desk.

"I don't know for sure who did it, but I know he's going to kill again on Halloween night," Darla said. Her eyes pleaded with me, begged for me to listen.

"You say you were murdered last year, right?" I said.

"That's right."

"But you don't know who did it," I said.

"Yes. That's right."

"Well, I mean, if you're dead, you're obvious proof of an after-life. Can't the big *G* help you any?" I said. "Because if He doesn't know who killed you—"

"Mr. Tartaglia, I'm trying to tell you. I'm not an angel."

"Oh? Okay then. Why—after nearly a whole year—are you coming to see me? I mean, I could have been looking into this for months. Why didn't you come and see me right after you died? Who knows, if so much time hadn't lapsed, we might have caught the person—that's saying I'm buying into this, which, by the way, I'm not—responsible for your death. Right?" I said.

"Mr. Tartaglia, when you are murdered you don't just come back. There's a very long process, it's tough to explain."

"Purgatory?" The 'way station' between heaven and hell. Catholics used to believe in this place. Recently, they've shunned the idea. I wonder why after so many centuries they didn't believe in it any more?

She nodded. "Purgatory is nonsense. I can't explain where I am, or how I got there. It's not purgatory though. You have to trust me."

"Trust you? With all my heart I do. Why should you feel differently?" I said.

"All right, Mr. Tartaglia, I know I'm asking for a lot from you, here. Let's just say there's a very long process you must go through after dying, you won't understand it until you have to go through it. But back to the

31

point, the cult only meets during the school year."

I wasn't listening and I didn't believe her. "I need for you to leave my office," I said, reaching to grab her arm. My hand passed through her, grabbed air. I spun around. Where were the mirrors? Where was the real Darla hiding?

I looked quickly around the office, found nothing odd or out of place. Darla sat patiently, stared, waited. "I know you don't believe me, but I'm not a ghost."

"That's good, because I don't believe in ghosts." I stood in front of the illusion, waved my hand through her. She wasn't transparent; I couldn't see through her. She looked solid, real. "It's a good trick, really."

"I'm a spirit, I guess you'd say *like* an angel, but I'm not an angel either. I haven't been to any place where angels exist," Darla said.

"Is that so," I said. "Angels are a pretty hot topic on earth right now," I moved my hand around behind her, on the sides. Tried to touch her hair, but couldn't. "Where is the light source coming from because you've got me stumped, I can't figure out how you're being projected."

"Mr. Tartaglia—"

"Call me Nick, please."

"Mr. Tartaglia, I'm serious. You have to listen to me. A young girl's life is in grave danger. She's going to be sacrificed," Darla said. She looked like she might start to cry. Her expression appeared genuine.

"Listen, I'm having fun and everything, truly impressed but I'm starving," I said, a hand across my belly. "I missed lunch remember?"

"Nick, you have to listen to me. Please, just hear me out."

"You're a ghost, right?" I asked.

"No. A spirit."

"Whatever," I said. "Is your spirit trapped here?" I smiled. "Or are you free to roam?"

"To roam?" Darla asked, confused by the question.

"Yeah, like I said, I'm hungry. If you really want to talk, then come along. I'll buy you a taco, or something." I stuffed my hands into my pockets, bounced on the balls of my feet. I knew I had her now. The gig was up.

"I'm not bound to this room but I am bound by time."

"Ah, time. Yeah, that always tends to ruin a schedule, gets in the way and everything," I said, scratched at the back of my ear. "Okay well if you're still here when I get back, we'll talk." I turned to go. Before shutting the office door, I looked back. Darla was gone, again.

Before leaving the agency I said to Betty: "Tell Ned, great trick."

32

"Whatever, Nick. Have a good night. Get plenty of sleep."

"I'm not going home, just out to grab a quick bite," I said.

I strolled down the hall mulling over the illusion. She looked Hollywood-real. I would have to give Ned a lot of credit, find out how he did it and see if I could borrow the equipment and freak the hell out of my parents some day.

Smiling, I waited for the elevator. The doors opened. Inside the otherwise empty car stood Darla.

"There you are," I said. "That was great. Great acting. Do you go to school for this?" I stepped on, reached to shake her hand, passed through what should have been warm-blooded flesh. "Jeez!" The elevator doors closed. "How is this happening?"

"This is not a trick. It's no illusion. I'm a spirit Nick, here, *begging* for your help."

My sanity was slipping. Real? Illusion? The question continued to replay itself in my head. I couldn't accept this image of Darla as being real. That was crazy, and yet, how could she disappear and reappear? How could Ned have known I would use the elevator and not the stairs? I suppressed an urge to laugh like Dr. Frankenstein at the moment he discovered his creation was alive. It's alive! Alive! A-ha-ha-ha!

"You're not going insane," Darla said, as if reading my mind. "It may feel that way, but you're not."

"Great," I said. "Okay, great. Thank you Doctor Darla. So you're a spirit here to save a girl from—what did you say—becoming a sacrifice?" I asked. "Why me, then? Out of all the police agencies, private investigators—why me?"

"Because. Before I was murdered my mother was going to come to you for help. She thought you might be able to help her save me." The words were spoken softly, sounded sincere. The spirit-girl looked truly troubled.

"From this killer?" I asked.

"From myself."

"From yourself. Of course," I said. I looked around the small elevator car. There were no mirrors, no extra lights.

"I was part of a cult on a college campus," Darla began to explain.

"Oh, a cult. Uh-huh, I see."

"My mother lost her nerve," Darla said. She looked at the ground. Embarrassed to look me in the eyes? "I don't blame her for not trying to help me. I mean, she did try, she just didn't get any professional help, someone like you, you know what I mean? She didn't know what was really going on.

33

She couldn't bring herself to call you. Then soon after the fact, I was found dead. A drug overdose—choked on my own vomit. They threw my body into the Erie Canal, made it look like I was so messed up from the drugs that I'd lost my balance, fell in," Darla said. She sounded defensive: "But I didn't take the drugs."

"No? Someone forced you to do drugs?" I laughed. Why was I talking to a figment of my imagination? That's what I believed now. There was no Darla except in the deep recesses of my mind. Somehow I'd brought a vague memory to life. Hell, I was just like Dr. Frankenstein then, wasn't I? Darla was my monster—albeit beautiful.

"Yes. Someone did force me, literally."

I sighed. This was too unreal. Forget lunch. I needed to see a doctor. "Look—"

"No, *you* look. It was too late for me. I died. But it's not too late for the other girl," Darla said, pointing an angry, trembling finger in my face. She started to cry.

"And who is this girl?" I heard myself asking and could not believe my ears.

"I don't know who she is. Not yet."

"Of course not," I said. Unbelievable. The elevator doors opened. I walked off. Darla walked beside me.

Holy Cow. Someone in the lobby would say something about the holographic image walking with me. No one stared at me. No one said as much as *boo.* They could all see the image, right? Or was I seriously losing some marbles here? I felt nauseous, closed my eyes and walked out the doors to the parking lot. Darla was gone.

I sat behind the steering wheel, started the engine and put the shifter in drive. Darla appeared, suddenly sitting beside me. "Jesus!"

"Sorry, Nick."

"Sorry? Sorry? If you're so sorry you'd put an end to this ridiculous game. It's not funny. I told you already, I'm not in the mood. So end it! Okay, just stop it!"

"Nick—"

"No. No, Nick. No, please listen. I'm done. I've played along with the whole stupid game!" I was really upset because, I knew there was no way Ned could be playing a trick. He could not project Darla's image so completely in my car. I had to be losing my mind, a few sandwiches short of a picnic.

Darla cried. "He chooses the girl on the night of the sacrifice. No one knows beforehand who it will be. I didn't know I was going to be chosen that night, and when I was, I wanted to run. I realized everything I'd done wrong the instant he picked me. I was part of an evil cult and I was about to die because of it. All I wanted was for my mother to come into that dark room and rescue me."

"Do I know your mother? Who is she that she was going to call me to try and save you from yourself?" I said. Asking the question meant I was accepting the situation and I was not accepting the situation. I was just asking the question. As a trained professional, it is my job—and second nature—to collect the facts. The only way to gather information is to ask questions. Then my brain processes the data, sorts through the mess and decides what is true and what isn't.

"To her, you were the only person she ever truly loved, the only person she ever wanted to be with. She wanted to spend the rest of her life with you. She trusted you," Darla said. She spoke with compassion.

"Oh yeah? You aren't really telling me anything here. Let's try to be a little more exact this time. Who was your mother?"

"Honestly?"

"Sure, why not. You've been honest with me up until now, why stop? Let's continue to be honest with each other," I said, hoping she understood the sarcasm. I felt the hairs on my neck stand on end. "How's that sound?"

"My mother was the only person *you* ever truly loved."

"What?" I said.

Before my eyes, Darla disappeared.

"Hey, hey! Let's not just disappear like that!" Goosebumps spread down my forearms. I groaned, slammed the car into park and jumped out. I felt eerie. "This is great. Just wonderful. What a day I'm having. I can't believe the day I'm having! Save someone jogging in the morning, lose my sanity in the afternoon." How was I supposed to believe what I'd just seen, everything I'd heard? "The only person I ever truly loved," I mumbled. "What kind of lame bullshit is that?"

In that instant, as if a flashbulb went off in my face, Karis came to mind. God, I hadn't thought of her in at least eighteen years—not since high school. Now I knew who Darla looked like. She looked exactly like her mother, like Karis.

35

Chapter 3

Karis Bristol and I had started dating in our junior year of high school. A love stronger than puppy love kept us together until graduation. The world-awaiting high school graduates drove us apart. Karis went to college in Miami; I took classes at the community college for two years, received a degree, then transferred to New York University.

Of course, back when we broke up, we vowed we'd stay friends. I haven't seen or heard from her since that good-bye so many years ago. Trying to remember all the good times we shared, I saw nothing in my mind's eye but cardboard images. The memories, wrapped in a rubber band, stuffed in a brain-cell shoebox in the back of my subconscious, were dusty, and the color faded.

Karis had been beautiful, though. That image came to mind clearly: Long, straight, auburn hair; dark eyes; full, pouty lips; long, sexy legs. How could I not sigh after conjuring up an image like that?

Not knowing if Karis even lived in Rochester, I drove to a payphone, left the car running, grabbed and scanned through the Bristols in a phone book dangling from a thick cord. The chances of her—or anyone—moving back to Rochester after living in Florida were slim. There weren't many listings for Bristol in the white pages. There was, however, a K. Bristol. Maybe she missed the snow? Might not even be her.

The address wasn't far. I knew the street.

I pulled into the empty driveway, sat there and stared at the house. It was a white cape with navy blue shutters. "Okay," I said. "This was a stupid idea anyway. What am I going to say if this is her home, 'Oh hey, hi Karis. How've you been? Really? Great. Oh, nothing. Someone claiming to be your dead daughter came to see me today. It got me thinking, and after all these years, I thought I might drop by and see how things have been going for you.'" Talking to myself has always been a little problem—not for me, but for those who happen to see and hear me doing it.

I put the car into reverse, but before backing out, I saw the front door open. Someone stood behind the mesh screen. Though I could not see the face of the person, I did see folded arms. "Oh God, it is Karis!" Her car must be in the garage.

Shutting the engine off, I ran a quick palm over the top of my hair, thankful it was still a full head. I got out of the car. I smiled and waved. The screen door opened.

Karis stepped out onto the front step. A hand went to her mouth, as if covering her surprise. "My God. Nick? Nicholas?"

"Karis," I said. My legs felt like frozen Jell-O. It didn't matter. Karis had jumped off the steps and was running toward me, arms spread wide, tears in her eyes, a large smile on those still-full, pouty lips. No make-up. Wearing a white T-shirt under an unbuttoned sky blue blouse, loose fitting stonewashed jeans and white canvas sneakers, she still looked terribly sexy.

She hugged me tightly. I hugged her, tighter. It felt great, wonderful.

"I can't believe you're here. I can't believe it," she was saying. She still held me, squeezed me with more strength than I would have thought possible. I smelled her hair, savored the scent. My hand held the back of her neck, the other wrapped around the small of her back.

"How are you?" I managed, weakly.

"You'll never believe this, but I've been thinking about you all day—all day!" Karis just stared at me, smiling. "You're coming in aren't you? I've got coffee made. I was just doing some research on the net." ·

"Research?"

"I'm a freelance writer." Karis shrugged.

"I thought you wanted to go into medicine?"

"I did, but when I finally got to school I took some English and literature classes and loved them. The next thing I knew, when the second semester came around, I was an English major. I enjoyed writing papers and have been writing ever since."

"That's fantastic. Hey, I used to date a famous writer," I said. I thought about telling her that I was trying to write a mystery and decided against it. It wasn't the time. I would wager a bet that everyone tells Karis they're trying to write a book. I didn't want to be like everyone else.

Keeping an arm around my waist, Karis led me toward her house. I wrapped an arm around her shoulders. "Do I get any royalties for that? Having been your inspiration, you know?"

Karis laughed, throwing her head back, exposing a lovely neck. A strong feeling exploded inside me. A feeling I hadn't felt in quite awhile steadily increased the beat of my heart. In an instant I knew what it was. I still loved Karis, not realizing how much I'd missed her, how empty my life has been all these years without her, until just now. Stephen King would call it *Ka-tet*; destiny or fate. The sudden, amazing realizations, felt shocking, but true, right.

At one o'clock, I'd thought my day ruined. Funny sometimes, how a day can turn one hundred and eighty degrees on you.

Karis' house, decorated in a country motif, possessed warmth, but felt empty. "This is beautiful," I said. In every room were hardwood floors polished to a brilliant shine and tasteful art depicting farmhouses, flowery meadows and rainbow colored landscapes hanging on the walls. A small television set was in the living room, a sofa and love seat sat against adjacent walls in full view of the TV.

"Thank you," Karis said. "I spend a lot of time in my house working. It's important I feel completely relaxed and comfortable."

"Well, that's how this place makes me feel."

"Can I get you a cup of coffee?" Only her fingertips were tucked into the front pockets of her jeans.

"You know, a cold glass of water sounds better, if you don't mind," I said. My throat felt dry, coffee would only leave a bitter taste in my mouth. I followed Karis into the kitchen. It's been years since we've seen each other and yet, I felt like I've seen her all along.

"I've got to ask," Karis said, grabbed a glass from a cupboard by the sink, filled it with water from a jug in the refrigerator. "Why are you here?" She opened the freezer, removed an ice tray, dropped three cubes into the glass and handed it to me. "Please, sit down."

"Thank you," I said, sat at the table, took a sip of freezing, refreshing water.

"I have to tell you, I really find it odd that I spend the whole morning thinking about you and then I see a strange car pull into my driveway and you get out." She let out a nervous sounding laugh. "Maybe I should start my own psychic network hotline?"

"If it pays the bills." I smiled. "Did you ever get married?" Subtle question.

"Why Nick? Are you here to start courting again?" She fluttered long eyelashes at me, poured a cup of coffee, sat at the table across from me and stared into my eyes. She dropped one elbow onto the table, rested her face on a clenched fist. In a serious voice, she said, "No. I never got married."

38

Something in her voice told me I'd touched upon a sore subject. "Me either. With my work, I don't even have a someone-special. It gets kind of lonely," I said, wondered why I'd said so much, took a sip of water so I'd shut up. Was Karis smiling at my statement, or could it be just my imagination?

"Nick, I've got to know, what is this about? I mean, I'm glad you're here. I can't tell you how good I feel just seeing you again. I thought I might never see you again. What's it been?" Karis asked, her eyes never looking away from mine.

"Nineteen, twenty years?" It sounded impossible even as my mind did the math. Numbers don't lie.

"Oh my God, I can't believe it." Silence sat between us for several moments, an awkward peace. "You look great. I mean, really terrific!"

"Thank you," I said, flattered. My weight was increasing each year, starting to show around the mid-section. Karis was too kind. She was the one who looked wonderful. Still possessing a thin and athletic figure. Her skin looked creamy and soft. Her eyes looked like the only things that had changed drastically. There was no magical glow in them. Back when we'd dated, the glow had always been there. It was an attractive feature, prominent. What had killed that glow? Innocence lost? Time?

A dead daughter?

"So why are you here, Nick?" She brought the question up again, this time her expression demanded a truthful answer.

"Well, the truth is—and it's going to sound bizarre and may be none of my business—but, the reason I'm here—"

"Nick, you always used to do this in high school," Karis said. She laughed nervously.

"Did what?"

"What you're doing now. Spit it out, get to the point."

"I'm a private investigator," I started.

"I know." Her look became somber. Her eyes lowered. She had seen my name perhaps in the phone book. Maybe at one point, like sometime last year, she had thought about calling me, or coming down to see me. Maybe to talk about Glory Days? Maybe to ask me to save her daughter.

"Yeah, well, I had a young girl come by my office this morning. S-she looked a lot like you—a mirror image of you, really. She claimed—now this is weird okay? Try to hear out my whole story, because I don't want you to think I'm crazy, all right?"

"Nick—"

"Okay. Okay. She claimed to be your daughter," I said.

39

Karis' hand slapped across her mouth. She cried, turned away.

"Karis," I said softly, touched her shoulder. "Karis—"

"I'm sorry. I'm sorry. It's just, Nick, my daughter is dead. She died almost a year ago," Karis said. Tears spilled from her eyes, rolled down her cheeks, dangled from her lips and chin. I stood up, walked over to her, knelt by her side, wrapped an arm around her shoulder.

I didn't think it was possible, couldn't believe the obvious. "I know this must be hard," I said, tried to sound like a professional, "but can I see a picture of your daughter?"

"Of Darla?"

Darla. "Please."

Karis took a moment to wipe away the tears with the backs of her hands. She stood up, tried to compose herself for my benefit. There was no need. "There's a picture of her in the living room, on the end table near the love seat, the one with the telephone on it. Would you mind—"

"No. I'll go and take a look at it in there," I said. I left the kitchen.

"How could someone do that?" I heard Karis say. "Pretend to be my daughter? What kind of a prank could this girl be playing?"

A sick prank, I thought, as I sat on the love seat and lifted the frame off the end table. The girl in the photograph was the girl in my office and I had no doubt. I studied the image, the eyes, lips, hair. No other girl could look that pretty. Still, there had to be someone who just amazingly resembled Darla. Chances of that? Slim. I've always gone with gut feeling. This time, I ignored my gut. Had to be a prank.

When I looked up, Karis was standing in the threshold between the kitchen and living room. "She was beautiful, wasn't she?"

"Looks exactly the way you did," I said.

Karis sat next to me, leaned her head on my shoulder. I felt her tears wet my shirt. "She was so smart, could have been anything in the world she wanted to be." Karis took the frame away from me and held it to her chest. "I know what you're thinking."

"You do?" I asked. At the moment, I was thinking only one thought: Comfort Karis, take away her inner pain.

"I moved to Florida right after graduation, rented an apartment not far from campus and worked as a waitress for the summer in this small diner. There was this guy, a regular. He came in nearly every morning for coffee and always sat in my section. We went out once. I thought I might love the guy. After that one night, he never came back to the restaurant and when I found out I was pregnant, I decided not to tell him. I took an extra year off before starting school. I moved back to Rochester, lived with my parents, had the baby then went to SUNY Monroe College part time."

"And the father?"

"I still don't know where he is and could care less. Darla and I were better off without him. He was a stranger. I don't think I would have married him anyway. It was a stupid, kid-like thing to do, you know? But, well, I've told you more than you probably wanted to know, huh?" Her cheeks turned red. Karis handed back the frame to me.

I looked into Darla's eyes in the picture, remembered the eyes of the girl in my office. "If you don't mind me asking, how did Darla die?"

"The official version, or the personal one?" Karis asked. She lifted her head, my shoulder suddenly felt cold. "The official version was that she drowned. She was going to school at Monroe. It was the beginning of her freshman year. She'd been drugged up, an overdose they told me. She was walking along the canal near campus, slipped on some rocks, or just lost her balance and fell into the water. They found her." Karis stopped. Her hand trembled. She held a hand over her mouth and gasped. She sucked air in, in jagged, quick breaths and let out a long, low sigh. "They found her body miles away from campus, up on the rocky canal bed. When her blood was tested they found the drugs she'd taken to be bad, laced with dangerous chemicals."

"And that's not how you think it happened?" I asked. I remembered what the spirit-Darla had told me. *Someone forced you to do drugs?* I'd asked her, laughing. *Yes*, she'd said, straight-faced, *someone did force me, literally.*

"I don't know what happened exactly, but I know my daughter," she said. "I knew her! I was going to come and see you, as a matter of fact, last year, but I lost my nerve. She needed help, I know. She was hanging with the wrong group of kids at school, you know? I was scared, but I never dreamed . . . I don't believe for a second that my daughter died from a drug overdose. I refuse to believe it."

Just as spirit-Darla had told me, though she never denied using drugs, she did deny taking them on the night in question.

"Why didn't you come to see me, Karis?"

"How could I? We hadn't seen each other in nearly two decades. I felt embarrassed. I know now I was wrong, that my pride might have—"

"You can't say that. It's not true. You couldn't possibly have known how this would have played out." She was blaming herself. This blame, I'd bet, was the reason the glow in her eyes was gone.

41

Karis sobbed. "I really think you could have helped her. I know you could have."

"Helped her how, Karis? What could I have done?" I asked. I already knew the answer.

She said, "Well, it was more than just some reckless kids on campus that she hung around with. Darla was involved with some sort of campus cult. They were a bad, raunchy satanic group if you ask me. I saw the change in Darla immediately. She didn't try to hide the fact that she'd joined this, *religion*, if you want to call it that. She did, she called it that. She always told me I should be happy for her because she'd found God, but I know she wasn't praying to the one in heaven. I knew it was an unhealthy faith from the start. Nick, you should have seen her, when she'd come home, she would be dressed in black. Always in black. She'd mumble these meaningless little prayers—meditate in the nude. Nick, they're a sick bunch and I know, from the deepest depths of my heart, I know they had something to do with her death. That was why I was going to come and see you. I wanted you to kidnap my daughter." Karis laughed. "Sounds pathetic, doesn't it?"

"Not really," I said. The Darla I had seen was dressed in white. Not black.

"I tried to talk to Darla, to get her to see what she was involved in for what it was, a satanic cult. She was blind to the truth, believed everything told to her by some high priest, whoever in Hell he is. I had no options. None. Except kidnapping her, you see. How could I come to your door and ask you to steal my daughter out of college. You would have thought I was crazy."

I said nothing. I wouldn't have thought she was crazy, but if I told Karis this, then she would just continue to blame herself for not coming to me for help. I didn't want her to be blaming herself anymore.

"Karis, this is really hard, but everything you told me just now is exactly what this person told me in my office," I said. "She even told me that you'd contemplated coming down to see me." She also said that I was the only person you ever really loved.

"So who is she?" Karis asked. The mystery was before us, the challenge unnerving.

"Like I said, she claims to be Darla and is an exact double of your daughter. The resemblance is uncanny." How could it be? Who was the girl in my office? Darla's spirit? It couldn't be. Did I tell Karis, *Oh yeah, I almost forgot to mention that my hands passed right through her.*

"What did this girl want?" My news was troubling Karis. I hated subjecting her to this. After all these years, we should be talking about better times.

"Truthfully? She wanted me to help her stop that same cult from sacrificing another girl," I managed. I held Karis' hand, gave it a squeeze.

"My God!" she said. I knew what she was thinking. She'd been right. Darla didn't overdose. She'd been sacrificed.

"At the time, I didn't believe this girl, whoever she is, but now I think I might," I said. Was it Darla's spirit? Could it really be a ghost? I had to keep an open mind, ignore the fact that ghosts and spirits don't come and talk to people and ask for help. Unless, I was finding, they really, really need it.

"Nick, what can you mean, you believe her? Darla's dead."

"I don't know exactly what's going on, but I'm going to dig around a little, see what comes out." I wrapped my arms around Karis, held her. She rested her head on my chest. "Something's going on, prank, or no prank. If a girl's life is in danger, then I have to try and save her. I plan to find out more about this cult, Karis. I'll find out what happened to Darla."

"This is weird," she said in a whisper. She sounded tired, depressed, like she might fall asleep.

Was she talking about the visitor I'd had, or us hugging? I didn't ask. It didn't matter. Both things I found *weird*. However, hugging Karis was the best weird I'd felt in a long, long time. The visit from spirit-Darla was just a freak-the-hell-out-of-me kind of weird.

Chapter 4

The promise was made. We'd be in touch, meet for lunch, talk about old times, talk about the *now*. I knew we would, too. Seeing Karis again left me weak in the knees.

Pulling out of her driveway, though, I wondered about the problem at hand. Who was the Darla I'd spoken to? Part of me believed she was the spirit of Karis' deceased daughter. A bigger part of me could not accept that. It didn't seem possible, wasn't logical, but then again, neither was love.

I decided to go back to the office, log onto the net and surf around the SUNY Monroe College web site and links. It would be the easiest way to launch a pro bono investigation. When I walked into the office, Betty looked shocked. "I didn't expect to see you back today, Nick. "

"Why? I told you I was just going out for a quick bite. " I smiled. "Any messages?"

"Yeah, Judy Swanson. She left a number, said it wasn't important if you didn't have time to call her back," Betty said, handed me a slip of paper. "And Ned's in his office. Actually, I told him you went home for the rest of the day. Want me to tell him you're here?"

"Is he busy?" I asked, slid the paper with Judy's number into my pocket.

"He shouldn't be. "

"I'll just knock on his door then," I said walking to his closed office door. No one else was around. Maybe Ned sent them all home after lunch. I knocked with two soft taps.

"Come in," Ned said.

I opened the door. "Busy?"

"No, Nick, come on in. I thought you went home for the day?"

I walked in, closed the door and stuffed my hands into my pockets. I loved his office. Everything was black, his furniture, the curtains and even the carpet. The walls were white, with what I called black-blob art. The framed images reminded me of drawings shown to patients in a psychiatric evaluation. The one I liked best hung on the wall behind Ned's desk, titled:

44

Splatter. In a way, they made me nervous. Every time I saw one of the paintings, I thought I saw something different in them. Maybe that was why Ned liked them so much. Always new conceptions conceived, true conversation pieces. "That's what Betty told me she told you. I told her I was just going out for a late lunch and that I'd be back. You send everyone else home, or what?"

"Yeah. It's dead around here. Why have people killing time sitting at their desk waiting for the phone to ring? If it rings, I'll call them all back. Right? Everything okay with you?" Ned asked. "Betty told me about what happened this morning. What a way to start the day. If you want, you can go on home, too. Things are still quiet around here. If anything big were to come up, I'd let you know." Ned waved his hand at the empty chair in front of his desk.

I sat down, stared at Ned and admired the man's good looks. In a way, Ned resembled President Bill Clinton, with a full head of wavy silver hair, thick silver eyebrows set over deep-blue eyes, small nose, rugged chin, a still solid, muscular build. Ned's voice had a gravel sound to it and he talked just louder than a whisper. "Thanks," I said, "but really I'm okay."

"Okay. If you're okay, then we're okay. What can I do for you?"

"Nothing. Earlier Betty said you asked about me," I said, feeling relieved. Betty had obviously held true to her promise and had not told Ned about Darla Bristol.

"I was just concerned because you hadn't shown up for work and we couldn't reach you at home. That's all. In fact, I wanted to congratulate you on closing out the Cappelli and Smyth cases. The Cappellis have sent over a bonus check," Ned said and flashed a smile full of white teeth.

The Cappellis owned a good-sized deli on Spencerport Road, in Gates. Someone was stealing from them. Cappelli hired me as an employee. I worked long hours and learned the tricks of the trade, so to speak. I met and became familiar with plenty of customers and with the rest of Cappelli's staff.

It didn't take me long to find that old Joseph Cappelli's seventeen year old nephew, Michael, was stealing the goods. Michael would casually drop wrapped food into a garbage pail, take the garbage to the dumpster, remove the food, set it behind the dumpster, return late at night and pick up his merchandise.

I followed Michael one night. The youngster had a girlfriend and a baby that no one seemed to know about. I snapped pictures of the small family, close enough to see them sitting around the kitchen table eating the food

Michael had taken from his uncle.

I confronted Michael. He told me his family would be upset with him if they knew the truth. Instead of telling everyone his situation and facing the shame, he hid his girlfriend and the baby—a son he'd named Joseph.

Joseph wasn't paying him much money. He didn't think a boy, seventeen, needed to make a million a year, Joseph had once told Michael when the boy had asked for a raise.

Old Cappelli was relieved to hear the reasons behind his nephew's thefts. He was honored to hear that his great-nephew was named after him.

Instead of firing Michael, Joseph made Michael manager of the deli on the condition he attend college and receive a business degree.

Joseph gave Michael enough money to put a down payment on an engagement ring, if—he'd told Michael—that was what he wanted to do.

Michael got engaged, no wedding date set . . . yet.

"Great," I said. "Nice family. Well, I better get going."

"A case?"

I didn't want to talk about the Bristols. Not yet. Not with Ned. "Nope. Just thought I'd work on some research." Ned knew I wanted to write a novel, a private investigator book. He thought the idea was ridiculous, the genre overdone to death. I disagreed. I'd read many books and enjoyed most all of them. I felt each writer had something unique to offer—a different twist in a saturated field. New perspectives.

Ned gave me a knowing smile. "Good luck. If you have any questions on how a PI goes about solving a case, don't be afraid to ask for a professional's help."

"Wow, was that funny Ned. Thanks, I'll keep it in mind." I gave him a friendly wink.

In my office, I sat behind my desk in front of my computer terminal. Web sites on Monroe were plentiful. I had trouble looking through them though, as my attention was continually drawn to the chair opposite my desk.

Yes. I was waiting for Darla to reappear. Expecting her to do so left me without an ounce of concentration. The suspense grew inside me. I could hardly take it, the waiting. Who was she? Where was she now? Could I, or should I, expect to see her again?

"Great," I mumbled. "I can't get anything done just sitting and staring at an empty chair all afternoon."

I remembered that Judy Swanson had called. Removing the paper that Betty had given me from my pocket, I dialed the number. A woman answered on the third ring, just as I was about to hang up.

"Hello?"

It was Judy. I easily recognized the voice. She still sounded uneasy.

"Judy? It's Nicholas Tartagllia."

"Nick? I'm surprised you called me back," she said, sounding more cheerful. I still heard a trace of anxiety in her words.

"Oh? Why are you surprised? I told you I'd be here for you. I wasn't just feeding you a line you know."

"I know now," she said. "Anyway, I—"

"What?"

"I might as well just say it," she said, as if speaking to herself. "I would like to make dinner for you one day this week, maybe Friday night?"

"That's completely not necessary," I said, remembering how beautiful she was. I started to hate myself for declining her generous offer.

"No, I know it's not necessary, but it's something I want to do to show my gratitude. You saved me from a nightmare that could have ended much differently. I hate even thinking about the *what ifs*. Nick, let me make you dinner," Judy said, quickly.

I hemmed and hawed. "I don't want you to go to any trouble," I finally said.

"It's no trouble. Believe me, it's something I want to do." I heard it then. Something in the tone of her voice had changed. She was interested. I'm a private investigator trained to pick up on these things.

"Well, all right then," I said. What else could I say?

She gave me directions to her house. We'd have dinner at her place on Friday, seven o'clock. I was to bring a bottle of wine. When I hung up the phone I felt good for one fleeting moment.

Then an image of Karis came to mind.

But what were the chances of Karis and I getting involved again? I honestly didn't know. If Karis wanted to, though, would I?

Of course I would.

Then what about Judy Swanson?

"I haven't got a clue," I said, shut my computer off. "One minute I'm alone for half my life, the next minute I've got to choose between two women."

No, not yet, Nick, something inside my head said. *You're way ahead of yourself. You don't know for sure if either of them like you. You only think they both do, you ass.*

My house, a small Victorian, hung on the edge of the suburbs, had a small front yard and an even smaller backyard. The detached garage sat at the end of the driveway. I never parked in it because too much junk and clutter occupied all the space. I always planned to clean it out, but never found the time to carry it through. However, a tentative schedule had mentally been made to begin restorations in the spring. (Only in mental-pencil, though).

While shutting the engine off, I climbed out of the car, locked the doors and walked up the front porch steps. Nothing but junk mail was in the box. Taking it and tucking it under my arm, I unlocked my door. I walked into the foyer, deactivated the alarm system with a four-digit code, and tossed the mail onto the sofa and said, "I'll sort through you guys when I find a minute."

I didn't realize just how humid it was outside until the stuffy, stagnate air in the house closed in around me. It felt difficult to breathe. I pulled the dangling chain to switch on the ceiling fan in the living room, loosened my tie and unbuttoned the top button on my shirt. "I'm going to start saving for central air," I said.

In the kitchen I grabbed a beer, twisted off the cap and took a long, much-needed, swallow. "Ahh," I gasped. "Now if a cold beer doesn't hit the spot, I can't imagine what would."

I walked with the beer back into the living room and plopped down on the recliner, snatched up the television remote and began surfing through the channels, knowing perfectly well that nothing worth watching would be on. "Nothing. Nothing. Nothing." I shut the television off.

Leaning forward in the recliner, I ran my hand up the back of my neck, through my hair. "God, I've got to get a pet so when I talk to myself, I don't sound so crazy."

"Nick, I've got to tell you," someone said, suddenly. I stood up, spun around. She was sitting on the stairs. "Dammit, Darla—"

"I thought you'd be working on my case, especially after talking with my mother," the girl said. She was dressed the same, elbows on her knees, chin on her knuckles.

"How did you get into my house," I demanded.

"Not this again. I thought we already went through this? You believed I was a spirit before, why not now?" Darla asked. "Nick, not even Ned could carry a trick this far."

I stared at the girl, the spirit—at Darla. "Oh yes he could," I said, not really believing my own words. "If he wanted to, he could."

"Could he, Nick? If he could, would he? He knows what kind of a morning you've had."

Of course Darla was speaking of Judy Swanson. I thought about her comments while taking steps toward her. She stood up. She reached out for me. I reached my fingertips out to her. We touched. I felt her skin for just an instant, then my hand passed through her. I pulled back, suddenly nervous, perhaps afraid. "Son of a bitch."

"There really is no time to kill, Nick. Please, find out who this girl is and save her. Because if you don't, I promise you, she will die. Please, Nick. Save her."

Darla was gone. She didn't become transparent and disappear, she didn't shimmy and fade. She simply was gone. Here one second, gone the next. I felt a finger of ice trace my spine, and shuddered.

Chapter 5

Darla had made her point the other day. I needed to get the ball rolling. Karis had filled me in on the basic details of her daughter's death and was adamant about the fact that her daughter did not overdose on drugs. Darla had claimed the same.

The quickest path to start researching could be made with one, reluctant phone call.

I knew Homicide's Detective Tommy Cerio's phone number by heart. I've never called my brother-in-law before, not to ask for help on a case, anyway. I felt funny doing so now, especially under these unusual circumstances.

Tommy was my sister Arline's husband. They just found out they were expecting, told the whole family just last weekend. Everyone was pretty excited. I know I was. I was going to become an uncle.

"Homicide, Detective O'Mara speaking," a woman said, answering Tommy's phone. I didn't really know O'Mara, we've talked once or twice. For some reason there was always static between us. She was probably attracted to me, couldn't handle her feelings. I know I thought she was pretty cute.

"I'm looking for Detective Cerio? Is he in?" I asked, as I drummed my fingertips on the coffee table. "It's not an emergency, or anything."

"Who's calling? I'm his partner, can I help you in anyway? Detective Cerio's away from his desk right now."

"This is his brother-in-law, Nick. Could you maybe have him give me a call at home? I'll be here the rest of the night, I imagine. Like I said, though. It's no emergency. I just had a question for him," I said.

"Sure, Nick," O'Mara said. "He has your number, right?"

"He does. Thanks." I hung up, went upstairs and brought the cordless with me into the bathroom so I could hear if it rang while I took a long, ice cold shower. It felt wonderful.

When I was standing naked in front of the fan in my bedroom the telephone rang. I'd left it in the bathroom and had to run down the hall to grab it. "Hello," I said. Despite being alone, I felt goofy running around the house without any clothes on. It was too damned hot to get dressed, though.

"Nick, it's Tommy. What's up?"

"How's my sister feeling?"

"Nauseous. It sounds funny, but I think I have sympathy-nausea," Tommy laughed.

"Really? I never heard that one before. How's everything since that incident with the Mafia and that paperboy? How are you feeling?" I asked. He'd been shot in the leg while saving a twenty-seven year old paperboy from the mob. The paperboy had witnessed a Mafia hit on his morning route and went to Tommy for help. The media made a circus out of the incident. Tommy had been somewhat of a hero in the papers: Homicide detective expecting new baby, risks life to save paperboy from mob.

"I feel all right. Leg still hurts, Delski's got me strapped to a desk. I hate it," Tommy said. Carl Delski was the police chief for the Rochester Police Department. He was a hard ass and would have a fit if he knew I was calling Tommy for help on a case. The locals don't like private investigators, they think we are a nuisance. Though our paths rarely crossed, I am under the impression Delski thinks all PIs are dishonest, dangerous and deranged. Other than that, though, he's a nice guy outside the office.

"Sorry to hear that."

"Is there something specific you wanted, Nick? Not that I'm all that busy pushing a pencil."

I couldn't imagine my brother-in-law sitting at a desk waiting for the phone to ring, doing office things like filing and changing the ink cartridge in the printer and getting Delski his coffee. "I've never asked a favor from you before, but I need one now. A small one," I said, holding my breath.

"And the favor is?"

"I don't know if you were called in on the case last year. Darla Bristol. She would have been a floater, Erie Canal. A Monroe student. Drug overdose or because of drugs used, fell in and drowned in the canal. She was found, maybe, several miles away from the college? Ring any bells?" I said. Opening dresser drawers, I took out a change of clothes, tossed them onto the bed, dreaded getting dressed.

"It sounds familiar. I was called on the scene. Young and pretty. I remember it, yeah. After the coroner did her thing, she ruled the death a drowning caused from a drug overdose. The girl lost her balance, fell into the water. No foul play detected."

"Can I get the police and coroner reports on the case?"

"What's up?" Tommy asked, ever the investigator. "You got something new?"

"Naw. Not really. The girl's mother just wants the matter looked into a little more, still in mourning, still searching for peace of mind, I guess," I said, only half-lying to my brother-in-law. The police, in general, didn't want private investigators working on potentially serious cases. It was a threat to them. No one other than a trained police officer should be able to solve a case that's just not solvable. No offense to my brother-in-law, but I am a better investigator than most of the officers on the force. On the other hand, I work one case at a time. I could dedicate myself completely to one cause.

"It was an overdose, Nick. I know the coroner. If something was wrong, she would have found it and said so," Tommy said, defending his own.

"I'm sure she would have. I'm not implying a haphazard job. I've just been hired and want to do all I can to be thorough, you know?" Pet the ego, stroke it. It's all a part of the game. I was a pretty good player. Piss no one off. It was my first, and most golden rule.

"Sure," Tommy said. "I got no problem with that. Let me see what I can come up with and how touchy the subject of getting the information to you might be. I might not be able to get you a copy, but if you have specific questions and if I have the file in front of me, then maybe I can just give you what you're looking for that way. Sound good enough?"

"Sounds great. I really appreciate it, Tommy," I said. "Tell Arline I said hi, all right?"

"Sure, Nick. Hey, I heard about you and the jogger. You done real good. Probably saved that girl's life, if not her life, her sanity."

"Thanks," I said, nothing more. Attention made me uncomfortable. How could he have heard about it already? I'd wager a bet that Officer Callister was still typing up the damned thing.

"Let me run through this and get back to you," Tommy said.

"All right, and thanks again. Take care of that leg—and my sister. By the way, got any names picked yet? I know Nicholas is a good one, should the tiny tyrant turn out to be a boy," I said, half-joking, half-hoping.

"Haven't given it a thought. I'm sure Arline has got a list already, though. If I get a chance, I'll sneak a peak and let you know if your name's on it." He was serious. He'd look, and if he could, try to add my name.

"Cool. Take it easy," I said and hung up, got dressed, collapsed on the bed   and   fell   asleep.

The sound of the telephone ringing woke me. I sat up in bed, grabbed the phone. "Hello?"

"It's me, Nick," Karis said. "I think I need to see you. I think I'm losing my mind and I have no one else to call. I'm going out of my head here, losing it. I'm losing it."

Karis sounded frantic. "Hold on, slow down," I said. "Where are you? Home?"

"Yeah. I'm home," she said, sounding more calm. Maybe talking to me had soothed her.

"Okay," I said, looked at the time on my alarm clock. 7:11 P.M. "I can be out to your house in fifteen minutes. Is that okay?"

"Thank you, Nick."

I hung up. What had upset Karis so much? She sounded scared, afraid, like she'd seen a . . . a ghost. Dammit Darla!

There would be no need to knock on the door. When I pulled into the driveway, Karis was standing in the doorway, arms folded, one hand near her mouth—perhaps she was chewing on her fingernails. She waved to me as I got out of my car. I waved back.

Karis opened the door. "Nick, I feel so foolish now," she said.

"What's going on?"

Karis laughed, covered her face. "Have you had dinner yet? I feel so stupid now, making you drive all the way out here, the least I can do is make you something to eat, if you'd like. I have a pot of water boiling. I *was* going to make spaghetti. I'm sure it's no where near as good as your mother's. I remember being intimidated by your mother back when we were dating. Whenever we were at your house, she always put out so much food, always had a few pounds of spaghetti ready, cookies, pies. God, sometimes I thought she just wanted me to get fat, or something."

I laughed at that. "I think bringing people around the house intimidated my mother. She was always embarrassed by her broken-English, the heavy Italian accent. If people were eating, they couldn't ask her questions, right? She knew it was impolite to talk with your mouth full, so she kept on feeding everyone and anyone I brought around, you know? Actually, I'm starving. Spaghetti sounds great if it's no trouble," I said, patting my belly.

"None at all. I'm glad you're staying," Karis said, holding the screen door open.

Walking into her house I knew something was still bothering her.

53

"How are your parents doing, anyway?" Karis asked.

"Great. They're doing great. They both retired and spend winters in Arizona," I said.

"Not Florida?"

"They don't care much for Florida. Too many old people, I guess." Karis laughed. I didn't think I'd said anything funny. I don't consider my parents to be old. Does anybody? "Karis, you were frantic when you called me. What was going on?"

We walked into the kitchen. She poured a box of spaghetti into the water in the pot and stirred. Leaning against the counter, I just watched her. She seemed to be ignoring my question, stood with her back to me.

"Karis," I pressed. "Karis—"

Karis turned around. She was crying, looked lost. I pulled her into my arms. Holding her felt wonderful, the sensation amazed me.

"I don't know if it's because you came around and dredged up all the memories I'd locked away, or what." She buried her face into my chest.

"What happened?" I asked, my tone soft.

"I saw Darla." She pulled out of the hug, looked me in the eyes. She seemed to be waiting for me to call her crazy. When I didn't say anything, Karis said, "She was here. She told me everything was going to be all right now."

Shit. This was too hard to accept; a ghost popping up all over the city. I believed it, but didn't want to. "Where was she?"

"Right here, in the kitchen." She pointed at a chair. "She sat right there and talked to me."

I let go of Karis, looked around the room, checked the ceiling corners, opened cupboard doors, parted curtains to inspect windowpanes. I found nothing out of the ordinary. Waving my hands over the chair where Darla supposedly sat, I wondered what the hell was going on.

"Nick, what are you doing?"

"I'm having trouble with this."

"I know my daughter died, Nick. I buried her. The girl sitting at the kitchen table was Darla." Karis looked sad, eyes filled with tears.

I thought of Darla being in my house, touching—or rather—passing my finger through her finger. Then she'd vanished. "Darla the spirit."

"I accept that."

"That easily?" I asked. It should be a comfort to me that someone else was seeing Darla the way I'd seen her. Confirmation that I wasn't insane.

"Yes." Karis went over to the kitchen table, stared at the empty chair as if waiting for her daughter to reappear. She sat in the one next to it. "She said you accepted it, too."

"That was before," I said.

"And you don't believe it now?"

"No. Yes. I had time to sleep on the matter. I was blaming stress this morning while I took a shower. Actually had myself going along with it, too. Karis, I don't know what the hell to believe right now."

"You're going to help her, right Nick?" Karis stood up, folded her arms, stared intently at me, waited for an answer.

Taking a deep breath, I said. "I've already started. I talked with my brother-in-law a few hours back. He's in homicide with the Rochester Police Department. He's digging up the file on Darla's case. He's going to give me a call as soon as he has something for me."

Karis shuddered, cupped her hands over her mouth and started to cry again. "Believe it or not, these are happy tears, Nick. I feel so much better knowing someone's finally going to help my daughter. I've felt so useless this past year. It's a horrible feeling to think you ought to be doing something, but you have no idea what."

Walking over to Karis, I wrapped my arms around her. "I'm going to do all I can," I said. "But no promises."

"I understand that." She kissed my cheek, pulled out of the hug, went to the stove. "Have a seat," she said calmly. "Dinner will be ready in a second."

The chair where the spirit-Darla sat might as well have been in another room. There was no way I planned to sit in it. I sat at the opposite end of the table. When Karis turned around, she noticed where I was sitting, and why, at once. She gave me a sly smile. I returned the gesture with a two-finger salute and a wink.

Chapter 6

Driving into work this morning, I did not see Judy Swanson out jogging, but didn't expect to. The realization of *why* Judy was not out jogging made me cringe. What a sick society we live in. This realization was not new. I thought about it often. Who's to blame? How can anyone truly say? Nurture, nature? I think it's a blend of both. What scares me is if something is not done to stop the acts of violence, they will continue to grow, breed like rats, and eventually become the accepted norm.

I drove to the back parking lot of Safehouse Investigations, strolled into the building, took the elevator up to the sixth floor, walked down the hall and through the glass doors.

"Betty, good morning," I said in a loud voice. "How are you?"

"Very well. Thank you, Nick. And you look considerably better, might I say," Betty said. She wore a bright red dress and red lipstick to match. The top of her desk was littered with folders.

"Thank you. I feel much better," I said. "Busy are we?"

"Nope," she said, chuckled. "Cleaning out drawers. Got to keep busy one way or another, right?" She grabbed together a stack of files, stood them up in her hands, then banged them on the drawer to keep them neat and aligned. She pushed back in her chair, pulled open a gray filing cabinet drawer and filed the folders.

"Wonderful." I started away.

"Oh, a detective Thomas Cerio called?" Betty said, retrieved a note from the corner of her desk hand it to me. "Just maybe, two minutes ago?"

"Tommy? Great," I said, looked at the note, then put it in my pocket.

"Want me to get him on the line for you?"

"No thanks. I'll call him myself a little later."

"Fine. If you'd like, I could check your office for ghosts before you go in there," Betty said, as she smiled and gave me a wink.

Ah, isn't she cute. There's nothing like being teased. "I should be all set, thank you."

At my office door, I hesitated. I glanced over my shoulder. Betty had come to gawk. I smiled. "I'm not afraid to go in. I was just trying to remember something," I said.

"Sure, Nick."

Pushing open the door, I gave Betty a look that said, *See, no fear!*

Quickly, I entered the office, closed the door. "She must think I'm crazy. I know I would, if I was her. And Nick, stop talking to yourself."

Sitting comfortably at the desk, I switched on the computer and dialed Tommy's phone number. It rang three times before someone answered it. "Homicide, Detective Cerio speaking."

"Tommy?"

"Nick. How are you?"

"Busy," I said. "You called me?"

"Yeah, I was able to get my hands on the information you requested. Got a minute?" I distinctly heard the sound of him shuffling through papers.

"Of course." I got comfortable in my chair, loosened my tie, crossed my leg over the top of my thigh, held the ankle. "Go ahead."

"Okay. Darla Bristol was pronounced dead of an overdose on illegal narcotics. Nick, it says here that her system had massive amounts of liquid cocaine—"

"Liquid cocaine? I've never heard of that."

"It's mostly used for injecting. Darla, it appears, ingested it. She drank it. She also had DOM in her system—"

"Never heard of DOM, either. Sorry." I mumbled, "In my day it was strictly pot. God I feel old."

I heard Tommy sigh. "DOM," he said, "is the correct name for the drug. The street name is Tranquillity?"

"That I've heard of," I said.

"Great, Nick. On top of those two drugs, she had a blood alcohol level of four point seven. It's no wonder she died. Her body couldn't possibly handle the amounts of drugs working in and against her system.

"The coroner states the time of death to have occurred roughly between midnight and noon the next afternoon. She was lucky to get it narrowed down to that proximity. I guess the tissue was pretty riddled even though she hadn't been in the water long. There's enough fish in the canal that they were able to do considerable damage. The body, because the water was so cold, froze her liver making it hard to determine an exact time of death. The body was found at noon, so the post times are a little *non*-exact, you know?"

Tommy said.

"Okay, this helps. There were no signs, or marks on her body that might indicate a struggle?" I asked. Darla had said she was forced to take the drugs. If someone tried to force me to take drugs, they'd physically need to hold my arms down, kneel on my chest and pry my mouth open.

"I have four photographs here, part of her file, they show bruises on Bristol's wrists and ankles. There's a paper clip holding the photos and a report together. The coroner wrote the report. She says the police, through their investigation, concluded that Darla was into S and M kind of things. Bondage, you know, pain, that kind of thing. The marks are consistent," Tommy explained.

"Can I get a copy of those photographs?" I asked. The marks might be consistent with kinky sexual habits, but could they also be considered as consistent to bruises caused by someone tying you down and pouring liquid cocaine and tranquillity into your mouth?

"Nick, they're strap burns on the wrists, like leather belts, what's to see? They're barely visible, just a hint of purple bruises, like they're healing," Tommy said.

"Or like they're fresh," I said. *They forced me to take the drugs*, Darla had told me. "Does it, by any chance, say from whom they got this reliable source of information? Because, I've met the girl. She didn't impress me as the kind of girl who might be into that kind of thing." I imagined Darla, the pretty young girl-spirit, sitting in my chair, dressed in white. She didn't look the S and M type, but neither did she look dumb enough to join a satanic cult.

"You knew her?" Tommy said, sounded suddenly sympathetic. Professional curiosity prompted him. "You didn't say that before. How'd you know her?"

"Well," I stumbled, "I'd met her once. I really knew the girl's mother, years ago. We went to high school together. So does it say who the police got their S and M information from?"

"Ah, the police report claims that her roommate made the comment about it. That's in the police report, now, not the coroner's report," Tommy said.

"I think I can keep the information between the two clear. Thanks. How about this, Tommy, did she have a boyfriend?"

After ten seconds Tommy said, "It doesn't say so here. Nothing I can tell from the report."

I heard it in my brother-in-law's voice, he found this odd, too. Without a known boyfriend, how could Darla participate in S and M activity? "Okay

Tommy. This is all great. One more small favor?"

"What's that, Nick?"

"What's the name of Darla Bristol's roommate?"

"Nick—"

"Come on, I could find out if I head over to the college and ask a million people. Save me some footwork here. You've got the name right in front of you, don't you?"

"You're going to owe me," Tommy said.

"I volunteer to be the first one to watch your rug rat. This is for free, mind you. This will allow you and Arline to go out and enjoy each other. May not sound important now but once that kid's here life will be different between the two of you. How's that sound? A little tempting?" I said. Some deal, I would watch their kid anytime, anyway. Tommy didn't know this, though.

"All right. Fair enough. Darla's roommate's name was . . . is, Maryjean D'Amonda. Maryjean is one word, *jean* is not a middle name."

I wrote it down. "Got it. Tommy I gotta run. I think I've finally got an investigation to conduct. Thanks for your help, bro. It's really been helpful."

"Hey Nick, if anything comes up—"

"Don't worry, Tommy. I'll keep you in the loop. See, this is how a working friendship gets started. You wash my back, I wash yours." Maybe he and I could work cases together, like in all those private investigator novels.

"I'm not washing anything of yours. This is not going to happen every time you have a new case, Nick. Remember that. You asked for a favor. Now you owe me. It doesn't mean we can bounce questions off one another all the time. Understand?"

I knew my brother-in-law. He was just trying to sound like the tough homicide detective. It was an act. "Sure Tommy. I understand perfectly. Bye-bye."

The conversation with Tommy proved intriguing. I logged onto the Internet, looked up Maryjean D'Amonda in the electronic phone book. No listing. No surprise. There were two full columns of D'Amonda's, however. And I was faced with one major question: Was Maryjean from Rochester?

She would be a sophomore at Monroe this year. Classes for the fall semester began at the end of August. I knew I needed to talk with Maryjean, but I also wanted to talk with the local church heads, as well. Who better to ask the down and dirty about a cult?

I switched off my computer, left the office.

"I'm going out to SUNY Monroe College. If anyone needs me I'll have the cell phone on," I said to Betty. She gave me a crooked smile. "What?"

"Nothing, Nick. Have fun."

The way Betty was staring at me, I could tell she'd thought I'd lost my marbles. Maybe I have. Before going anywhere, I knew I needed to stop home and change from my work clothes into a pair of jeans and sneakers.

As I suspected, the State University buzzed with life and youthful activity. The college was set up with the dorms outlining the rear of the cigar shaped campus. Classroom buildings, set in the center, faced a cobblestone walk and were equipped with wheelchair ramps and stairs.

Unfortunately, the visitor's parking lot was full. I would have to drive out to the student parking lot. This entailed parking on the opposite side of the railroad tracks near one of the two gymnasiums, Tuttle South.

Walking from the parking lot, up toward the library—where the bridge extended over the railroad tracks—I felt a sense of awe for the students around me. Sure I missed the social activity of college life, but I also missed the learning.

One thing about college was that students could be ageless, no one seemed to give my presence a second thought as a group of students skated by on roller blades, knap-sacks slung over their shoulders.

The mental plan for the day unfolded in my mind. First, try to find Maryjean D'Amonda. Perhaps I'd look up the school president, or even the vice president. Next, I'd want to talk with the editor of the school's newspaper, *The Monroe Reporter*. If there were time, maybe I'd talk to a local preacher.

Lots to do. I glanced at my watch, saw there was an entire day to do it in. Should be enough time. Only time would tell.

Chapter 7

Spying a small cluster of girls huddled and talking, I approached. Instead of an excuse me, I said, "Hey, any of you know Maryjean D'Amonda?" It wasn't exactly a large school, but this approach was still a long shot at best. However, it was a quick way to get started.

First, they all stared at me as if I didn't belong. A few of the girls turned away, as if my question was part of a line I might be feeding them. One girl snarled, "No. Should we?"

Either freshman snobs thinking a title of *queen* followed them over from high school or college seniors flaunting their new mental crowning. "Hey," I said, "thanks anyway."

Someone tapped my shoulder. I turned around and faced a young girl. She was dressed in black boots and black jeans with a black belt with a large black iron belt buckle. She wore a black T-shirt—no sleeves, a black studded necklace strap—like a bull dog might wear, dyed black hair, a nose ring in each nostril, multiple earrings in both ears and an earring piercing each eye brow. "Hey," she said.

"Yeah?" I asked. I could not help but stare in amusement.

"You're looking for Maryjean D'Amonda?" she said, looking around as she hitched her knap-sack up over one shoulder. She gave me a nervous smile.

"I am." I spoke softly, casually stuffing a hand into my front pocket as I shifted my weight from one foot to the other. "You know her?"

"You police?" She asked. I noticed small breasts under the tight fitting T-shirt. No bra.

"No. Do I look like police?" Dumb question, I know. Had to ask it, though.

"Yeah. Look at the way you're dressed, man. Got a cigarette?" she said.

"I do."

"Let's smoke. We'll talk."

Grabbing my cigarettes and a pack of matches from the breast pocket of my shirt, I could not believe what I was hearing. This girl acted like a spy. I had the feeling I was wasting my time. She'd suckered me out of a smoke. "You know," I said, handed her a cigarette. "I'm only looking for Maryjean. She's not in any trouble, not with me. But it is very important that I talk with her." I handed her a business card.

She eyed me suspiciously, stuck the butt between her lips and waited for a light. Striking the match, I offered her the flame first, then lit my own. She looked at the card next, studied it and stared at me some more. She didn't comment on the card, as she tucked it into her back pocket. She took a long drag on her cigarette and exhaled as she looked around campus. "Is this about the Tenth House? Are you with them?"

The Tenth House? "Not that I'm aware of." What was the right answer to her obvious probe-like question.

"Oh? Me neither," she said, took another long drag.

"And what's your name?"

"Scar."

"Scar? Lovely. Your parents must have spent a long time on that one," I said.

"You are the police," Scar said, turning away, ready to run.

Risking an assault charge, I grabbed her arm. "I'm not with the police. I wasn't lying to you. Why are you so tense? Is Maryjean in some kind of trouble where she needs to be afraid of the police?"

Scar stared at me, took another drag and ignored my question. "Let's walk."

"Where to?" I asked. Though I found Scar oddly entertaining, I didn't want to waste the entire morning with her. Especially if she could not produce any answers. I needed information.

"The Student Union. It's like a cafeteria and lounge. We can sit in there." Scar started to walk away. I was left with two choices, follow her or head off blindly on my own and hope I run into someone else who might know Maryjean.

Going out on my own would seem foolish, especially if Scar really did know Ms. D'Amonda.

"Hot today, huh?" Scar said as I quickly caught up to her and walked along side her. "Humid as hell. I'm a sophomore and a Criminal Justice major with a minor in English."

"How do you know Maryjean?" I asked, while scanning over the faces of kids passing by. In a bizarre way, they all resembled one another with the same haircuts, same ill-fitted clothes and same acne.

"She's my—ah, shoot. They saw me," Scar said suddenly. I heard her swallow hard.

"Who saw you?"

"Look, I don't want us to separate suspiciously, so I'm going to say good-bye normal-like. Okay? No scene," Scar said softly. She took a quick drag on her cigarette, dropped it to the ground and used the toe of her boot to crush the lit end. She stood on those toes and kissed me hard on the lips, her hands held tight to the back of my head. I thought my eyes might pop, so I closed them. When the kiss ended, I thought I couldn't talk. Scar had caught me completely off guard.

Finally I managed, "What's going on?" I dropped my cigarette to the ground, too, crushed the head. I tried not to look mad or scared.

"You going to be around?" she asked. "Around campus I mean, Magnum PI?"

"I should be," I said. Scar shot me a stern look. "I'll be around, but it's not Magnum. I'm going to swing by *The Monroe Reporter*. I have more work to do around campus."

"I'll catch up with you later, maybe not today, but later. Okay, Nicholas Tartaglia?"

"Wait, before you go. What's this Tenth House?"

"I thought it was the reason why you were looking for Maryjean," Scar said.

"Is it something I should know about? Because, I've never heard of it, doesn't even sound familiar," I said. Again I pulled my pack of cigarettes out, took one and offered another to Scar. She, of course, accepted.

"You should know about it!" she said. Her tone was very serious. I sensed an anxiety in her answer, as well. "The name should sound off a freaking alarm in your head. The Tenth House is nothing to screw around with. Remember that," Scar said, waited for me to light her cigarette. I cupped the flame and held it to her lips. She puffed on the butt and blew smoke out of her mouth.

"What is the Tenth House, Scar?" I asked.

Again she ignored my question. "Thanks for the smokes. I'll be broke before the end of the semester, won't even have enough for a pack of cigarettes, know what I mean?"

I shrugged. I knew what she meant. For the second time, she stood on tippy toes and kissed me softer this time. "See ya later," she said, winking as she turned and walked away.

Glancing around, still feeling a tingling sensation in my lips and through my body, I could not find any group of people watching us, not even after that rather strong display of physical emotion. Schizophrenic? Maybe.

How long I stood there, stunned, I don't know. All at once I realized I knew I needed to move or risk turning to stone.

The newspaper was run from the bowels of the building where most of the English and literature classes were taught. At the bottom of the stairs was the door to the journalism room. Printed on a frosted glass door in fancy black scrawl were the words: *The Monroe Reporter*. Knocking, I turned the knob and walked in. "Hello," I called out. No one answered.

Looking around, I was amazed to see the amount of computer terminals set up in the room. Ten laser printers, side by side, sat on a long table in the rear. "Anyone here?"

Strolling around, I glanced at everything, looking for anything. In a corner of the room was a rack filled with back issues of the weekly newspaper. I grabbed several copies and looked at the printing dates. There were no windows in the room. The light overhead was dim; reading any particular article would give me a headache.

"Can I help you?" someone asked. I turned around, saw a young woman who bared an uncanny resemblance to novelist Patricia Cornwell. Short, straight, dark brown hair with blond highlights, worn over the ears. She wore round, gold-rimmed glasses over dark eyes, little make-up. "My name's Patricia Helms, I'm the senior editor for the paper," she said as she came forward and held out her hand.

"I'm Nicholas Tartaglia. Nick," I said as we shook hands.

"Freshman? Interested in a spot on *The Monroe Reporter*?" Helms asked. "We're always looking for someone new with a fresh voice. Are you a journalist major?" Her smile was cordial. Her eyes took in my clothes. I thought I looked fine. Though no one, I'll admit, was dressed like me.

"Um, no. Not really," I said. Patricia, obviously strong, confident, gave me an odd look—one I was getting used to receiving. "I needed to ask some questions, and I thought someone on the paper, you maybe, might be the one I need to talk to."

Patricia laughed. "That's ironic. Usually, it's me and my staff asking the questions." She sat on a table, crossed her ankles and folded her hands on her lap. "Shoot. What's on your mind? You with another paper?"

"No. I'm not a journalist. I was looking for information on the Tenth House. Could you provide me with anything?" I asked. Patricia shifted her weight very slightly, body tensed. I caught the movement.

"The Tenth House? No, it's not something I'm familiar with. What is it, exactly?" she asked. I could tell she was lying, good at it, but lying just the same. Why lie though?

"I don't know, exactly. That's why I'm here. That's where the question is coming from."

Patricia slid off the table. "Look, I might be a journalist, but that doesn't mean I have the answers to everything." She tried to laugh. It sounded forced. "If you find out what it is and want to come back, maybe we can look into it. Right now, I don't have the time to put any leg work into . . . what did you call it, the Tenth House?"

"Right. So, you've never heard of it?" I said. I would accept that answer for now. Move on. Question number two: "Okay, how about Darla Bristol? Does that name ring a bell?"

"It does," Patricia Helms said, slowly. "I've heard it, can't remember where. Why? What about her?"

"She was a student here, a freshman last year. Pretty. Died of a supposed drug overdose last October. Her body was found in the canal." I spoke quickly reciting basic facts.

"God, that. And who are you exactly?" Patricia said. She looked distraught, suddenly. She was waiting for my answer. She wasn't going to talk to just anyone, it seemed.

"A friend of Darla's mother," I said. I gave her a business card.

She looked at the card, didn't question my friendship, or the fact that I was a private investigator. My answers seemed to satisfy the editor for the moment. "Yeah," Patricia said. "I remember when that happened. I wasn't the reporter on that case, though."

"Oh? Who was?"

"I have no idea," Patricia said. "Listen, I really am busy. I work on tight deadlines, especially between classes and the paper, you know? I've got to whip the next edition into shape. I hope you understand? I also hope you find what you're looking for. Right now, I need to get to work."

I'd been wrong. She wasn't going to talk to anyone.

She was terminating our conversation. I thanked her for her time. "Hey," I said, still holding a stack of *The Monroe Reporter* back issues. "Can I read through some of these? I know you don't remember who wrote the Bristol lead," I said, wanted to add: *And are a little too lazy to look into it for me.* "But I'll bet the story's in one of these issues." I smiled. "Easy to find."

"Those can't leave this room and right now I've got to lock up. I have to interview someone. Our meeting is in ten minutes." She held out her hand. I gave her the newspapers.

I shrugged. "I'm sure back copies can be found on file in the library, huh?"

"Of course. Feel free. If you find what you're looking for let me know. I'll be glad to do all I can to help you."

It felt like the room temperature dropped fifteen degrees. It should have felt good considering the heat outside. It didn't. I had the chills. "Sure, thanks. You've been very helpful, Ms. Helms."

She stood by the door waiting for me to leave. I walked past her, out into the hall. She closed and locked the door behind her. "Who have you got an interview with?" I asked, trying to make small talk and using it to continue my probing.

"The student council members. They have budget talks tonight, I want to get a feel for how things might look for the school year," Patricia said. We walked up the stairs together. "Look Mr. Tartaglia, I hope I didn't seem rude back there."

"Rude? No. Call me Nick, though."

"Listen, I knew Darla Bristol. We weren't friends or anything, but I knew her."

How? I wanted to ask, waited. She was giving me something. If I pulled, she might fall silent. As long as she was willing to talk, I needed to be willing to listen.

"It was a real bad thing, what happened to her. It's a shame."

"What is?" I asked.

"That she got into drugs. She probably thought she could handle it, got in over her head. I don't know. It happens to a lot of people. I mean, everyone tries drugs. I know I have, but I also knew I would never become addicted. I always thought of myself as stronger than that. If you would have asked me before Darla's accident, I would have said that I thought she was stronger, too." Patricia sighed. We'd reached the top of the stairs. I pulled open the door. "I mean it when I say, good luck. If you need anything, really, let me know. You know where to find me. I'm down there almost every night sometimes, and when there's a deadline to beat—all night."

"Okay, thanks. Good luck with your interview," I said. We stepped outside.

"My what?"

"The interview with the council," I reminded her.

"Oh that. Yeah, thanks." She smiled and stared at me for a moment.

She walked off. She had a very attractive figure and I could not help but watch her walk until I could no longer differentiate her from the rest of the student bodies.

"Okay, now where to?" I asked, stuffed my hands into my pockets and started walking toward the faculty building across the way from the Student Union.

While I walked, I wondered where Scar might have taken off to? Did she still plan on going to the Student Union? I changed direction, decided a bite to eat for lunch might hit the spot right about now.

Entering the Union from the rear, I was suddenly face to face with a flyer-filled cork board hallway. Many of the ads, I noticed, urged students to apply for credit cards, most proclaiming, No Student Shall Be Turned Down!

Odd. Most students were like Scar—and myself when I was attending college—broke. How would I have managed a monthly credit card bill on top of my weekly drinking expenses? Shaking my head, I pressed on.

Down the next hallway, an easel stood holding a chalkboard. 101 BSU. The school's highly acclaimed alternative radio station. The door was open. Walking in I noticed the large collection of compact discs in the room behind the glass where the DJ operated the station.

A kid with long hair on the left side of his head, shaved bare on the right, sat talking passionately into a microphone. I could not hear what the topic was, but hung around, arms folded, watching. The DJ continued to talk. He must have felt my eyes on him as he looked up and stared.

I waved.

He gave me a look that said, *What the hell do you want,* dufus!

I left.

In the heart of the Union I saw an information and ticket sales booth over by a small grouping of wall-mounted pay phones and a spiral staircase. Past the booth was a lounge area littered with sofas, love seats, chairs, coffee tables, end tables and an assortment of magazines. Behind the lounge was the dinning area for the cafeteria. People walked through a door at the back of the dining area and came out at the opposite end with trays full of food.

Suddenly starving, I moved to the back of the line, grabbed a tray, some silverware and a small stack of napkins. The guy in front of me was talking to the guy in front of him. They went back and forth talking about an upcoming, off-campus party.

I ordered a cheeseburger, fries and a salad, filled a large cup with Dr. Pepper, closed a lid over the cup, took a straw from a bin, paid for my food and found a centrally located table.

Pouring a packet of catsup over my fries, I glanced casually around the Union. From where I sat I could see the information booth, spiral staircase, pay phones, lounge and the doors leading to the campus courtyard.

Though I looked around for a proverbial clue, it was Scar I hoped to see. Realizing she was nowhere to be found, or purposely avoiding being seen by me, I ate quickly and decided to get on with the investigation.

The president of the school could not see me now. He was off campus at a meeting, his secretary told me. Her name was Mrs. Stavinski. I tried to schedule an appointment with him for later today.

"That's no good. He's not coming back. The meeting he's in is an all day affair," the secretary informed me. She looked like the exact opposite of my Betty. This woman was old, full of wrinkles, silver hair and a thin smile, streaked with cocky attitude.

"So?"

"So, you need to schedule an appointment with him for another time," she said smiling as she reached for her coffee mug.

"When would be a good time to make an appointment?"

The secretary regarded me for a moment, as if wondering why I wouldn't just go away. "And you're a student here?"

"No, I'm not," I said.

"I see. Are you a reporter?" Mrs. Stavinski asked.

"No ma'am, I'm afraid not," I answered.

"May I ask why it is that you wish to speak with President Granatta?" She continued to smile, looked royally annoyed.

"Sure you can, only I can't tell you. Client privileges, you understand I'm sure," I said, perhaps leading her to believe I was an attorney, though the way I was dressed may have left a trace of doubt in her mind.

"I see. Well, how does tomorrow afternoon sound? One o'clock? I can schedule in about ten minutes, will that do?" Mrs. Stavinski said.

Glancing at my wristwatch, I smiled, looked up. "Should be a wonderful time. I look forward to it."

"And your name?" she asked.

"Nicholas Tartaglia." Mrs. Stavinski wrote it down. I left.

In my car, I sat for a moment, heels of my hands pressed firmly over my eyelids. A headache was growing, pulsing. It had been a long day. Despite lunch, I felt hungry still. Very tired and ready for a long nap, I tried to decide what to do next.

Driving around the outskirts of campus I found a Catholic Church, St. Anthony's. I decided to stop and call on the priest in charge.

Chapter 8

A beautiful statue of the Virgin Mary, dressed in a white gown and sky-blue robe, stood out on the front lawn in front of the sanctuary, arms spread, a Rosary dangling from between the fingers of her right hand. The graceful woman's head was tilted slightly as she looked at the world around her. Studying the expression on her face, I saw sadness. It was the same expression I found on all statues of the Blessed Mother. Who could blame her? Her son had been taken from her and sacrificed.

The church, shaped like a large farmhouse, was white with a black shingled roof. A large steeple rose into the sky, a giant cross at the top rose higher. Stained glass windows and rose bushes decorated the exterior sides.

Entering the church through large wooden doors, I turned and faced more statues behind rows of lit candles. The statue of Joseph, Mary's husband, was set in a headstone-shaped hole in the battleship gray wall. He wore a brown cloak, a rope tied around his waist. His feet were bare. St. Anthony stood in a mirrored hole opposite Joseph, dressed in a white gown, red vest-like robe draping over sandals. His arms were outstretched, welcoming, his eyes looked to heaven.

Outside, the heat and humidity had reached an unbearable level—at least unbearable to me. Inside the sanctuary it was cool. It felt refreshing but was also dark, a little eerie.

Fifty candles, on two wrought iron tables, sat in front of each statue. Most of the candles burned. To light a candle, you donated money into a collection box. One was mounted to the head of each table. Candles were lit with something resembling raw spaghetti from a box.

I stood in front of the statue of St. Anthony, hands in my pocket.

I thought of Darla. Her spirit seemed trapped between this world and the next. I took a few bills out of my pocket, dropped them into the box and lit a candle in her honor. I whispered: "Here's to God's speed, Darla. Amen."

Walking through another set of doors into the church, I marveled at the rows of pews sectioned in halves filling the room of worship. The altar possessed more statues, including one of Christ, hanging, suspended from the ceiling, nailed to the cross. I could see no wires, or string. Another miracle, I guessed. From somewhere I smelled incense burning, or were the candles I'd lit scented? "Hello?"

"Hello? Can I help you," a man's voice said. I looked all around. He was up in the choir box; a balcony above the back quarter of the church. The priest leaned over the balcony's edge and smiled down at me.

"Ah, I'm not sure, really. I just needed to talk to you for a little while, ask you some questions. If you have the time, of course." I dipped my fingers into the Holy Water in the marble bowl mounted to the wall near the doors. I made the sign of the cross with wet fingertips, felt a tingling sensation on my skin—as I always did when touching the blessed water to my flesh.

"Of course. I'll be right down," the priest said.

"Thank you Father. Take your time." I walked to the center of the room, the front of the altar. I stared at the podium where a huge Bible sat closed. A microphone stood on a stand beside the podium, angled toward an invisible speaker.

I stared at the image of Christ on the cross. "God," I whispered, "is Darla with you?"

Hearing footsteps behind me, I turned to watch the priest walk down the center aisle. He stood five-eight with dark, slicked back hair. Twilight blue eyes bulged enough to be noticed from sunken sockets. He was clean-shaven, dressed in the traditional black shirt, white collar, black slacks and shoes. Like his eyes, the priest's belly bulged just enough to be noticed. He walked slowly, talking to a man in his late fifties, I'd guess. The man wore navy blue overalls, carrying a six-foot ladder on his shoulder and a tool belt around his waist. The maintenance man's hair was silver, his skin looked soft and showed signs of wrinkles. His eyes were a gentle shade of blue, almost gray.

The priest explained to the man what work still needed to be done, pointing at the altar, then to the back of the church. I couldn't hear everything being said, but I overheard enough to know the guy in the overalls worked for the priest. "When you're done there, Zach, come and see me. I might have a few little things that really need to be looked at before next Sunday's Mass," the priest said.

"Sure thing, Father. I might run over and grab a burger later. You want me to bring you anything back? You want to come?" Zach asked.

"Let me know before you go, I'll go with you," the priest said. He turned away from the maintenance man. He tried not to get caught looking me over. "Now, what exactly is it that I can do for you?" the priest asked. He stood beside me, smiling. He said, "I'm Father Paul, by the way." He held out his hand. I shook it.

"Nicholas Tartaglia," I said. "You can call me, Nick. Anyway Father, I have some questions I need to ask, but the reasons for asking them are a little hard to believe," I said, snorted. "I even feel funny trying to explain myself. It's, well, kind of supernatural, you might say, the things I need to talk about." Over the priest's shoulder I noticed the Stations of the Cross mounted to the wall between stain glass windowpanes. The remaining stations, I guessed, were mounted to the wall behind me.

"Son," the priest said, "I'm a man who's based his whole life on believing in the unseen. Faith. It's called Faith. And if you, Nick, believe in what you're doing, then who am I to question your faith."

I smiled.

"You're not a student from the college, are you?" He asked.

"No."

"And you're not a member of this parish?"

"No. Is that a problem, Father?"

"Of course it's not. I was just curious. I'd hate to think you were and I didn't recognize you. We can talk in my office if you'd like? Come on, follow me." He placed his hand on the small of my back and led me to the altar. We kneeled, made the sign of the cross, stepped onto the altar and walked through a side door, down a dark hallway. It led to a closed door.

Father Paul opened the door revealing a plush, well-lit living room and office. A large cherry oak desk, computer and pair of filing cabinets sat in the back corner of the room. A sofa, love seat and recliner encircled a fireplace. The room was filled with books on wall-to-wall shelves. Lamps stood in every corner and sat on end tables, though none were on; large windows with the curtains parted provided plenty of natural light.

"Have a seat," the priest told me. "Can I interest you in something to drink? How about a glass of lemonade with some ice? I know it's hot out there."

"Sounds great. Nice and cool in here," I said.

"Central Air." He left the room, returned a moment later with two, tall glasses of lemonade with a slice of lemon in each. He handed me one. I took a long sip and held the glass with both hands. Waited. He sat down in the black leather, well cushioned, reclining chair. He wriggled around, getting comfortable. After he settled in, he stared at me and folded his hands across his small belly. "So, what can I do for you, Nick?"

"Sitting here right now, I feel pretty foolish." I laughed, took another sip of lemonade. "I mean, the past few days have skirted along the edges of surrealism, you know? I find everything a little hard to accept, so why I thought you'd believe me anymore than I believe myself is a little crazy." There is a long pause. I couldn't believe I just mentioned Darla. Standing up, I set the glass down on the end table nearest me. "I don't think I should be here, Father Paul, and I'm sorry to have wasted so much of your time."

Father Paul did not move. "Nick, do you have time to hear a story?"

A parable? I wanted to ask. "Yeah. I do," I said.

"Sit back down. I promise you it's not a long one, but I think it may help brake the *proverbial* ice here. Okay?"

I sat down.

Father Paul took a deep breath. I realized what a good-looking man he truly was. I don't think I've ever seen eyes like his on anyone else before. His features were strong, defined. The cleft in his chin, I'd missed seeing earlier, stood out. His nose was narrowly proportioned to the size of his oval face and slightly puffed cheeks. I liked this priest, he reminded me of my own father.

"Are you familiar with the church in Greece, down at the end of Mt. Read? There's a small cemetery around it?" Father Paul asked.

"The library? I mean, they turned that church into a library, right?"

"That's the one," Father Paul said. "Well, one Sunday night, a long time ago, a young priest was in the study—very much like this one, only smaller. He was enjoying a tumbler, one tumbler, mind you, of bourbon and reading passages from the Holy Scripture

. "He was new to the priesthood and new to the parish. It seemed like everything that was said that day, in his first sermon, came out wrong. Nothing had gone right. He began to question his chosen life, wondered if he'd made a vocational error. He still believed in the main Guy, just began to think he should be serving Him from the *opposite* side of the altar.

"Anyway, it had been a long, unproductive day and the priest just needed to relax and collect his thoughts." Father Paul crossed his legs. He looked away from me to the window. His lips thinned, brow creased, as he appeared to drag the memory out of some recess in his mind. I waited for him to go on.

"Like some bad cliché, it was raining horribly that night. Thunder boomed, lighting flashed. The young priest was thankful for the time he had to spend alone. Reading, thinking and questioning. Then there was a knock on the door. Reluctantly, the priest set his Bible and drink down, went to the window, parted curtains with the back of his hand, but couldn't see who was on the front step. He went to the door and opened it.

"Standing there in a red rain coat was a little girl, no more than seven. Despite the hood on her coat, she was soaked and her hair was drenched."

"What are you doing here?" the priest asked. He looked over the girl's head, out into the night. The sound of thunder began to roll, it grew louder and let out a bang. The sky was torn in shreds as the fingers of a skeleton danced across the heavens and lit the night. "Come in, get out of the rain!"

"I can't. It's my mother, she's dying. The phones are down. She needs to see you," the little girl said quickly. Rain water dripped from her bangs into her eyes. She made no move to wipe her eyes. "Please, come quickly."

"I need to grab my Bible and a rain jacket. Step inside while I get them," the priest said. He ran about the study searching for the things that he thought he might need. A woman was dying, needed her Last-Rite's read to her. He had never performed such a task. He felt panicked, nervous and nauseated. "Okay, where are we going?"

"Follow me, we'll run through the cemetery. It's a short-cut," the little girl said. She looked excited, anxious.

"Hurry then, I'm right behind you," the priest said. He followed her as best he could. The little girl was younger, faster. She weaned around the tombstones like a lab-mouse in a maze-study. Her home, the cheese. "Slow down," the priest shouted into the night. His words lost, unable to compete with the obstreperous thunder. "Little girl, slow down please."

The girl seemed to hear him. She slowed. Bending low to study a grave marker, she turned to see how far away the priest was. She stood up straight and ran again. The priest did not think he could run much more. The ground was saturated, he slipped and slid, but kept his balance and pressed on. A stitch in his side caused him to moan and hold the area while he ran.

Then he lost sight of the girl. She had vanished. The priest felt desperate. He tried to run faster and thankfully saw a lone house, a cape—lights on in the lower level. The sight of the house gave the priest a small burst of energy. He felt the urgency, perhaps, radiating from the home.

He made it to the back door, knocked, waited. The door opened.

"Father," an old man said. What hair he had on his head was white. His skin, including the top of his head was filled with various sized brown liver spots. "I can't believe you're here. The lines are down, I've been trying to call you. My wife, she's very sick, dying."

The priest felt an odd sensation begin to grow in his belly. The little girl was seven, eight at the most he rationed. She had told him that her mother was ill, dying. Yet the man standing in front of him was at least seventy, or perhaps older. There could be no way he was the father of the little girl. "Your wife?"

"Yes," the old man said. "Please come in, see my wife, talk to her. Your words will give her hope. She needs some hope right now. She's a good Christian woman, mind you, but it's been a while since we've been to church. She hasn't been out of bed in nearly two years. That makes her scared. Tell her there's no reason for her to be scared, that God understands her circumstances, that he won't keep her out of heaven because she's been ill and hasn't been to church. Will you tell her that?"

"Of course I will," the priest said.

"Father, how did you know my wife needed you?"

"You can thank the little girl for coming and getting me. She's the reason I'm here." The priest shrugged off his raincoat.

The old man took it, hung it in the coat closet. "Little girl?"

"Why yes. She told me her mother was dying, that she needed me. At least that had been what I thought she said. But what she must have said was that her grandmother was dying."

"We have no grandchildren," the man said.

The priest saw it then. It was on the wall, an antique looking photograph of the little girl who had come to his church, begging for his help. "This is her," the priest said, pointing to the photograph. "She was the little girl who came to get me."

The old man's pale face turned whiter. "That's our daughter, Father. She died when she was seven years old. It couldn't have been our Marlene."

The priest stared at the picture. It was the girl who had come to get him.

When the priest finished reading the dying woman her Last Rites, he started back to the church, walking through the cemetery. His newly learned short cut. He'd promised the elderly couple he would return after Monday's morning mass to see how everyone was feeling.

The rain had stopped. A thick fog rolled across the ground and engulfed the tombstones. In the distance, he saw someone sitting on top of a marker. "You," he called, quickened his step.

The child slid off the gravestone and ran into the woods, disappeared in the dense fog. He heard her laugh. The sound of it gave the young priest chills. He didn't run after her though. Instead, he walked toward where the child had been sitting.

The priest saw that something was on the tombstone. When he reached it, he gasped and knelt to pick the red raincoat up from the ground. He nearly screamed when he read the inscription on the headstone.
Marlene Canters 1920-1927.

I felt a chill race down my spine, realized I had been holding my breath, sitting on the edge of the sofa cushion. The story had me, caught me off guard. Father Paul was a wonderful storyteller, knew how to keep the pace. Timing. Delivery.
"You believe that story?" Father Paul asked.
"Do you?"
"Yes, with all my heart. I can't say for sure, but I've always suspected that God sent that little girl to the priest. A sign, perhaps. The young priest's faith was restored that evening. Not that he didn't still question it from time to time. I suppose we all do. But he never thought of doing any other kind of work. He was dedicated to serving God, then, and helping bring light to others." Father Paul reached for his lemonade, took a long drink, set the glass down.
"Was that young priest you, Father Paul?"
A twinkle in the eye that said, *Can't put one past you, Mister PI.* "Yes, Nick. It was me."
Did I believe it? I suppose. It sounded absurd and off the wall, I know. I've heard "off the wall" ghost stories, straight from the stock library of *X-Files* and *The Twilight Zone*.
"So do you see what I'm saying? About having faith in the unexplainable?"
Taking a deep breath, I realized it was my turn. Father Paul had earned my trust. I explained everything to him. I started with the ride into work on that morning, the rescue of Judy Swanson, and finished with my coming to St. Anthony's. While speaking, I studied the priest's expression, waiting to see the look that would tell me I'd gone too far.
Father Paul was a man I would not want to play poker with. His facial expression never changed. He listened without asking a question, without nodding. When I was done. I'd taken up nearly an hour of his time. "I'm sorry," I said. "I didn't mean to take so much of your time."
"There's nothing to be sorry for, Nick," Father Paul said. "If I had other plans, we either would have rescheduled our little meeting, or I would have rescheduled the other. As it is, I don't have to be anywhere. I do have an

appointment, marriage counseling, in roughly forty-five minutes, though."

I stood up. I didn't know what else to do. There wasn't much else to say. My lemonade glass was empty. I couldn't remember drinking it all. "Do you think I'm crazy?"

Father Paul sat comfortably in his chair, hands folded across his mid section. "Crazy? No. Troubled? Yes."

"That means you don't believe my story?" I asked.

"I didn't say that. Actually, I think I believe every word of it. When I say you're troubled, I mean you have yourself in the middle of an extremely bizarre situation and a potentially dangerous one, too. I know of the Tenth House. I'll never forget hearing about Darla Bristol when she was found dead," Father Paul said.

Did I expect the priest to believe my story? Of course not. The fact that he did, gave me an unexplainable odd feeling. Maybe I'd been hoping Father Paul would tell me I was off my rocker, not the sharpest knife in the drawer. Since he wasn't, I wasn't sure how to react. I fell back on basic instinct. I asked, "What can you tell me about the Tenth House?"

We both sat down.

"That's a tough one. Let's start with the name, all right? The Tenth House is like a constellation. You know, star clusters studied by astrologers and astronomers? It's said that anyone born under this sign, is the devil. The Tenth House is the devil's house. So the group of believers you're looking for are satanic worshipers. This cult, that's what I call it—similar to a David Koresh cult—meets frequently. Where? I have no idea. Who runs the show? I don't know the answer to that question either. So how do I know they meet frequently? Let me try to explain," Father Paul said. He stood up, stuffed his hands into his pockets and walked to the window. He pulled the blinds open all the way, as if suddenly afraid of the darkness gathered in the corners of his room. He leaned against the wall, stared out toward the parking lot. "If we said the cult was like the wind, then you could say the wind is always around, even on a hot, stagnate day like today, right?"

"Okay." I wasn't sure what he meant. I thought if I let him keep talking, without asking questions, that he would explain himself. After all, his job consisted of talking coherently so that everyone he spoke to understood what he was saying.

"Now, when the wind picks up, you feel it. When there's going to be a storm," he paused, turning as he walked toward me. We stood toe to toe, nose to nose. "When there's going to be a storm you not only feel it, but you sense it. The darkness that comes before the sky opens up. The wind stops moving all together, the air gets thicker, heavier. There's not much you can do but hide, watch and wait to see how much damage gets done."

I understood what he was saying. I was hoping for a little more detail, something a little more substantial.

"I know what you might be thinking," Father Paul said. "How can a priest know an evil cult exists right outside his doors and talk about hiding; do nothing to try and put a stop to it."

I hadn't been thinking that. It was a damned good question, though. I accepted full credit for the thought. "I wasn't sure how to go about asking it," I said.

"There was a confrontation between me—the church really—and the cult."

"You had words?"

"Had words? No. Nothing as luxurious as having words. No. When I came to this parish, oh in eighty-eight, I was not warned about the Tenth House. The priest leaving was old. He was retiring. He never said a word, and I can understand why. No one would believe him, right?"

"I guess. What's his name? Maybe I can look him up, ask him some questions."

"Father Frank."

"Father Frank," I said. "He have a last name?"

"He did. I can't think of it right now, but that doesn't matter. He died a few years back. Natural causes. You don't hear that one too often nowadays. His heart just stopped one night. He was in his nineties.

"Anyway, I always loved moving to a new church. It was a challenge; get the followers to have more faith and more trust in God. This parish was not healthy when I got here. Anorexic. Father Frank, in his day from what I understand, was quite a speaker. People flocked from all around to hear him talk. But, as he got older, his fire died some. His heart was still in the job, I gather, but the zealous vigor and energy couldn't be. Know what I mean?"

"I do." I hated the thought of growing old.

"Where was I going with this?"

"You were building up the tension in your story, leading it toward the climactic confrontation."

"You a writer, or an investigator?" He laughed.

"Both, I guess you might say." I laughed, too.

"Well," Father Paul said, "I needed to do something to bring people back into the fold. I started asking questions to those who showed up every Sunday morning. Things like, What do the people want? What can I do to help this town? The main answer I received in return to my inquiry was to stop and get rid of the Tenth House."

This was either in eighty-eight, or eighty-nine, I reasoned. The cult has been around for over ten years. That's amazing. "They've been around a long time then, huh?"

"Longer, I'd imagine." Father Paul went back to his chair, sat. "I started a personal crusade against the House. I made sure a reporter from the newspaper and the college paper interviewed me. I was on channel thirteen, even. Every Sunday, more and more people filled the pews. They knew I had issues, things to say. I became quite popular. Mind you, I wasn't looking to get famous. I was looking to fill the church so I could preach and teach them about God."

"I understand." It amazed me, the sincerity in Father Paul's words. He cared and it was obvious.

"Cutting to the chase, on the altar one early Sunday morning before Mass, I found a skinned dog. It wasn't dead. It's muscles and bones were exposed. It was horrible. It looked like one of those illustrations in a medical textbook showing the inner tissues of the body. It was weird, the dog looked at me with no eyelids. It was panting a mile a minute, dying, in terrible pain. I knew it would die from shock."

"What did you do?" I asked. "How'd it get there? I mean, don't you lock the church doors?"

"The church doors are locked, yes. I have no idea how they got in. How does a thief get into a locked house or car? I called the police. They came right away. They said that the locks looked fine. No one had tampered with them. All they did, really, was inspect the area around the dead bolts for scratches. I could have done that. But the police brought a veterinarian, too. By the time they arrived though, the dog was beyond saving. I said a prayer for the animal, even though I don't really believe in animals having souls." Father Paul slid forward in his chair. He rested his elbows on his knees, folded his hands together. "I think I prayed, not so much for the dog, but for me. I was scared. I knew, right from that moment, I knew I was being warned. It was a pretty clear, evident warning, wouldn't you agree?"

My throat felt dry. I was captured in the tale. I nodded.

"The police got the dog off the altar. I quickly scrubbed the area, trying to rid the altar of the bloody mess. People would be arriving for the morning service. Finally, I draped a running carpet down the altar.

"I greeted people at the door that morning, as I did every Sunday. One couple looked distraught and their daughter, Melissa, who was six at the time, was crying terribly. The father, I can't remember his name, was going to take his family home. They couldn't stay. He told me they thought they could sit through Mass, but it was too painful for their daughter. Her dog was missing."

I swallowed. I pictured the heart-broken little girl. Her dog had been taken and tortured. It would be better for her to believe the dog had run away. "Did you convince them to stay?"

"Why would I? No, I thought it might be easier for us all if they go, too. Well, the father sent his wife and daughter back to the car. He came up to me, asked if we could talk. Sure, I'd told him. He handed me a small envelope, said it was pinned to the morning newspaper. My name was on the flap. He hadn't opened it. The man stared at me, maybe waiting for me to open it right then and there in front of him. He didn't know I knew about the dog, so he just thought it was odd getting an envelope addressed to me with the paper. It was odd, I'll admit, but I knew right at that moment what the letter might say."

Father Paul looked nervous, anxious, sick. I wanted to tell him to stop, that he didn't need to go on if he wasn't ready. I couldn't. I needed to hear what he had to say.

"I simply tucked the envelope into my back pocket and thanked him. He gave me a quizzical look, raised his eyebrows in defeat and walked after his family. I had to wait until after church before I could read what had been written and stuffed into that envelope. I swear I could feel it burning against my buttocks," Father Paul smiled.

"What did it say? Did you save the letter?" I asked.

"I didn't save the letter, no. It was evil. I didn't need anything evil in my possession. I read the brief note once, then burned the paper and the envelope."

"What did it say?" I pressed.

"The note said just this: *Next time it will be Melissa.*"

Shit. "And you knew it was them, the Tenth House?" It was a stupid question. I was sorry I asked it.

"Not a doubt in my mind."

I gave Father Paul my card, told him if he ran into any members of the cult, or if he had any tips, to give me a call. Before I left, I got around to asking a few more cult-specific questions, like: Is the cult a registered religion? Is it a group that was initially after a tax break? Could the church have started out as a front to launder money for some business? Since I knew drugs were involved, I wondered if the cult made drugs and sold them? Father Paul looked at me, a gleam in his eye and said something like, *You know Nick, those were questions I never got around to thinking of. They're good questions. If you want*, he'd told me, *I'll look into some of that for you.* He said then with a laugh, *I kind of like the idea of playing Father Doweling.* I told him if he found himself with some extra time on his hands, to go ahead, but that I didn't want him getting involved if he thought it might be dangerous for any of the people in his parish. He assured me he'd be discreet in his inquires, *besides, it'll make me feel good to know I'm back in the battle,* he'd said. A man's got to be fighting against something, doesn't he? I had to admit, though, it doesn't feel so bad fighting an enemy when you have an friend fighting beside you.

Then we wished each other the best of luck. Father Paul said God was in our corner. He told me to come around if I needed anything, any help at all. He was as anxious to rid the town of its cancer as I was to save the next girl scheduled to die. He'd call me if he came up with anything.

When I left the church, I drove back to the college, circled around the campus a few times hoping I'd spot Patricia or Scar. If either were around, I couldn't see them.

Who had Scar been afraid of? It was more than one person at the school. Who had seen her? She had said: *Ah shoot. They saw me.* Who, they? I didn't have Scar's real name, so I could not officially look her up anywhere. She'd be easier to find than Maryjean. Asking around campus for a Scar might be more effective in striking a chord in someone's memory. I know if someone asked me a hundred years from now if I'd ever met a person named Scar, I'd be able to vividly recall the wild young thing I'd met today.

Chapter 9

The next morning at work, Betty told me Ned was in his office and wanted to see me first thing. I wasn't fully awake yet. I missed seeing Judy Swanson out jogging on my way into work. I think seeing her woke me, and kept me up for the day. God, I hoped she'd start running again.

In my office, I glanced quickly at the answering machine. There were no new messages. I dropped my sports coat over the back of my chair and walked across the way to Ned's door, knocked softly three times. Ned said: "Come in."

"You wanted to see me, boss?" I walked into the room, closed the door behind me. He was dressed in a dark suit, as usual. I hated that. He made me feel like I should wear a suit, too. I didn't, he just made me feel like I should. Comfort came, for me, in nice, loose fitting jeans, a dress shirt, or in the winter a turtleneck and always a sports coat. Today, I just happened to be wearing taupe slacks, loafers and a denim blue dress shirt.

"Hey Nick, take a seat," he said, leaned back comfortably in his chair, laced his fingers together, placed his hands behind his head. "I got a call the other day from this company," Ned started. I sat slouched in the chair and crossed my feet at the ankles. "They've been receiving outrageous telephone bills, full of 1-900 charges. They wanted me to catch the person making the calls."

"Couldn't they just have 900 block on the line?" I asked. I enjoyed talking with Ned. He always ran cases by me. Either he appreciated my input, liked to test me, or needed a sound board to help him puzzle through a mystery, or maybe a bit of the three.

"They could, were about to, but realized they wanted to catch and confront the person responsible. They felt the situation should not simply get by-passed, or over looked. They wanted, in essence, to right the wrong."

"Well, they must know from what phone the calls are being made from," I said. It would seem obvious then who was making the calls.

"They do, but it's a centrally located phone at the front desk. People use it all day," Ned explained.

"Right." I strained for a thought. I needed a new cup of coffee; the full cup I'd brought with me on the ride to work sat on the dash in my car, two thirds full, cold as ice. "How often have these calls been made?"

"Three times in two months."

"Three times? That's it?"

"The total bill for the three calls is just over three thousand dollars."

"Get out of here," I said. "How about just give out memo's to everyone who works there, even the cleaning staff and any supply vendors? Maybe call a meeting and explain some consequences to the group if the calls continue?"

"Did it. They've done that." Ned smirked. He was playing a game, definitely testing me.

"Well, were the calls being made all over the country or to one particular number? If they were going all over the country, it might be harder to pinpoint a specific employee. However, if all the calls were being made to like, 1-900-Spank-It, I'd start looking at all the male employees." I worked out the thoughts while I spoke. Ned was looking for quick thinking. I waited for his reaction.

"Let's say the 900 number is generic, like a psychic line, or daily horoscope listing. I'd wager a bet that it's an even share of males to females who call those numbers. What then?"

"Ah," I said, as I stood up, held my chin pinched between thumb and forefinger, the other hand stuffed into a pocket. I paced around the office. "Is it a psychic line?"

"Actually, no. It's a gambler's line. Picks Lotto numbers, baseball games, Vegas odds, that kind of thing. I called the number. Betty's gonna flip when she gets the phone bill. She'll think I've developed a gambling problem." He laughed.

There was no laugh from me. I was working on the mystery. A thought came to mind. "Nice point. Anyone working for the company have a gambling problem?"

"No. I did an extensive background check. Most haven't even been up to Niagara Falls Casino, yet," Ned explained.

"Does this company receive a lot of front door deliveries? Small packages that might require an employee signature?"

Ned sat up, leaned into his desk. "Sometimes. Yes."

Where was I going with this? "Maybe," I said, felt like a lawyer questioning a witness during a trial. "Maybe a delivery guy shows up, a package under his arm, tells the person he has a delivery for Joe Schmo. Person near the desk tells the guy that no Joe Schmo works at the company," I said, paused, thought.

"Yes. Go on," Ned urged.

"Well, the delivery guy gets all flustered, says he needs to call his boss, clear up the big mess." I slip the other hand into my pocket now. The mystery solved in my mind. I just needed to complete the telling of the tale. "Who's going to tell a delivery guy that he can't use the phone. The guy calls the 900 number—his number. A number he set up with the phone company as his own business. He waits for the charges to add up while he listens to his own recorded messages. If he's smart he's set his line up with a hundred-dollar minimum for the first minute, maybe fifty, sixty bucks for every minute thereafter. He stays on the line, pretends he clearing up the delivery schedule with his boss. When he's sure he's made a fortune, he hangs up, thanks the person behind the desk and leaves. Wham, he's off to the next office building, same package, same scam." I was so proud of myself, I pulled my hands out of my pockets and clapped them together.

"Beautiful. Wonderful." He smiled like a proud father. I'd done good by him. "You working on anything new?"

"Kinda. Nothing big, really. Why?"

Ned laughed. "Nothing big, huh? I got three calls on my voice mail last night. People wanting to know if you're who you say you are."

"Three calls, really? Who?"

"Only a Father Paul from St. Anthony's gave his name. The other two all said you asked them some questions, gave them a card. They wouldn't leave a name." This didn't seem to concern Ned. People were funny about their privacy.

"And they all asked the same basic question?"

"Basically."

"Huh. That's interesting. Were the anonymous ones women?"

"Yup. What's up?" Ned asked.

"I'm not really sure," I said. It was the truth, sugar coated, but the truth.

"Give me a WAG," Ned said.

"WAG?"

"A wild ass guess." He smiled.

"Never heard that one before," I admitted.

"Use it in your book. I'm sure you'll find a way to work it in," Ned said confidently.

"I can give you a SWAG," I said, smiled.

84

"SWAG?"

"Yeah. A *scientific* wild ass guess." Ned laughed. I told him, without mentioning Darla, that an old friend from high school wanted the death of her daughter looked into. I gave him some background on the work I'd done, leaving out the supernatural happenings. I told my boss that I'd been in touch with the police, my brother-in-law, Detective Cerio. "So," I wrapped it up, "I'm guessing the calls came in from Scar and Patricia."

"Sounds like a pretty educated guess to me," Ned said. He'd asked me to guess who called and I did. "You getting paid for this, Nick, or how are you working it?"

Ned Baxter did not like to take on friends or family for clients. It was always harder to collect fees due. It was a reasonable rule. I'd broken it. "Yes," I lied. "We're getting paid."

"You didn't offer your old girlfriend a break?"

If I were charging her at all, I would have offered a break. "A small one. If it's a problem, take the what's owed out of my wages."

"Not a problem, Nick. Just asking," Ned said. "Scar, huh? Sounds like she might be a little odd. You making up the kisses? I've been in this business a long time, nothing like that ever happened to me. Never met a female named Scar, either, though."

"With a wholesome name like Scar, how could I possibly make any of it up?" I laughed.

"Get back to work, Nick. Go on and get back to work."

Back to work, right. I left Ned's office and locked myself in mine. There were several things I could do to get the day started. The most obvious would be heading back up to the college and nose around some more. My little talk with Father Paul still left a tingle of apprehension in my spine. It sounded like the Tenth House has been around for many, many years, decades possibly.

Scar was another person I looked forward to running into again. She was part of the story. How exactly, it was too soon to tell. On that note, I thought Patricia, the school's newspaper editor, was a little suspicious, but then again, aren't most reporters? Aren't most college students?

I had an appointment set with the school's president. I glanced at the clock on my wall. It wasn't even nine, I was scheduled to meet with Jeffrey Granatta at one. I wouldn't want to keep the biggest man on campus waiting.

I leaned back in my chair. Where has Darla-the-ghost been hiding? If she dared to show herself again, I had questions about her life and death that only she could provide the answers to.

For starters, I could not picture Darla involved in wild, kinky sex. And who introduced Darla to the ways of the Tenth House? Maryjean? A boyfriend, maybe the kid that liked to tie her up, whip her, hurt her for the pleasures of sexual fulfillment?

I thought of Scar. She seemed to be willing to talk, to help. Sure, someone, or some group of *someones* had scared her off, but . . .

My telephone rang. I picked it up. "Yeah?"

It was Betty. "There's a call on line one. It's a girl. She won't give me her name. She sounds kind of young. You want to take it?"

I thought of Darla. Could a spirit use a phone? "Sure. I'll take it." I pressed the flashing light for line one. "This is Nicholas Tartaglia. How can I help you?"

"No kidding, you really are a private eye?" she said. It was Scar. I recognized the voice immediately and matched it to the level of excitement in the way she spoke. "I thought you were just busting my chops the other day, you know? Reworking an ancient pick-up line. I swore to myself you were just a student."

A student. I look that young? Cool. "My school days were over years ago," I said. I pictured Scar, dressed in black. I remembered her kiss. A tingle made it's way down my belly, to below my naval. "What's going on? Or did you call just to check my credentials."

"No, I called to check your credentials yesterday, I'm calling now to see if you want to meet me today for lunch," she said.

"You're too young for me," I said, half-joking.

"Don't flatter yourself. You kiss good and everything, but you're a little too straight, if you know what I mean."

I didn't. "No. Not really."

"Look," Scar said. "I'm not picking you up. I knew you were looking for Maryjean, Darla's old roommate. I happen to know you're still looking for her. I can help, lead you right to her, but I need to hear what's going on, you know? So meet me for lunch, all right? We can go to the Student Union. You can buy me a sandwich and some fries. How does that sound? We can pick up where we left off, all right, sound good?" Scar asked.

"It sounds," I said, shook my head and leaned forward into my desk, "like a date."

"A date? I thought I already told you not to flatter yourself. You ever been to college? Of course you have, smart guy that you are. Try to remember back to those—what do people in your age group call it, Golden Days? If you thought school was expensive then, try going to college now. It's very expensive, Nick. Very expensive. If I got information you want, the least you can do is spring for a lousy lunch and a few butts. Hell, you've got to give a little, Nick. You can't go through life being a taker. Take. Take. Take. For one thing, people won't like you—no matter how cute you are. See what I'm saying, Nick? Learn to give a little here."

"I thought you said you were a criminal justice major?"

"I did, but it's the minor in English talking. Lunch at eleven. In the Union. I'll meet you by the information booth, all right? Look, I must be going. I have a test at nine thirty, and I want to do a little more studying."

"I'll see you at eleven, then. Hey," I said.

"What?"

"Good luck on your test," I said. I tried to picture Scar, maybe lying belly down on her bed in her dorm room, a text book opened in front of her, a pink highlighter in her hand, reading and studying. The image was hard to conjure up in my mind. Why? I have no idea. Scar wore dark clothing, wore dark make-up. Those were physical attributes and had nothing at all to do with the girl's mind.

A criminal justice major. A minor in English. Interesting.

"Hey Nick?"

"Yeah, what?"

She teased me. "'Yeah, what'. Try to dress a little more appropriately today. Buy yourself a used knap-sack, or something, you know? Stick some books in there. If you're going to be hanging out with me, I can't have you looking like a weirdo, all right? People will think you're a cop. Or worse, a private investigator."

"I understand, don't look like an idiot," I assured her. "I'll swing by a thrift shop. How's that?"

"Now you're talking. See ya in a couple of hours." She hung up.

The only thrift store I knew of was in Henrietta. I drove south on I390, got off at the Jefferson Road exit and headed west toward Marketplace Mall. Traffic looked light, where normally it was heavy most of the day. The community college, less than a mile north on West Henrietta Road, which intersected Jefferson and several businesses, were the main provisions for the bottle-neck traffic in the streets.

It was a beautiful morning. The sun was bright, only a few cotton balls littered a blue sky. The man on the radio just said the temperature. Eighty-eight. The humidity level, ninety percent. Damn, it was going to be a scorcher. The weatherman left Mother Nature a challenge. He said the high today would peak in the nineties. I hoped not. It had been extremely hot and humid all summer. All winter long I prayed for the sun, but sometimes enough is enough! Fall, only days away, did not show any signs of beginning.

At a red light, just past the Mall, I stopped and waited. My cell phone rang. My sport coat was folded and in the passenger seat. I pulled the phone out of the special pocket I'd had sown into the hem of my coat. "Nicholas Tartaglia," I said. No one responded. After a few seconds, the line went dead. I set the phone down between my legs, sure that the connection was bad and the caller would try again. The light turned green. No one called back.

There it was, up on the right. An old converted record store, an ancient place. The Thrift Store, as it was appropriately called, was spray painted on the front window in big, bubbly, psychedelic letters. The parking lot was crowded. I pulled in, tried to find an empty spot up front, couldn't, drove around back and parked my car between a rusted, beaten station wagon and a brand new, bright red Mustang.

I grabbed my coat, slipped it on, despite the heat, and placed the phone in the special pocket. In the store I found clothes on racks that reminded me of the things in my closet from back when I still lived home with mom and dad. "Man," I mumbled, "I can't believe I'm going to buy this stuff." A shirt hung on a hanger caught my eye because it was so ugly. I held it by the sleeves and looked at it with disgust. I decided to buy it. I finally took it off the hanger and strolled around the store in search of pants to match—or mismatch.

Along my journey, I happened across a knap-sack. It was a knap-sack, but so many patches had been sown onto it, that I thought calling it a patch-sack might be more appropriate. I grabbed it. It was too ugly not to be fashionable.

"Anything I can help you with, sir?"

Sir. God, I hated being called that. It made me feel old. I turned to look at the girl waiting on me. She had more rings piercing her nose than Jupiter. "Thank you *Miss*, but, I should be all right."

"Hey, whatever," the young girl said and walked away. She was dressed in a flower-patterned piece of drop cloth. I was sure there was a figure hiding somewhere under the garment. She had on men's black dress socks and sandals. What a flattering choice in style. A real voice in the world of fashion.

I hung the shirt I'd chosen back on the rack and grabbed an even more horrible looking shirt. Folded on a table I found a pair of jeans, flaring bell-bottoms. "In for a shirt, in for an ensemble." I brought the items up to the register.

"This it man?" He was a young boy with sideburns that came to a point, stretching from his ears to a point at his chin.

"Should be," I said.

"Wild shirt. This new?"

Nothing in the store was new. It was a thrift shop. I thought that was the concept, to buy old, used clothing. "Huh?"

"They just put this out there? I wish I'd seen it. I'd a bought it for sure." He held my shirt up to his face, studied it intently. "I can't believe I didn't see this thing out there."

I was touched he liked my clothes. I still had a sense of style. "Listen, I'm only going to wear it a few times. I'll bring it back."

"Really?"

"Sure. How much do I owe here?" He told me. I paid as I promised the begging kid I'd bring the shirt back when I didn't want it anymore, and left.

Outside, it already felt hotter than it had before I went into the store. I climbed into the car, looked at the time, knew I had plenty left before my meeting with Jeffrey Granatta, the school president. The only problem I faced: Where to change? Opening the glove compartment, I removed a leather ankle holster, and from the trunk, in a locked box, a Charter Under-cover .38 Special. I put my Glock in the box, locked it and closed the trunk. With my bag of clothing, I went back in to the store.

"Bringing the shirt back," the kid at the register asked, eyes glowing, mouth open.

"I don't think so. Look, I need to change, all right? I want to wear the clothes I just bought." I looked around the store for a dressing room.

"Oh, sure, man. Go right to the back of the store. There's a few rooms back there."

In one of the rooms, I changed quickly, removed my shoulder holster and strapped on the ankle one. I transferred the gun from my chest to my leg. The pants flared so much at the bottom, I was embarrassed. At least no one would notice a gun on my leg. I slipped on the shirt, studied myself in the mirror, wanted to throw up, but held it in. I put my regular clothes and shoulder holster into the bag, then left.

Chapter 10

Pulling onto campus and wanting to fit in, I decided once again to cruise down to the student parking lot. I drove past the two gymnasiums and parked in the large lot across from the football field—way the hell away from any classrooms. Getting out of the car and locking the doors, I slung the knapsack, filled with triple-A books from the glove compartment along with my normal clothing—to change back into for the meeting with the president— over my shoulder and started across the field toward the railroad tracks.

I felt like a fool and looked like one, too. I thought the pants were too big, although the kid at the thrift store assured me the fit was exactly as it should be. The shirt smelled funny, but not bad like body odor. The smell was more like a combination of Tide and pot smoke.

Students were all over the place. I walked with my hands stuffed in my pockets and head down. No one seemed to notice me. I was blending. Nick "the Chameleon" Tartaglia, Private Investigator. No autographs, please.

Despite the size of the campus, I feared getting lost. As I passed over the football field, crossed the railroad tracks and started past three high-rise dorm buildings, I realized I knew exactly where I was. It felt good to be on a college campus again and I could not help but feel like a student ready to learn, waiting to challenge the world, youthful.

With purpose and renewed confidence, I walked to the Student Union, head up. People gave me nods and I nodded back. Someone said, "Hey, Jack." I said: "Hey." The hardest thing so far, was trying not to stare at all the young, beautiful girls all around me. Back when I was in school I used to hear men say that the hardest thing about getting older is not being able to stare at the young ladies. I'd laugh at them, but, damn, I *don't* remember girls looking like this when I was their age. Full figures, exposed navels, long hair and milky skin.

Anyway, the Union was dead ahead, just past the center of campus where three flagpoles extended into the sky. I gazed quickly up to see three limp, motionless flags. The American flag was in the center on the tallest pole, the New York state flag and the school flag were on poles of equal height on either side of the ol' red, white and blue.

I took the stairs two at a time to the Union's rear entrance, just as I had done the other day. I did not bother to stop and observe the radio DJ, but instead I passed right by without even glancing in. I was mad at him.

Plenty of students crowded around the information booth. I did not see Scar among them. Ten minutes early I looked around and admired the electricity passing through the room. It touched all of the students, animated them in one way or another. I was grounded, receiving a slight shock now and then, but nothing compared to the voltage passing through everyone around me. The need and want for knowledge was tremendous!

In my college days I'd felt alive and vibrant, even if I spent most of the time complaining about one thing or another, but I couldn't wait to graduate. The day after graduation, I remember sitting in a chair in my parents' living room. The television was on but I wasn't listening. I was lost in one repetitive thought: *Now what do I do with my life?*

"Nick," Scar said. She was standing behind me. I spun around. "You been waiting long?" she asked.

"Seconds," I said. Scar smiled. I liked her smile. Despite her young age, there was something about her that fascinated me. She was not beautiful, but pretty. It was truly hard to judge the extent of her looks with all the pierced body parts and dark make-up. "What have you got for me?"

"The test?" she said as she looped an arm in mine and led me toward the food court.

"Test?"

"The one I was studying for?" she said.

Small talk. I got it. "Oh," I said. "That test. How did it go?"

"Without sounding too full of myself, I'm pretty sure I aced it." There was that smile again. She was looking up at me with glassy eyes. I think little Miss Scar has a crush on me.

"Glad to hear it," I said. "Hungry?"

"Like a bull." We got in line. "I like the clothes, especially the shirt. Can I have it?"

"It's spoken for," I said, smiled. She didn't smile, she looked offended. "What's good here? I had a burger the other day. That wasn't bad."

"I'm a vegetarian. I usually get the grilled cheese." We both grabbed trays and slid them down the railing track. She grabbed a cup of french fries, poured vinegar into the cup. "I learned this in Canada," she said.

I grabbed a cup of fries and poured vinegar. "I learned this from someone who used to work in a carnival."

91

After I paid for lunch, we took our trays to a table in the corner. She wanted seclusion. I thought it made us more conspicuous. We stuck out. Was Scar putting me on? Did she, maybe, want us to stick out? I couldn't rule out the possibility. I've only known her for two days, and if that time were translated into minutes, then I've only known Scar less than half an hour. That was too short a time to decide whose team she played on. Right now, I planned to leave her in the middle of the fence. The more I learn about her, the more I can judge where she belongs.

"How do you like school?" I asked while eating a french fry. For the meal, I ordered a hamburger. I was too hungry to risk buying something that might not taste good. I was happy with the burger, I'll stick with that.

"I do, but I'd rather just graduate and get on the force, you know?"

"Yeah. I remember feeling that way," I said. "Don't rush it though. You'll have the rest of your life to work."

"You sound like my father." Ignoring her sneer, I picked up my hamburger and took a big bite. "How can you eat that garbage? It's bad enough you bought it under the pretense that it's cow beef. The chances are better, though, that you're eating some old, worn out horse."

That comment made it difficult to swallow my food. I managed, though. "Well, thanks for the conversation. What's say we eat now and talk after, huh?" I stared at the sandwich, not sure I could take another bite. Horse? Couldn't rule it out. Budgets were tight for educational institutions.

She picked up a triangular slice of grilled cheese sandwich. "You got a girl friend, Nick."

"That's none of your business. For the record though, no."

"Want one?"

"Nope."

"Why not? I think we could be pretty good together."

"I'm too busy," I said, smiled. "But just for an appendage to the record, I think we'd be pretty good together, too." I returned the flattering gesture.

"Ah hell, it's because you think I'm too young. That's the main reason, isn't it?"

I shrugged. No sense lying to her. "You could say that."

"I'm twenty. How old are you? Thirty-nine?"

"Yep. On the nose."

"So what's a nineteen year difference? It's nothing. My parents got married, a ten year gap between them. My mother was older than my father," she said. She was hurt. I saw the pain clearly in her eyes. She was trying to hide it, unfortunately, this made the expression more prominent.

She dropped her grilled cheese onto the plate. I guess I caused her to loose her appetite. Touché.

"I'm sorry, Scar."

"I'm not going to just give up, though. Fair enough?"

"Fair enough," I said. This challenge pacified her. She leaned forward. "Down to business?" I said.

"Down to business."

"Now, you called me, but I still have some questions from the last time we saw each other," I said, taking a small bite of my hamburger—it wasn't bad. I might be able to eat it after all. In truth, if it was horse, then that horse tasted damned good. "Remember? You got all nervous, said they saw you— or us?"

"Yeah."

"Who saw us?"

"No one. I didn't know who you were. You could have been some weirdo. I wanted to do some checking on you, first—you know that kind of thing. I wasn't going to just lead you to Maryjean without knowing out who you were." Scar smiled.

"You really are a criminal justice major, huh?" I returned the smile, intrigued I must admit. "So you know Maryjean?"

"We're roommates this year."

"Roommates? On campus?"

"Nope. We rent a half house just off campus." Scar munched on a few french fries dripping vinegar. She looked around the room. "I didn't come right out and tell Maryjean that you were looking for her. She's still upset. She and Darla were pretty good friends. It was traumatic to hear she had died."

I had an entire line of questions mentally mapped out. I wasn't sure if Scar would be the one to ask. Tommy Cerio had said that Darla was into S and M. They knew this because of Darla's roommate, Maryjean. The question should be asked to Maryjean then. Not to Scar.

"Bottom line, can you arrange it so Maryjean and I can meet? Someplace that feels safe for her. I have some specific questions about Darla and her life that I really need to ask her." I still needed Scar. Maryjean would be simple to find knowing she lived in a rented half house somewhere just off campus. Scar was Maryjean's roommate, though and if I played it right, she would be my lubricated in.

"I think I can do that. She doesn't go out much, occasionally, but not often enough to dismiss the fact she's truly a homebody." Scar laughed.

93

"You know, it's because of her I spend so much time studying. If I didn't have Maryjean for a roommate and a friend, I'd be out partying all the time and failing miserably, I'm sure."

"I don't know," I said. "You seem like a pretty smart girl to me."

"I might be smart, but I love to party. Maryjean keeps me straight."

I wanted to ask: Straight, how?

We threw away our garbage, saving the french fries, and set the food trays on top of the garbage containers. We walked out of the Union, back into the heat, munching on fries. "Can't believe this heat," I muttered.

"Don't like it hot?" She teased, looked up at me with large eyes, lids batting. I left the innuendo unanswered. "Anyway," she said when I didn't take the bait, "thanks for lunch."

"You're very welcome. You got class now?"

She shrugged. "Not yet. You got to meet with the school president?"

"I do."

We walked a little more, but I didn't know where she was leading me. I doubted she knew. "Want me to call you after I talk with Maryjean and see how she feels about getting together with you?"

"I'd appreciate that. I really would." I had finished my fries and still felt hungry. Scar, as if reading my mind, offered up her cup. I took it and ate her fries.

"You going to talk with the president of this college dressed like that?"

"I got a change of clothing in the patch-sack."

"Patch-sack?"

"It's what I thought I might call it," I said.

"You always make up names for your things?"

I let the sly remark slide. I wasn't baited that easily. If she pulled me into her little sexual advances, then she'd be winning her game. There were morals at stake. I couldn't lose so early in the first quarter. We walked for a few more seconds. I glanced at my watch. "I gotta run," I said.

"Me too."

Was she going to pop me a kiss again? "Hey, Scar?"

"Yeah?"

"What's your real name?" I asked.

She stood on her toes, kissed my cheek, then my lips, held my neck in her hand and whispered in my ear. "Never on a first date. I'm not that kind of girl."

Chapter 11

Mrs. Stavinski sat with a stern expression on her face, the phone to her ear, held in place with her shoulder. She had a pencil in her right hand and was tapping the tip like a drumstick against the thumb of her left. "Uh huh. Right. So if you call back tomorrow, I should have that information for you. Okay. Bye now." She hung up and looked at me, forced a smile. "Can I help you?"

"I'm here to see Mr. Granatta?" I said.

"Do you have an appointment, sir?" Mrs. Stavinski asked.

"I should. You made it for me the other day. The name's Nicholas Tartaglia." I smiled, hoping my charm would work. She didn't return the smile. She just grunted and used the pencil tip as a pointer to scroll down through the appointment book in front of her.

"Mr. Tartaglia. Here you are. If you want to have a seat, Mr. Granatta will be with you shortly."

"Thank you," I said. I moved to the small waiting area. Several chairs and a sofa surrounded a coffee table, the surface littered with a variety of magazines and a few old copies of *The Monroe Reporter*.

I picked a June issue of the school newspaper and scanned the headlines. Nothing gripping or eye-catching. There was an article on Maureen Kingman who works in the bookstore, taking first prize in a national poetry contest. Her poem will be published in an anthology and she will receive a check for five thousand dollars. In another earth-shattering story, a professor announces his early retirement. I yawned.

My telephone rang. Mrs. Stavinski looked up from her desk and shot me an annoying glance. I pulled the phone out of my pocket, answered while flashing the secretary an apologetic grin. "Hello?"

No one answered. I heard the calling party hang up. I hung up. The phone rang again. "Hello?" I said. "Hello?"

No one.

"If you're done," Mrs. Stavinski said, as if I were playing with a toy,

"Mr. Granatta will see you now."

I closed the phone, put it away, stood up and tossed the newspaper back onto the coffee table. "I'm always ready, Mrs. Stavinski."

She knocked once on the president's door, then opened it. "Go right on in and have a seat."

"Thank you," I said. Once I was in President Jeffrey Granatta's office, Mrs. Stavinski closed the door behind me. Where was Granatta? I hadn't heard the phone ring in the reception area, so how did Stavinski know he was ready to see me?

Looking around the office I felt inadequate as a human being. Diplomas from many schools were cluttered together, mounted in expensive frames, and hung on one wall. Pictures of celebrities, both the Hollywood type and political, hung on another wall. One man, the center point of every photo, stood shaking hands with, or was being hugged by the famous. I guessed the reoccurring man in every picture must be Jeffrey Granatta.

He looked to be handsome with black, silver hair, thick eyebrows and dark eyes. A long distinguished nose with full lips was noticeable in each photograph. He seemed to have an athletic built with a bright smile. As I was examining these pictures, a door opened. "Mr. Granatta?" I said.

"That's right. And you're?"

"Nicholas Tartaglia, private investigator." We shook hands. I explained to him the reason behind my visit.

"And you're working for Darla Bristol's mother, right?" Granatta asked me as he smoothed his black tie against his white shirt. He reached for the arm of his chair and sat down. He pressed the fingertips of his right hand to the ones on his left and leaned back in his chair as he blatantly studied me.

Here's where I should say, *No, I'm working for Darla. She's the one who hired me.* "That's correct." Without being asked, I sat in the chair on the opposite side of the president's desk. "She believes that her daughter's death was not a mere case of drug overdose, falling into the canal and drowning."

"She doesn't?" Granatta snorted.

"Do you remember her?"

"I didn't know Darla, personally. We have thousands of students enrolled and rarely do I get to meet more than a large handful. And even then, I might recall their face, but remember their names? Not likely."

"Well," I said, crossed my legs, "I'm not here to ask you personal questions about Darla."

"You're not?"

"No. I want to know if you're at all familiar with a local cult? Quite possibly, it's campus oriented. They call themselves the Tenth House," I said. Jump to the punch, watch for an expression change. Granatta was good. He simply continued to stare. I waited.

"That's absurd," he said, while he shifted uncomfortably in his chair. "I can't honestly say I know anything about a local or campus cult."

Never trust anybody who uses a word like, *honestly*. "The name doesn't sound familiar? Ring a bell? Anything?"

"No. No, I don't think I've ever heard of a Tenth House. Now, the fraternities on campus get a little wild; huge parties running all weekend long, hazing—even though they're not supposed to, we know they do. There's an occasional fight between the football team and the wrestlers, but to say there's a cult at work here," he laughed, "no. I've never heard anyone mention anything about a cult, and frankly, I'm trying to figure what you might possibly be trying to get at."

I ignored his vague question. "Darla Bristol had no previous record with the police. She'd never been arrested for drugs before."

"Going from high school to college is a major transition. Kids leave home for the first time, live in a building full of other kids from a variety of social and economical backgrounds. They begin to go through a process of emotions, like anxiousness. They know they're at school but can't believe it. Freedom reeks from everywhere and everything. They realize there is no one to answer to. They live it up. We expect them to. Then after a few weeks, hopefully, they settle into a routine. Classes get started and the professors bog them down with work. Overwhelming. All the classes, all the social events, being away from home, it starts to get to them. It's a tremendous amount of pressure. Did you attend college, Mr. Tartaglia?"

"Call me Nick, please. I graduated from NYU. And I understand the process of emotions that a student might stagger through, but I think I'm missing your point." I really wasn't. I just wanted to hear the head honcho speak his mind without beating around the proverbial bush.

"Drugs, Nick. Drugs often come into play. Beer and whiskey are drugs. More kids become alcoholics while in college than at any other age. That's a sobering fact. Some kids, though, turn to the use of narcotic drugs. Pot smoking, acid, you know? It's a sad truth and there is little we can do to prevent it. If kids want drugs, they'll get them.   "I'm not going to sit here and tell you that our campus security has a Drug Task Force and that we cooperate with the local police in frequent drug searches and aid in drug busts because it isn't an episode of COPS around here. It's a school, a facility for learning. Unfortunately, it's the entire process that is part of the experience and in essence, *is* the learning."

Wow, can this guy blow smoke out his ass. "I understand what you're saying," I said. I couldn't bare to have him continue. He'd a made a small point, but had used a mouthful of words to do so. "Just the same, I'm not happy with the police reports. Like Darla's mother, I'm not convinced Darla's death was an accident." I thought of the strap marks on Darla's wrists, the ones Tommy Cerio had mentioned. It was easier to believe Darla was tied down and forced to ingest drugs, than it is for me to believe the young girl was into wild and kinky sex. The police, on the other hand, accepted the fact that Darla was a drug addict. *To them*, S and M would just be par for the course then.

Jeffrey Granatta displayed a pacifying smile. "Bottom line, Mr. Tartaglia?"

"Bottom line. I want your permission to roam around campus, posing as a student," I said. "I know most of your classes are sized for a hundred kids or more, so I figure slipping in and sitting in the back row shouldn't draw much attention."

"I see. And you will be observing who, exactly?"

"A few students in particular, as of now. In a few days, after I've gotten somewhere, who knows. I'm not sure who's involved with this cult yet, maybe no one else," I said, but I didn't believe it. There were plenty of people involved. I didn't want to tell the president that, though. I didn't want him to think he was facing an epidemic.

"Uh-huh."

I wasn't going to offer to pay for classes. "I need you to help round up a couple of class schedules, too, if it's not against the rules. If you can't, I can always follow the people I need to and learn their schedule, but then I'll be hanging around campus that much longer." I knew Granatta would want me away from his school as soon as possible. "I have a few people on campus I'd like to spend time observing. Three people, really. If I sit in on some classes, since I won't be paying, I promise not to learn anything." I held up two fingers. "Scout's honor."

"It's three."

"What's three?" I asked.

"Scout's honor is three fingers." Granatta showed me.

I raised up a third finger. "I was never a scout."

Granatta washed his hands over his face. "Really? I wouldn't have guessed."

"So, what do you say? Can you help me arrange this?"

Granatta sat for a moment in silence. He reached across his desk and pressed a button. The intercom box came to animated life, talked like Mrs. Stavinski with static, "Yes Mr. Granatta?"

The president positioned his mouth over the box. "Mrs. Stavinski? I'm going to need your help going through a few student class schedules. Can you get registration on the line for me?"

"Thank you," I said. "I appreciate your help."

"Just conduct your investigation discreetly, please! All right?"

"I promise," I said, holding up three fingers. "Do you think they would take someone like me? At my age?"

Frustrated, the president sighed. "Who, Mr. Tartaglia?"

"The scouts," I said matter of factly. "I've always wanted to join."

Chapter 12

Besides Arline, I have another sister, Julia. She's a few years younger than me. She lives on the opposite side of the Genesee River in Webster. I talk with her now and then, but not nearly as often as I'd like and rarely of the things I'd want to talk about. We go through an improvisational skit that comes out sounding rehearsed. How are you? Fine. Work? Good. Did you talk to Arline today? No, have you?

Lately, I find myself thinking about Julia because of Arline. Arline is having a baby, but a few years back, Julia's baby died during delivery. I'll never forget that night being at the hospital with expectations of the newest family member to be born, anxiously waiting to meet the new baby, only to find that we never would. Unfortunately, Julia had developed gestational diabetes during pregnancy. This disease caused the baby to grow at an unhealthy rate. When they weighed him at the hospital, Baby Peter tipped the scales at fifteen pounds.

I saw him, held him, kissed his fingers. Handsome, chubby, chubby cheeks, dark hair, silky skin. There will always be the 'what ifs'. I don't think about them, or try my best not to. God has His reasons for taking my nephew, I'm sure, but we would have loved him and taken good care of him no matter what. Maybe it's better this way. Baby Peter will always be innocent, untouched and perfect. At the funeral my father said to a church full of family and friends that Baby Peter would have been a tough kid, a boy to be reckoned with. I thought so too. My father also said that Peter set a blazing trail into heaven in the hopes that we would all follow along one day and meet with him there. I want to go to heaven when I die, I need to meet my nephew.

After the Mass we went to Holy Sepulchre Cemetery on Lake Avenue behind Kodak Park. Baby Peter was to be buried in Garden thirty-six. The cemetery was beautiful, full of weeping willows, maples and Fir trees. The lawn was bright green and immaculately manicured. There were several monument-sized headstones and statues around, while rows of more traditionally sized headstones covered the landscape. Wreaths and flowers were everywhere.

Over the years, people have died but I've never visited a grave after the funeral. Since Peter's death, I've faithfully come to see him at least once a month. I like to spend time with him. For never having the chance to know him, I sure miss him an awful lot. Love knows no boundaries. It is unconditional.

Today, before going to the cemetery I stopped at the grocery store, bought a bottle of soda, a candy bar and a book. As I parked the car along an arm in the maze of roads stretching throughout the cemetery, I grabbed the bag and walked down to where my nephew slept; a beautiful location, backed up to a row of hip-high hedges.

His headstone was gray granite, nothing flashy. The engraving on the stone showed an angel playing a bugle floating over the name, date and words quoted from the Bible. I sat on the grass next to the small piece of earth that was his home.

"Hey there, little buddy," I said. Speaking out loud to my nephew felt natural. It helped. To just sit here and think thoughts felt impersonal. I liked to believe he could hear me. "What a week." I filled Baby Peter in on all that had happened to me, starting with the rescue of Judy Swanson to my encounter with a visitor from the spirit world. "Do you know Darla?" Of course Peter didn't answer me. I knew he wouldn't. Still, if Darla could communicate from the *great beyond*, why not my own nephew? "I'm trying real hard, Peter, to accept everything that's going on here. It's hard, you know? Ghosts, spirits, whatever." I picked at the grass, threw the blades away, picked some more. "I just . . . I'm looking for answers to solve a mystery and I know there's truth to Darla's story, but, working for a spirit, that's kind of bizarre. What do you think, Peter, bizarre? I'll tell you what, if Ned ever found out the truth he'd have me committed, or worse, he'd fire me."

Looking around, I noticed there was not a cloud in the sky. The cemetery was unusually empty. I seemed to be the only person visiting a loved one.

Taking the bottle and candy bar out of the bag, I opened them both, took a long drink and finished half the soda. I took a big bite from the candy bar and said: "But that's enough about me, Pete, and my weird week. I know what you're waiting for." I took the book I'd bought out of the bag and tucked it under my leg so it wouldn't blow away. I opened the Dr. Seuss story to the first page. "*Green Eggs and Ham*, by Dr. Seuss," I read. "This one's my favorite. I think you'll like it, too," I said. "I am Sam. I am Sam. Sam I am."

As I pulled into my driveway, I realized it had been a long day and I was tired. Though many things got accomplished and I was getting somewhere, I still felt as though this investigation was moving in slow motion.

Nothing was in the mailbox. Carrying the sport coat and the knap-sack slung over my shoulder, I unlocked the front door and entered the house. I closed and locked the door behind me, tossed the coat and sack onto the sofa. Shrugging off the shoulder holster, I noticed the flashing red light on the answering machine. Five messages waited for me.

The first one was Judy Swanson. "We still on for tomorrow? I hope so. If not, give me call." She said her number. I didn't erase the message.

"We're still on," I said to the machine.

The second one was from Karis. "Hey Nick. I was just thinking about you, what you might be doing. I hate just sitting here doing nothing. If you can think of anything I can do to help—let me know. Hey, have you seen her lately?"

I knew whom she meant. Darla. No. I haven't seen her. Dealing with the supernatural was new to me, felt odd and just a little unsettling. Though seeing her again might prove useful in preserving my sanity, it also may scare the hell out of me.

"Well," Karis said, "give me a call, or stop over whenever. Bye."

I swallowed. I stared at the machine. Poor Karis. I couldn't imagine the tormenting pain she must be suffering.

The last three messages were hang-ups. "Great. Probably the same person who's been doing phone-pranks to my cellular." I deleted the hang-ups. "I need a shower," I said to no one. I went into the garage with a mug. I'd converted an old refrigerator into a bar, kept a half keg of beer inside, drilled a hole through the side and mounted a tap. It worked perfectly. I got the idea from Uncle Tony, a man who truly loved his beer. Filling my mug, I brought it with me into the bathroom. I started the water running, stripped out of my clothes, stepped in, stood under the spray and set the beer down in the soap holder.

After the shower I dressed in jeans, no socks or shirt, and went into the kitchen. I picked the phone up and called Karis. It rang four times. Her answering machine picked up. I waited for the beep, left a brief message and said, "No. I haven't seen her either."

It was time for dinner and I was hungry. I pulled open the refrigerator and stared at shelves full of nothing. I wasn't sure what I was in the mood for, but I did know I didn't want what was in there. I closed the door and went to the cupboards. As I opened one, the doorbell rang.

It was almost seven o'clock. I went to the door and checked through the peephole. In my line of work, you are bound to make enemies. I know I've made plenty. I always kept the doors locked. Karis stood on the front step. She was holding a casserole dish, potholders on her hands. "Son of a bitch," I whispered with delight and opened the door.

Karis smiled, stared at me with a funny expression, her eyebrows arched as she made eye contact.

I didn't have a shirt on, I realized. "Hey, Karis. Come on in," I said, pushing open the screen door.

She stared at my chest, not my eyes. "I thought you might be hungry. I left a message on your machine. It was a cowardly kind of message. I really wanted to ask you over for dinner, but I choked. I'd already made all the food because I didn't plan on chickening out." She looked embarrassed. "Hungry?"

"Like a horse," I said. "Why don't you set that on the kitchen table and I'll go slip into something a little more comfortable." I laughed and disappeared down the hall. In my drawers there seemed to be fifteen different shirts to choose from. None of them looked right. "I can't believe I feel this nervous," I said. "Relax. She's, like, a client." I put on a metal blue T-shirt. In the top drawer I found and put on a pair of white tube socks.

Now that I was fully dressed, I felt hot, sweaty and in need of another shower. I went back down the hall. Karis was in the kitchen, setting the table for two. I stood at the end of the hall for a moment and watched her. God, she's beautiful.

I clapped my hands together and walked into the kitchen. "Smells wonderful."

"I like to make casseroles. They're easy."

"Says *you*. Can I get you a glass of wine? A beer?"

"A beer sounds good," she said. Ah, a girl after my own heart. "If you don't use a glass, I don't need one either."

"It's on tap," I said. "But if you really like your beer from a bottle, I can have it poured into one?" I teased.

"That's fine." She laughed, too.

I ran back into the garage with my mug and one for Karis. I filled them and sat at the table. We ate mostly in silence, but I felt at ease around her.

The Tenth House

The casserole was as delicious as it smelled. I told Karis this after helping myself to and eating a healthy third serving.

"I guess you do like it," she said, flattered.

Her glass was empty, so was mine. "Need another beer?"

Karis stood up, grabbed her glass and mine. "I'll fill them." She went out into the garage and returned with two full glasses.

"Want to go sit in the living room?" I asked. I hoped it didn't come out sounding too forward. I wasn't making a pass, only wanted to be more comfortable. She accepted. I followed her into the room, we sat next to each other on the sofa, but not too close. "Want some music?"

"What do you like. When we were in school you were such a head-banger, all that loud rock music. I never really cared for it," Karis said.

She smiled as I made my way to the entertainment center. I pressed open the glass doors, turned on the stereo. "You never said anything. What kind of music did you like, then?" I asked, realizing I should have asked her that question a hundred years ago.

"Country," she said. She snickered, embarrassed.

"Country's pretty hot now," I said, "but *then*?"

"I know there was no Garth Brooks then, but really the music style hasn't changed, only the artists." She was right. I grabbed a Vince Gill, Clint Black and Trisha Yearwood CD and popped them into the carousel, pressed the Play in Random button. I set the volume and sat back on the sofa.

"I like country, too." I said.

"Get out of here!" She didn't believe me. The music started, then she believed me.

"I like alternative, too. I guess I like a bit of everything, everything except dance music. I hate that."

"Do you dance?"

"No."

"Maybe that's why you don't like dance music," Karis said.

"Do you dance?"

"I used to. I haven't . . . in a while."

Awkward silence filled the room and began to linger. I didn't want the night to die young. I was enjoying Karis' company too much to have it all end so soon, I knew I needed to say something. "Written anything interesting lately?"

"I have. It's interesting to me, but I'm sure it would bore the hell out of you," Karis said, took a sip of beer. She smiled modestly.

"Try me."

"Well, it's an article I've been asked to write for a lady who's son died of anorexia. He was in his twenties. He suffered horribly, not just from his disease, but from treatment he'd received—and didn't receive—at a hospital here in New York." Karis came to life. Her face reflected excitement. She enjoyed talking about her work. I actually enjoyed hearing about it.

"A real writer, wow. I'd love to read some of your work," I told her. She looked so beautiful I couldn't help wanting to lean over and kiss her. I'd settle for reaching over and holding her hand.

Something in her eyes told me she was feeling the same way.

The telephone rang, as it always will at the most inopportune times. "Let the machine get it," I said, my voice hoarse, dry with anticipation. Excitement stirred in my body. We reached for each other until the tips of our fingers touched.

The answering machine clicked on. Judy Swanson's voice said, "Nick, you never called me back. I just need to know if you're still coming over for dinner tomorrow. Let me know just so I'm not home waiting for you. Okay? Good-night."

I closed my eyes tightly as if anticipating a hard punch in the gut. When I opened them, Karis was on her feet. She looked like she was trying to hide her anger and disappointment.

I know I didn't need to explain myself, but felt like I had to. I stumbled a few times with an opening line.

"Forget it," Karis said. "This whole thing is crazy anyway. I don't know how I feel, or what I'm feeling. My life is in shambles. Maybe I'm just grabbing for stability. Because it's you, maybe I'm just trying to sink and hide in the past."

It was a logical explanation. It hurt. Was I only a time vehicle to her? Who was I to question her?

"Karis—"

"Please don't. It's late, I have to get home. I have some line editing to get started on. Deadline's Monday. I had a nice night. Thanks for the beer."

"Wait," I said. "Your dish."

She waited. I got it and gave it to her. "Judy's the girl I saved the other day, the jogger." It sounded lame, but I was trying. "There's nothing going on between us."

"Then she's just like me," Karis said. "Because there's nothing going on between us either. I'm sorry Nick. That sounds harsh and insensitive, but I'm not mad. I'm just confused. Can you understand that?"

I nodded. "I can. I'm sorry if you think I was trying to rush things. I wasn't."

"I know you weren't. I'm the one that showed up uninvited on your doorstep, not the other way around. So I'm sorry if you think I was trying to lead you on. I wasn't." Karis bit her lip, tears rolled down her cheeks. "I just didn't want to be alone. I've been so lonely this last year."

I hugged her tightly. "We'll get through this mess. And you can show up on my doorstep anytime you want. No invitation needed, ever."

Karis gave me a small kiss on the cheek. "Give me a call, okay?" She left after I promised to keep her posted. Not once had she mentioned her daughter. I realized that Karis just needed a night away from it all. I felt good knowing the night she spent away, was spent with me.

I drank down what was left of my beer, then filled the mug again. I lit a cigarette, sat in the recliner and switched on the television with the remote control. While channel surfing, I sipped at my beer until it was gone, smoked a second cigarette and then, finally, I must have fallen asleep with the television on.

Chapter 13

Something rang, a fire alarm, maybe. I jumped up and fell to the floor. Where was I? I didn't know. Seeing the television set and shaking my head I realized I was still in my living room and had fallen out of the recliner. What woke me up? The telephone wasn't ringing. The smoke alarm wasn't going off.

The doorbell sounded. I stood up, still feeling groggy. I looked at the time displayed on the VCR, 1:53 AM. I grabbed my gun as I went to the door and looked out the peephole. "What the hell?" I opened the door. "Tommy, what are you doing here?" I said to my brother-in-law. He was wearing a badge on the lapel of his suit coat.

"I got called on a case."

"Delski let you out?" I asked. "Come on in."

He came in. "I told him I was somehow connected to it already."

"And that was enough for him? Where's your partner?"

"She's in the car."

"Tell her to come in, I'll put on some coffee, or something." If he was on a case, what in the hell was he doing at my place at this ungodly hour?

"We can't stay, actually, we want you to come with us," Tommy said. "You're connected to this mess, too."

"I am?"

"That's right. We got a call about a college girl, lives in a rented house just off campus."

First thought: Oh shit, Scar's dead.

"The victim was Maryjean D'Amonda. Dead. A knife was through the chest. She was found in her bedroom. Roommate found her." Tommy had his hands balled into fists, planted on his hips. He had a thick head of brown hair, large dark eyes. He stood at roughly five-eleven. Weighed no more than one hundred and ninety pounds, mostly muscle.

"The roommate is Scar."

"That's what she told us. Real name's Eleanor."

Never would have guessed it. Eleanor? "Where is she now? At the station?"

"Yeah."

"She's not a suspect, is she?" I asked.

"No. Not yet. But we aren't ruling her out. We aren't going to rule anything out. I knew you were looking into this. Scar brought your name up so the chief wants you involved, too."

"What, I'm a suspect?"

"Don't be an ass, Nick. Delski wants to compare notes, find out what the hell's going on."

"Let me get ready. I'll only take a second."

"I'll be in the car," Tommy said.

I ran into the bathroom and brushed my teeth and hair. I slipped on my shoulder holster, secured the gun in place, put on my sport coat and shoes. I was as ready as I could be on a moment's notice.

My mind was a whirlwind of emotion. Questions crowded and filled every crevice in this brain of mine. I had no answers to pacify myself. I'd have to go through the motions with Rochester's finest and see what comes of it.

I locked up and walked quickly down the drive-way to their car, the passenger window was down, I leaned on the door. "Hey, Deanna," I said. Though I'd only met her once, Deanna O'Mara left a lasting impression on me because I could tell she was tough, knew her business. She wasn't only Tommy's newest partner, she was also new to the force, fresh out of the academy. She was shorter than Tommy, blond hair, blue eyes—cute. She looked young, eighteen, nineteen. Tommy told me she was only a year younger than him. That surprised me.

"How are you, Nick?" She asked.

"A little confused."

"Join the group," Tommy said. He backed out of the driveway. I got into my car and followed behind the homicide detectives.

Scar, or should I say, Eleanor—ah hell, Scar—was sitting in Carl Delski's office. A female officer sat with her.

"She's being questioned?" I asked.

I could see her through the windows that made up Delski's office walls. She had her hands folded in her lap. She was crying, not bothering to wipe away the tears. She may be twenty, but right now, she looked like a frightened teenager.

"No. Officer Bonnet is just sitting with her for comfort," Deanna said.

"You don't want her to get away, huh?" I said.

"That too," Tommy said.

Scar still had all her earrings and nose rings on. Did she sleep with them in? "Is it all right if I go talk with her?"

Tommy looked hesitant. She was an unofficial suspect. "She hasn't been charged with anything, right," I said.

"Right," Deanna said.

"So, until she's charged—"

"Go ahead," Tommy said. "You guys can have a few minutes. Deanna and I need to see Delski, anyway. Forensics should be finished with the scene. Hopefully Delski will have some kind of a report, prints or something."

"So I can go talk with her?"

"A few minutes," Deanna said. "Okay?

"Sure. Thanks." Scar saw me. She smiled, wiped away her tears. More came. She gave up. I went into the office. "Want me to sit with you for a while."

She nodded. Officer Bonnet stood up, looked out into the hall, then silently left. I sat in the chair next to her. I touched her leg, squeezed her knee. She fell into my arms, sobbed. Her tears soaked through my T-shirt. Her breath was hot. I held her tight, rubbed her back. I didn't whisper *It's all right*, because I'd be lying at this point.

When she stopped crying, I planned to ask her what had happened. She cried for twenty minutes. I was afraid Tommy and Deanna would come back and ask me to leave before I had a chance to talk with Scar.

I took some tissues out of the box on Delski's desk, handed them to Scar. "Some mess, huh?"

Scar tried to smile. She blew her nose, gave me an apologetic look for having to do so. "Maryjean's dead," Scar said. "Oh my God, I can't believe she's dead. I saw her. She was on the floor in her bedroom. Oh God, it was awful. I'll never be able to sleep again!"

I thought I knew how she must be feeling. I'd seen many dead people in my time as a private investigator. You never adjust after seeing the body of a person who's been murdered. The image kind of stays with you forever. Your nightmares enhance the images, then distort them. Scar would fall asleep again, at some point, but I didn't think she'd ever sleep as deeply. Of all the bodies I've seen, none have been of a best friend or roommate.

There wasn't much to say. I kept quiet and let Scar ramble on while I rubbed her back.

Tommy came to the door. Scar's face was still buried in my chest. He silently signaled with a head-shrug for me to follow him, then walked away.

"Scar, listen, I'll be right back, okay? Is there anything I can get for you? Are you thirsty?" I asked, holding her shoulders. Her mascara had run, streaking down her cheeks. She looked like Alice Cooper.

"I just want to be alone. I just want to get out of here," she said, sounding weak.

"I'll be right back," I said, again. I stood up, took the box of tissue off Delski's desk and set it on the chair I'd been sitting in. As I walked out of the office, Officer Bonnet came back in. She knelt in front of Scar, took the girl's hands into her own.

I always found myself thinking, *Now this is a nice precinct.*

Tommy was at the end of the hall with Deanna and the chief, Carl Delski. He was a large black man who looked and sounded meaner than he really was. His tightly curled black hair was covered with an epidemic of gray. He suffered a receding hairline. With his curly hair and a big, pear shaped nose he looked like a Koala.

"Chief, you remember Nicholas Tartaglia?" Tommy asked Delski.

The chief just shrugged. He didn't look happy. I couldn't blame him. I put my hand out any way. "How've you been, Chief Delski?"

His large, strong hand enveloped my own. We shook hands. "All right, Nick. A little bent out of sorts tonight, though. I came in when I heard about the D'Amonda girl. You were asking about her, weren't you?"

We were out in the center aisle of the police station. Colored cubicles lined both sides. Not many people were around. It was the middle of the night. Still, I would have preferred going somewhere and talking. If this was where the chief wanted to talk, though, then it was fine with me. After all, Scar was in his office.

"No," I said.

"No?" the chief mimicked. "Did you not ask Detective Cerio about Ms. D'Amonda?" He looked angry. I knew his bark was supposed to be worse than the bite, but with the look raging in his eyes and mannerism, I couldn't help but wonder.

"I asked him about Darla Bristol. She died of a supposed drug overdose, fell into the canal and was found on the rocks along the canal, miles away from campus," I said. "Darla was roommates with Maryjean D'Amonda

110

their freshman year. Maryjean's name is in the police file associated with the Bristol case."

"What case? There's no case," Delski said. "Bristol was a drug user, running with some gang."

"It was a religious cult, not a gang. I doubt they were worshipping the big guy upstairs, either." I smirked.

"Whatever," Delski said, his voice louder. Louder still, "So who do you think you are nosing your way around campus, asking questions?"

"I was asked by my client—"

"Your client? Who's that?" Delski shouted. "Who hired you, Nick?"

"Darla's mother. Karis." I looked at Tommy and Deanna. They stood behind their chief, hands folded in front of them. They were silent, looked like mannequins. Poorly dressed mannequins.

Delski was silent. He massaged his chin, thinking. "Let's go sit down and get some coffee. Forensics should have something soon. We've got uniforms talking to the neighbors around the house the girls rented. Someone's trying to get a hold of the home owner, some guy lives in Florida." Delski looked at me. "I'm not pissed at you, Nick. I'm pissed at this whole stinking situation."

"I can understand that chief. I'll help in any way I can."

While we walked toward a break room with three round tables, thirty chairs, three vending machines, the chief said, "Did you talk with Maryjean?"

"Scar was—"

"Scar?"

"Eleanor, sir?" I said. He nodded. "She was going to set something up so we could talk. She knew I was a private investigator and said she'd help me. Do you think she had anything to do with it?"

"I can't say yet, Nick," Delski said. "This is serious. We have to take many things into consideration."

"Like what," I asked, pulled out a chair and sat down.

"Coffee, Nick?" Tommy asked. He was at one of the vending machines, a bunch of coins in his hand.

"Thanks, but no thanks." I hated the taste of coffee from a vending machine. I always wound up with a cup full of grounds. What I really wanted was a soda. I didn't have any change and wasn't about to ask my brother-in-law for the money. "I'm all set."

A man walked into the break room. He was dressed in jeans, a T-shirt and white sneakers. He was balding, hair in a brush cut. It didn't look like it would ever grow in. He looked at me, then to the police chief. "Carl," he said.

Carl stood up. "What have you got?"

"There were prints all over the place. It's a college house, you know. They probably had parties there every weekend. D'Amonda's prints and her roommates were everywhere, on just about everything. But there were too many others everywhere and on everything, you know?" The man looked nervous as he stuffed his hands into his pockets. He looked like he wanted to sit down. The chief didn't ask him to. He stood where he was and bounced up and down on the balls of his feet.

"What about the knife," Tommy asked, stepping forward.

"Only the victim's. She may have been trying to pull it out, you know?"

"Suicide?" Deanna asked, while folding her arms.

"I wouldn't think so. The blade is right in the middle of the chest. It's buried up to the hilt. You'd have to be strong, not to mention one crazy bastard to stuff a knife that deep into your own chest," the man said. "Not to mention, penetration looks straight. How could someone stab themselves in the chest without an angle to the blade? Wouldn't be an easy thing to do." By this time I knew he was part of the forensics team. "We did discover a butcher's knife missing from a block in the kitchen. It's probably the murder weapon. We'll still do the testing, just for the sake of being thorough. I mean, you find a butcher knife in a girl's chest and one missing from the block in the kitchen, you don't have to have a college degree to figure that one out. But, like I said, we'll complete the ballistics and fax over our report."

"Still, that's not enough evidence to book the girl. We need prints, too," Tommy said. He looked to his chief.

"We'll have to let her go. O'Mara, can you handle that?"

"Sure chief."

Delski turned to me. "We still need to compare notes. Not now, it's too late. Tomorrow though."

"Saturday?" I said.

"Today, Nick. After we all get a little sleep. Come back after lunch." He left.

I looked at Tommy. "I can give Scar a ride home," I said.

"She can't go home, Nick. The house is roped off. It's a murder scene."

Oh yeah, I forgot. "I'll give her a lift to wherever, then."

Tommy shrugged. "Fine."

Detective Deanna O'Mara left the room. She was going to release Scar.

"Tommy," I said. "Can I get a look at the report?"

"On D'Amonda?"

"Yeah."

"It's a murder case, Nick. You know I can't give you anything out of there," Tommy said. He walked out of the break room. I followed at his heels like a shadow.

"Tommy, we're on the same side, here. Right? I'm involved in this. Now, unless things have changed, I'm not a suspect. You know me better than that," I begged.

"You're a civilian. I'm sorry, Nick. I respect the work you do, but it's not enough. There are things in that report that only the police and the killer knows about. We can't have that information getting out," he said. He sounded apologetic. I knew he was sincere.

"I'm not going to blab, and you know that."

"It doesn't matter, Nick. I can't show it to you and even if I could, I wouldn't."

"How's my sister going to like that. You letting me go after a hard-core killer. You know a lot about the killer. I know nothing. You might as well blindfold me, take me for a ride and let me out in the middle of the express-way."

"Don't be so dramatic. I don't have time for it. If you're giving Scar a ride home, then get her out of here."

"You going to keep an eye on her?" I asked.

"Of course."

"Tell her the police-thing: Don't leave town?"

"Yeah."

"Good." I smiled.

"Why is that good?" Tommy asked.

"Because. I don't think she killed D'Amonda. I think whoever did is going to come back and try to kill Scar. I'll feel better knowing she has some people keeping an eye on her. It's like a free bodyguard service," I said.

"I hope you're right about her. Kid dresses funny, but that seems to be about it. My gut tells me she didn't do it either. She's too genuinely broken up. I've seen actresses before, none as convincing," Tommy said.

"I don't think she's acting."

"We'll see."

I left Tommy and went looking for my stray.

Chapter 14

Scar sat quietly in the car, fastened her seat belt without a word. I was afraid she might be slipping into shock. I started the engine. "Scar," I said, spoke softly. "Where can I take you?"

She didn't answer me. "Are you from Rochester? Do you have family around here?"

"I'm from Horseheads," she said. That was a few hours away. I don't think the chief would like me driving his only suspect in a murder case to Horseheads.

"No one around here? Do you know anyone on campus, maybe crash for a few nights in a dorm room?" I asked. It sounded like a reasonable question. Maybe she had a boyfriend, or some girlfriends who wouldn't mind her hanging around.

"No."

"No?" I asked. "No one."

"Maryjean was my only friend." She cried, cupped her hands over her face.

"I see," I said, though I found it hard to believe. I was stuck now. What do I do? Put her up in a hotel? That would be crazy. I put the car in reverse and pulled out of the precinct parking lot. I couldn't spot the tail, but was sure the police were following.

"Where are you going?" Scar asked.

"My house. You can stay with me for a couple of days," I said. "I've got a real comfortable couch."

"You don't have to do that. Bring me back to the college, I'll find somewhere to go. Someone will let me stay with them," she said.

"Nah. Then they'll drill you all night with questions. You don't need that."

"Thanks, Nick. I mean it. Thank you."

"I know this is a hard time, Scar. A terrible time, but I'm doing this for two reasons," I said, sounding stern.

"I know."

"You do?"

"You want my help. I'll help you. I'll tell you what you need to know. What questions I can't answer, I will point you to the people who can. That sound fair?" Scar was crying while she spoke. It was apparent she was suffering inside.

"Fair," I whispered.

Scar folded her hand into a fist, rested it against her ear and laid her head down on the door. She fell quickly asleep. I drove home on autopilot, there was too much to think about. My mind asked me questions that I didn't have the answers to. It was very, very frustrating.

A shard of a plan began to form in my brain. It was sharp, but that was a two-fold concept. I could either cut with it, or be cut by it. I thought of a character from a Tom Piccirilli novel. Submerged in a mystery, digging into a girl's past, running into obstacles, and pressing on.

When we got home, I made the sofa up with a clean sheet, a top sheet and a light blanket. I slept with three pillows. I liked two under my head, one to hug. I kept the hug pillow and sacrificed one of the others, thinking Scar could use it.

While I worked as a hotel maid, Scar used my bathroom to get ready for bed. I let her have one of my T-shirt's to sleep in. When she came out of the bathroom, my heart skipped a beat. The make up she'd been wearing had been washed off, her skin looked raw, but soft and milky. I thought the T-shirt would be longer. It came down just past her waist, leaving thighs fully exposed. They were nice.

"So you don't sleep with those rings," I said. I needed to talk to keep from staring.

"I left them on the corner of the bathroom counter, in the corner, I hope that's okay?" She said, sounding sad. She looked beat.

"That's fine." I fluffed her pillow, tossed it against the arm of the sofa.

"That looks great," she said, pointed to the bed I'd made. "I didn't think I'd be able to sleep again, but right now, it's all I can think about doing."

"I understand," I said. "Here, come with me."

I led Scar down the hall to my bedroom, switched on the light. I was giving her my room. She looked like she might protest. "Make yourself at home. If you need anything, like if you get hungry, just go get something to eat. Don't wake me up to make you a sandwich, because I won't do it. If you want one, you make one. My kitchen has the same basic layout as anyone else's. Silverware is in the drawer by the sink, plates and glasses are in cupboards over the counter. Sound simple enough?"

"Uh-huh."

"All right, then. Goodnight, Scar. I'll see you in the morning."

"Nick?" she said. "I would have been fine on the couch."

"I know you would have," I said, turned to leave.

"Nick?"

"Yeah, Scar?"

"My name's Eleanor," she said.

"Thank you. You telling me that, means a lot."

"But I don't ever, ever want to hear you call me that." She said softly, closed the bedroom door. I stood in the hallway and smiled. "Good night, Scar." I went down the hall and flopped onto the sofa, too lazy to change into PJ's, not to mention, my pajamas were in my bedroom with a half naked girl. No, sleeping in jeans would be just fine . . . for tonight.

I couldn't sleep. From the coat closet, I grabbed my knap-sack. I unzipped it and pulled out the class schedules I'd asked Jeffrey Granatta for. I crumpled up Maryjean D'Amonda's and looked closely at the one for Patricia Helms. She had a nine o'clock class this morning. It was almost five now. Leaving Scar alone might not be the best thing, but I still had a job to do.

I put the schedules back into the knap-sack and tried to sleep. If I was up in time, I'd head out to the college, if I overslept, fine. I closed my eyes, prayed for dreams and not nightmares.

The smell of eggs, bacon and coffee brought me out of the realms of sleep. Groggily, I propped myself up on an elbow and looked around my own living room. Déjà vu, I thought. Only hours ago Tommy Cerio had been at the door when I'd been asleep in the chair and woke up disoriented. I shook my head and ran fingers like a brush through my hair.

Scar had to be making breakfast. Standing up, I noticed the smell of food more strongly. I was starving. I stumbled into the kitchen. Scar was leaning over the table, sipping coffee, flipping through the newspaper. She looked showered, her hair still wet, her nose rings were back in place. She wore the clothes she'd had on yesterday.

"I was going to let you sleep until everything was ready," she said, smiling. "Cup of coffee?"

"Sounds perfect," I said. I looked at the time on the microwave oven. "God, it's almost ten."

"What time you normally get up?"

"I don't know, five? Five-thirty? I better call work," I said then picked up the phone and dialed. "Hello, Betty?"

"Nick? What happened, you get lucky last night?" Betty asked, laughing. I could picture her sitting at her desk, leaning back comfortably, a mystery novel close at hand.

"Nah, I over slept," I said.

"You like cheese in your omelets?" Scar asked.

I covered the mouthpiece on the phone. "Shh," I said to Scar.

Betty gave me a hard time. "Who's that, Nick? Your alarm clock?"

"It's not like that, Betty. It's a long, serious story. Tell Ned I'll either be in real late, or I'll see him on Monday. I think I'll be working the whole weekend," I said. Scar smiled at me as she listened to my end of the conversation. I didn't like the smile, she reminded me of a wife. I wasn't married. If I were, she'd be older than Scar.

"Nick, I thought you were going to be taking it a little easy. Ned told me you were working on something for an old friend. When you finish that case, take a long vacation," Betty said. So concerned, such a mother.

"You make it sound so simple."

"It is simple, Nick. Ned gives me three weeks vacation every year, and every year I use all three weeks. That's why they were given to me, so I could use them to get away, relax. You really ought to try it. The whole time you've been with us, you haven't taken more than a few days here and a few there," she said. She sounded like a boxer losing a fight she never had a chance to win.

"I'll think on it."

"You promise?"

"I promise. Will you give Ned my message?" I asked.

"I'm a secretary, aren't I?"

"That you are. Thanks dear." I hung up. Scar had the food scooped and on the table.

"I just took a guess that you always sit at the head of the table," Scar said.

I sat where the food was. "I live alone, Scar. Anywhere I sit is the head of the table." Taking my fork, using the edge, I cut off a piece of omelet and ate it. Wonderful. It melted in my mouth. I tasted three different kinds of cheese, finely diced peppers and onions.

"Well?" Scar asked.

I shrugged, my mouth full, finished chewing and shrugged again. "It's okay. I've had better."

She threw her potholder at me and laughed. "You bastard!"

Scar filled her plate with omelet, sat down next to me and started eating. "I need to see Maryjean's family. I should have been there last night when the police told them, but I couldn't. I wouldn't have been able to handle seeing them. I was acting selfish, I know."

"I don't think they'll be upset with you," I said.

"Unless they think I killed her," Scar said.

"Why would you say that?"

"Well, that's what the police think, isn't it? I'm not stupid. Maryjean and I were the only ones home last night. I had the television on, but I wasn't really watching it. I was studying. I was on the couch, you know, book open on my knees and every once in a while I'd hear laughing, and I'd turn to see what was happening. Maryjean, right after we ate dinner, said she was beat— she was going to take a shower and get to bed early. It wasn't odd, that was Maryjean. She was always tired. And that's it."

"That's it?" I asked. I thought I might have missed something.

"I mean, yeah. I didn't hear anything, no fight—if there was one, no screaming. No one came through the front or back door. I was right there in the living room, I would have seen, not to mention they'd have to walk through the living room to get to the stairs. It's a colonial."

"Uh-huh. So you're telling me you and Maryjean were alone? No one broke in? You didn't hear anything, no sounds of struggling, no screaming?"

"That's right."

"The television was on, was it on loud?"

"Not so loud I wouldn't hear someone screaming for help," Scar said.

"Okay, okay, so finish the story," I said. I was beginning to see why the chief of police liked the idea of Scar being a suspect. Her story was thin, not impossible, just thin. She could not provide an alibi. There were no signs of forced entry into the house. The only thing on Scar's side was the fact that many sets of finger prints were littered through out the house and only D'Amonda's were on the murder weapon.

Scar trembled as she continued. "I shut the television off around midnight, I was tired too. I was looking at the words in the book, but not reading them. Everything was becoming a blur.

"So I went upstairs. I was going to go into the bathroom and get ready for bed, but Maryjean's bedroom door was open. I called out to her, because she never slept with her door open, in fact she always slept with it closed and locked. I used to hate that. I'd tell her it was dangerous. She never listened.

She never answered me.

"I wasn't scared or anything at this time, I just thought it was odd, so I was going to go into her room and say something like, 'Hey, what are you afraid of, the bogeyman?'" Scar laughed. "She was on her bed, naked and lying on her back. The knife, oh God, the knife handle was all I saw, only I didn't know that's what it was at the time. There was blood all over her chest. Her white sheets were soaked in it.

"I started screaming, I remember, so hard and loud and long, I thought I was going to pass out. I wanted to go over to her, hold her, you know? I wanted to grab the knife and pull it out of her chest, but I couldn't." Scar cried, buried her face in her hands. I reached over and rubbed her back. "She was my best friend and I couldn't even go over to comfort her. What if she was still alive and I could have saved her."

"It doesn't sound like you could have," I said. I hadn't seen the photographs from the murder scene yet. The way Scar described it all, I wasn't sure if I wanted to. "Scar, there was nothing you could have done."

"I could have heard something and helped her!"

"But you said you didn't hear anything?"

"I didn't. I didn't and that's driving me crazy, Nick. I'm going out of my mind here! Now every time I try to remember, I think there is a noise— only I ignore it. Then I tell myself, you only hear that noise now, because you know she was murdered. There was no noise. But the other half of my brain insists, no, no, there was a noise, but you were too lazy to see if everything was all right!

Scar held her head in her hands now. Her fingers rolled into fists, clumping tufts of hair into the palms. I hoped she didn't pull any out. She seemed on the edge.

"You just need time," I said, hoping I sounded sincere and not like a bad cliché. "Of course everything is going to seem fuzzy right now. In a few days I bet you'll have a better idea whether or not you heard a sound. Don't let yourself dwell on it right now. Okay? It *will* drive you crazy."

Scar looked at me like I was crazy. Did I say the wrong thing? Her look softened. She released her hair, rested her cheeks in her palms, her elbows on the table. She blubbered. I got off the chair and knelt by her. She hugged my neck tightly and cried on my back.

"I want to call her family," Scar said. "Hell, I need to call my own."

I agreed. She should call her family. "Did you know Maryjean's parents at all? Are they from around here?"

"LeRoy," she said. About forty minutes south. "I knew them. After

Maryjean lost Darla last year, she spent a lot of time with me. We didn't live together then, but she would take me home with her on long weekends. This school year just started, but I was really looking forward to seeing her family. I hadn't seen them all summer long," Scar explained.

"You can use my phone to call," I said. "Call your family. Let them know what's going on, tell them you're staying with a friend, so they won't worry. Give them my number. I need to go shower and get dressed. I get the feeling today is going to be a very busy day." I remembered the messages on the machine. I still hadn't called Judy Swanson back.

"Nick?" Scar said. "Thanks."

Chapter 15

I dropped Scar off at the D'Amonda residence in LeRoy. The family was glad to hear from her. They wanted her with the family. Scar seemed relieved. I was too. I needed to get back to work, having Scar in my house left me feeling obligated to spend time with her. I was a busy, busy man. I didn't have time for Scar right now. She was a strong kid, she'd be all right. It sounded heartless, I know, but its nothing less than the truth. People were dying, young innocent girls. Thanks to Darla, I was involved and it was up to me to stop the killings.

Sacrifices. The Tenth House. I needed to find out more about this cult. I couldn't say for sure if they were connected to Maryjean's murder. A burning itch in the pit of my belly told me they were. Information would be the only way to begin to scratch it.

I'd given Scar another one of my cards. It had my cell phone number on it. I told her to call if she needed anything, a ride, to spend the night, anything. She promised she would.

I needed to see Tommy. A thought had come to mind and I needed someone professional to share it with. Driving to the police station I used my phone to call my answering machine at the office. There were two messages. Both were hang-ups.

Normally, I get a lot of hang-ups. Lately, though they're all I've been getting. It was annoying. I'd hate to get an unlisted number. If people need to get a hold of me, I would like to think I am readily available.

At the precinct, I parked in back where the police officers and detectives parked. There were too many cars in the lot to see if Tommy's was around. All the cars looked alike. I couldn't even be sure what color Tommy's car was. Most of the cars here were white.

I went in the back door. The police in the room gave me odd looks, none tried to stop me. Most knew who I was and didn't like me because I was a private investigator. They thought I was just a hot dog. I wanted to be one of them, it was *them* who wouldn't let me join.

Knowing where Tommy's cubicle was, I didn't need to stop and ask for directions. I went up a small flight of stairs, out into a maze of cubicles. I was at the start of the maze, Chief Delski's office was at the finish. Tommy and Deanna sat somewhere in the middle.

Weaving in and out, here and there, and in no time at all I found them. Out of respect I knocked on the frame of the cubicle. "Excuse me," I said.

Tommy had his head cradled in his hand. He was flipping through a report. He worked with an intensity I admired. Deanna, sitting with her back to me, was the mirror image of her mentor. Their desks faced each other. "You guys look like you haven't gone home, yet?"

They both looked over at me, looking annoyed. "We haven't gone home," Deanna said. She still looked cute, frustrated, but cute.

"What is it, Nick? We've got work to do here."

And I didn't? "Just something I was thinking," I said. "I didn't see the coroner's report, or the murder scene or anything, but I've got a few questions that might give us an answer."

"Okay, Columbo, what are your questions?" Tommy asked. He was a tough cop, but a nice guy. Open minded. I liked that. He took help wherever he could get it; he didn't seem the type who'd be afraid to ask for it, either.

"I talked with Scar," I said.

"Good," Deanna said. "We figured you would."

"Any chance she confessed?"

"No, Tommy. She didn't." I took a deep breath, knelt between the two desks where they were butted together. "Now, Scar told me she was watching television."

"Yeah, and didn't hear a thing," Deanna said.

"That's very possible," I said.

"I'm not going to sit here and argue with you," Deanna said. "Sorry. Let's hear what you have, then I'll argue with you," she finished, folded her arms and smiled.

"Thank you. Anyway, she doesn't hear any struggling, there's no screams, no one broke in, right?"

"Right. House was secure, all the windows, doors were locked. Except for all the prints in the house, it doesn't seem likely that anyone else was in that house. Right?"

"Right," Tommy said. "That's how we see it. That's why we don't want Scar leaving town."

I smiled. "I think it was suicide."

Tommy and Deanna both shook their heads at me. "Suicide's already been ruled out. The knife went in *too* straight and *too* deep to be a self inflicted stab wound."

"I need to see the house. I think I can prove it was a suicide and not a murder."

"Oh," Deanna said, "and why do you think you can do this?"

It was a hunch, but I wasn't going to admit to that. If I'm wrong, they'll be expecting that. I won't look so bad. If I'm right, I'll be surprising them. I'll look like one smart private eye.

"What have you got, Nick?" Tommy asked. I had his attention. I knew I would.

"Look," I said, "why don't you call the chief. I was supposed to meet with him today, anyway. I can go through this once, save us all a lot of time. Okay? But then, just between the three of us, I need to get down there and see the scene. Deal?"

"What deal? If you have information on a murder case, you have to come forth with it. If you don't you could be arrested for obstructing justice. There are no deals, Nick. We don't have to show you anything."

I smiled. "That's if you're investigating a murder case, Mister Brother-in-law."

"It is a murder case, Nick," Tommy said. I was wearing him out. I didn't mean to, it just happened.

"I think it was suicide."

Tommy stood up. "Let me go get the chief."

Tommy drove, Deanna sat beside him. I sat in back. Delski thought the link with Maryjean's death and Darla's was a little too coincidental. Everything I told them, I said, Karis Bristol had told me. I didn't mention the fact that the spirit of Darla had hired me. I don't think that would lend credibility to the story, and might leave me looking less than able.

"What else have you got on this cult?" Deanna asked.

"Only what I told the two of you and the chief," I said. There was no reason to withhold any information back. In mystery novels and movies, the private investigator always withholds evidence, keeps an ace in the hole. To me, that seemed foolish. I work hard and don't mind sharing what I learn. If someone were to die, I'd feel responsible for trying to do it alone. With all the police around, there was no reason for me to be doing it alone.

We pulled onto College Street. The houses were old, huge. I loved them. No one made houses like these anymore. Large colonials, Victorians, front porches, pillars. Without ever being in any of these houses, I could still imagine the gleaming hardwood floors, gumwood trim, big rooms and plenty of closet space, along with finished attics. The downfall was the college. I would not want to live this close to a college. Every weekend I'd be worried about drunken kids fighting on my front lawn, and vandalizing my car. Not that college kids are trouble, but drunk kids could be.

Halfway down the street we pulled into a driveway. It was the worst looking house on the street. It was in desperate need of painting. The wood on the front porch was warped, the top step broken. I followed Tommy and Deanna into the house.

The outside had me fooled. I expected to find a mess inside. Never judge a book by its cover. In the front foyer was a grandfather clock, an ottoman, a vase with plastic flowers sitting on a doily. Some abstract art hung on the walls following up the staircase to the second level. A small chandelier hung over my head. "This is kind of nice," I mumbled.

"This room here is where Eleanor was supposedly watching television while her roommate was being murdered," Deanna said. She led me into the living room. In here I saw a sofa, love seat and recliner chair. In the center of the room, a coffee table set on an oriental looking area rug, and the hardwood floors gleamed. A large entertainment center housed a puny sized television set that left it looking out of place. Three lamps sat on natural wood end tables.

"Place is all done getting dusted, right?" I asked. Tommy said that it was. I picked up the remote control, turned the television on, set the volume at what I considered to be a normal level. I tossed the remote onto the sofa. "Okay. Now what?"

"Upstairs, Nick," Tommy said. I followed them upstairs.

"This is Eleanor's room," Deanna pointed out.

I looked in. Seeing the room told me more about Scar than I would have ever guessed. Her hard look, dressed in black, nose rings, were all an act. She was not hard, or a freak. She was a smart kid, liked the normal things, Unicorns and lighthouses. Her bedroom had a bed with a frilly, flowered bedspread. Tasteful art was on her walls. She had to be the one to hang the drawings on the stairway. I stepped into the room, looked closer at the drawing. ES was written in the bottom right hand corner. Eleanor Scar? Was she the artist?

Across the hall was Maryjean's room. Tommy switched on the light. The scene still looked gruesome. The bed had not been touched, the sheets were still covered in blood.

124

I walked closer to where Maryjean was found dead. I turned around slowly, looking at the room. Two dressers were pushed together, but not so they touched. I continued to search around the room for more possible signs. Right now, the dressers looked to be about right.

"What are you looking for?" Tommy asked.

I might as well give it a try. "Wait here, let me run downstairs real quick."

In the kitchen I found a knife block on the counter by the sink. One knife, the butcher knife, was missing. I grabbed the chef's knife and went back up to Maryjean's bedroom. Tommy and Deanna stared at me oddly.

Keeping quiet, I wedged the handle of the knife between the two dressers. It fit in place snugly, stood erect with the tip of the blade pointing to ten o'clock. "Now, I'm not saying this was exactly how it was done," I said.

"How what was done?" Deanna asked.

"Suicide," Tommy said.

"If the doors were locked, windows, too; if Scar—Eleanor—was downstairs watching television and claims not to have heard a fight, or a struggle, suicide is very plausible. But the coroner didn't think the victim could have penetrated her own chest with such force and still have the blade go into the body as straight as it did, right?" I was on a roll. It felt right. I could imagine Maryjean doing the things I said. "She set the butcher's knife between the dressers, like I did. Then, when she's ready, she just throws herself onto the blade."

"Ah God," Deanna moaned. She squirmed. "Why on earth would someone do that?"

"I have one theory. I asked Scar to ask Maryjean if she would talk to me about Darla and the Tenth House."

"That cult?" Tommy asked.

"Like I told you, Darla was involved with them and that's part of the reason why I don't think Darla overdosed on drugs. However, in this case, I don't think Maryjean was murdered," I said.

"So, you disagree with the police on two cases. Why aren't I surprised?" Tommy asked.

"Maryjean was a part of the cult, it's obvious," I said. "When Scar asked her to talk to me, Maryjean must have told someone else. That someone else might have told the kid to kill herself—for the integrity of the church, or some such bullshit."

"Kill yourself for the church? Is that the best you've got for motive?" Deanna asked, looking disgusted. She kept her arms folded while she talked.

"She's dead isn't she?" I said.

"The police are still looking into murder as the cause, Nick," Tommy said. "Your idea has merit, but it won't fly. I don't think the chief'll buy it either."

I stared at the knife wedged between the dressers. I could picture Maryjean praying silently before impaling herself. The thrust would knock the wind out of her, she wouldn't be able to scream. She would lose her balance, stumble backwards, fall on the bed and die.

"Well," I said. "I hope you know what you're doing. I'm going to continue my investigation under the assumption that Maryjean committed suicide. As far as I'm concerned, though, whoever gave her the order to kill herself is responsible for her death. I think we're dealing with a Charlie Manson copycat here. He has everyone else do the dirty work. His hands never get bloody. But this person is a genius. I'll guarantee it. A master mind."

Tommy and Deanna stared at me. I think I successfully planted a seed in each of their minds. They would talk about my theory in great lengths after they dropped me off at the precinct.

I was right. They knew it, pride kept them from admitting it.

Chapter 16

On my way to Judy Swanson's I stopped off at Harvey's Liquor Store. It was one of many small businesses sandwiched between a Wegmans Super Store grocery market and a Chase-Pitkin. On the left of Harvey's was a place to get your hair cut, on the right, a bagel-shop cafe.

I felt comfortable in pair of loose fitting jeans and a short-sleeve pullover top with three buttons down the front, no collar. I wore sneakers. Casual is better. This wasn't really a date. We weren't going out, she was just making me dinner.

I grabbed a bottle of red and a bottle of white wine, not sure what was on the menu for dinner. On a whim, I ran into the bagel shop and bought a dozen assorted bagels and three different types of cream cheese.

On the way back to the car, my cell phone rang. My hands were full. I shuffled the bag of bagels under my arm, grabbed the phone. "Hello, Nicholas Tartaglia?"

"You're dead, Mr. Tartaglia." The caller hung up. The voice had been distorted. I couldn't be sure if it was a man or a woman threatening me. I dialed *69. The prerecorded operator told me that she was unable to contact the last caller. Slipping the phone back into my coat pocket, I wondered who it could have been. It could be anyone. I've been poking my nose into other people's business for over five years and making lots of enemies. I hand my PI cards out to everyone I encounter.

Still, I assumed the call was related to my present case. Perhaps it was a member of the Tenth House trying to scare me off. I do not scare easy. Somehow, unbeknownst to me, I must be getting close to a nerve. The problem: When had I'd gotten close? Who had I gotten close to?

Judy lived in Greece, by the canal. Her driveway was long, the house large. She had a front man-made pond with a bridge arching over it. In the daylight, I'd bet it was full of ducks and birds.

I parked next to a two year old, red BMW. Did she own, or lease? Either way, I'd never be able to afford the payments.

No one was at the door when I got out of the car. The walkway was cobblestone and led to the steps at the front door. I rang the bell, listened to the loud, long chime and waited. After a few moments, the door opened.

Judy Swanson looked stunning, wearing her blond hair down instead of in a ponytail. She had on a white top and black jeans that fit her body snugly, but didn't strangle. She had on very little make-up—a touch of rouge on her cheeks, soft red lipstick and a little mascara. She was perhaps one of the few women I've ever met who actually realized she didn't need to cake-on the cosmetics.

"I'm glad you called me back," Judy said, opening the door.

"I'm sorry it wasn't right away. I've been tied up in a rather involving case," I made excuses. The interior of the house was even more beautiful than the outside. I loved the ambiance. She had the light dimmed, soft music coming from everywhere. I spotted speakers mounted in a corner of the ceiling in every room.

I felt the central air-conditioning upon entering her house and was immediately thankful for it. It wasn't terribly hot out, but I was still sweating a little. Maybe I was nervous. I don't know, I wouldn't admit it to it. I plead the fifth.

"That's all right," Judy said. She sounded nervous, also. Could she be as nervous as I could? Doubt it. We were on her territory. She knew the floor plans. She could only lead. I could only follow. "I'm just glad you didn't cancel."

I smiled. "How've you been?" We both knew what I was asking.

Her look turned somber. "I'm doing pretty well. I haven't been to work all this week. The officer, Callister, he calls me all the time. I like him, he looks gruff but he's not. There's going to be a trial because he has you and me to testify."

"That's good. That's what we want. I'll give Callister a call, get the low-down."

There was a moment of awkward silence. "Can I take your bags?" Judy suddenly asked.

"Oh, yeah. Yes." I handed her the bottles. "I brought a red and a white wine. I wasn't sure what you had planned."

"I'm going to grill steaks outside on the deck. Does that sound all right?"

"Wonderful," I said. I held up the bag in my other hand. "I bought some bagels."

Judy took the bags.

"There's some cream cheese in there, too. Might want to stick it in the refrigerator."

"I love bagels, but I never buy them. At work, on Fridays, this lady comes in with bagels and sets up a little area in the office with an empty coffee mug. People just drop in money, you know? Then she picks up the money and uses it to buy bagels the following week." She smiled. She looked embarrassed, like she was mad at herself for talking so much. I liked it. It told me she was comfortable with me in her house.

"You never did tell me where you work," I said as we walked into her kitchen. It was huge. Most everything was white, the floors, the appliances and the counters. Some things were black, like the knife block, the coffeepot and the microwave.

"I'm a paralegal. I work for a large firm downtown, across the street from The Democrat and Chronicle." She placed the wine and the three containers of cream cheese in the refrigerator. "Can I get you something to drink? I have a white and red wine, wouldn't you know. I also have cognac, or—"

"A cognac sounds nice," I said. "This really is a beautiful home."

"Thank you. I've worked very hard to get it. At first, when I bought it, it owned me, not the other way around. But my hard work has paid off. I've got a good job with a strong firm. I like the people I work for and they seem to appreciate and respect my talents," she said. She sounded quite proud and she should be. I know I was impressed.

It was a three-tier deck stepping down to a lawn that reminded me of a golf course; small hills, a pond and bright, green grass. The only thing missing were the sand traps. I hated sand traps. They ruined my game.

"I'm sorry if I'm repeating myself, but this is incredible," I said, took a sip of my drink and leaned on the rail. Though it wasn't terribly late, the moon was bright. It hung in a starlit sky resembling too perfect an image, like a backdrop used for a motion picture.

I tried to do the actual cooking. Judy wouldn't let me. She made me sit on some patio furniture while she fired up the grill. She wore a red and white checkered apron. She handled the utensils like a barbecue pro. The scent of the steaks made my stomach growl and my mouth water. I found I could not wait for them to get done.

We small-talked, then decided to eat outside. It was too good a night to waste sitting in a kitchen. I made trips back and forth from the kitchen following Judy's lead. She'd made a Greek salad, loaded with black olives and Fetta cheese. She had potatoes baking. I picked up the red wine and we set the patio table.

"Medium-well," Judy said, taking both our plates, setting a steak on each. She gave me back my plate and set hers down next to me. She shut off the gas on the grill, then sat down. I would have told her to leave it on a while, let the grease cook off, but decided against it. Her house, her grill.

"Great. Thanks," I said, while filling our glasses with chilled wine. "I suppose I should make a corny toast?"

Judy giggled. "If you'd like."

"To justice," I said, looking into her eyes while I spoke. They were like crystal. She was staring at me like she wanted to kiss. I wanted to kiss her. I leaned in, she leaned closer. I felt my pulse quicken.

This wasn't right. The mood was, the atmosphere around us was; the moon, the heat, the cognac, but it still wasn't right. I didn't know Judy. I was attracted to her, physically stimulated by her, but I didn't know her.

Great. What a time to develop a sense of morals. Just wonderful.

I knew in my heart, not knowing Judy did not keep me from kissing Judy. Actually, it was the thought of Karis that stopped me. I wanted to be with Karis. If I haven't blown it, I could assume Karis wanted to be with me.

"I'm sorry," I said, Judy's eyes had been closed in preparation and anticipation of our first kiss. They opened. She looked immediately embarrassed.

"No, I'm sorry. I don't know what came over me, I'm sorry."

"It's not like that, I am very attracted to you, you're beautiful and sexy, but I have someone else, a girlfriend."

"Oh, you have one of those?"

"Just bought one." I laughed. Judy didn't.

"You must think I'm like this all the time. I'm not, I swear. I just have this feeling about you, a feeling I can't explain," Judy said. She rested her elbows on the table, held her wineglass in both hands, but didn't take a sip. She looked up to the heavens, perhaps she was looking for the face in the moon.

"Maybe you feel that way because of the way we met."

"I guess."

Dinner was ruined. We both knew it. Neither of us wanted to eat. We both ate though. We ate everything. Keeping food in our mouths kept us from talking.

When I got home, I called Karis, let the phone ring four times. No one answered. It was almost ten o'clock. She might have been sleeping. I hung up. Two minutes later, the telephone rang, I picked it up, hoped. "Karis?"

"Karis? No, it's *me*, Nick. I need a ride. Please come and get me."

"Where are you, Scar?"

"Where you dropped me off."

"You're kidding me? You can't just spend the night there? What's going on?"

"Nick, they think I had something to do with her death. There was a phone call not too long ago. Maryjean's father answered it. I watched him from across the room because he was staring right at me. They'd been getting phone calls all day, you know? I hated to see the family go through the pain of retelling their story every time someone called. I thought Maryjean's dad was just looking my way, not staring, until his eyes narrowed, you know? Then I knew. He was, like, burning a hole in my head with this intense stare," Scar said. She was crying. "When he hung up, he came right over to me. Maryjean's mother was hanging on his arm saying, like, Honey, what is it? What's wrong. But he didn't answer her. His hands were clenched in fists, down at his side. He gets right in my face and starts yelling that he wants me the hell out of his house." Scar cried harder. It sounded like she was having trouble controlling her emotions.

"Where exactly are you now?" I asked. "You're not still in their house, are you?"

"God no. I left as fast as I could. I just started running down the street and kept on running until I came to this, I don't know, some little convenient store. It's called," I heard her cup her hand over the phone and ask someone the proper name of the store. "Nick, the place is called, Come and Get It. It's on the corner of Raleigh and Madison. Nick, will you come and get me, please?"

"Of course. We'll talk more when I get there. I'll leave right now."

On the expressway, I drove the speed limit. I knew Scar was upset, but getting a speeding ticket wouldn't make me very happy. Not enjoying the ride, I took time to think. So much had happened in the last few days, I haven't had any time for reflection. There was more going on than I realized. Things, good and bad, were set in motion around me. There was no way I could be aware of it all. I found that thought sobering.

The one obvious puzzle: The phone calls. I'd received one, so had Mr. D'Amonda. Same person? Most likely. How did this person know Scar was

131

at the D'Amonda home? Someone must have put a tail on me. Was I being watched? Was anyone following me now?

Checking my rearview mirror, I was relieved to see that I was the sole car out on the road. Two cars were ahead of me.

Then there was Karis. She was on my mind, fighting for space in the front of my brain and holding her own. She wasn't going to be satisfied on hold in the dark recesses of my mind. As I thought about her, I realized there might still be something between us. I know I felt something. I thought Karis felt something, too, or was I just hoping she did? Only time will tell, as the old cliché goes. I wouldn't want to rush things. Everything should happen in its own time and at its own pace. Slow and easy—that was fine with me.

While thinking of Karis, I noticed headlights in the rearview mirror. Although the car was far, far behind, paranoia bubbled in my belly. Cars drive on the expressway everyday, that was the purpose of them. Just because it was late at night, didn't mean that me and the two cars ahead of me, owned the road.

Fancying myself as a mystery writer, I couldn't help but envision one of the cars ahead of me using a two way radio, telling the guy in the car behind me, to "come up slowly on Mr. Tartaglia. We don't want him to think he's being followed. I'll get off at the next exit, you keep behind him for a few miles, pass him, and I'll get back on the expressway at the Leigh High Station ramp."

Paranoid. I know. But seeing the right directional blink on the car ahead of me, watching as the car left the expressway, I couldn't help but think I was right, either. "Just great," I said to myself, getting caught up in my thoughts.

If I really was being followed, there wasn't much I could do about it. They must know where I'm headed, considering they'd be my best guess to the ones responsible for the threatening phone call.

I slowed to thirty-five miles an hour. The car behind me came onto my rear, flashed the bright lights, switched lanes and pulled up along side me. I looked over, into the other car. It appeared to be a young, college-aged boy with a brush cut. A girl's garter hung around his rearview mirror. He stared at me and gave me the finger. What a nice boy. I gave it back. Give and take, that's how things work. I can't always be getting the finger without giving it to others. That would be rude. The kid sped away.

I had to wonder now, had he been following me?

Pulling into *Come and Get It*, I saw Scar inside the little store. She looked to be talking with the cashier. I couldn't see the cashier; racks of lunch-size potato chip bags blocked the person's face.

I beeped the horn three times. My cheeks felt hot. Jealousy? Nah, that's crazy.

I pressed long and hard on the horn when Scar didn't respond to the first few beeps. "Come on. I don't have all night you know," I yelled in the car even though the windows were up.

She waved to the cashier, came out of the store and hopped into the car.

"You don't look too upset," I said to her.

She slammed the door and buckled her seatbelt. "Go to hell, Nick. You don't know what I've been through."

"That's part of the reason why I'm here. I want you to tell me."

"Start driving. Get me out of this stinking town. I'll talk while we drive," she said and started crying.

Scar was silent for quite a while. She'd stopped crying by the time we were back on the expressway. I kept my eye out for cars. Again, none were around. Okay, I admitted to myself, maybe I'd overreacted. No one was following me. Not now, anyway.

Finally, I asked, "Do you have any idea who was on the phone when Mr. D'Amonda answered, or what was said?"

"I don't know who it was that called, but I think I know what was said. When Maryjean's father hung up, he came right at me. He looked like he wanted to kill me. I was really scared, Nick. I thought he might start punching me in the face or something," Scar said.

Outside, the bland scenery could not hold my interest. I found myself looking away from the road, watching Scar as she retold the story with animated hand gestures. "And what? What did he say?"

"You knew they were going to kill her! This guy on the phone just told me you were a part of her death. You're in my house and you are responsible for my daughter's death?" Then Scar continued, "Then he started to swear at me and everyone tried to get him to back off, but they all still looked at me in this weird way—like maybe they believed what Maryjean's father was saying—that somehow I was a part of her death."

"I can't imagine." I wanted to ask, *Were you?*

"Then he starts rambling," Scar went on, "Instead of helping my daughter, he tells me, you turn the other way. I told him, I had no idea what he was talking about, but it's too late, this guy was beyond listening. Maryjean's mother was trying to lead me out of the room. The two of us got into the kitchen and then she's crying and I'm crying. I told her I didn't know what her husband was talking about. She told me that, right now, it might be easier if I just left."

"So you did?"

"So I did. I walked right out the kitchen door, down to that store and called you. I didn't know who else to call."

The question sat in my mind like a rock. Now, I kept my eyes on the road. My stomach muscles kept tightening and relaxing and tightening again. She was staring at me, I could tell. Maybe waiting for me to say something. She wanted me to say something, I'm sure. I had nothing to say. There was, however, this question I wanted to ask.

"I don't believe this," Scar said. "You want to know if I had anything to do with her death, don't you? You want to ask me if I knew about her dying?" She cried. "I didn't hear anyone in the house. I never heard her scream! I was on the couch just watching television. I didn't see or hear anything!"

"I think Maryjean committed suicide, Scar."

"What? She killed herself?"

"That's what I believe, and I think I've persuaded the police to investigate the possibility, too. That would explain why you didn't hear a struggle, it may even explain why you didn't hear a scream. The knife was big. When she stabbed herself it would have been like getting punched in the stomach, only a lot more painful and deadly. So the wind could have been knocked out of her. She wouldn't be able to scream." It all made so much sense. I had to wonder why Tommy and Deanna did not think of it themselves. That was academic. I had their attention now and that was all that mattered.

"So you believe me then?"

"I believe that you didn't hear her scream, that there was no struggle, yes."

"What are you having trouble believing then?"

"That you didn't know your roommate was a part of the Tenth House cult," I said, my voice flat. I waited a few seconds, letting the implications of my statement sink in. "Scar?"

"What Nick?"

"Are you a part of the Tenth House, too?" There. I'd asked my question. Now I had to wait it out and fear Scar's answer.

She looked away from me and out the window. When she looked back, tears were in her eyes, but she wasn't sobbing. "No, I'm not you stupid bastard. Do you think I've been playing some little game?"

"Yes."

"Go to hell!"

"Tell me what's going on Scar! There's things going on here, that's why you've been so helpful, isn't it? You need me for something, don't you? What's going on?"

She broke down, crying harder than I'd ever see a person cry before. She couldn't possibly be acting. She had me feeling like an idiot for yelling at her. "I'm not falling for your sympathy-act," I said, wanting to reach out and touch her.

"I told you to go to hell!"

"Scar, whether you wanted it or not, I'm your friend now. We're friends," I said.

"That's crazy. You're doing your job. You, you *jerk*. You needed me! I was your link to Darla Bristol. There's nothing more. You needed me. Don't feed me some line about being my friend. I know who my friend was and she's dead!"

I couldn't lose the upper hand. She was good. She was trying to mislead the conversation by creating a diversion. "Why did you need me, Scar? When you found out I was a private eye investigating Darla's death. The Tenth House had you pull me in. I need to know why?"

"Pulled you in? I am not your mother. I didn't pull you in, I tried to help you," she insisted.

"Why?"

She didn't answer. I needed to get off the expressway, I was traveling at over sixty miles an hour and not paying a bit of attention to the road. "Scar, answer me!"

"Don't you yell at me," she said, punching me hard in the arm.

"Scar—"

"Let me out!"

"I'm not letting you out, we're on the expressway in the middle of the night, fool!" I yelled.

She unfastened her seat belt and opened her door.

The sound of driving filled the car, a wild wind whipped around loose papers in my car. I grabbed Scar with one hand, yanked her as close to me as I could. I swerved the car left, the motion jerked the car door closed.

"That was absolutely the most stupid thing in the world to do. What in the hell were you thinking? Were you going to jump, Scar? Was that your answer, jumping? Who would you blame on your way out? Me?" I asked.

When I spoke again, I mimicked her voice in mockery: "That nasty Nick made me so mad I had to jump out of his car and kill myself!"

"Get lost!"

"No, Scar, I won't get lost. You're going to talk to me."

She curled into a ball, lying on the front seat. She put her feet against the door and her head on my lap. "I'm going to sleep now," she whispered. "I don't feel like talking."

I didn't blame her. "Scar?"

"I said, I don't feel like talking, Nick."

"No matter what, you are my friend." I thought I saw her lips form into a hint of a smile. It was enough for me. I ignored her when she told me to drop dead.

When we got home, I ran up to the front steps, unlocked and opened the door. I carried Scar into the house, cradled in my arms like a five-year-old. She was either a heavy sleeper, or faking it, because she didn't so much as stir as I placed her in my bed, removed her shoes and socks and covered her with the top sheet.

I stood over her for a minute, admired her pretty face while she slept. She was going to be a knockout when she reached her mid twenties and lost a few of those rings piercing her body.

An urge passed through me to lean over and kiss her forehead in a father-like fashion. She was pretty, sexy, I was afraid if I started with a kiss on the forehead, I might not be able to control myself.

Turning off the bedroom light and closing the door behind me, I thought, *am I a* pervert, *or just frustrated*?

I lit a cigarette in the kitchen, took a beer out of the refrigerator and an ashtray from off the counter. I went into the living room. I wasn't in the mood for television. I sat in the dark and stared at the burning tip of the cigarette. It glowed bright, hot orange like a beacon. It reminded me of hell. I smoked two more, finished my one beer and decided to call it a day. Tomorrow was Saturday. There was so much that needed to be done, but I thought I might sit around the house and do nothing.

I was on a case, not getting paid and hired by a ghost. The only thing normal in that statement was that I was on a case. I've always gotten paid and a ghost has never hired me. It feels like months ago that Darla was in my office, begging me to look into her murder. It seems like months ago since I've seen Karis.

Looking into Darla's death has taken me down avenues I never would have guessed. No road is ever straight, no matter how straight it might appear.

I think Maryjean and Darla's deaths are related. The Tenth House is one bad group, so I've gathered. If they don't want me talking to someone, they have that person commit suicide. That's power. It's sick, but it's power. Who possessed that kind of power?

That was the bonding thread of the mystery. If I find the cult leader, bring him, or in a more diverse world, her, down, then I have won the battle. Another leader will take the fallen one's place, of course, but someone else will have to deal with that.

Right now, I was only interested in bringing Darla's killer to justice.

For the second night in a row, I slept fully clothed on the sofa.

Chapter 17

When I woke up the following morning, I expected to smell breakfast cooking. There was no such smell. I rolled off the couch, felt stiff in the neck and throughout my back. Stretching, I walked into the bathroom, freshened up and brushed my teeth.

In the kitchen I lit a cigarette and started a pot of coffee. I didn't normally eat breakfast, not because I didn't like it, but because I was too lazy. If there weren't someone who was going to make it for me, I'd just as soon starve until lunch. Then I'd buy a hamburger and fries, or something.

While the coffee brewed, I tiptoed down the hall, peeked into my bedroom. Scar looked to still be asleep. I thought about waking her, getting her moving, but I had nothing planned for the day so why should I care if she slept the morning away?

I could see slits of sunlight peeking in through the gap in the blinds. I opened the front door to grab the newspaper and yelled, slamming the door shut. "Oh my God," I gasped. I took a moment to catch my breath before I opened the door again.

It hung by its foot from the awning over my front step. "What the hell," I said, looking at the skinned animal. I wasn't sure what it was, a cat, maybe, or a raccoon. It was hard to tell with out any fur. The thing was still alive, barely, panting fast. It's eyes looked like they were bulging. There were no eyelids. The eyes *had* to look that way. The sight of its body—muscles, tendons, fat blood vessels—made me want to throw up. It looked like meat at a butcher shop, only pulsating.

Now what do I do?

I grabbed the phone. I was thinking of Father Paul and what happened with the dog on his altar, but it wasn't him I planned to call. Maybe I would stop in and see him later. I obviously had more questions for him.

"What's going on out here?" Scar asked.

She was dressed in yesterday's clothes, which happened to be the clothes she'd been wearing two days ago. I had to get this kid home so she could change. "Go take a shower," I said, dialing.

"I heard you scream, are you okay?" She asked.

"Wonderful. Now go take a shower," I said. I was trying to sound calm. It wasn't working. I could see my own hands shaking. I didn't want her to see the animal.

"Nick, my God, Nick, what is it?"

"Go take a shower, Scar," I said, my voice a whisper, my teeth clenched together. "Go on!"

"Bastard!" She said, stormed off. I heard the bathroom door slam closed and the lock click. I felt bad, but, dammit, she wasn't listening. She may hate me, but she'll get over it.

"Arline, how are you feeling?"

"Good, Nick. How are you? Why are you calling so early?" My sister asked me. I felt bad I hadn't been over for a while. I was due for a visit. I've just been so busy, but that's no excuse. I didn't tell her any of my thoughts. I thought of the breathing animal hanging from a foot in front of my door, the poor things bulging eyes.

"I need to talk to Tommy, is he in?"

"No, he's not. He left for work early this morning. He tells me you're involved with this case, Nick. It sounds like a dangerous one, please be careful, because I don't want to spend every day worrying over the two of you," she said. But she would. We both knew it.

"We'll be careful. I'm a pro. I'll take extra good care of your husband. He may need watching over." I laughed.

"You can try him at work, Nick. Okay? And hey, when are you going to come over?" She missed me, isn't that sweet?

"Soon. I promise. I gotta go, sis. I'll get a hold of you. Bye." I hung up, called the precinct. "I need to speak with Detective Cerio, please. Yes, it's important. No, there hasn't been a murder—but I'm working with him on a murder case. Yes. Nicholas Tartaglia. The private eye, that's right." He'd heard of me. "Great. Thanks." He put me on hold.

Tommy came on the line. "Nick? What's up?"

"I'll make it fast, I don't want to hold you up," I said, hoping the sarcasm was evident in my tone. "There's a half-dead, skinned raccoon hanging by a foot in front of my door. I'm going to guess it has to do with the Tenth House. Maybe I've hit a nerve with them. Want me to take it down, toss it out?"

"No. No. Don't touch it. I'll be down with a team. We'll look the area over. I doubt we'll turn anything up, but it's worth investigating. Thanks for thinking to call."

"Just doing what I can," I said. "Hey, Tommy, can I take Eleanor back to her place? She needs clothes. She's been wearing the same crap for two days now."

"Yeah. Just stay out of the D'Amonda room. We're almost all set in there. If there's a policeman around, keeping an eye on the place, tell him you cleared this with me. Sound good?" Tommy said.

"Good enough. Thanks."

We hung up. I went back to the front step and kept from looking at the thing in my doorway. I grabbed the paper, closed the front door and locked it. In the kitchen I poured a cup of coffee and lit another cigarette. I had the feeling I was in for a rough day.

Cradling my head in my hands, I tried not to think, and tried not to set my hair on fire with my cigarette. Feeling eyes on me, I looked up. Scar stood in the hall, looking into the kitchen. She was wearing one of my Miami Dolphin's T-shirts, no bra, a pair of my jeans that looked huge on her, but that was the style nowadays anyway, wasn't it?

"I'm sorry I yelled at you," I said. "Want some coffee?"

"I want an explanation," she said. She sounded hurt, but mostly angry. "Just last night you argued with me, trying to convince me we were friends. You know that when I fell asleep in the car, I felt good. I'd made a new friend. I don't have any friends, Nick. You saying we were friends meant the world to me. I know now you didn't mean it," she said.

"Of course I did—"

"Bullshit. Friends don't treat each other the way you just treated me," she yelled, pointed a menacing finger at me. She walked into the kitchen. "That's not how it works. I've read books, I've watched *Beverly Hills 90210*, and I know how friends are supposed to act towards one another. You didn't act like a friend when you were yelling at me. You acted like a complete jerk!"

I took a long drag on the end of the cigarette, held in the smoke, let it flow throw my lungs and relax me while it sped up my heartbeat. When I exhaled, I said, "There's a dying animal strung up outside my door." She gasped, her eyes narrowed. Maybe she didn't believe me. "The police are on their way. I didn't want you to see it. I got nervous, panicked. I was trying to protect you. I went about it the wrong way. You're an adult. You don't need protecting, so maybe I didn't need to divert you. Just the same, you're my friend, you've had a rough couple of days. So, I'm sorry." I took another drag.

Scar looked a little embarrassed. "There's really a dead animal out there, on your step?"

"Yup."

"My God, who? Why?"

"I think it's a warning. Someone, or some group of someone is trying to tell me to keep my nose out of their business." I took a sip of coffee.

"The Tenth House?"

"That's my guess."

"Are you going to stop what you're doing?" Scar asked.

"No. Do you think I should?"

"I don't know. That's kind of scary. I think I'd stop."

I shrugged. "If I stop, then I'm not very good at my job and I'd need to look for a new career. I've got bills. I don't have time to go out looking for a new job. I like what I'm doing now, anyway. I think I'll stay on the case," I said.

Her features softened. She sat at the table. "Anymore coffee?"

"Fresh pot," I said. She could get her own coffee. After all her shouting, I had a headache.

She stood up, poured a cup of coffee, stole one of my cigarettes from the pack, lit it and sat down next to me. "I'm sorry, Nick."

I looked at her. She was staring intently at me. I smiled. "Forget it. We're all wound a little tight, huh?"

"To the breaking point, I'd say," she said.

"Maryjean was involved with the Tenth House, wasn't she?" I knew she was. I needed to hear it from Scar. Confirmation. It explained a lot. It also made me wonder. Just how much trust should I put in Scar? Was she a part of the cult? If she was, what in the world should I do about it?

The doorbell rang.

Opening the front door I saw Tommy and his partner, Deanna. A man with a camera was taking Polaroid pictures from a variety of angles. I closed the door and went out through the garage. Scar waited inside. The sun was out, shinning bright, but it was not a hot morning. Summer was ending, fall was on the fringe of claiming its rite of passage. Squinting, I nodded silent hellos.

"This how you found it, Nick?" Deanna asked.

"Ah, no, I took off the tuxedo it was wearing, didn't want it to get ruined," I said.

"Don't be a wise-ass, Nick," Tommy said.

"Sorry. Just a little unnerved at the moment. It's a weird feeling to see just how vulnerable you are. I mean, I was inside sleeping on the sofa, right on the other side of the door, while someone was stringing a raccoon to my awning," I said, stuffed my hands into my pockets.

"It is alarming, isn't it?" Deanna said. She was taking notes and stopped long enough to watch my reaction.

"Yes. That's what I just said." She wrote some more.

"You think the Tenth House was involved with this?"

Father Paul would swear to it, I was sure. "This happened some years back, I guess."

"What did?" Tommy asked.

"A dog was found on the altar at St. Anthony's church. It was skinned, the police were called." I didn't think I needed to retell the entire story. They were the police, they could do a little research on their own, draw their own conclusion.

"And you think the two are related?" Tommy asked.

"More than ninety percent sure," I said.

"What are you going to do then? It's an obvious warning, Nick. Whoever is involved with everything here, knows you—or knows of you. Apparently, they don't like you around. It's a pretty serious warning, I'd say," Tommy said.

"It is, and I'll listen to the warning, but it won't stop me from continuing my investigation," I said.

"I didn't think it would. Just do me a favor, Nick," Tommy said.

"What's that?"

"Be careful. I'd hate to have to tell my wife I let you die."

"That's funny, just this morning I promised her I'd look out for *you*."

We laughed. I don't think either of us saw anything funny.

On the drive back to Scar's place many thoughts cluttered in my brain. I needed a big bare wall and a million squares of paper, the ones with the sticky backs. I could jot down thoughts, stick them to the wall, move them around, set up a logical flow, solve the mystery.

Nothing is that simple.

It was hard *not* to think everyone I've met so far is a suspect. They all were. Except the dead ones.

Tommy and Deanna and the coroner agreed with me. Maryjean's death was a suicide. Officially, the police were closing her case. What was there for them to solve? I was on my own. My brother-in-law knew what I was up to and said not to hesitate to call him if I needed any help or information. It was an offer I planned to keep in mind.

I hated to think of the priest as a suspect. Father Paul had been wonderful retelling the ancient ghost story of a little girl, a red raincoat, a rainy night and a cemetery. I knew the tale sounded familiar. I'd first heard it back when I was thirteen years old and had a paper route. I hated riding my bicycle by the cemetery because of that same story, told by someone else.

Father Paul was a suspect on my list. He ran a church, the Tenth House might be a cult, but it had a religious—albeit satanic—undertone. Father Paul knew plenty about heaven and hell. Who better to be a leader?

It was more than that, though. Why, if Father Paul was trying to put the Tenth House out of business, did he just give up his fight? Sure he'd been threatened and he didn't want any harm to come to any of his parishioners, but I can't see quitting the quest. He didn't impress me as a man who surrenders. He looked strong and strong willed.

I don't know. Father Paul is just one square of paper up on the wall.

Then, without names, I have another person who the leader of the cult is *not*. The high priest of the Tenth House is not a college student. Obvious reasons lead me to this conclusion. One, in order for the leader to be a student, then every four years maximum, you'd have to find a new leader. Leaders like the one we're talking about, are not born every four years. Two, reread number one.

A third square of paper would just say, hot. I'm hot on the trail of the case and I know this because of the threatening phone call and the raccoon on my front step. The funny thing is from which way is the heat coming? I haven't the foggiest. I spoke to someone who doesn't want me speaking to anyone else. My questions are making people nervous, but who have I really been asking questions, too?

The president of the school, Mr. Jeffrey Granatta.

He seemed a likely suspect in that he's been with the school forever. He knows the students. He knows the campus, all of its nooks and crannies. He was a man who thrived on power—look at who and where he is today.

The last few days have been amazingly hectic, but productive—productive without me knowing it. Here I thought I was getting nowhere, when all along I've been picking up pieces. Placing those pieces on the table and fitting them together is an entirely different process, of course, but at least I had the pieces to play with.

"You sure are quiet. What are you thinking of?" Scar asked.

"Everything. You name it, I've been thinking it."

"So, you're working for Darla's mother? We never really got a chance to talk about your case," she said, sounding like an adult for the first time since I met her. It almost made me laugh. If I wasn't in such a pissy mood, I might even have smiled.

"I don't remember wanting to discuss my case," I sneered.

"Oh, you want to ask all the questions, but not have to answer any in return?" Scar asked. She folded her arms across her chest. "Well?"

"Well, what? I thought it was a rhetorical question. You just asked it for the sake of asking it. I didn't think you wanted an answer," I said.

"Believe it or not, I know what rhetoric means," she said. "I was just asking you a question. I'm just as scared as you are," she confessed for the both of us.

"I never said I was scared."

"Oh sure."

"'Oh sure', what? I'm not scared. This is my job. This is what I do every day," I said. Actually, usually, married women hire me to follow around their husbands. But hell, that could be every bit as dangerous as tracking down a satanic cult leader -slash- murderer.

Scar looked offended. She leaned back, looked out the window to avoid looking at me. "Scar," I said.

"Forget it. I don't get you, Nick. That's twice. Twice, I tried to believe you and your lame friendship line. God, how could I be so stupid. I'm just a pawn in your game."

"That's not true," I said. Why did I give this kid such a hard time? Could it be because I was physically attracted to her? I was. I needed to keep her at arms length in order to control my animal instincts. Keeping her at arms length meant keeping her angry with me, didn't it?

It did. "Scar, I'm sorry I've been an idiot."

She didn't seem convinced. My apology must not have sounded sincere enough. I took a deep breath, checking my rearview mirror. We were at her house. I glanced over and saw her body tense. I touched her wrist, her fingers wrapped around my hand like a five legged octopus (are those legs on an octopus?) and squeezed tightly.

"Hold on," I said. "Let's sit here for a minute."

She didn't turn to look at me. Maybe she was expecting an elaborate

144

apology, I don't know. What she couldn't be expecting is what I began to tell her. "In a way, I'm working for Karis, Darla's mother. In another way, I'm working directly for Darla."

I caught her attention. She turned away from the window and looked at me. I wouldn't say she was crying, but tears had recently rolled down her cheeks. "What's that supposed to mean?" she asked.

I told her. I started at the beginning and ended in the middle—which is where I considered this case to be right now. We weren't at the beginning anymore, but neither were we close to a resolution. We were in the middle.

"You talked to Darla Bristol?" Scar asked. She didn't sound like she might be mocking me.. "She was in your office and asked you to take on her case, to solve her murder. And you believed her?"

"Not right away, I told you that. It's not every day a client from the Stephen King Clinic passes through my door. You had to see it though, Scar," I said, could feel the excitement grow inside me. "She was solid, sitting in my chair, and my hand went right through her fingers. That's a bizarre feeling."

"I'll bet. Are you sure you weren't drugged."

I cocked my head in disappointment.

"Sorry," she said. "Just a question."

"Understandable. For a while I did think I was going crazy. I'm still not so sure I haven't."

"You haven't," Scar said. "I think you're the most sane person I've ever met."

"Gee, thanks."

"Thank you for telling me all of this," Scar said, spoke softly. She still held my hand. I could tell she was debating whether or not to let go of it. I was debating whether or not I wanted her to let go of it.

Our eyes met.

I stared into more than her eyes. I thought I saw . . . Eleanor. We were going to kiss. It was coming. We both leaned in. I saw her moist lips inflate a little, pucker. I self-consciously licked mine. My body was responding even to the thought of a kiss. I shouldn't let it happen, but I was only human and I'd already proved my strength against Judy Swanson, another woman I wanted and could have had.

It wasn't a quest. Having sex with Scar would mean more to me than having it with Judy.

There was still Karis. Nothing formal between us, but would I be able to pursue a relationship with her after a fling with Scar? Would a fling with

145

Scar, because that's all it would be is a physical fling, be fair to Scar?

I didn't know. I'd have to think about it after the kiss.

We moved in closer, as if in slow motion, our eyes closed at the same time.

A loud knock startled me. I turned to my window. A bulging stomach in a cop's uniform blocked the view. A nightstick, gripped in a chubby hand, batted against the window again. I rolled it down. "What the hell do you think you're doing? This here's a murder scene," the police officer said. "Get out of the driveway and move it along."

"Ah, officer, my name is Nicholas Tartaglia. I'm with Scar. She lives here. Detective Tommy Cerio said we could swing by and pick up some of her things."

"Oh he did, huh? Do you have any ID?"

I showed him.

"A private investigator, huh?" He snorted. I was insulted. "Go on, get what you need. Stay out of the D'Amonda room, whatever you do."

"We will," I said, opened my door. "Watch my car while we're in there. I'd hate to have some college punks try to steal it."

"Like hell I will, loser." He went down the driveway, hopped into his cruiser and pulled away quickly.

I knew that would get rid of him. "Come on," I said, saw the disappointment in her face and something else contorting her features. Maybe it was because she saw the look of relief in my expression?

"I'm going back to classes on Monday," she said.

"How can you? I mean, you have the funeral this afternoon—"

"Me? Aren't you coming with me?"

I had so much to do. There was private investigator stuff that I needed to get started on. Answers didn't just fall into place. You had to find answers by asking the right people, the right questions. Then there was an entire process of sorting and sifting through the answers looking to make sense out of the entire mess. So if I didn't start asking questions, I'd be where I was now. Nowhere. "Sure. If you want me to come."

"Maybe I shouldn't even go, after last night, you know?"

"I think you should go," I said. "You're saying good-bye to a friend, it has nothing to do with the family. They may see how badly they overreacted if you show up and they may apologize."

"They don't need to apologize," Scar said, pushing open the front door. The house smelled like stale coffee. The place needed to be vacuumed. Instead of being empty for days, it felt as though it had been vacant for years. A haunted house. Was the spirit of Maryjean around? Would she ask me to solve her suicide, too?

"Spooky," Scar said.

"You took the words out of my mouth."

"I'm going to grab some things and we can get out of here. How does that sound?"

"Like a plan to me." I followed her up the stairs to her bedroom. It was difficult not to see the yellow police tape closing off Maryjean's room. The sheets on the unmade bed were still bloodstained. How long before they cleared that room out and sent everything down as evidence?

Ah, they wouldn't. You don't need evidence for a suicide.

Maybe it would be up to Scar—or the owner of the house—to clean up the mess. God, what an awful job that'll be. I'd have to remember to ask Tommy what the situation is.

While Scar grabbed clothing, I asked, "Are you sure you want to go back to classes on Monday? Maybe you might just want to go home, see your parents for awhile. You know, that might be the best thing to get you through all of this."

"Why, you don't want me at your place?"

"No, I don't care if you stay with me for awhile, but that's just it. You can only stay with me for awhile. I mean, you can't just move in with me." I laughed. The thought was funny. Scar wasn't laughing. "Don't tell me you thought you'd just live with me the rest of the year?"

"No. I didn't really think that," Scar said, stopped packing and sat on her bed. I sat beside her. "I guess I don't know what I thought. Maybe I've been trying not to think. You ever do that? Just try not to think about anything and just hope all your problems will disappear?"

"I sure do. Sometimes I use a little booze to help speed along the process, but you know what?" I pulled a couple of cigarettes out of the pack, lit them both in my mouth and handed Scar one.

"What," she said, taking a drag.

"When I get sober, nothing's changed, except I have the same problems I had before *and* a splitting headache."

Scar smiled as she stuck the butt between her lips. She stood up and went back to emptying clothes out of her drawer. "You like someone else, don't you? That's why you didn't kiss me in the car."

"I didn't kiss you in the car because a fat policeman was standing outside my door ready to beat my head to a pulp." I sat back on the bed, leaned against the headboard and kept my feet on the ground.

147

"You didn't kiss me after he left because you have a girlfriend, don't you?"

"I don't. But—"

"But what?"

"There is this woman I know, I knew her a long time ago, and I think she's pretty cool."

"'Pretty cool', that's how you'd describe her?" Scar asked. She stopped packing again, leaned against an open sock drawer and just stared at me, waiting.

"Yeah. See, we dated in high school. We're not really together, you know? Not yet." I said. "She's Darla's mother. Her name's Karis."

"So, Karis, does she know you like her?"

"I thought so. I think so, yeah." I remembered Karis leaving mad the other night. She left mad, because she liked me and wasn't too keen on the idea of me having dinner with another woman. She had been jealous.

"So what have you done to tell her you dig her?" Scar asked. Somehow she had become my psychiatrist, or my friend.

"Nothing really."

"That isn't going to help," she said.

"Tell me about it. I know I should do something to actually get the ball rolling, but I don't know what. I'm no good at the whole dating ritual. Never was. That's probably why I'm still single," I said. Talking about and thinking of Karis was getting me flustered.

"I'll help," she said.

"I don't need help," I said.

She tossed some socks into a suitcase, closed her drawer, closed her suitcase and zipped it shut. "Yeah, you do, Nick." She went to her closet and took out two nice dresses, kept them on hangers as she draped them over her arm. She stooped down and grabbed a couple of pairs of dress shoes to match. "Ready?"

Maybe she was right. I've always worked things alone. That's a lonely way to live. "Born that way," I mumbled. I stood up, grabbed her bag and we got the hell out of that spooky house without so much as a glance into Maryjean's room.

Outside, the sun shown brightly, the sky clear, the wind blew softly. "Nice day," I said.

Scar snorted. "Yeah. Too bad we have to spoil it by getting ready for a funeral."

Chapter 18

The funeral was at a large Catholic Church in LeRoy. The stained glass windows displayed abstract art, depicting Christ at different stages of his life; as a baby in His mother's arms; as a boy preaching to a large gathering; as a man with His apostles; on the cross dying for our sins.

Despite the size of the church, every pew was filled. Maryjean had a large family and many friends. I was overwhelmed. Scar clung tightly to my arm. We'd both dressed in black trying to blend in. Scar worried her roommate's parents might spot her and make a scene. We both wanted to avoid a scene. I assured her there wouldn't be one.

In the center isle, up by the altar, sat the casket on a gurney with wheels. The priest, followed by two altar boys, carried an incense burner on a chain. Waving it back and forth, the scent of the incense surrounded the casket. The smoke lingered up to where ceiling fans sent the fragrance spinning throughout the church. The priest prayed, sending the soul to heaven. Some people cried.

The service lasted for an hour, and there was not a dry eye left in the church, including mine. I hated these things.

When it ended, everyone filed out behind the casket and headed to the cemetery. Scar and I decided to pass on the cemetery. Instead we pulled up to the drive-thru of a fast food joint, ordered some burgers, fries and milk shakes. We weren't especially hungry, it was just something to do.

We found a park and parked. We got out of the car with our bag of food and walked over to a picnic table. We sat down and ate fast while swatting at bees and flies. "I hate eating outside," I said. There wasn't much else to say. Scar looked lost. She was upset. Her friend had killed herself. I knew she felt responsible. "It wasn't your fault," I finally said. We'd never really talked about it. Sometimes it was easier to ignore things than to confront them. I could ignore something forever. I would convince myself that everything was fine. I didn't want to do that with Scar. She needed someone, a friend, and I was her friend, I was someone.

Scar dropped a half-eaten hamburger onto the wrapper. "The hell it wasn't."

I looked around the park. We were alone. I'd finished my lunch. It sat in my gut like a rock. I crumpled the wrappers and stuck them in the paper bag. "When's the last time you sat on a swing?" Scar gave me a confused look. I was forced to elaborate. "Come on. We'll swing, we'll talk. It'll make everything less formal. Besides," I said, hoping I had suggested the right thing to do, "I think I can swing higher than you!"

Scar let a small smile spread across her face. I loved that smile, slightly regretted not getting to kiss those lips. "Try it!"

We raced to the swings, sat next to each other, kicked off and started pumping our legs. At first we kept in perfect rhythm, it was all very sexual; up, down, up down, in, out, in, out.

I knew we would have been good together, synchronized. By the look on Scar's face, our possible compatibility wasn't lost on her, either.

She was winning, swinging higher. She was laughing.

"You know how we became friends?" Scar finally said, I knew she was talking about Maryjean.

"How?" I tried to catch up, pumping my legs with everything I had. She still swung higher. She weighed less, which was the reason I guessed, stoking my ego.

"A party. I forget where it was, but I was pretty messed up. Not drugs or anything, just a lot of beer and a few shots of vodka. Or it was the other way around, a lot of vodka and a few beers. I don't know, that just goes to show how truly messed up I was.

"God, I haven't had a shot of vodka in a long time. Straight, you know. I drink it straight."

"I didn't think you were old enough to drink."

"Ha-ha, smart ass. When you went to college, were you old enough to drink?"

"No."

"Did you."

Yes. "We're not talking about me."

"We're not talking about me, either. We're talking about how I met Maryjean," Scar said.

I laughed. "No, you're talking about you and how drunk you were at a college party."

"Shut up, would ya?" Scar said, then went silent for several minutes. I gave her time, didn't prod and poke for more of the story. She would tell me when she was ready. It was her choice. I know talking helps people clear things up in their own heads. I, on the other hand, rarely talk, despite knowing the psychology of baring one's heart and soul. Most of the relationships I'd been involved in ended because I never opened up.

Suddenly Scar started: "I remember coming out the house and falling onto the grass. I remember falling because it was like, in slow motion. The ground didn't rush up to meet my face or anything. I felt more like a glider airplane, you know, like one of those things John Denver crashed in?"

I said, "I know what you mean."

"I never went up in one, but when I fell onto the grass, I imagined that's how it would feel to land in one. Wobbling from side to side as the wind tips the wings and then a smooth touch down." She laughed. "Weird, huh? But that's why I remember it, because it was so weird."

I'd been drunk many times, fell down twice as many, never did I remember falling down in a way such as she just described. Of course, I always wound up face down in a parking lot, or on loose gravel. Girls. They have all the luck.

"Well, someone picked me up and got me back to the dorm. I woke up the next morning in my room, in my bed. I would never have known it was her, Maryjean, who helped me, except when I went for breakfast that morning, she came over to me and said something like, 'Glad to see you're still breathing. I felt kind of funny leaving you alone, didn't want you to choke on your own puke'." Scar laughed. "I assured her I was not the type that puked. Maryjean said, 'You just pass out, right'?"

This time I laughed.

"We ate breakfast together, talked and hit it off." Scar had stopped swinging somewhere along the way. She sat with the tips of her toes on the dirt ground, her ass drooping over the back end of the swing. Her arms were wrapped around the swing's chains. She was looking down, I couldn't tell really if her eyes were open or closed.

I heard her sob. Her fingertips touched her forehead, her body trembling as she cried. I went over and knelt in front of her. She fell into my arms, onto her knees, crying into my shoulder. The tighter I held her, the harder she seemed to cry. I wanted to make her pain go away, but I didn't know how, so I kissed the top of her head.

She kissed my neck, rubbed my back. I returned the rub, kissed her on the left temple, then the right.

One thing started to lead to another. I wanted her. There was no question about it. It was easy to say no to Judy Swanson, despite her beauty and physical attributes. I didn't know her. I knew Scar. I liked Scar. There was an obvious chemistry between us. I didn't want to say no to her. "No," I said. I took her wrists and pulled her arms away from me. She never looked away from my eyes. We studied each other.

"But I thought—"

"I can't let it happen," I said. Although I wanted to remain true to the thought of a relationship with Karis, but that wasn't what stopped me from having sex with Scar. "I really think we've developed a friendship. If we do this, we'll ruin it. You might think I have a lot of friends, but I don't. I have a career. There are people I know and people who know me, but that is it really. I've enjoyed being with you these last few days. Sure, I'll admit to the sexual tension but I think that's okay, that it might even be healthy."

Scar looked at me for a long, silent minute then she started to laugh.

"What's so funny?" I said, feeling self-conscious.

"I've never heard a guy turn down sex because it might ruin a friendship."

I lifted her up and we walked back to my car, our arms wrapped around each other. She was crying again, and laughing. I thought I might have had something in my eye, and wiped away some moisture with the back of my hand. I didn't think Scar caught the motion. I don't know. Someday I might ask her.

"God, now what do we do?" Scar asked. We were at my house, parked in the driveway. Neither of us seemed to remember how to move. We sat there, the radio on quietly, competing with the hiss of the air conditioning.

Finally we mustered up the strength to head in. Scar looked tired. I suggested she go take a nap and she agreed it might be the best thing for her right now. I looked at my answering machine. There were no new messages. I was thankful for the break. I didn't need to hear anymore hang-ups. I knew I would need to get a hold of Tommy though, and see how he was coming along with his investigation.

I lit up a cigarette and dropped into the recliner. I smoked the cigarette slowly, taking long drags on the filter, holding in the smoke, studying the burning tip while the smoke filled my lungs and circulated through my system. God, it felt wonderful and relaxing in a way no non-smoker could ever know.

With the cigarette smoked, I had nothing better to do but lace my fingers together, put my hands behind my head, close my eyes and fall asleep.

A knock at the door woke me. I didn't know how long I slept, I hadn't looked at the time when I closed my eyes, but it felt like I'd just closed them. Judging from the shadows in the room, I'd been asleep a while. Peeking out the front window, I saw Karis' car in the driveway and Karis on the steps at the door.

I opened the door. "Karis," I said, excited to see her.

"Nick, I just wanted to apologize about a few nights ago. I stormed out of here like an idiot. I guess I felt jealous. Why? I don't know." She was saying all of this on my front step, her fingers fidgeting with the shoulder strap on her purse.

"Come in," I said, moving out of the way. She came in. I took her purse, placed it on the chair.

"I don't want to bother you."

"I was just going to step out on my back porch and have a cigarette. You smoke still?"

"Started up a little over a year ago. I guess you can figure out why," she said, digging through her purse. She pulled out a pack of cigarettes in a leather case with a lighter in a small pocket.

We went outside, stood on my porch and smoked in silence for several minutes. I caught Karis staring at me. I knew she had a question and wondered when she might ask it. While I waited, I also wondered what Scar might be doing. Hopefully, she was still asleep. I know I didn't turn her down on purpose, but she might feel rejected. I didn't want to upset her by having her meet Karis.

Maybe I should wake her, call her out and introduce the two of them. It would avoid an awkward first meeting, kind of force things to progress and move forward. It seemed like the right thing to do. In fact I knew it was the right thing to do because it would be a hard thing to do. Whenever you're confronted with a choice, the hardest one to pick, is usually the right—or most moral—one.

"What's wrong, Nick?" Karis asked. We stood side by side, rested our elbows on the rail. I stared out over my back yard—God, it needed cutting. When would I find the time? "Nick?"

"There was a suicide a few nights back," I said. I told Karis about Maryjean D'Amonda, Scar, Father Paul from St. Anthony's and Mr. Granatta from the college. Karis listened intensely. She didn't flinch when I told her Scar had spent a few nights with me. I did not know if I explained it clearly enough, that Scar was still going to be spending a few nights with me.

"That's great you helped her out," Karis said. "I always knew you'd

153

make a great father."

Guilt, like you could not imagine, balled itself up into a fist and punched me in the stomach. We'd almost had sex, some father. "I suppose," I managed saying while feeling guilty.

"So have you heard back from the priest?"

"No. Not yet."

"Well, maybe if you don't hear from him in a couple of days, give him a call?"

"That's a good idea," I said.

Karis moved a little bit away from me, stood up straight, and stiff and said, "I got mad the other night, when that Judy called, because well, because I wanted there to be something between us. When you came over to see me last week, I felt something in me. It was more than I felt before, when we dated a hundred years ago. It was something fresh, new. It's hard to explain, but that's how I felt."

I knew what she meant. I'd felt it, too. I felt it now.

"I've never made a first move in my life. Showing up at your door with dinner—God, I must have driven past your house fifteen times before I finally pulled in your driveway. I was so nervous, I thought I'd get sick." She laughed. She looked at me as if studying my expression. "I want there to be something between us, Nick. I know it's crazy, but I think I'm still in love with you, only more." She swallowed, licked her lips and looked away from me.

I moved in, wrapped my arms around her and hugged her tight. "Sounds like you just got yourself a boyfriend, you over-aggressive hussy."

"Hussy?" She laughed, slapped my chest playfully, and rose on her tiptoes to kiss my neck.

I tilted her chin up and landed a wet one on her lips.

We just stood there, our lips pressed together. It felt like the most erotic kiss I'd ever experienced. Her arms wrapped around me, my arms around her. We began to sway, never breaking the bond locking us together. We moved, as one to the sliding glass doors, back into the kitchen. She was ready. I was ready. We wanted each other.

"Hi guys," Scar said. She was sitting at the table eating a bowl of cereal, looking less like the woman she was just a short while ago, and more like the teenage daughter I never had.

Karis was embarrassed, I could tell. "Oh, hi. You must be, Scar is it?"

"Scar it is," Scar said sounding friendly enough. They shook hands. I wanted to die. I knew there could not be enough air in my house for the three of us to all be breathing at the same time. That scared me. I couldn't imagine dying of suffocation. It seemed like a long, drawn out way to die. I wished for a burglar with an assault rifle to come through the front door and kill me.

I ended up making coffee for the three of us. We sat around the table for an hour making small talk. Each minute I heard Scar become more and more sarcastic. It was subtle, but I heard the tones. She was like a time bomb, the timer set and the seconds ticking away. She'd blow soon if I didn't do something quick.

Karis must have started to catch on, maybe felt the tension building in the room. She stood up and went over to put her cup in the sink. "I have to get going," she said to me, making a face. I wasn't sure exactly what the face meant, but I had a pretty good idea.

"I'll walk you out," I said.

"It was nice meeting you," Karis said to Scar.

Sounding like a child, Scar said, "You, too, ma'am."

Ma'am? Great. I was in trouble.

Outside by Karis' car, I said, "I'm sorry—"

"That's all right. She has a crush on you," Karis said.

"You think?"

"Yup. Take it easy on her, she's just a kid," Karis said. "Want to try and get together tomorrow, maybe take in a movie, or if you want, come over to my house for a little while?" She kissed me hard on the mouth, reminding me of the things we'd been about to do before Scar crashed through the picture.

"I'll bring wine?"

"Sounds good. I'll make, what? Pasta?"

Women always wanted to cook pasta for me. Was it because I was Italian? "That'd be perfect," I said. We kissed again. She got in her car. I stayed in the driveway until she drove out of sight.

I took a deep breath before going back into the house. The wrath of Scar.

Walking into the house I noticed Scar was ignoring me. She still sat in the kitchen, her elbows on the table, her hands balled into fists, her cheeks on her knuckles. She did not turn to look and see who had come in or closed the front door. Of course, she could safely guess it was me. I think it took tremendous concentration and focus not to look, just the same. People are nosy. It's human nature.

155

In the kitchen I stared at the bowl of soggy cereal Scar had abandoned when Karis and I came in from the back deck. It looked horrible. Scar played with the spoon, anything to keep from looking at me. If she took a spoonful, I'd gag. "Scar," I said. "I know you're upset."

"I'm not upset." The voice was placid. I knew better. Underneath the current was raging. If I lost my balance the undertow would grab me, pull me down and drown me. "Why would I be upset, Nick. Get real. Don't be so freaking full of yourself. She's cute. Pretty, really, not at all what I expected."

Her words sounded good, felt encouraging. I smelled a trap. If I agreed, Scar would cry, or swear, or break things, or leave angry. I pretended she said nothing. "Scar, look—"

"I'm not upset, Nick. I'm just hurt. I really thought we might have something together. At the park, I thought, this is it, he's going to kiss me. I knew if we kissed, you'd fall in love with me," Scar said. She wasn't trying to sound conceited. She was just speaking her true feelings. She was right.

"Maybe I knew that, too," I said. "Maybe that's why I couldn't let that happen."

"But why, Nick? You're really not that much older than me," Scar was saying. She started to cry. Her hands refused to wipe away the tears. I went to the table, knelt beside her and took her hands. "Why don't you want to love me?" she said.

"Because," I said, speaking softly, "I'm in love with Karis."

Scar laughed. It didn't sound bitter. "Oh. I have to get to bed. I have school in the morning."

I looked at the time. It wasn't even time for dinner. "Goodnight," I said.

She left the kitchen. I heard the bedroom door close. I grabbed the pack of cigarettes and lighter off the counter and filled a frosted mug with beer from the keg. Out on the back deck I smoked and drank and wondered how my life had become so confusing in one week.

The feeling left me inspired, oddly enough. I went back into the house and down into the basement where I had a small office set up. I switched on the computer and flipped open a notebook.

I had turned my basement into an office with the help of hired labor. I was good with a gun and good at thinking on my feet. I was terrible with a hammer or any kind of power tool.

A false ceiling, some eggshell-white colored paneling, a tan carpeted floor, some drawings and framed photographs of lighthouses and some Miami Dolphins paraphernalia. There were bookshelves all around the room,

156

filled with hardcover books I've read and a few I never got around to reading. Presto! An office worth writing a mystery novel in.

The notebook pages were filled with ideas and character names for the mystery novel I'd always wanted to write. I stared at the blank computer page. I wanted to write an intriguing tale of suspense with characters down and out, plots that twisted this way and that. No one would be able to guess the events that unfolded during the climactic ending. I'd read literally hundreds of books by authors like Lawrence Block, Robert B. Parker, Jonathan Kellerman, John Sanford. They were the best and made writing look easy. (I blame them for that. I also should know better. Writing is not easy; it's an act).

Now, I wondered, who should die and how? I'll worry about the *who did it* and *why* later. After twenty minutes in my office, I'd written no more than a boring opening paragraph. I wasn't going to give up. I just didn't have a story in mind yet. I needed to work on a plot. There had to be a murder at the beginning, then my detective, Grant R. Philips, would begin his investigation. That much I knew.

I lit up a cigarette and picked out a book from the shelf of books behind the desk. It was a novel written by another fantastic writer, Robert Tolins. I sat back, opened it and started reading it for the second time. Without meaning to offend Mr. Tolins, I think I fell asleep before I finished reading the first chapter.

Chapter 19

Scar didn't have a car. I gave her a ride to school. We had to go a little early because I needed to stop in at the office. We made plans to meet for lunch in the Student Union.

It had been a long weekend, little rest involved. It was Monday and I had detecting to do and couldn't let something insignificant, like feeling tired, slow me up. I didn't want to let my client, Darla, down. Business was at hand. I was pumped and ready to get my hands dirty.

Clichés, how could you not love them?

Betty sat with her back to the Safehouse door. She was stroking away at the keys on the keyboard, typing up a report or something. I watched her for a moment and then cleared my throat. She stopped, turned and smiled. "God, Nick. You scared me."

"Sorry," I said. "What's going on?"

"Things have picked up, a little, anyway. Ned wants to see you," she said.

"He's in already?"

"Came in just a few minutes ago. He didn't look mad, but maybe preoccupied. I asked him what was up and he just said, 'If Nick comes in this morning, tell him to see me'."

"That's it?"

"Yeah, but it's the way he said it," Betty said. "Want me to buzz him, tell him you're in?"

"I want to stop in my office real quick. Then I'll go see him."

"He really said he wanted to see you right away. To me that sounds important."

"I know, he wasn't mad, just looked preoccupied," I said.

Betty shrugged. "Yup. Let me know what's up."

I winked and walked past some of the other cubicles in the office. All empty. Things were picking up some, Betty had said. That was good.

In my office I called Tommy Cerio, as I stood by the desk. I wasn't in the mood to sit.

As luck would have it, he answered the phone himself.

"Detective Cerio, homicide."

"Tommy, it's Nick."

"What's new?" Tommy asked.

"With D'Amonda dead, I don't have Darla's boyfriend's name," I said, honestly. "I still need to talk to him. I know you must have his name in the official report. You gave me Maryjean's name."

"Look Nick, I'm a little busy. Helping you out with the Bristol case was all right when I was stuck at the desk pushing a pencil until the chief said it was okay for me to get back out on the street, but, I've got a pretty heavy caseload," Tommy said.

"Just a name, you don't even have to read to me what was in the report."

"I don't even have to give you a name," Tommy said. I heard papers crinkling. "Hold on a minute, I still got the file in my desk here."

"Thanks, bro. I appreciate it."

"Right."

There were a couple minutes of silence. Tommy sighed, "All right, Nick, got a pen?"

"I have like, photographic hearing—a *soundographic* memory, you might say. I just made those words up." I smiled.

"Whatever. The kid's name is Kenneth Brackman."

"Kenny Brackman. Got it, Tommy. Thanks. I owe you one."

"I'm not keeping score, Nick, but the total is far greater than one. Remember that," Tommy said. "Oh and Nick?"

"Yeah?"

"D'Amonda? She was a suicide. Good call."

"I'm sure you would have found out after the autopsy," I said, modest as usual.

"Probably, but you saved us time. We could have spent a few days out looking for a killer who didn't exist. So, anyway, thanks."

"You got it, Tommy." We hung up. I left my office, went across the way to Ned's office. His door was closed. I knocked for good measure.

"Come in," I heard Ned say. I went in, closed the door. "Have a seat." I knew right away what Betty meant by preoccupied. "What's up?"

"Don't you look professional," he said.

"Like undercover work," I said. I was dressed in loose jeans, an oversized T-shirt, under a hunter green dress shirt. I left the baseball cap in the car. Good thing. "I'm heading over to the college after I do some things around the office. Why can't we dress like this all the time?"

"I can't afford a new wardrobe." He laughed.

I laughed. We stared at each other. The laughing stopped. He had something serious on his mind. I could see it in his eyes; the tightening of his jaw muscles as his tongue practiced forming words behind closed lips.

"I got a disturbing phone call yesterday. The voice was masked. I couldn't really tell if it was a guy or a girl talking. That bothers me." He leaned back in his own chair behind his desk. His elbows rested on the armrests; his fingertips from both hands tapped the desk while he spoke.

"It would bother me, too," I said, thinking of the annoying phone calls I'd been receiving. I didn't mention the calls to Ned. At this point, he didn't need to know about them because they didn't mean anything. Besides, the case hasn't been solved. "The person obviously said something," I said. "What? Was it troubling?"

"That depends," Ned said.

"On?"

"If the things I was told are true."

It was getting to be like pulling teeth. I didn't have time for this. I didn't mind being a sounding board, but I was on a case and anxious to get back to the college campus. There were some things and some people I wanted to look into a little more deeply. I decided to play along, though. "And those things were?"

"Let me be blunt, Nick, all right?"

"It would save us some time."

"Who's hired you for this case you're currently on?"

Ah shit. To lie, or not to lie. I choose to stall. "Why?"

"I mean, if I went out into the lobby right now and asked Betty to pull out the application form your client filled out, whose name would be written on line one of the form?" Ned looked anxious. He didn't like what he was doing, but needed to follow through. I understood his dilemma.

"Ned, what's this about?"

"Don't dick me around, Nick. Whose name is on that line?"

"I don't believe I had her fill out the form yet, Ned. I told you. She's kind of a friend," I said. I was still telling the truth. Darla had not filled out the form, and in a way she was a friend. A dead one, but still, I knew her mother. Any friend of Karis is a friend of mine.

Ned slapped his hands on the desktop, jumped out of his chair, leaned across the desk and yelled his question at me for a third time. I knew I could not pussyfoot around any longer.

"Darla Bristol."

"The dead girl?"

"Yes."

"She's your client?"

"Yes."

"She hired you?"

"Yes."

"A dead girl hired you, Nick? A dead girl? Explain this to me, because right now, I don't believe my ears. I can honestly say that I don't believe what I'm hearing." He laughed. Nothing was funny. He was upset.

"Ned, I didn't believe it either," I started to say, when Ned didn't cut me off with more yelling, I knew he was waiting for me to continue. "I came into work and she was in my office, sitting in the chair. I went back and forth with Betty about a woman being in my office, but she kept insisting—"

"What? Betty knew you were talking to ghosts? Son of a bitch," Ned said, folded his arms. I realized then he was letting me tell my side of the story, but only for the sake of letting me tell my side of the story. At this point, it didn't matter. He'd asked me a question and I was going to answer it.

"She knows. I asked her, as a favor to me, not to mention it. She doesn't know I took Darla's case," I said. Hearing it out loud made me cringed.

"Oh, she's not aware that you took on a ghost's case?"

"Ned—"

"Nick, I want you to drop the things you're working on and take a couple of weeks off," he said.

Behind him, transparent as hell, Darla appeared. I wanted to scream at her, to tell her to get lost. What if I told Ned to turn, would he see her? If he couldn't see her, he'd really think I was crazy. Besides, Darla was shaking her head no.

"No?" I said out loud.

"No? No? Nick, this is serious," Ned said, thinking I had told him no. Two weeks off sounded wonderful. I would have said no to him anyway, so it didn't matter.

"I can't," I said. Darla smiled folding her hands together in prayer. She mouthed the words, Thank You. I flashed her a wink.

"What the hell was that?" Ned asked. I thought he could see Darla, then realized he meant the wink.

"Something in my eye. It's out now. Thanks for worrying."

"Take some time off. I'll even buy you a plane ticket to anywhere you want to go. It's not a gift, Nick, consider it part of your medical insurance. It's like, like—"

"Therapy," I said.

"For lack of a better word. Yes."

I stood up. "It may all sound funny, but at this point, does it matter who hired me? Ned, I'm involved in something serious. This Tenth House is evil, they're an evil cult. Did you get my message about the raccoon?"

"Yes," Ned said. "That's immaterial now. Who's going to pay you? Look, I know you might be helping, but, believe it or not, Safehouse Investigations is a business. We do what we do, not because we're like the Three Musketeers. We do it to make money. It's sounds heartless—"

"Yes. It does."

"Well, I'm sorry Nick. I want you to drop what you're working on and take some time off." Ned stood up too. He walked around to the front of his desk and sat one cheek on the corner. "Right now."

Standing behind the chair I'd been sitting in, I rested my hands on the back and shook my head. "I'm sorry, I can't."

"I've got another assignment. If you don't want to go on vacation, then you can get started on the new job. Today. How's that sound?"

"Not interested."

"Then you're fired."

"Just like that?" I couldn't believe Ned was firing me.

"That caller I told you about? The person said they were going to call the paper, tell reporters you took on a case for a ghost. This may not be the biggest or fanciest investigation company, but it's mine, Nick. I worked very hard to get where I am. Sure, your stunt with the ghost—"

"It's not a stunt."

"Maybe you don't think so," Ned said, "but the press will. They'll either write you off as a crazy employee, or they'll claim we're pulling a stunt for free advertising. Either way a piece like that might generate a lot of phone calls, some of them from real potential clients, but most of the calls, Nick, most of the calls will be from kooks. There'll be woman wanting you to contact their dead cats, people looking into finding out winning lotto numbers. We don't need all kinds of crazy calls. I don't want my investigation company to turn into a joke. That's what your stunt—"

"It's not a stunt."

"Whatever. I know you might think you believe what you're telling me. This stunt will turn my company into a joke. Look, usually I'd say any

162

publicity is good publicity. But how can I claim to be a serious agency if we're acting like ghost-busters? I know you can see where I'm coming from. I can't have that. I won't let that happen. When and if the press actually calls, I'm going to deny any truth to their story. I'd like to tell them that you do work for me, Nick, that you couldn't possibly be working for a ghost because you've been down in Disneyland for the last few weeks."

"You want to lie to the press?"

"They lie all the time."

I feigned shock.

"Cut the crap, Nick. We're friends, I mean, we've known each other for years. I need you, I bounce ideas off you. I'm trying to help you here. I want to help. But this has got to be your last chance. Will you go and visit the famous rodent in Florida, or start on the new assignment?"

"I won't start the new assignment and it's tornado season in Florida," I said. Who had called him? The question was beginning to eat away at me. I needed a cup of coffee. I was pissed off.

"Nick—"

"I'll make it easy on you, Ned. We're old friends—"

"Don't do this," Ned pleaded.

"I quit."

I didn't feel well. I liked Ned, my job, and I didn't want to quit. I don't think he wanted me to go. He pushed an ultimatum in my face, forcing me to make a choice. I would have quit regardless of the case. It was the principle I was fighting for.

Jobless. God, now I was on a whole new set of statistic sheets.

I needed that coffee more than ever.

Deciding to get a cup on campus, I drove to the college with the windows down and the radio on. I smoked cigarette after cigarette, feeling more upset about quitting than I ever would have imagined. It wasn't that I could not find another job, I was sure I could, it was that I enjoyed working for and with Ned.

When I walked out, I told Betty I'd be back for my things. She started to cry.

When I got to the student lot I wasn't as upset about having to park way the hell away from the campus. I looked forward to the solitude of a long, quiet walk. I grabbed a black Miami Dolphins baseball cap and my knapsack. I had my ankle holster in the glove compartment. I strapped it on, slipped the gun in place, got out of the car, locked the doors, and started my walk.

Slate gray clouds blanketed the sky and blocked the sun. The depressing weather fit my mood, so I couldn't complain. If it had been sunny, I would have felt worse because there'd be no way to enjoy the day.

Chapter 20

In the Union lounge, two and a half-hours before lunch when I was to meet with Scar, I sat on a comfortable sofa sipping French vanilla gourmet coffee. On one of the tables were five copies of the school paper, *The Monroe Reporter.* I picked one up and thumbed through it. There was nothing in there about Maryjean D'Amonda's death. Perhaps it missed the paper's deadline. I would have to make a point of getting next week's copy, I was anxious to read what might be written about the former student.

Unzipping my knap-sack, I dug around inside for the copy of Patricia Helms' class schedule, found it, and quickly studied it. She was in a communication class over in the Edmund North building. I had no clue where that might be. The class ended in ten minutes. That should be enough time to consult a campus map and get to where I needed to be.

Finishing the coffee, sticking the free copy of the newspaper into my knap-sack, I stood and walked over to the Information counter. The girl behind the counter was on the phone, talking excitedly about a party she'd attended over the weekend. She held a finger up to me to tell me she'd just be a minute. I didn't want to break her train of thought, but noticed a small stack of maps on a table behind her and so I pointed to them. The girl followed my finger, pointed to the maps too and looked at me. I nodded. She took two or three of them and handed them over. I thanked her. She winked.

The map was printed on one side of a normal size sheet of paper. A list of phone numbers and campus departments were printed on the opposite side. While I made my way toward the building housing Patricia's communications class, I wondered how I might find Mr. Brackman. I got lucky before when Scar happened to walk by when I was first looking for Maryjean D'Amonda.

Would Scar know Kenny? I never asked her. I had planned on asking Maryjean. Now that Maryjean was dead, I had nothing to lose by asking Scar, did I?

One question kept going through my mind. Who told Ned about Darla employing my services? It was a troubling question because only three people knew the truth. The three people that had this information, I trusted. To think one of them betrayed me felt awful. It made my stomach churn.

Just recently I had told Scar about Darla. Sure, she had time to call Ned, tell him about Darla, but why would she? I hated to think she might be like some double agent, working for the cult and sucking information from me.

It was possible. I couldn't doubt the possibility just because I like her. I would have to be on guard and extra observant around her.

Walking past the library, I noticed a group of students going in, laughing, enjoying college life. It was its own community, a seemingly safe and out of reach place, tucked far away from the dirty fingers of "my" society. I envied them, missed my own golden days of irresponsibility.

As I continued to walk, I thought of when I first talked with Darla and how I'd gone to see Karis. She knew the truth, hell, her daughter had shown up at her kitchen table. Why would Karis call Ned and tell him that I'm working for her dead daughter? No. That didn't sound right. She wouldn't. I think it's safe to take Karis right off the list of suspects.

Coming up on the front of dorm buildings, I looked at decorated windows. In more than one I saw a triangle with a straight beam of light passing through the geometric figure and spilling out the opposite side in a spectrum of refracted light. It was hard to believe that Pink Floyd was still popular college music. I suppose the songs were timeless. People depressed could remain depressed cranking up any of the titles found on The Wall; a bottle of vodka, a dark dorm room and a Pink Floyd CD playing. Memories.

I stopped in front of three high-rise dorm buildings and glanced at the map. I realized I'd gone the wrong way. All the class buildings were now behind me. Hard not to feel stupid, I stood there with a map in two hands, looking up at the buildings and back over my shoulder. Quickly, I folded the map and stuck it in my pocket. The building I was looking for should be on my left. I walked briskly and with purpose—so I wouldn't appear lost. However, I did notice one thing: I was either not the only one lost, or someone was following me.

As I briskly walked, I thought of the only other person I had told about Darla. . .

But that couldn't be, either. Why would Father Paul call Ned? Curiouser and curiouser. It didn't make sense, no more sense than Scar and Karis. If I had to accuse someone of being a fink, it wouldn't have been any of them.

When you look for questions, be careful, you might find answers you don't like. Who said that? I can't remember. Maybe it was me. I don't think so. Despite being a private investigator, I didn't consider myself to be all that philosophical. Only detectives in novels were good at quotes and poetry—basically your all around dream Jeopardy contestant.

Father Paul. I made a mental note to try and stop in and see him one more time. Just to chat, a friendly visit.

He was the one who told me about the dog on his altar and then I find the raccoon. Was he trying to warn me first by telling me a fictitious story about a warning he'd received? When I didn't stop snooping, he actually did have someone kill, skin and dangle a raccoon in front of my door?

It sounded plausible. I needed to keep asking myself and others questions. There's no way to come up with answers if there aren't any questions.

Walking up the ramp to the Edmund North Building, I looked around, hoping to spot my tail. I had to reason this out. Of course I was being followed. Whoever it was, was good. I'd been trying to spot my tail since entering the Student Union. Maybe it was more than one person? Nah. That sounded too complicated. I should know better, though. Never underestimate anyone, or in this case, any cult.

Inside Edmund North the floors were hidden under navy blue carpeting, the walls white, potted trees and plants and small study areas encircled the several auditorium sized class rooms. Classes were still going on, the hall was mostly empty except for a few lone kids sitting here and there, reading, writing, or sleeping.

I found the classroom listed on the schedule print out where Patricia should be.

Seeing Patricia only the one time, I worried about not recognizing her. When the students filed out of the room, I stood back and looked at each one. After a good three minutes, the flow of students leaving thinned to an occasional trickle. Patricia had not been among them.

Stepping into the room was like walking into a movie theater. The hundred or so chairs were aligned in two rows, split by the center aisle-way. One armrest on each chair transformed into a small desktop. The floor declined leading to a dark stage where an overhead projector sat next to a podium. The podium was on, notes presumably from the class, were projected up onto a pull-down screen. I saw only one other person in the room, down in the front row, apparently still copying down the notes from the screen.

I strolled slowly down to the front. I saw the short, straight, brown hair, tucked back over the ear. As I got closer I noticed the gold-rimmed glasses. Ah, it was my Patricia.

I cleared my throat. She looked over at me. I stood, smiling, hands in my pockets. "Ms. Helms," I said.

"Mr. Tartaglia," she said. I was a bit surprised to see she'd remembered my name.

"I thought I said you could call me Nick?"

"Maybe you did, maybe I just don't want to call you by your first name," she said looking back to the screen, her lips moved as she read a sentence. She went to work writing that sentence in immaculate handwriting in her spiral notebook. When she finished, she closed the notebook, slipped it into her knap-sack and put her pen into a pouch on the pack.

"How's everything going with the paper? I just grabbed a copy of the latest issue, but haven't had the chance to sit and read it. Looks good, a lot of color. I remember when papers were in black and white." I laughed. She just continued to get ready to leave. "Ancient, I know."

I followed her while she ignored my presence. Finally, outside the room, she stopped suddenly and spun around. "Do you have a reason for following me, or are you just hanging around to kill time. If you've got a specific question, ask it, otherwise, I don't have time to just stand around and chat."

Hostile. Why, though? "I just wanted to talk to you a little more about things. Heard about Maryjean D'Amonda, I'll bet."

"Of course," she said, looking defeated. I'd struck a nerve. "Look, I'd really prefer not to talk to you. But if I must, I won't do it here. Not out in the open like this."

"Okay. Where? When?"

She sighed, as if I was asking her out on a date and she was telling me to get lost, only I wouldn't. "I live on campus, in the high-rise dorm."

"Which one, I saw three."

"The one in the middle. It's called Kerrington. I'm on the top floor—not that it matters, I have to actually come down and let you in. The front door to all the dorms is locked. Only the people who live in the building have a key." She rambled. She looked at her wristwatch. I was waiting for her to say she had to run, another class awaited. I had a copy of her schedule. She didn't have another class until after noon. So far, she hasn't lied.

"When?"

"I don't know. Tomorrow?"

"Not soon enough."

"Tonight? It can't be now. I'm busy. I have another two classes after lunch. I'm really pretty busy," she said.

"We all are, Ms. Helms."

"Don't call me that. I really hate it."

"Try Mr. Tartaglia. I always end up looking around, expecting to see my father," I said.

She laughed. Then she smiled. The smile stayed on her face. "Come to the dorm at, I don't know, how's nine sound?"

"Like a perfect time. I promise not to take much of your time."

"Right," she said.

She slung her knap-sack over her shoulder and walked away. As I watched her go, I noticed her rump sway rhythmically. Was she doing that on purpose? She had to know I was watching her. I decided she was doing it on purpose, but whatever the reason, it didn't matter.

For the sake of doing something useful while waiting for my lunch date with Scar, I roamed around campus asking students if they knew Kenneth Brackman. No one, so far, had ever heard of him. This didn't surprise me. There were thousands of students living on campus, and if, let's say, Kenny commuted then he would know even less people.

If he commuted, then there might be a listing for him and his parents in the phone book.

Starting to feel comfortable with the campus layout, I walked back to the Student Union and went right over to the pay phones across from the information and ticket sales counter. There had been a phone book there last time, but now it was gone.

The same girl was behind the counter and still gabbing on the phone. I played the part of a mime and indicated that I wanted to use the phone but needed a telephone book. It became more like charades. She was pretty good, too, I'd bet the life of a party. She guessed what I needed on the first round of pantomimes and handed me both the white and yellow pages. I took the white pages and started flipping through the book.

The girl behind the counter seemed annoyed, as if I might be trying to invade her privacy and listen in on her conversation. She stuck a finger in her ear and turned away from me, while the phone cord was wrapping around her back.

I found a listing for fifteen Brackmans. No Kenneths or K. Brackmans. I didn't want to start copying names and phone numbers right here at the counter. I would have to work on it . . . I was going to say at the office, but I forgot. I don't have an office anymore. I would have to work on it at home, tonight, before my meeting with Patricia Helms.

I closed the book and slid both back across the counter. The girl did not turn around. I thanked her back and walked away. There was still time to kill. I knew I could ask around a little more about Kenneth, I might get lucky and someone will know him, but I didn't feel like it. I was starting to feel very tired.

I went to the phone, dialed Karis' number and hoped she would answer. She did. "Hello?"

"Karis? It's me."

"Nick, how are you? We still on for tonight?"

"That's what I'm calling about. I have an appointment at nine—"

"Oh," she said, "I see. That's all right."

"No, look, I don't want to back out, I want to see if we can make it for a little earlier, like maybe dinner at five?"

"What about the movie?" She asked.

"I'll rent one. What do you like?"

"Surprise me. You know Nick, I'm really looking forward to this," she said, sounded bashful. I could just picture her standing in her kitchen, cheeks red, hands tangled in the telephone cord.

"Me too, Karis. I gotta run. I'll see you at five."

When I hung up the phone, the hairs on the back of my neck stood on end. I could tell that whoever was following me was close. I stood still, my hand still on the phone. I hoped it looked like I was thinking. All at once I spun around.

One kid leaned against the wall by the information booth. His arms were folded, his legs folded at the ankles. He was handsome in a boyish kind of way, like Michael J. Fox or Rob Lowe. His hair was light brown, his eyebrows thick and darker than the mop on his head. His eyes were blue. He was dressed very much like yours truly; with a baseball cap on backwards, loose jeans and an unbuttoned solid brown dress shirt over a white thermal undershirt. He also wore hiking boots.

He was staring right at me. I walked over to him.

I felt my stomach muscles tighten a little. I wanted to be ready for the unexpected. I kept my knees loose, ready to spring, duck, or dive. I casually rolled my shoulders. Stay loose. Stay loose.

"Problem?" I asked him.

"Depends. I hear you been looking for me, if that's so, then we might have a problem," the kid said, his voice was more gruff than his appearance.

"You Brackman?"

He held out both hands. "Found me."

170

I laughed a small laugh. "Don't be so modest. You, Kenny, found me."

"I only just started asking about you, I don't know, less than an hour ago," I said.

"Word gets around fast," he said, shrugged. "You asked a kid who I tutor. No big networking system."

Kenny tutors students. Interesting. "What's your major?"

"Is it your business?"

"It's not."

"Right." He stared at me. "Physical Education. I want to be a coach. High school football, or something." He had the build to go with the dream: Tall, big shoulders, muscles bulging. His hair was a little long—not as long as mine was. His eyes were evenly set in his face under a slightly protruding brow. Large lips framed straight white teeth. He could be a gym teacher, I thought, or a model. Whichever.

"Want to take a walk?" I said. "Pretty nice day. Hate to be inside the whole time, you know?"

"I don't have class until one. Yeah, a walk sounds good. What are you, a cop or something like that?"

"Something like that," I said, smiling. He looked at me funny. He was waiting for an answer. "I'm a private detective."

"And you're looking for me because?"

"Because you were dating Darla Bristol when she died."

Kenneth's hard-nose look changed. His shoulders slumped. He closed his eyes. He took his hands out of the pockets in his jeans and clasped his hands together. "I was dating her, yeah. But I wasn't with her the night she died."

I heard the love and anguish in his voice. He was still dealing with her death, I'd be willing to bet, and not handling it well. "How long had you known her?"

"Long. We went to high school together. We didn't date in high school, or anything. You know, we'd pass by each other in the halls and say hi, that kind of stuff. Then, when we both came here, we were the only people we knew, you know? So we kind of bonded. We would hang out, went to orientation together, out for pizza. Next thing you know, we're holding hands and calling each other on the phone." He stopped walking and looked at the sky. When he finally looked away and looked at me, I saw he was crying. "I really loved her."

171

"So why didn't you get her to stop taking drugs."

"I didn't know she was. As far as I knew, she was real religious."

"And that didn't bother you?" I said.

"Why should it. I believe in God."

"Did you ever go to church with her?"

"I believe in God, you know, like I said, but I wasn't—and still ain't—into going to church. I don't know, I really find it kind of boring." Kenneth started to walk again. I stayed by his side.

"Where were you the night Darla died?"

"Home. I'd gone home for the weekend. It was a friend's stag party. That's kind of funny, you know. Here I am a freshman in college, and a buddy I graduated with from high school is getting married. The girl wasn't even pregnant. Isn't that funny?"

I didn't think so. "Did the two of you have a sexual relationship?" It was a personal question, but I needed to get down to business. Halloween wasn't too far off. A girl's life hung in the balance. The cult was warning me off. I'd lost my job. Things needed to start happening fast. I didn't have the time to finesse answers out of Coach here.

"I don't think that's really your business."

"It is. Trust me," I said, spoke with a firm voice. I wanted him to know, I might not be police, but I was just as serious, if not more. He must have understood.

He blushed. "Yes. We had sex. You know, I thought for sure she wouldn't put out, being religious and all. But, well, as long as we're talking about it, Darla—she was the exact opposite as you might expect. She was very sexual. Horny all the time."

It was hard hearing this. I pictured the ghost-girl in my office. She didn't look like a nymphomaniac. Karis would be upset, I'm sure, if she ever heard this about her daughter (rest assured I wasn't going to be the one to tell her, either).

"You say this like it might have bothered you, did it?" I asked.

"Would it bother you?"

Bad question. I didn't want to answer it. "We're not talking about me, Kenny. I am asking you how you felt about being with a girl who wanted sex all the time. How did you feel about it?"

"Like, *great*, is the only word I can think off. Tired. I felt tired and great." He looked at me, expected sympathy.

"You used to tie her up." I made it a statement. I wanted him to know I already knew. I wasn't asking him a question.

Kenny looked away. "I went through all this, you know. The police asked me all these questions."

"I know."

"So why can't you just read whatever they wrote up in their reports? Why do you have to come here and bring up all these . . . these, things!" He was crying. His hands were balled into fists. He took a deep breath and settled down. "One night," he said, "She told me to like, use my socks and tie her wrists to the bedposts." He laughed. "I thought she was pulling my leg, you know? She wasn't the first girl I'd ever been with, but I hadn't been with many. Tying someone to the bed. It just sounded so weird, but it excited me." He stuffed his hands into his pockets. Maybe he was waiting for me to say something. I kept quiet. He would tell the story in his own words now. I had pricked the memory bubble, the memory had no where to go except out the hole I'd created.

"Darla was different. I don't want to make it sound like she was a slut, because she wasn't. She told me she just wanted to try something different. I was all for it, you know? Something different, who wouldn't be?"

I nodded. It was the closest I'd come to a verbal response.

"On my birthday, she bought me two leather straps. They were like, dog collars, only they had an extra loop that secured to the posts. They were great, I mean, we used them right away." He smiled at the memory.

"Look," he said. "I never hurt her."

"But you wanted to. When she was strapped to your bed, you wanted to hurt her. She had marks on her wrists, struggle marks, consistent with someone trying to break free of restraints."

"No. The bands were never tight. They held her wrists, but if she wanted to, she could always just slip her hands out. I swear," Kenny said.

I believed him.

"We had a good time together," Kenny said. "I don't just mean sex. We went to movies, out to eat, studied, we were a regular couple with an extraordinary sex life. I loved her."

I believed him. "What do you know about the Tenth House, Kenny?"

"Her church, that cult? I found out it was a cult only after she was dead. I swear I never knew."

"What would you have done, had you known? Would you have tried to get her out?" I asked.

"I don't know. I doubt it." It was an honest answer. "She seemed to like it there. I mean, as far as I know, they never killed any animals, or sacrificed any people or any crazy thing like that, right?"

"As far as you know, right." I pulled out a business card, handed it over. "I want you to call me if you think of anything that might help."

"You think she was murdered, huh? That's really why you're here. You don't think she just took too many drugs and drowned. Am I right?"

"You're right."

"Will you do *me* a favor?"

I knew what was coming. "Sure," I said. "What?"

"If you find anything out, let me know. I think I'll sleep better if I can give this mess some closure." Kenny tried to smile. His lips quivered. I patted him on the back. "You'll let me know?"

"I'll let you know." I had one more question. I felt like Columbo. "Kenny, one more thing?"

"Yeah?"

"When was the last time you used the cuffs?"

He shrugged. "I don't know, three weeks before Darla died. End of September, first week of October maybe. We liked them, you know, but we didn't use them all the time."

"Yeah. Sure. Okay," I said. I would have to call Tommy, find out how recent the marks on Darla's wrists had been when the autopsy had been performed.

"Look," he said. "I gotta run." He tucked the card into his pocket, put out his hand. I shook it. He ran off. I watched him until I could no longer differentiate his figure from the other students swarming about.

The dark sky threatened rain. It was time to meet with Scar for lunch. My stomach growled. I felt hungry.

174

Chapter 21

Scar looked tired. She was standing by the cafeteria line, her hands folded in front of her. She was leaning against a wall and looking around, perhaps searching for me. When I got closer, she saw me. Her eyes widened and she waved. I smiled back.

"I thought you weren't going to show," Scar said.

"I'm not late," I said.

"I know, I just had this feeling that you weren't going to show. Sounds a little paranoid, huh?"

"A little." She made me think, where the hell is she going to live? We haven't talked about it yet, but she couldn't stay with me forever. Sooner or later she would need to start looking for a new apartment, or see about moving into a dorm on campus. We had a lot to discuss, and I would have to be the one to bring up the topic. I would, too. When the time was right. Right now, the time didn't feel right.

"Hungry?"

"Yes."

We went through the line. I grabbed a chicken salad sandwich with potato chips and a large *Mr. Pibb.* Scar paid for a salad and an order of french fries. She covered the fries with vinegar. When we sat down, I stole two of those fries.

"You like them that way?" she said.

"Reminds me of when I used to go to carnivals. Always put vinegar on the fries. It's funny though, I never put them on my fries anywhere else, only at carnivals." I took a bite of my sandwich. "Do you want some of my chips?"

"I'll pass. How was your morning?"

"Very interesting," I said.

"Oh? How?"

"Well, for starters, I got fired—"

"Oh God, Nick," Scar said. "How? Why?"

"Because I wouldn't get away from this case, basically, because someone

called my boss and told him a ghost had hired me to look into her death. I
guess Ned wasn't too happy about me working for a spirit. Can't blame him,
really. The one thing I can't figure though," I said, then paused for a minute
while taking another bite of my sandwich.

"Is?"

"Is, who called him in the first place. Only three people knew Darla
hired me."

"And I'm one of the three?" Scar asked, while pushing her salad to the
side. She stood up. She said, "You're indirectly asking me if I called your
stupid boss?"

I didn't want to have a scene, but if she wanted one, I wasn't going to
stop her. Sometimes when people lie, they make a scene to divert attention.
I'm not saying Scar was going to lie, I'm just stating a little well known fact.

"I haven't accused you of anything—"

"You sure as hell have!"

I folded my hands and leaned back. "You about done?"

She stared at me, rolled her eyes, then sat down. "You're an ass, Nick, a
real ass." She was talking in a calm voice. "How can you accuse me that
way, like you're Columbo or something? That sucks. Do you have any idea
how that makes me feel? Do you?"

"I was going to just ask you. And I still will, because, with the whole
scene you just made, you never said if you did or didn't call Baxter." She
looked angry all over again, but kept silent. "Scar, did you call Ned Baxter
and tell him Darla hired me to solve her murder?"

She laughed, it wasn't a happy sounding laugh. "No, jerk. I wouldn't
do that."

"I really didn't think you would," I said.

"You just had to ask. It's your job."

"Exactly. Now eat your salad before it gets cold." It was a joke. She
didn't laugh.

After my lunch with Scar everything on campus seemed pretty much
concluded. Scar was going to stay late and use resources in the library to
conduct research on a paper she needed to write. She would take a cab to my
place when she was done. She had a key. I'd given her one.

I drove to St. Anthony's, ready for confession time. Only I didn't plan to
be the one confessing. I figured if I applied enough pressure, Father Paul
would come clean and tell me just what in the hell was going on.

A question that bothered me, and I kept asking myself, was: Could Father Paul be the high priest in the Tenth House? The answer I might end up with scared me. He was a man who was supposed to be full of morals. If you couldn't count on a man of the cloth for the truth, where then, were we all headed?

I entered the church and stopped by the candles. I stood there a moment then decided to drop five dollars into the collection box. I lit two candles, one for Darla and one for Maryjean. I didn't say a prayer. I went through the doors into the church. The large room was empty. I walked to the center isle and stared at the altar. I turned to look at the choir balcony, where Father Paul had been last time. The balcony was empty.

The church felt dark despite the sun pouring in through the stained glass windows. Someone, other than the statues, was watching me. Slowly rotating, I tried to see everything. There was much to see and I could see no one. No one was hiding on the altar, behind the rows of pews or up in the choir balcony. So why was I so sure I was being watched?

"Father Paul," I finally called out. "Hello?" No one answered. I knew the rectory was just across the parking lot. If Father Paul wasn't in the church there would be a good chance he was at his home.

I left the church. Stepping outside the bright light caused me to squint. Walking across the parking lot to the rectory building, I realized Father Paul had to be the loose link. He called Ned. I was fairly certain it wasn't Scar. I hadn't confronted Karis yet—though I would at five, when we had dinner—but I felt safe assuming she was grateful I was looking into her daughter's death. She wouldn't try to get me in trouble with my boss. Father Paul is the only person who I didn't really know. Sure he was a priest but they had priests in the Tenth House, too.

The rectory was a brick building that had the same design as the church but without a vaulted roof. I rang the doorbell that mimicked the chime of the bell in the steeple. The sound made me laugh. No one answered, so after a few minutes, I rang it again.

I looked around the lot. Mine was the only vehicle around. As I walked around to the back of the rectory I noticed a driveway leading up to a garage. The door was closed. I decided to peek in the window when I heard the sound of power tools.

Through the garage window I saw Father Paul dressed in jeans and a tank top. He wore a heavy apron and large safety goggles. He was bent over a table saw working on a piece of wood.

In between the sound of the saw, I tried to knock on the side door. After

177

a while, he heard me, lifted his goggles and stared my way. He came to the door and opened it.

"Mr. Tartaglia? Nick, isn't it?" He looked genuinely pleased to see me.

"Good memory," I said. "A carpenter, too?"

"Always liked working with wood, creating things. And, the line of work I'm in, I've always admired carpenters." He smiled.

"I guess you would."

"Is there something I can do for you?" He asked, stepping out of the garage. Either he wanted fresh air, or he didn't want me to see what he was working on. He closed the door behind him, took the goggles off his head and sweat dripped into his eyes. "Hot in there. Nice out here, though."

In the shade along the side of the garage was a cooler. Father Paul went over, opened it and pulled out two cans of soda. He offered me one. I took it. We went around to the back of the garage where there was a small patio and some patio furniture. We sat.

"The other morning I found a skinned raccoon hanging from my gutter," I told the priest, taking a long refreshing sip of soda. "It scared me pretty good, seeing it just hanging there and still alive."

"I know the feeling." Father Paul said while he rested his arms on the armrests of his chair, as if bracing himself. Closing his eyes, he tilted his head back so his face could absorb some sunlight. "I'll never forget finding the dog on the altar. I suppose this experience is something you won't forget, either."

"I don't suppose I will," I said. "Have you been able to find any other information out about the Tenth House? Remember, you said you would."

"You wanted to know if the cult was a registered religion. I called the Bishop, had him look into it for me. He told me he'd never heard of them, but would do some looking around. He got back to me that same night. They're not registered, and so that answers the second question you asked," Father Paul said. He no longer worshipped the sun, but looked at me. He held the soda can between his thighs.

"Which was?" I said.

"If the Tenth House was set up for tax-break purposes. If they weren't a recognized church, they wouldn't qualify for tax breaks. Right?"

"Right," I said.

"I have a feeling, Nick—do you want to hear it?"

"If you're sharing fresh insight and ideas, I'm always receptive," I said.

"I think the cult is college oriented."

College oriented? There's a thought I'd missed, despite the obvious college following. "But who would run it? Not a student, the leader would graduate every four years."

"So?"

"So, they'd have to train, and pass the torch. That doesn't feel right."

"Doesn't have to be a student running the cult, then, does it?" Father Paul said.

He had a point. "Then who?"

"I'm not the PI." Father Paul closed his eyes again and looked to the sky. The sun hid behind a cloud. Darkness forced the priest to open his eyes. "And the last thing you asked me to look into was a front, a place for drug dealers. Again, if the church isn't registered, there's no chance to use it for laundry."

"No. There wouldn't be, huh?"

"I think the Tenth House is a serious, evil cult. Plain and simple, these people are devil worshipers with no ulterior motive and that, Nick, is one scary thought." Father Paul stood up. I did, too. "I hope what I've told you helps."

"I think it will," I said. "Oh, one other thing."

"Yes?"

"Have you shared my story with anyone, the story about Darla Bristol being in my office?"

"Tell anyone?" Father Paul said. "I'm not sure what you mean?"

"No? It's really a simple question Father. Here, let me make it a little simpler to understand. I told you a story of how Darla Bristol hired me to look into her death. Did you tell anyone else that story?" I was getting angry. I heard my voice get louder with each word I spoke. I was almost shouting. "Did you, Father, call my boss and tell him I was working for a ghost?"

Father Paul smiled and shook his head. "Why would I do that?"

"That's exactly why I'm asking you, to figure out why you would."

"But I wouldn't. Who else have you told your story too?" Always the guiding hand. Never did the finger point in his direction, I was beginning to realize.

"Not many. Two other people know. One of them is Darla's mother. I truly don't believe she would have told my boss I was doing work for a ghost." My hands were fisted, pressed hard on my hips.

"And the other?" Father Paul asked as if he'd told a joke and was waiting for me to get the punchline.

Scar.

Just great. "I gotta go, Father. Thanks for your time."

"Nick, I don't know exactly what you're up against, but it's tearing you apart. I'd have to be blind not to see that. You know, we always have extra seats in church on Sunday. I'd love to see you drop by," he said. We shook hands.

"I just might take you up on that offer."

"Anytime you need to come by, Nick, come by. You don't have to call or anything."

This was his way of telling me he had nothing to hide. Did that mean he did?

Despite feeling excited about the upcoming dinner date with Karis, the case was bringing me down. After talking with Father Paul, I drove home, showered and smoked three cigarettes and tried to relax the twitching nerves in my belly. Partly, I was nervous about having a romantic dinner with Karis because I didn't know how to be romantic. I only knew how to be me, but somehow that didn't seem good enough. I never thought I measured up. The other part of my nervousness seemed more obvious. Father Paul. He'd done his research and gave me answers. I would still double check the information he'd given me. It was my nature, and I didn't trust him. I had no reason at this point to trust him.

I brushed my teeth and realized it wasn't even four o'clock yet. So I smoked two more cigarettes out on my deck. I couldn't relax, but knew I needed to.

The telephone rang. I went into the house and grabbed the cordless. "Hello?"

"Mr. Tartaglia?"

"Yes." It was a woman's voice.

"I need you to stay away from the Tenth House." It didn't sound like a threat, but more like a request.

"And you are?"

"It doesn't matter who I am. Please, leave it alone or you'll get a lot of people hurt, a lot of innocent people. You've got to listen to me." She was begging me, perhaps disguising her voice.

"Are you talking through a handkerchief."

"Don't play games—"

"But this has been a game since the beginning, I just want to understand the rules."

"Mr. Tartaglia, please. I'm warning you," she said.

"No, you're asking me. Look, if you're stuck on the inside and want out, maybe I can help you." I said. I picked up my cigarette.

"You can't. You're aggravating the church. You're upsetting the high priest."

"Now we're getting somewhere. Who is the high priest?"

"I can't talk to you Nick."

"So now it's Nick?" I teased. "Hello? Hello?" She was gone. "Figures. I got to remember not to be such a wise ass." I sat down, leaned back in the chair, smoked my cigarette and thought about the muffled voice I'd just heard.

I knew it from somewhere, but couldn't place it. Obviously the woman who called thought I might recognize her voice, that's why she choose to disguise it. But where did I know it from?

Finally giving up, I went back into the house, locked the sliding glass door and brushed my teeth again. The last thing I wanted was to smell like smoke. I'll admit, it's a disgusting fragrance.

181

Chapter 22

I promised Karis I would bring wine and a video. Karis said she'd make pasta. I was hungry, I had not eaten since lunch. (Most people don't. I'm not like most people. I usually pick between meals. It's a bad habit but it's something I'm good at.)

I knocked on the door. She yelled from somewhere in the house that it was open. I walked in closing and locking the door behind me. I reminded myself to tell her that it was never a good idea to leave the front door unlocked. Of course she would argue that she was expecting someone and I would retort with, that doesn't matter. Maybe we'd argue. No, I wasn't in the mood to argue, so I chose not to say anything right now.

Karis came out of the kitchen looking wonderfully sexy in a pair of loose fitting blue jeans, white canvas sneakers and a unbuttoned blue blouse over a white tank top. Her hair was worn in a ponytail, pulled back off her forehead and away from her ears. "How was your day?" she said. I suddenly felt married. That felt wonderful.

"The worst. Absolutely horrible," I said.

She laughed. "I'm sorry. It's not funny that you had a bad day, it's just, I don't know, feels funny how natural this all feels to me."

I laughed a little. "It does feel natural." I want it to be natural.

She took the bottle of wine. "Oh, nice."

"I just grabbed one, really. I picked red. I don't know all that much about wine. It's not a super expensive bottle and it wasn't cheap." I felt self-conscious, didn't know what to do with my hands. I stuffed them into my pockets.

"It's perfect." She went into the kitchen. She didn't ask me to follow her so I stayed where I was.

When she came back into the family room she had two glasses of wine. She handed one to me. We stood there. "Why don't we sit on the sofa for a minute. The water's not quite boiling yet. You can tell me all about your horrible day."

We sat. I didn't really feel like talking. I wasn't known for opening up.

182

Karis knew this. So why did she think I would open up now?

"Nick," she prodded. "What happened today?"

"I lost my job."

"My God, how?"

I told her. "Karis, I don't have any idea who told Ned about Darla."

"Was it the girl?"

"It could have been," I said.

"Is she still living with you?"

"Yes."

"And the priest?"

"He might have, I don't know. Both he and Scar have been so helpful, out of the way helpful, you know? It makes everything that much more difficult to decipher. Dammit, I'm usually a pretty good judge of character, too." I was talking, and thinking and it hurt. The wine helped but not much.

Karis reached over and rubbed my thigh.

That was it.

We forgot about the water boiling. We were boiling. The pot spilled.

Spinning spaghetti onto my fork and while Karis sprinkled more grated Romano cheese over hers, I said, "This is wonderful sauce."

"Thank you," Karis said. She began twirling her fork around. "Nick?"

I finished chewing. I hated to talk during dinner. Living alone, I never had to worry about this. I always ate in silence. If I wanted to talk to myself, I didn't have table manners to concern myself with. "Yes?"

"This is going to sound so insensitive, God, I hope you don't hate me for asking it this way, but—"

"Since I've been fired, will I still look into Darla's death? You better believe it. I may not be Spencer for Hire, or Matthew Scudder, but I'm pretty damned good at what I do."

"Who?"

"Characters from some of the best written mysteries. It's not important. Listen, someone wants me to leave this case alone. It's because Darla didn't die accidentally. She was murdered and we both know that, and the person or persons responsible know it. So, I'm getting close. Hitting nerves. It's driving the cult crazy. I'm terribly close, too." I briefly told Karis about the phone call I'd received earlier.

"And you think the girl calling is a part of the cult?" Karis asked.

"That's my guess. And she's scared, or someone—like the high priest—

has put her up to calling me. It might be a different way to apply pressure. You know, like telling me if I don't back off innocent people are going to die. It worked on the priest. They killed a dog and left it on his altar, and in a note told him next time it would be a little girl from his parish."

"God." She dropped her fork. I must have killed her appetite.

"Sorry." I set my fork down. "But he stopped his digging, left the cult alone, and apparently they left the members of his church alone."

"Unless he's the high priest," Karis said.

"Right. Unless he's the high priest."

"And not to confuse you more, Nick, but—"

"But what?" I said.

"Where was Scar when you got this phone call?" Karis asked. She picked up her wine, held it to her lips and just gave me an intense stare from over the rim of the glass.

"At . . . she was at school," I said, closed my eyes. My world was spinning. "My God, Karis. I feel like I'm drowning in some whirlpool here. I can't find a way out."

"Maybe there's only one way out." Now she took a sip.

"Oh, and how's that?"

"Become a member of the Tenth House."

Holy shit, Batman.

It was a nice night. After dinner Karis and I held hands and walked around her block. Streetlights lit the way, and though it was not late, the moon was out. The moon's presence helped a little when it wasn't hiding behind passing clouds.

"What are you going to do?" Karis asked me.

"I'm not sure how, but I figure I'll find some link on campus, someone who can tell me when and where the cult meets. I don't know how exactly to pretend I'm interested. Am I supposed to walk around with a skinned animal over my shoulder?" I said.

"That's not exactly what I meant."

"Oh?"

"I meant about work. What will you do now that you aren't with Safehouse?"

"Well, I've always wanted to open my own office. I think that would be pretty cool," I said. It was true I'd always dreamed of running a one-man show in some office above a tattoo parlor or something.

"Why don't you?"

"Front money, client list, ego. I don't know, there are a lot of reasons why I can't."

"But aren't there just as many why you should?" Karis said. "Like being unemployed, for one?"

"That is a big one, isn't it. I don't know. I'll toss the idea around some. Maybe I will." I let go of her hand. She looked at me quickly, as if I slapped her. Then I slipped it around her waist. We stopped walking. I pulled her in close. "I would need a sexy secretary. Someone to fetch my coffee."

"You mean someone to chase around your desk," Karis said.

"That too."

"Maybe someone you could bounce idea's off of? Someone who'll listen to all your zany plots and conspiracies?" Karis continued to say, slyly.

"That too."

"I'd be interested in that job," she said. She smiled and kissed me.

"Oh would you?" I said and kissed the tip of her nose.

Then her expression changed. She looked serious. "I'd get to bring my laptop into work, and when things were slow I could write. That would be my one big rule. I would need time to write. Not to mention, I'd work for free."

"You're serious aren't you?"

"As serious as you are about starting your own agency," Karis said.

"But maybe I am serious about starting my own agency."

"Then I'm serious about being your secretary."

We kissed again. "I'll have to give it some thought," I said.

"About hiring me as your sexy secretary, you bastard," she said playfully slapping at my shoulders.

"No, I mean about opening my own place."

"I think you should."

"I think I might."

"Good."

"Good," I said. We walked with purpose back to her place. This time we didn't make it to the sofa. We fell to the floor just inside the house enough to kick-close the front door.

By eight forty-five, I had to call it a night. It was amazing that time had gone by so quickly, and how much we'd done in that short time. Karis wanted me to stay the night and I wanted to stay.

"I have to go," I said. I still had a meeting with Patricia Helms in her dorm room at nine. There was something inside me, professional instinct, which told me I shouldn't miss talking with her. I explained this to Karis.

"Duty calls," she said. "Do you want to come back after?"

I did. "No. You get some rest and I'll give you a call tomorrow."

We were in her living room, my shoes on. She sat on the arm of her love seat, her arms wrapped around my waist. It was a futile attempt at keeping me in her house. Her arms were strong. She almost kept me. I broke the link delicately, walking closer to the door.

"Nick?"

I had never looked away from her. Our eyes had been locked together for hours. "Yeah?"

"I have a silly question. I know it is but I still want to ask it. Okay?"

"Of course." We held hands.

"What did all of this mean for us? Maybe I should ask it this way. What did all of tonight mean to you? Because, if, well, you see for me—"

I leaned in and kissed her. It stopped her from rambling. I liked her rambling. It was cute and turned me on. "I love you," I said. Hopefully, for now, those three words would give her the answer she was looking for.

"God, Nick. I love you, too." She stood up and hugged me. "Come back tonight," she whispered in my ear. "Even if you're tired. It would be great to have you sleeping next to me."

How could I say no to that? "What are you going to do, leave the door unlocked?"

"I'll get you one of my spare keys."

She did and I slid it onto my ring. We kissed again and then I started toward Monroe, my mind on matters other than my job. My God, I was in love. I haven't really been in love, well, since the last time I was in love with Karis.

Chapter 23

I was tired of parking way out in the college boonies. It was late at night. I figured I could slide into a parking spot closer to the dorms and not get hassled. It was understandable during the day that the professors and staff want choice parking spots, but at nine o'clock, what harm could I be doing by parking not fifty yards from high rise dorm buildings?

When I got out of the car I locked the doors. I wasn't dressed like a student any longer. I had on what I'd been wearing for my date with Karis. To most, I might resemble a cop - slash - writer wannabe.

Some students were out, but mostly the campus was quiet. I entered the front vestibule. It was secured. I needed to ring Patricia's room, found her name on a panel of doorbells and gave her a buzz. After a few seconds her voice filled the tiny room.

"Who is it?"

"Nicholas Tartaglia," I said. The narrow hallway was crowded. Weaving between the rush of students, I made my way to just past the vestibule. On the opposite side of the locked doors, the walls were lined with key-lock mailboxes that I guessed belonged to the students.

There was a loud buzzing. I pulled open the door and waited for it to close behind me. Walking past the mailboxes and into the lobby, I wasn't surprised to find so much activity going on. Three sofas, over filled with students, were positioned in front of a wall-mounted television set. In silence, the gathered group watched a television show. I recognized the voices of the characters on the program but couldn't recall the show's name. It was an emergency room drama. In addition to the television crowd, two ping pong tables were in use, a billiards game was well under way, several video machines were occupied, a chess and a checkers game were being played out and lastly, all around the lobby lone students read or wrote.

Although I wasn't dressed like a student, no one gave me a second look.

I walked slowly around noticing the shine from the white tiles and that the walls were windows with partially closed curtains. I noticed a peg board filled with flyers pinned to any exposed space available, even if it meant

covering another flyer entirely with information printed on them about anything and everything: Roommate needed, Ride needed, Credit Cards for
Students, Lost knap-sack—no name found.

Patricia Helms came downstairs. She was dressed in a gray sweat suit.
The pants were tight, clinging to her body, the top was oversized and hung
down to her thighs. She did not have socks on. Her toenails were painted
red. She smiled, a small smile, when she saw me. Without any hellos, she
waved for me to follow her.

I took one last look behind me and started up the stairs.

Patrica's dorm room was small, but private. "My roommate dropped out
after the second week. They never filleed her space. I have this room all to
myself." She was proud. The walls were decorated with movie posters.
Intelligent thrillers, I'd say, despite the oxymoron.

"You like movies?" It was a dumb question, but an important one. I
wanted to break the ice between us, get her talking. What better way, but to
have the person talk about something you know they love.

"With a passion. I read a lot, too," she said, pointed to one of two closets
filled with books. "I've read 'em all. Most are mine. I buy them. I hate to
go to the library and then have to give back a good book. I've been reading
thrillers forever. I have an amazing collection at home. My mother always
asks me why I keep all the books. She asked me if I planned to go back and
read them some day. I told her I might, but you know what? There's always
a new book to read. There's never a time where I don't have something else
to read. So why keep them? Because I love books and someday, I just might
go back and read them." She said.

She was drunk. The signs were not hard to see. She rambled, a little
slurred speech. Great.

I looked around her room, on the desk, beside her computer, next to the
hard drive was a half-empty bottle of Southern Comfort.

She must have seen what I was looking at. "Want a swig?"

"No. Thank you." This was going to make my line of questions a little
hard for her to follow, I imagined. "What do you like to be called, Patricia, or
Patty?"

"Patricia. Being called Patty makes me feel like a hamburger, or sau-
sage, or something." She giggled as she sat on her bed. "You want to sit?"

I pulled out the chair at her desk and sat. "Patricia, I don't want to beat
around the bush here. I know you know some things about the Tenth House."

"Why would you think that?" She tried to look serious and it worked until a hiccup escaped her lips. She covered her mouth with long slender fingers with red polish on the nails, matching the color on her toes. She started giggling again.

"What do you know?"

There was a long silence. Patricia had stopped giggling. She tried to stand up and fell back onto the bed. She tried again. I helped this time. She got to her feet and walked around the bed to the window. She pulled open the blinds. She pushed open the window a few inches and breathed in the fresh, night air. "You know why I want to be a reporter?"

I leaned back, got comfortable. If Patricia had something to tell me, she wasn't going to volunteer anything easily. We were going to play games. I was sober though, so I thought I might have a good chance at winning. I have the patience of a dead person. I can wait forever to get what I want. She was drunk, wanted to talk, maybe liked to hear herself talk—the way most drunks do. Fine by me. I was here to listen. I couldn't be sure I'd hear anything revealing, but at least I'd be here to sort through the garbled sounds. "No," I said. "Why?"

"Guess."

It shouldn't be too hard. "Because you like to read?"

"Perfect. True intuition. I like to read, so naturally I want to be a writer. You'd think it would be simple, writing a story, wouldn't you?"

Actually, I knew from experience that writing a story is anything but simple.

"It's not," she assured me. "Plots have to be complex, characters three dimensional, all the webs of the story need to tie together neatly at the end. God, it's infuriating to read a book where the author makes everything look so natural and easy."

"That's their job, making fiction appear real."

"I know that, but I don't understand how. I mean, I think I'm creative. I take all these writing classes and attend stupid workshops taught by writers who couldn't make it as writers. Some of it's great, but most of it is pathetic." She sat on the window ledge, blocked the steady, cool breeze. "With journalism, I can write and it will be published. It's not creative, and I'll probably never get my own column. But you want to know something? That's okay, because I think I like what I'm doing."

I smiled. She was getting at something, making a point somewhere. I just wasn't sure what she was getting at, where the point was being made. I had to ask, "And what is it that you're doing, Patricia?"

"Investigative reporting."

"You called me today, didn't you?"

She turned away to look out the window. The gesture gave her away. She was guilty. I hadn't been sure until just that moment, but I thought I'd ask. I knew the voice on the phone had sounded familiar, but not familiar enough to place it. If it had been Scar calling me, even disguised, I would have known. The same goes if it had been Karis, or one of my sisters or my mother. Some voices you just know, if you know the person the voice belongs to well enough.

"I don't know how, exactly, but I got into the middle of things."

"What's that mean?" I asked. She was still looking out the window, her knees drawn up to her chest, arms wrapped around her legs. She didn't sound drunk anymore, just sad, depressed.

"I don't know. It means I stumbled onto something, a lead, a story. I enrolled in school here, my head full of ideals. I was going to do *so* well, graduate in the top percent of the class, make dean's list. I mean, I'm doing all right, holding down a three-oh average," Patricia said. She slid her legs down, walked over to her desk, pulled open the center drawer took out a pack of cigarettes, offered me one.

"I've got my own," I said. We both lit up. "A three-oh's good, some would say, very good." Smoke escaped my lips while I talked.

"I suppose." Patricia set out an ashtray for me, but took a Styrofoam cup, poured some southern hospitality into it and took it and the bottle back to the window ledge, she got comfortable in the same position she'd been sitting in before. "But it's not dean's list material. The only place I excel," she said, as she tapped the ash end of her butt into the cup, then took a long swig from the bottle, "is working on the paper. I love it. Deadlines, headlines, the important feeling I have when I go places no one else can get to because I'm with the paper. You know? There's power to be had being with the press."

"I guess there would be."

"No guessing about it, there is." She smiled. She sat smoking and drinking as she stared out the window.

"Did you know Darla Bristol," I asked outright.

"Not at first, not before she joined the Tenth House."

She was a member of the cult. I knew it.

"Why'd you call me?" I asked, but had a good idea what the answer was. I waited.

"When I joined with the House, I didn't know exactly what it was, or what it was about—just that it was off beat, that college kids were drawn to it, but nobody talked about it. It was like an elite club. I wanted to be a part of it, naturally, because it sounded so elite and exclusive. But, as a to-be-reporter, wouldn't it be great to get the inside report? I felt like a spy, and it was easy to pull off, because I was truly fascinated and interested in seeing what the cult had to offer." She was staring at me. Her eyes looked intense. She didn't seem to blink. "I have to admit, I was pretty wrapped up in it all and not as a reporter, either. I mean, we did these drugs that just made you feel incredible and invincible. All through high school, I never touched a drug. I drank beer, sure. Some wine, you know. But I never smoked a cigarette," she held up the butt between her fingers, "and I never smoked any pot. I still don't really do pot, but I like the tripping stuff they give us during Mass."

She watched me, I was sure she was waiting for the disapproving look she was sure I'd give. I controlled my expression, knowing I wasn't in a position to judge. "What about why you called me?" I tried to keep her on track. She was straying, albeit, into interesting territory, but straying just the same.

"I told you I didn't know Darla Bristol, and I didn't until she became a part of the cult. Then we were sisters, you know. Secret sisters. That's how it was. Not just like you hear a priest say in church: Brothers and Sisters. I mean like real sisters. We talked all the time, did homework together, but not just us, all the girls in the cult. We all hung out and talked about guy trouble or what professor was a prick. It was great," she said. She started to cry, took a long drag on the cigarette and dropped it into her cup with a hiss.

"So what happened?"

"I hit bottom. One night, I got to mass late and missed the drug plate that gets passed around. At every mass, the high priest assembles a plate of pills and passes them around to all the members. You take whatever you want and as much as you want."

"Free?" I asked.

"Nothing's free, Nick. You should know that. Nothing good is ever free. At the end of each service, there was a priest at the back door. You dropped in donations. Nick, I never dropped in less than a twenty and never took more than enough pills for the night." She asked me to toss her the pack of cigarettes and her lighter. I walked them over to her, afraid she'd lean forward to catch them and fall on her face. I lit the cigarette for her and lit another for myself. I sat on the foot of the bed, closer to her. She was fascinating and she knew how to tell a story, to keep the listener's attention riveted. I thought, if she could write like she talked, she'd make a fine novelist someday.

"So, you were saying," I said, when Patricia seemed to be lost looking out the window.

"I was saying, one night I got to mass late, missed the drug plate. I witnessed the mass straight. It was the scariest fucking thing I've ever been through. The scariest thing in the world." Her hands trembled while she spoke. She kept biting her lip.

"Why? What did you see?" I had so many questions. Now was not the time to ask them, I realized. Patricia didn't want to be interviewed. She wanted a friend. She needed to talk. She truly had a story to tell. I decided to back off and listen. After tomorrow, I could ask her any questions I wanted.

She looked at me, our eyes locked. Anger filled her expression. "Nick, they tortured animals. I mean, even when I was stoned, I knew they did this to animals, but stoned, it didn't seem to matter."

I thought of Father Paul's dog and my raccoon.

"People would have sex with a dog, I don't just mean a few, I mean most of the kids had sex with the animal. They get in line, strip out of their clothes and stand there in a line. Guys and girls. I've got to tell you, Nick, I don't remember ever doing that—having sex with an animal—but, God, I must have. That makes me sick. I get so sick thinking about that. What have I done? But it's worse, you know. It gets worse. While they screwed this animal, some other students skinned the thing."

My stomach churned.

She cried. It was hard to understand her. "They would cut it's face, a long slice from like cheek, up over the forehead, to cheek and pull away the fur and skin. They peeled the skin away and the thing howled and cried." Her shoulders shuddered. She could barely hold the cigarette. I stood, took it out of her hands and dropped it into the cup.

She came to me and hugged me tightly and started to kiss and lick my neck.

I tried to push her away. When I finally managed to get her off me, she was asleep. I gave her a little shake, "Patricia," I said. "Patty!"

Nothing. She'd passed out.

I put her to bed, kept her on her side, covered her with just the bed sheet, closed and locked her window. I sat in the desk chair a moment, stared at her and wondered: *Now what?*

The computer was on. Three spiral notebooks sat on the desk. I reached over grasped the handle for the drawer, expecting it to be locked. Instead it opened. "Ah-ha!" I felt like a heel, taking advantage of a drunken girl this way.

I was going to go through her drawers and there wasn't a thing anybody could do to stop me.

Until the knock on the door.

Dammit. I didn't even get time to scan through file names on her hard drive.

I stood and went to the door. It was a girl. Someone from the Tenth House, I had to wonder. I smiled. "She's sleeping!"

"Who are you?"

"Her brother." I didn't sound very convincing.

"She doesn't have a brother."

"We just found out about each other."

She pushed me out of the way. "Where's Patricia. She better be all right!"

The girl started screaming for help and ran into the bedroom. People were coming out of their own rooms and into the hall to see what the commotion might be about. I just shrugged. Everyone was staring at me. I guess I stood out.

The girl who had practically screamed *fire* came out of Patricia's bedroom. "Who are you?" She asked me again. She looked like a rodent, short, thin, long straight, greasy hair in a pony tail. Her complexion was olive, her eyes like onyx and beady. Her mouth seemed to come to a rounded point, jetting out to match tips with the end of her sloped nose.

I gave her a business card. "You can call me Nick. All my friends do."

"I think you'd better leave, asshole."

"Why would you call me that? You don't even know who I am."

"You're Nicholas Tartaglia, Private Investigator for Safehouse Investigations."

"You retain what you read very well. I bet you scored high on your SAT's." I smiled. The girl did not smile back.

"What are you doing in Patty's room?"

"Ah, she hates being called that. Feels like a hamburger. She prefers Patricia," I said. "And Patricia invited me over, even let me into the building. Half the people who live here were in the lobby when she came to lead me up here."

"So?"

"So, you were looking for an explanation. I just gave you one."

"I mean, what did you want with her?" The girl asked. God, she reminded me of a weasel. "What would Patricia want with a private detective?"

"She lost one of her class assignments, thought I might be able to track it down. I'm good at that kind of thing."

"I'm calling the police."

"If you've lost something, you don't have to call them, I can look for it."

"I wouldn't hire you if you were the only bloody hound alive."

"That's blood hound," I said, correcting her again.

"Not after I get through with you. It would be *bloody* hound."

Tenth House material for sure, I realized. I didn't want to get Patricia into trouble. Look what happened with Maryjean. I needed Patricia to keep from killing herself, or getting herself killed. I was into something serious. Maybe Tommy and Deanna would want to jump in and give a hand. I made a mental note to call them first thing in the morning.

"Look," I said, hoping I sounded serious and sincere. "Patricia saw me around campus, asking people questions. She came up to me, wanted to know what paper I write for. I told her I wasn't a reporter, but a private investigator—"

"I like private dick better," she hissed.

"Good, you wouldn't want to display that kind of affection publicly anyway. You can be arrested for it." Too good to pass up. I got an evil look. I pressed on, "Patricia was fascinated, wanted to ask me questions, maybe do a little expose in the school paper. I told her it sounded cool. So we made plans to meet for the interview."

"And she'd told you late at night in her dorm room? Sounds thin, Dick, I mean, Nick."

I shrugged. "Whatever. It's the truth. Ask her yourself."

"She's passed out."

"Gee. You'll just have to wait until the morning then." I smiled, apologetically.

"I want you to leave or I'll call the RA. He has a black belt, got it in Judo."

"Really? I have one, too. Got mine in Wal-Mart."

I left.

On my windshield, campus security had left me an early Christmas present. A parking ticket. How thoughtful. I could clearly see how my car, in the otherwise empty lot, could be keeping people from finding a parking space. Well, I thought as I tucked the ticket into my pocket, now I would have to find something nice for them, to return the gesture.

I could hardly wait to get back to Karis, but I needed to stop home first. I wanted to grab a change of clothes, my toothbrush, check my messages, check on Scar, have a beer and smoke a cigarette in my chair.

Sounds more confusing than it will turn out to be, I was sure.

While I drove home, I couldn't help wonder if Patricia Helms might be in danger. If the weasel girl were actually a sister in the cult, she would tell the high priest that Patricia had been talking to me. The high priest knew who I was, seeing how he sent me a present just recently.

He would become infuriated and might kill her or ask her to kill herself. Would she? Was she still dependent on the drugs? Was that how he kept them in the cult, got them to participate? Did anyone ever just drop out? What happened the night Darla died?

Then there was Darla's concern, the reason she hired me in the first place: Who was the Tenth House planning to sacrifice on Halloween night? Is there anyway to save that girl from a horrible death?

I didn't realize it, but I was home. I was sitting in the car in the driveway, the engine off. It's funny and scary when things like that happen. I don't remember driving home and yet, there I was. It was dangerous, a mental black out. I'd made it home, but I was lucky. What if someone crossed the road without looking for traffic. Would my reflexes have caught it? Would I have been able to stop the car?

I didn't know. I would like to think, yes.

In the house, I found Scar asleep in my spot. She'd made up the sofa like a bed. She had a blanket, but it only went as high as her knees. It looked like she had kicked it down. She was wearing one of my T-shirts again.

Trying not to wake her, I went into the kitchen. There was a note on the table from Scar. She was telling me she had some macaroni and cheese in the microwave. The gesture made me smile. I opened the refrigerator and pulled out a beer and opened it. Grabbed a pack of cigarettes off the breadbox and lit one.

I sat at the table and looked out the sliding glass doors. Things were terribly wrong. I had a bad feeling things were only going to get terribly worse.

After I smoked most of the cigarette and the fun was gone, I let it burn in the ashtray and pressed play on the answering machine by the kitchen phone and lowered the volume on the side of the machine.

There was only one message. It was from Ned. "Nick," Ned said. "Nick, let's get together and talk some of this over. I got a little hot and said some things, and you said some things, but we've been working together for years. We're friends. I know I didn't give you a chance, and I apologize. Come on in, in the morning. We'll go out for breakfast. Show me what you got on the case, all right? Call me at least. Nick, I'm sorry man."

Good man. Big heart. I pressed delete, erasing the message. That part of my life was over. I didn't need to work for a man who didn't trust me, who wouldn't give me the benefit of the doubt right off. I was going to talk with Karis again, if she was serious, then I was serious. I was a licensed PI. I could rent a small office, she could be my secretary. I would love chasing her around the desk, on the condition of course, that she let me catch her once in a while.

It was almost midnight. I grabbed some clothes, tossed them into a duffel bag, wrote a little note to Scar, taped it to the back of her hand and left, locking the dead bolt behind me.

I drove slowly toward Karis' place and found myself stopping at the cemetery. When I'd been young, I would never have gone to a cemetery at night. It would have been too scary. I'd been afraid of ghosts and monsters and grave robbers and of any other thing my imagination could think of.

It's funny, after Baby Peter's death, I didn't think of the cemetery as a place for monsters anymore. It became like a large apartment complex. Nothing in the cemetery made my skin crawl anymore, not even the large, drooping trees with knuckled bark or the tilted headstones from the late eighteen-hundreds.

I didn't have any reason for stopping in to see Baby Peter, just wanted to say goodnight.

Parking my car and walking across the grass, I wondered exactly what my nephew might think of me, getting his birds-eye view and all. I hoped he liked me, and the person who I envisioned myself being.

Kneeling by his grave marker, I felt a warm feeling fill me. "God, sometimes I feel so empty and alone. Isn't that crazy? Here I am surrounded by all of these people, running here and running there, messages on the machine, mail in the box, not a minute to myself and I feel all alone. It's a horrible feeling, Peter. I hate it." I felt like I might cry. Sometimes I did this, cried. But only in front of my nephew. He didn't mind if I cried. He liked me, for me.

I imagined my nephew, the way I'd seen him that night in the hospital. I don't think he would ever age in my mind. He'd always be the big beautiful baby I remembered him being. I pressed two of my fingers to my lips, kissed them then pressed them against the earth. "Goodnight, tiger."

I stood, tears still coming from my eyes, and I walked back to my car.

There must be a purpose for everything. I like to believe that. It just seems a shame to go through life without really knowing what that purpose is exactly. A real shame.

On my way out of the cemetery, a thought came to me. There was someone I needed to speak with badly, but had no way of getting in touch with her. I pulled the car up to the front office and ran up into the foyer. Though the doors were locked, plotted maps printed on a three-page flier sat in a wood carved box by the door. I grabbed one and ran back to my car. I sat there with the dome light on flipped past the first two pages of detailed maps of the cemetery and looked at the list of names alphabetically listed on the back of the third page. I saw Peter's name, touched it with my thumb. Right in the middle of the first column was the name I'd hoped to find. Darla Bristol was in eighty-seven Meadow Lands.

I consulted the map on the first few pages, found the Meadow Lands and drove to it. I found the plot, beautifully located under the drooping arms of a large Willow tree. The headstone was black. I read the words etched into rock, and sat by the grave.

"Well now, it's a fine mess you've gotten me into, Ollie," I said, smiled, grabbed a handful of grass and tossed it. "You reeled me in and left me to hang myself on the line, Darla. I kind of expected a partner in this deal, thought you might be working with me, you know? Batman and Batgirl? Hansel and Gretel."

For some reason, I felt a little funny talking to Darla. It wasn't the same as talking with my nephew. "Don't hesitate to come and help out, now."

I looked around. It was late. Karis would be wondering about me. "I'm in love with your mom," I said. "I hope that's all right with you. She seems to feel the same way about me. It's hard to believe we were in love once so many years ago and nothing ever came of it. I wouldn't say we fell out of love, it just must have stagnated or something. I don't know really. It's kind of funny, but I can't remember what happened between us. But, I was like what? Eighteen? How could I know what my feelings were, what everything meant? I couldn't. Shit, most of the time, I don't now."

Closing my eyes, I searched for meaning, found none, like always, and became agitated. "Darla, are you going to show yourself again? It would be so much easier if I could parade you around, have you perform a few parlor tricks. I feel like I'm getting no where!"

"That's not true," a voice said.

I opened my eyes. Darla Bristol sat on the opposite side of her grave. She gave me a smile. She was dressed in a white night gown, looked lovely, looked like her mother did when she was her age.

"Darla—"

"Nick, you've made a lot of headway. Look at all you've uncovered."

"Like what?"

"When I came to your office and told you I'd been murdered, you didn't believe me, did you? But you do now. You know I wasn't lying to you. I was murdered by the Tenth House and you know this to be true.

"Yeah, I mean, sure I found out some things, but I have so many questions."

"I have confidence in you. You'll find your answers. You'll keep the cult from sacrificing another girl. I know you will."

"How can you be so sure?"

"I can feel it."

We were silent a moment. I thought if I didn't keep the conversation going, Darla would just disappear. I didn't want her to leave, but I had nothing else to say. She wasn't going to give me answers. So what questions could I ask?

The wind blew gently. The long branches of the tree swayed. Millions of stars were visible in the sky. The moon, opaque behind a thin mass of fast moving clouds, was nearly full.

"How are things on your side?" I finally asked, looked away from the branches and the sky, to find that indeed Darla was gone.

Chapter 24

Karis waited up for me. She let me in. The first thing I did, after we kissed, is handed her back the house key. Her sofa had a blanket on it, a half-eaten bowl of popcorn on the cushion and a can of soda on the end table. The television was on.

"I missed you," Karis said. "I don't know why, but I've been worried about you ever since you left. I think this whole mess is getting to me. In a way, I wish all of this—this investigation—never got started. I never believed my daughter died innocently, I always thought there was something more. You've proven to me her death wasn't an accident. I'm happy with that for some reason, it's closure enough for me. Nick, I'm asking you to quit the case."

She was hurting. I saw it in her eyes. I could also feel it in the way she hadn't stopped hugging me since I handed back her key. "Karis, I can't. You didn't hire me. Your daughter did. You know that. There's a girl who might die at the end of October if I don't find out who this high priest is and put an end to this crazy cult."

"But what if you can't, Nick? I mean, you've been warned to leave it alone. What if they put an end to you? That's a real question. These people are crazy. They're serious and they're crazy." She was crying as she let go of my waist and turned to hide her face.

I held her shoulders and rubbed her back with my thumbs. I kissed the side of her neck. "I can't let another girl die, Karis. I don't want to see another family suffer the kind of loss you're suffering through. I wouldn't be able to live with myself."

She turned and wrapped her arms around me again. "I don't really want you to stop, Nick. I just want you to promise me you won't get killed. You have to promise me you won't die."

"It would be an empty promise," I said.

"I'm a shallow person."

That was anything but true. "Then I promise to live forever."

"Oh, I knew you would. Thank you," she said as she gave me a squeeze, then led me to the sofa. "Want some of this popcorn?"

"Not really, but I'll take a beer if you've got one?"

"I'll get it," she said. I got up before she could and grabbed two. I handed one to her. We opened them at the same time. "You want to tell me about what happened tonight."

"Not tonight, no. I'm beat."

"Do you want to go to bed?"

"It sounds like a good idea," I said. She was staring at me. I wanted to kiss her. I wanted to make love to her. How could I, after telling her I was too tired to talk?

Apparently reading my mind, Karis said, "I know you're too tired to talk." She slid closer, touched my leg. "But —"

She fell asleep after making love. I wanted to, but couldn't. My mind wouldn't let me. I kept thinking about Patricia, sure I'd placed her in harm's way. Before our meeting, I didn't know she was a member of the cult. Maybe I had an idea, but nothing to actually go by.

I cupped my hands behind my head. The sound of Karis peacefully breathing beside me felt relaxing. Staring at the ceiling in the darkness, with a little moonlight streaming through a slight part in the curtains, I remembered back to a time when. . .

Every year the town of Greece sponsored an Italian festival. It ran for one week at the beginning of summer. Large tents were pitched in the front corner of Greece Ridge Mall. Beer trucks lined the tent backs; restaurants, jewelry dealers and souvenir vendors rented booths in the main tent. Eight-foot tables were set up in rows, end to end, with hundreds of folding chairs. There was no private sitting. Hey, we're Italian. Family. Everyone eats together, right?

Bands played on stage at the front of the tent. A postage stamp dance floor filled with people of all ages shaking to the Tarantella and the Hooky-Poky, (now a days they have added the Macgarania).

Aromas from a variety of foods filled the air, leaving one constantly hungry. There was always at least one stand selling calameri and clams, hamburgers and hot dogs, submarine sandwiches, bagels with cream cheese, calzones, or spaghetti. Beer was sold by the glass or pitcher, wine by the glass or bottle.

On the grass outside the tents, but still close enough to hear the music to shake your booty, people engaged in Bocci Ball games. They also danced, laughed and sat around and talked.

I went every year, ate too much, and despite being under age, drank too much.

It was easy to get served when you were not old enough. To enter the festival you payed a cover price. If you were twenty-one, you received a band clipped to your wrist. The color of the bands changed nightly to discourage people from hanging onto their bands. I remember driving around the parking lot earlier in the day. People leaving the festival would remove their bands and throw them out. Finding one was easy.

Once in the festival, I would take the band I'd found out of my pocket and fastened it around my wrist. Instantly old enough to drink.

The people serving beer could care less if you were twenty-one. As long as you could flash a wristband, they were satisfied.

On one night, the guy's I'd gone with were dancing up by the band with a couple of girls. I'd left the tent for air, walked around, looking for people I might know, saying hello to anyone who passed by, hoping to meet a girl.

I saw Madison, a girl from my math class. She was with three other girls. They all looked cute. What better place to help the odds along? I strolled over, hands in my pocket. I felt suddenly shy and stupid. It was obvious why I was coming over, so I stopped half way there, and looked around.

Madison, surprisingly enough, walked over to me.

"Hey, Nick," she said. She was sloshed, a band on her wrist. We were the same age.

"Hey, Madison. What's happening?" The others had come over, too. I said hi to them. They all said hello.

The smallest, and cutest, stood back, seemed not at all interested in me. She looked around the festival, appearing bored. I couldn't take my eyes off her. She had long, straight hair under a black cowboy hat, was dressed in tight pants, a loose fitting T-shirt, and the words on the decal had been in French. I had no idea what it said.

Madison and I did some small talk. The other girls with her seemed interested in getting to know me. I was preoccupied, though. I was looking at the little French girl.

"You're drooling," Madison said.

"Am I? Who is she?" I whispered.

"Name's Karis. She came to the school in March. You probably never got a chance to meet her? Want to?"

"You want to see if she's at all interested, first?"

201

"You're acting like a baby," Madison teased.

"Just see," I pleaded.

Madison was tactful. She grabbed Karis by the arm and pulled her up to me. She said to Karis, "See, Karis, he's interested in you, too."

That's why they came over to see me. Karis had spotted me first, asked Madison who *I* was. Hot damn.

Karis and I stayed with her friends for a while. I tried to engage her in conversation. Sometimes it worked, but mostly she stayed quiet. Madison scraped information out of her, asked me questions, too. "So, you dating anyone, Nick?"

"No."

"How about you, Karis?"

Karis just shook her head and turned away. She was smiling, though. I could tell. She wasn't drunk, didn't drink much, I found out later.

The Chicken Dance came on. That was my favorite. I grabbed her cowboy hat, put it on my head. "May I have this dance, Ma'am," I said in my best western drawl, as I made a clicking noise on one side of my cheeks.

"I don't think so," Karis had said.

"Ah, go on," Madison said, and gave her a push.

I took her hand and kind of dragged her out onto the floor. It wasn't as crowded as you might expect, especially for a song as popular as the Chicken Dance. Everyone dancing though, loved the dance and we all had a good four minutes together.

When the song ended, Karis couldn't seem to stop smiling. She reached for her hat, I moved my head away. "Fun, huh?" I asked.

"It was all right."

We spent the rest of the night talking, standing or sitting under a big tree, just past the Bocci games. We kissed at the end of the night, a slow, long and incredibly passionate kiss.

Madison came for her. Their ride was waiting. Karis wanted her hat back.

"No," I told her. "It's insurance."

"Insurance?"

"That I'll see you again," I said. "I give you back your hat, you have no reason to come looking for me." She took a pen out of her purse, wrote her phone number down on a torn square of paper.

"Take care of my hat," she said.

We kissed quickly, Madison's mom was waiting. "I'm glad we met," I said, it sounded dumb, but it was sincere.

"Me, too."

"What are you staring at?" Karis asked suddenly, jerking me out of the memory.

Why think of then, when I had her with me now. "I'm just remembering the night we met."

"The Italian Festival? I've never forgotten a moment from that night." I couldn't see her, but thought I heard a smile in the tone of her words. "You know, I haven't been to one since after graduation. How about you?"

"I go every year. I love the Calamari. Every time I go, I sit by that tree, you know?"

"You do?" Karis asked, pulling herself up onto an elbow. She rested her chin on her fist. Her fingers twirled the hair on my chest.

"Every year."

She kissed me. "I really do love you, Nick. God, I think I always have."

"We wasted a lot of time."

"Don't remind me."

"Look, I might be changing the subject here, but I've been thinking," I said.

"Yeah, about what?"

"I'm going to open my own agency. Whether you were serious before, or not—"

"I was serious," she said, sounded seductive. She pressed her body closer to mine. Her face was so close that the tips of our noses touched. "I want to work under you."

"I want you to work under me, if you really want to."

She touched me. She was driving me crazy. I loved it. "Oh yeah, I really want to."

"Okay then," I said, trying to sound calm, cool and collective.

"Okay then, climb on up boss," my new employee ordered. As her humble employer, I obeyed.

When morning came, I was the first one up. I spent several minutes just staring at Karis. She slept on her stomach, both arms under her pillow. The sheet was up over her rear. I was tempted to lean down and kiss her back, but I let her sleep.

Instead, I took a shower and dressed in the clean clothes I'd brought. I brushed my teeth and went into the kitchen to start a pot of coffee. I fished around in her refrigerator, found a carton of eggs, cheese, peppers and milk. I had what I needed. I began pulling out my ingredients and set them all on the counter by the stove.

I grabbed a frying pan, buttered up the surface, and made some Santa Fe omelets. I could not find the toaster and decided we would have to forego the toast with our breakfast. I set the table, opened the front door—half expecting to see a skinned animal hanging by the hind legs—and grabbed the morning newspaper.

The sky looked dark and gray, threatened rain. On the front page of the newspaper, I saw that my meteorology skills were in tune. Eighty percent chance of rain, it read. Cold, fifty degrees for a low.

Fifty, I thought. Damn. It'll be winter before we know it.

I went back into the kitchen. Karis was there, a rosy red robe wrapped around a—I'd wager a bet—naked body. She had a four-slice toaster out and was just filing the ports. "I looked everywhere for it, I swear," I said. I walked up behind her, wrapped my arms around her. She reached up and I held her in my arms.

"I keep it hidden. I don't want you to learn your way around to quickly. You might find you don't need me anymore," she said. We kissed. She'd recently brushed her teeth; her breath was fresh.

"Have a seat," I said. "It's just about ready."

"No. You have a seat, pour yourself some coffee. I'll finish up here," Karis said, reaching for the plastic spatula.

I didn't argue. I poured two cups of coffee. Filled my cup with sugar and milk. I lit a cigarette. "It's gonna rain," I said after a long stretch of silence.

"Is that what we're reduced to after a night of love making?"

"What? Reduced to what?"

"Talk about the weather?"

"I wasn't being formal, I was just stating a fact. The weather's important. People base their days on the weather, trips, vacation spots. Let's face it. Talking about the weather may sound impersonal, but it's a serious topic that often goes without discussion."

Karis was laughing, the back of her hand covering her mouth. "You're crazy."

Shrugging, as if satisfied with my speech, I took a quick puff on the cigarette. "Just so we understand each other," I said.

Chapter 25

I got out of the car and walked down the driveway with my duffel bag slung over my shoulder, and grabbed the mail. Feeling the chill in the air there was not a doubt in my mind it would rain, and it *would* get down into the fifties, too. The weather was indeed serious business.

I expected to see Scar asleep on the sofa when I entered my house. She wasn't, but she'd left the blanket there. She'd left for school, I assumed. I would have a talk with her later. She was staying with me, rent free. The least she could do is keep the place clean.

I set the mail down on the kitchen table and picked up a loose sheet of paper with writing on it. I knew who it was from the minute I spotted it. A sense of dread filled my belly. My lungs tightened. It was suddenly hard to breathe. The note read simply:

> *thank you, nick,*
> *you have chosen our present for this Halloween.*

The note wasn't signed. The only capitol letter was the H in Halloween. It was printed in pencil, very sloppy. I thought the author of the note had used the opposite hand than they normally used for writing to keep it from being analyzed by police.

They had Scar. She was going to be the sacrifice at the end of next month. I had been warned, the raccoon would have scared off most people, but not me. It was a sound warning, but I'd ignored it. Now they had Scar. She was going to pay for my stubbornness with her life.

Feeling dizzy, I pulled out one of the chairs at the table and sat. Then I jumped out of the chair and ran out the front door. I looked at the doorframe for signs of forced entry. None of the paint had been chipped around the doorknob area. The dead bolt had normal looking key scratches, but nothing out of the ordinary.

I moved down the front lawn, and checked the windows, including the ones on the ground that lead into the basement. None of the glass had been broken. I tugged and pushed. Nothing opened. In the backyard, up on the deck, I gave the sliding glass doors leading into the kitchen a few good pulls, inspected the track to see if it had been tampered with.

Everything looked untouched. I leaned on the deck rail and stared into the gray sky. It opened and rained on me. Thunder boomed and lighting flashed.

There was no use standing outside getting wet. I ran back around to the front door and went back into the kitchen.

I needed help. I'd never felt more alone, or helpless, than I did right now.

My first thought was to call my brother-in-law. Maybe he could help me. I grabbed the phone and called him. The phone rang three times. There was a click sound, and then the telephone was ringing a little bit different. I knew my call was being transferred.

"Homicide, Johnson speaking?"

"Johnson? I'm looking for Detective Cerio. He around?" I said. I tried to sound in control. My stomach was churning. I thought I might be sick. I hoped Scar was all right, safe and not undergoing any torture. Horrible scenarios played out in my mind. I tried not to think anymore. Thinking only made things worse. "I'm his brother-in-law, it's a police matter, though. I really need to talk with him."

"You the private eye?" Johnson said.

"That's me," I said.

"Cerio talks about you all the time, man," Johnson said.

"Don't believe all you hear," I said in my defense.

"We get a lot of private eyes calling us, you know. They're usually annoying little pricks, but Cerio, he likes you. He always tells us how professional you are. He says some other nice things, too, but I ain't gonna swell your head. Don't know you well enough to do that, just thought you might like to hear some nice words."

"I did. Thank you."

"But he's not in. He and O'Mara got called out a while ago. Body found in the Genesee. One of those little boys. Remember the two fell in a few days ago?" Johnson said.

"I read about it. They think it was a homicide?"

"Don't know, that's why they're checking."

"Can you do me a favor? Could you have him give me call? It's very important," I said.

"Police matter, you said, right? You want some help, I'll give you some."

"Thanks Johnson, the gesture means a lot. Someday, I may actually take you up on that offer. I'm going into business for myself," I said, but wasn't sure why. Building bridges, perhaps?

"Good luck. I'll give him your message. He got a number to get you at?"

I said Tommy would, but gave him my cell phone number again, just in case. "I'll keep that with me, so if he just wants to call the cell phone first—"

"Okay," Johnson said. "Good luck, man."

We hung up. I'd wasted time. No closer to saving Scar than I had been ten minutes ago. Where would the bastards have taken her? I would bet, not to their church. They had to assume I knew where it was, though I didn't.

I lit a cigarette and paced around the kitchen. Did they take Scar because I'd gone to see Patricia Helms? Because I'd blatantly disregarded their warning? If so, then Scar's disappearance was all my fault.

It was hard to handle. As a private investigator for the last five years, I've been assigned many cases, have seen many odd and bizarre things, but I've never been responsible for another's life. Mostly I followed husbands for wives who suspected infidelity. (Valentine's day has always been the busiest day of the year.) Occasionally, I did actual undercover work, like I did for the Cappelli's. Never have I been involved with a murder and, needless to say, never have I worked for a ghost.

In a way, I might have been playing a game. The irresistible private eye, a wise ass. I had been a wise ass to the girl in Patricia's dorm, the weasel. Could my fun-guy attitude and quirky remarks have gotten Scar into trouble?

It was likely, even probable. I'd never learn. Life wasn't a game, not for real, as I often liked to pretend it was. Real people get hurt, have real feelings. Maybe it's my fault, maybe I don't have any true feelings, or morals, or soul?

Right then, I knew I felt like an empty shell. A heart beating in the dark.

"Shut up. Shut up. Feel sorry for yourself later, ass face." I had my gun in my duffel bag. I took it and the shoulder holster out and went into the bedroom and changed clothes. I slipped into a black pullover shirt with a collar, three buttons down the front, loose fitting black jeans and a black belt with a small silver buckle. I checked the clip. It was full. No reason why it shouldn't be. I have never fired it, except at the range.

The cell phone was charging its battery on the adapter. I grabbed it and slipped it into the special pocket in my light tweed, black sport coat. I put on the coat, left the room and stood near the sofa. I kicked at the blanket, got down on my knees and studied the area.

I was looking for anything. A hair, a match, blood. There was none of these things.

Standing there with my hands on my hips, I wasn't that surprised. I knew how they got in. It was simple. They knocked, or rang the doorbell. Scar either opened the door without reservations, or she knew the person standing on my front step and let them in.

That would explain why the locks hadn't been jimmied, or the windows smashed.

Spinning around my living room, I looked at everything. Nothing looked out of place, though I would guarantee the place had been tossed. It would be a beautiful opportunity for them to get a look at who I am. I had to admit, I'm surprised they didn't trash the place. I wouldn't have put that past them. Maybe some devil graffiti on the walls, goat blood smeared on the carpet and sofa, the kitchen table smashed and the legs used like a baseball bat to smash anything smashable.

But then again, maybe they didn't have time. It's possible they didn't come for Scar until the morning, when they were certain I wasn't coming home from Karis'.

Karis. Shit. I picked up the phone on the end table, dialed. Karis answered on the second ring. "Karis? It's me," I said. "Everything okay?"

"I was just about to ask you the same thing."

"Scar's gone. She's been taken. It's a lot to explain."

"Are you coming here? Can you tell me over the phone what's going on?"

"I have another person I need to check up on. I'll call you. Listen, don't open your door to anyone. I have no clue what's really going on here, but I don't like it," I said. I pulled my gun out of the holster, checked the clip again. Yep. Still loaded.

"Nick. Nick, you're scaring me a little."

"Karis, I think it's time to be scared." I didn't want to tell her about the note. She didn't need to hear it. But she needed to hear me warn her. She would take me seriously, I thought. "You know what's a better idea?"

"You're not going to tell me to leave town for a few days."

"No," I said. "I was going to tell you to leave town for as long as it takes until I get this cleared up."

"But what if you don't? What if you can't clear it up? Am I supposed to just keep calling you every week and ask you when I can come home?" she said.

"If I can't get this cleared up," I said, "then you won't have anyone to call."

She knew I wasn't being melodramatic. The cult was an actual evil force and powerful. They had killed her daughter. They had stolen Scar. They skinned and had sex with animals. I couldn't wait to get my hands on them. Couldn't wait!

"Nick, God, please, don't try to do this alone!"

"I won't. I'm not. I've called the police," I said. I had not told her about the note. I had picked up, had held it in both hands. I was an idiot. We could never dust it for prints. No one would be able to obtain a clean set of prints after I manhandled the thing.

"Should I really leave town?" Karis said.

"I think you should."

"I can't, Nick. I won't. If we're really going to work together, you can't send me away every time you have a hairy case. That wouldn't be right, would it?"

"No, it wouldn't."

"I'm staying, Nick. And more than that, I'll be here. You come by, call—if you need me to do some legwork, I will," Karis said. God I loved her.

"Okay, okay. In a way, a selfish way mind you, I'm glad you're staying. I'd hate to miss you so soon after getting together. I'm going to bring you a single shot shotgun. I can show you how to use it easily. I'll feel better knowing you're barricaded away safely, but more importantly, armed."

Karis said. "First, I'm glad I'm staying, too. Second, I've got a shot-gun. Bought it years ago."

"Know how to use it?"

"Load it, wait—if I need to, I point and shoot."

"Sounds like you've been certified."

We said we loved each other and hung up.

Lighting a cigarette I stood by the opened front door and stared out at my street of neighbors. Just down the road a garage door opened. A late model Oldsmobile backed out of the garage and pulled out of the driveway and drove away. I thought all police, detective, and lawyer work amounted to the same thing. Research. History. Luck. All three of those could be obtained by knocking on doors and asking questions.

I finished my cigarette and went first to the front door of my neighbor on the left.

Mrs. Finnely was in her fifties, widowed. She had three sons who all moved out of state after graduating from college. One was a pharmacist, the other a veterinarian and the third worked for *Kodak* in Colorado.

Knocking on her door I glanced at my watch. It was ten o'clock. Ms. Finnely should be up. I remembered her telling me that she was plagued by insomnia most nights. She'd get to bed late, wake up early, drink her first cup of coffee in the dark and wait for the newspaper.

Her door opened. The woman, handsome with silver hair and a strong chin, with thick black-silver eyebrows, smiled as she opened her door. "Nick, how have you been?"

"Okay, Mrs. Finnely," I said. I didn't want to ask her how she was for the simple fact that she'd tell me. I didn't have time to listen to all her gripes, aches and pains. Any other day I would and gladly. Mrs. Finnely was a, for lack of a better word, swell person. "You up early still?"

"Every morning at four. Can't sleep worth—"

"Did you see any cars in my driveway? Hear any strange noises last night, or early this morning?"

"Why, not that I can remember. Why? Were you burglarized, Nick? Oh dear God, what is this city coming to?"

I wanted to tell her it was more than Rochester. It was the world. What was this world coming to? "I had a young girl staying with me," I said.

"I've seen her. Is she your niece?" She gave me a look that told me I should be ashamed of myself.

"Sort of," I said. "It was nothing like you might be thinking. She's part of a case I'm working on. Her roommate in college killed herself. She needed a place to stay. Somehow, she ended up spending a couple of nights at my place and hasn't made an effort to look elsewhere. The story's a little longer than that, but you get the idea."

"And someone broke into your place? Did they get much?"

"They got the girl, Mrs. Finnely."

The widow gasped. She clapped both hands over her mouth. She looked like she might start crying. "No, Nick, I'm sorry, no. I didn't see or hear anything."

"Are you sure?" Sometimes people see and hear things, but don't realize it. "Were you up late last night?"

"At least until midnight. I watched that Jay Leno. I like him."

"Then you went right to bed? You didn't go around checking the windows and doors to make sure the house was locked up?" I said.

"I did, but I don't remember looking out the windows. I know I didn't hear anything Nick. If I'd heard anything, I'd be at my window in a flash. I don't like to admit it, but under most circumstances, I'm a pretty nosy lady. What else do I have to do with my time. I read every Daniel Steel book there is, twice, some of them. As fast as she can crank them out, I can read them," Mrs. Finnely said. She was wringing her hands together. I'd upset her, made her nervous. "Did you call the police?"

"Yes. They may come around asking you the same questions later," I said, sounded apologetic.

"That's good. This way it'll give me more time to think. If I remember something, I still have your business card, do you want me to give you a call?" She said.

"I'd appreciate that. Call on the cell phone. I expect to be out most of the day. I'll have that with me," I said. "And Mrs. Finnely, I don't want to scare you at all, but keep the house locked up, all right? Don't just open the door to anyone. In fact, when the police come around, if you feel funny about opening the door, get their name and badge number and call 911. Ask the operator if those people are really at your address."

"You can do that?"

"You should do that. Crazy people dress like the police sometimes."

"God. This city," Ms. Finnely said. "What is it coming to."

Daniel and Louise Schemere lived to the right of me. They didn't have kids, and are in their early forties. On a few summer nights, when we've all been in our backyards together, we've drank beers by the chain link fence separating the property lines.

Daniel was a mechanic at *Sears*. He worked on brakes and shocks. Louise worked at the blood lab, jabbing people with needles and taking samples all day long. I couldn't imagine inflicting that kind of pain on people every day, five days a week. She seemed, if not happy, content with her job.

Together, they pulled in a pretty good income and had the *toys* to show it. Snowmobiles for winter, with a cabin up in the Thousand Islands and Jet Skis for the summer to cruise around on Lake Ontario.

Louise drove a *Jeep*. (A vehicle I have longed to have and to drive until death do we part, but have never gotten around to buying). She kept it in mint condition. It was turquoise with a black, Snap-On shell. Daniel drove a *Legend*. Black with black leather, all the bells and whistles. A tough looking car.

Neither automobiles were in the driveway, nor were they in the garage I saw when I cupped my hands over my eyes and spied through the window. I rang the doorbell anyway. I had nothing but time to lose.

I waited two minutes. Rang the bell again, and waited another two minutes.

No one was home.

I talked with a few more neighbors. No one saw anything out of the ordinary, though they all knew Scar was staying with me. Like Mrs. Finnely, they all made me feel like I should be ashamed of myself. After the third explanation, I got tired of defending my morals. I let them think what they wanted because they would go ahead and think what they wanted anyway.

Sitting on my front step smoking a cigarette, I bowed my head and watched a couple of ants run across the walkway into the grass. My cell phone rang. I pulled it out of my sport coat pocket and said, "Hello?"

"Nick, it's Tommy. What's up?"

"Maryjean's roommate, Eleanor, Scar?"

"Yeah. Yeah. I know her. Get with it," he said.

"She's gone."

"Nick—"

"I mean she was kidnapped. Someone came to my house yesterday—"

"She's still staying with you?" Tommy said. He sounded like my neighbors.

"Give me a break, okay, Tommy."

"I'm sorry. What's going on?" He sounded serious.

I told him everything.

"And you touched the note? That's not good, but I'd guess there weren't traceable fingerprints on it anyway. Everybody knows to wear gloves now a days. Still. I'd like to come down with a team and go through your place. I'll let the chief in on it all and Deanna and I will be over shortly," he said.

"Bring doughnuts," I said and hung up.

212

Chapter 26

A team dusting for prints was in my house. They'd taken a fresh sample of mine—though my prints were on file, it was part of being a registered private investigator—to use in comparison to those they might find.

Tommy, Deanna and I were on the front lawn. I was smoking. Deanna was trying to stand up-wind. She still swatted at the smoke. "Do you mind?" She said.

"We're outside," I told her. "One of the only places left where an honest American can still smoke a cigarette."

"That'll be against the law soon, too," she assured me.

I took a long drag. "Yeah? Well right now it isn't."

Tommy, like a parent with two fighting children, stepped in, "Okay. Shut up the both of you. Nick, tell me again what you did last night and everything right up until the time you got home. Then we'll go through each step you went through from the time you pulled into your driveway this morning."

I told him, said that I had spent the night with Karis Bristol, but left out the details of the night. I finished up, for a second time, with talking to neighbors and sitting on the step waiting for the police.

"What new information do you have about the cult," Deanna O'Mara asked. She was concentrating. It was time to work. She wouldn't bicker back and forth with me anymore, not during the investigation.

"That's just it. I found out bits and pieces of this and that, but I can't make too much sense of the information," I said.

"But somebody's fearful, maybe thinking you already made some kind of a connection," Tommy said.

"That's what I was thinking."

"But you haven't," Deanna asked.

"No. I haven't." I had ideas, theories, clues, things going on in my mind. Nothing concrete. I didn't want to start throwing around accusations. I wanted Tommy and Deanna to help, but I needed to do some more digging on my own first.

"Cerio, O'Mara?" a police officer from inside my house called through the screen on my storm door. "You two might want to come in here, take a look at this."

I followed the two detectives into the house.

"What have you got?" Tommy asked.

"Close the curtains," the male police officer said. Another policewoman pulled closed my curtains. "Shut the lights."

Tommy reached and switched off the lights.

"I imagine the darker, the better—I'm not sure what we'll see, but I know what I found on the wall," the cop said, explaining.

He held up a flashlight. It had a black bulb screwed in. He switched it on.

The walls and the ceiling in my living room came to life in the form of art.

The walls and ceiling glowed. "What the hell?" I said.

"What is it?" Tommy asked.

"*Tide* detergent," the policewoman said. "We came across traces when we were dusting for prints. But I wouldn't have expected this."

The *Tide* was undetected under normal lighting circumstances. The rays of a black light set the room aglow like a nightclub. The ceiling had been painted to resemble a Halloween mural. A large pumpkin, complete with triangle shaped carved eyes, nose and mouth had a knife buried in its forehead. Pumpkin juice, or maybe blood, was simulated with dripping drops of *Tide*.

On the walls was an altar, candles in the corners, a robed figure stood arms outstretched, palms up, face hidden under the hood of a cloak.

"Looks like a paintbrush was used. I just found some bristle hairs," the policewoman said. She'd examined the wall portrait. With latex gloves on, she used a pair of tweezers to remove the hairs. She slipped them into a small paper bag. Nobody used plastic bags. They sweat and spoil evidence.

Like I'd suspected, several police officers in uniform went door to door, canvassing my neighborhood. They'd ask many of the same questions I had. I'd warned all the neighbors that the police would be by. They'd be ready and maybe remember something they forgot to tell me about. I hoped someone would remember something.

"The Schemere's next door," I told Tommy, "weren't home when I stopped by. They both get out of work around five. Maybe someone can swing by there later this evening?"

"We'll take care of it," Tommy said. "Give me your feeling here, Nick.

Are these freaks going to ask for a ransom? Could this be another warning like with the raccoon?"

"I wish. No, I think I blew the warning. I think they're serious. You read the note, I've chosen their present for Halloween. Scar's going to be sacrificed, if we can't find her first," I said. My stomach muscles tightened.

"Darla Bristol was murdered then," Tommy said. He wasn't asking a question. "I'm going to need to talk with the chief. I think we'll have to reopen the Bristol file, get some more brass involved."

"I don't want to be asked to step aside, Tommy. I won't, anyway."

"Nick—"

"I can't just let this go. I'm not trying to be a hot dog. You know me, Tommy. I'm not reckless. This is important. I'm responsible for Scar. I have to help her. I know I can. If you try to make me stay in my house with the doors locked, I'll go crazy," I said. Tommy knew I was serious. I saw it in his face.

"I'm going to do what I can. If the chief thinks you're interfering—"

"Screw the chief, Tommy. I'm either in and a part of the team, or I'm on my own. Either way, I won't back off."

I parked in the faculty lot, grabbed my knap-sack and dug through it for the class schedules the school's president had given me. I found Patricia Helms, scanned it. She would be in Viet Nam literature right now, in Fenton Hall.

Running, I found Fenton Hall, ran up the stairs and went in. She was in room 117. That was a sub room, I took the stairs down. The room numbers were on nameplate plaques in white on black over the doors.

The professor in room 117 was at the head of the class. The room had maybe forty students. I walked tentatively in, looked at the faces.

"Can I help you?" The professor was clearly annoyed.

"Ah," I mumbled, walked up to him. "I'm looking for Patricia Helms. Is she in—"

"Ms. Helms? Ms. Helms?" He stood on his tiptoes and glanced around the room. "I don't see her, he said. Anything I can help you with?"

I gave him a card. "If she shows up, have her call me."

I started out.

"Mr. Tartaglia?"

I stopped.

"Is she all right," he asked, sounding genuinely concerned.

"I hope so."

Parking as close to the high rise dorm buildings on campus as I could get, I growled as I watched a green school security guard pull up in front of my parking space. I reached into my sport coat, pulled out my wallet.

"You can't park there, buddy." The man behind the wheel looked young. Maybe he was a senior at the school, a criminal justice major, working co-op with the campus police. Good training, I thought, but I had no time for games.

I flashed him my ID badge. It didn't look anything like a police badge, wasn't meant to. "I'm on business here. I don't have time to cross that bridge. If you have to write me up, leave the ticket where I can see it."

Walking around the car, I heard a car door open and without looking back, guessed I was about to receive another parking ticket.

In the cubby of Patricia Helms' building, I rang her room. Waited. I rang again. Nothing. I began pushing all the different doorbells, confident someone would let me in. A few voices filled the cubby over the speaker asking who was there. I didn't answer. Someone finally buzzed me in without checking.

The lobby was quiet. The television was on, the sound off, a student crashed on the sofa. Two students played ping-pong. The ball bounced back and forth over the net. Most of the kids, I'd guess, were in class.

I ran up the stairs and down the hall. At Patricia's door, I knocked.

"Can I help you?" A female voice asked from behind me. I expected to see the little weasel girl. I turned. It was not the weasel.

"I'm looking for Patricia Helms," I said. I pulled out my wallet.

"How did you get in here?"

I gave her a card, showed her my badge. "Look, I have reason to believe Patricia might be in danger—"

"In her room?"

"In her room, or if she's not in her room, she might be in danger wherever she is. I need to find her. I have to make sure she's all right," I said.

The girl stared at me. She looked me over and started down the hall. She knocked on a door. A young man came out. He wore no top, sweat pants, no socks, no shoes. "Yeah?"

"This guy says he's a private eye, looking for Patricia," the girl with my card explained.

"How'd he get in the building," he asked.

216

"I don't know."

He looked over her, at me. I showed him my private investigator badge. "How'd you get in the building?"

"Are you the resident advisor?" I said.

"I'm the RA, yeah." He came out of his room, tried to look intimidating, muscles flexed. If I remembered correctly, I'd been informed that he was a black belt in Judo. He looked healthy enough to do some serious damage. I didn't want to fight him. "How'd you get in?"

"Someone buzzed me in," I said.

"You know someone else in the building?"

"No. Look, I'm worried about Patricia. Do you have a key to her place?" I said.

"I can't just invade her privacy because you're worried about someone. This card, that badge, they don't mean a thing. I can buy one of those badges—"

"Look, buddy—"

"Hank."

"Look, Hank.. If she's hurt in there, we don't want to be wasting any time. I've knocked and she doesn't answer. I rang her bell and she doesn't answer," I said.

"How about class? This is a college you know. Most kids are in class learning."

"Not her," I said. "She would have been in Viet Nam lit. I checked. She wasn't."

I saw confusion contort Hank's features. He was faced with indecision. "I'll open it," he said. "Only I'm going in."

"Fine. Grab your keys and shake it."

Hank ducked into his room and came back out within fifteen seconds. He had a large, full key ring. He jingled them around, found the one he was looking for and unlocked the door. He knocked before opening the door. "Pat? Pat, it's me, Hank. I'm coming in, all right? Pat? Patricia?"

He pushed the door open and went in slowly. He came back out into the hall. The girl that had confronted me was standing next to me. Her arms were folded. She looked upset. Scared. A few others had gathered in the hall.

"Ah God! Help!"

I bolted into the room, looked around the suite. I went to the bedroom where I expected to see a bloody mess. "Hank?"

"The bathroom. Someone call 911 now! We need an ambulance."

The Tenth House

I went to the bathroom. The girl next to me had picked up the phone in the suite.

On the baby blue tiled floor, sprawled on her belly, was Patricia Helms. Hank held a pill bottle in his hands. The prescription label had been torn off. "She must have taken these," he said.

"She breathing?" I said.

"Barely."

"Do you know CPR in case she stops?"

"Yes," Hank said.

I kept her on her belly, stuffed my finger down her throat and tickled her tonsils. Her stomach muscles tightened, her shoulders moved. She was heaving. I pulled my finger out, gave her a chance to catch her breath, then tickled the tonsils some more.

She made a retching sound. I tried to pull my hand out, but wasn't quick enough.

She vomited spewed puke. I grabbed her and moved her away from the mess she'd just made.

People had filled the bathroom to watch. "Get out of here! Come on, move it, move it!"

Hank sprang into action, started to work the crowd. He knew them, would be better at controlling them.

The smell of puke assaulted my nostrils. Acid and tangy.

Patricia coughed, managed to get up on her knees. She moaned out a few words. I had no clue what she was saying. In her vomit I could see a large handful of undigested pills. The medics would take those as samples, figure out what she'd taken if she could not talk well enough to tell them.

"It's all right," I whispered. I grabbed a towel off the rack, wet it with cold water and rubbed it along her forehead. "Help is on the way."

Without using my finger, Patricia managed to throw up on her own.

When the medics and the police arrived, I gave Hank all the credit. Patting Hank on the back I said, "If Hank here hadn't of acted as quickly and as heroically as he did, that young girl would not be alive today."

"And how do you fit into this," the inquiring police officer wanted to know. It had to look funny to him, I'd be surprised if it didn't. Here I was, this private investigator, in a dorm room on campus looking for a girl who just happened to be in the process of killing herself.

He was short, fat, balding, but intuitive. I liked him even though I

218

wouldn't be able to help him. "I can't tell you that."

"I'm afraid you're going to have to do better than that," the officer told me. "See, I got a lot of paper work to fill out. If she'd a died, I'd have less, might not care why you were here. But she lived, so I got twice as much work. My chief hates blank spots on the paper work. I've got to do my best to fill all those spots in. See my problem?"

"Can't you write bigger?"

"Don't try to be funny."

"I don't. It comes naturally," I smiled.

"Look—"

"If you have any questions, you can talk with a Detective Tommy Cerio. You know him?"

"Sure," the officer said. He scratched at his balding head. "How's he fit into this?"

I gave him one of my cards. "I really don't have time to explain. You give him a call, ask him about me. He'll fill you in on anything necessary, I'm sure."

"I can't just let you walk away, Mr. Tartaglia. I mean, I know who you are—I've heard of you—but I can't just let you leave." It wasn't a threat, didn't sound like a threat. The old cop had his job to do and I wasn't making it easy on him.

"But you don't have any reason to detain me. There's been no crime committed here. Attempted suicide is *not* against the law. Suicide is. See what I'm saying? No law's been broken so you can't keep me," I said. I shook the officer's hand and Hank's. "And this man deserves some kind of special recognition." I gave Hank a wink.

"He'll be put in for the Annual Citizen Award Ceremonies."

"Great. Great. Let me know how that turns out," I said and left the building.

I made a special note to swing by the hospital in a few hours. I needed to talk with Patricia. Our conversation from the night before had fallen short of complete when the young college student had fallen asleep, or passed out.

Walking out of the dorm, behind the paramedics, I thought about the first meeting Darla and I had in my office when she appeared out of thin air. There was something she had told me, that I couldn't remember. It was important, I could feel it now, but there would have been no way of knowing it then.

It had to do with the Tenth House. The House.

She had said something about the cult only meeting while college was in session. Did that mean they stopped worship in the summer months? Over Christmas and Easter breaks? That didn't sound right, unless the head of the little religious group was a professor or member of the faculty's staff. It couldn't be a student, I had decided a while back, because students come and go. The Tenth House had roots, a foundation. It was tended to, organized, not wild and chaotic.

A faculty or staff member?

It tasted right in my mouth. There was one person who might be able to help me. My good friend, Mr. Granatta.

Unless, of course, he was the man I was looking for. Power. Control. Lust.

It was early in the day. There might be a million things I needed to do, things that would help me find Scar. Right now, talking to the president of the college seemed like the first and best way to start this investigation since talking with Patricia Helms had been placed on the back burner for a while.

I walked swiftly across campus to the building where, hopefully, the president would be sitting in his office with nothing to do—just waiting for someone like me to come and throw some excitement into his day. I would do this easily by accusing one or all of the people employed by the college of leading a satanic cult that catered to the students on campus.

God, this man was just going to love me.

Chapter 27

Mrs. Stavinski, looking as old as ever, looked up from her paperwork when she saw me coming. She recognized me, maybe not remembering my name, but definitely the face. I could tell from her smile that she couldn't recall from where she might know me.

"Yes?" The receptionist asked.

"I need to speak with President Granatta," I said. Her look changed. I think she remembered where she knew me from.

"Weren't you just in to see him not too long ago?"

"I've missed him," I said. She didn't see the humor in my comment. "I have some information that I need to discuss with him. It's rather important, and in this risking the chance to sound over dramatic, time is of the essence." I rocked on the balls of my feet. She wasn't moving. My vague specifics didn't seem informative enough to cure her curiosity.

"And what is the utter emergency in regards to? If I remember correctly, you are not even a student here."

"Your memory works wonderfully," I complimented her. "But I didn't realize that Jeffrey was restricted to only visitors of the student body."

"He's not."

"Then I'm missing the problem," I said. "And frankly Mrs. Stavinski, I don't see why you have any reason to hassle me every time I come in here. I'm a pretty pleasant person. I like people, get along well with them, but for some reason we can't get along. Why?"

"Because," she said with a straight face. "You're a wise ass, Mr. Tartaglia."

"Ah, you remembered my name." I whispered, "but your language has shattered the wholesome image you project." My lips formed into a wide tooth-filled smile.

"He's not in," she said after a long silence. She hated me. The hate, like heat, could almost be felt radiating from her aura. I told her so.

"I just wish we could start over."

"Would you care to make an appointment?" She was trying to keep her composure. I had the distinct feeling that somehow, I was getting under her skin. She might be old, but she still strove to behave like a lady. I respected this, and told her as much.

"I'll pass on the appointment, though. They're too restricting. My life's a little too hectic right now to be locked in to any specific time frame. Do me a favor, will you? Tell Mr. Granatta—"

"President Granatta."

"Tell him, I'll be back, that it's important. Tell him I need to speak to him at length about the death of Darla Bristol," I stopped. "Are you writing this down? I've got a bit of information that I really need passed along."

"No need."

"Okay. Good. I see you want to continue to exercise that fine memory of yours. Anyway, I need to talk to Jeff at great lengths about the murder of Darla Bristol—"

"She wasn't murdered," Mrs. Stavinski said.

"Oh, but she was, and the case is being reopened as we speak. I have some friends on the force," I bragged.

"That fact that you have friends, I find difficult to swallow."

"The dentures must get in the way," I said. I didn't miss a beat. "And the Maryjean D'Amonda suicide, and I'll also want to talk to him about Patricia Helms' attempted suicide."

"Mr. Tartaglia, Patricia Helms did not attempt suicide," Mrs. Stavinski said. She was standing now. Her face was beat red. She had her hands balled into fists. Those fists were pressed hard enough against her hips to drain the pink color from her skin.

"Oh, I guess you haven't heard yet. I just left her dorm, helped the police figure how to go about filling out a report. The RA in the dorm, Hank? Wonderful kid. He's going to be a hero. I bet he's on the news or something."

"Your charade—"

"No charade, Mrs. Stavinski, and I'm not playing a game. I've had my fun with you, and believe me it was fun, but I don't have time for these adverse dialogue skits. There's another student whose life is in grave danger. She was kidnapped. I can't get into anything more specific because I'm not sure if her family has been notified yet. The police are doing what they can, and aside from you setting up barriers, I'm doing what I can to help save a young girl's life. I need to talk with Granatta and soon, please give him my message." I turned and started out of the office.

Before I reached the door, I heard a very serious, maybe even sorry woman say, "I will Mr. Tartaglia."

Chapter 28

I used the cell phone to call Karis while I walked back to my car. "Hey," I said.

"Nick, what's going on?"

"The girl I came out to see last night, Patricia Helms? She tried to commit suicide. I found her in the bathroom with an empty pill bottle near her," I said.

"Oh, God."

"She was unconscious. Me and the dorm RA revived her. Paramedics and police came. They think she'll be all right. Do me a favor, they took her down to Strong. Will you keep tabs on her? If they move her into a room, send up some flowers or something. You want my credit card number?" I said.

"I can handle the fee, forget about it."

"I'll find a way to pay you back," I said.

"I can help you come up with a method of payment."

"I'll bet you can."

"So, it's like we're working together already, huh? I kind of like it," Karis said. "I feel good getting my hands dirty."

It *was* a good feeling, doing something to help others. "I'm not sure what my next move is going to be, but I've got the cell phone, you can reach me anytime. For now, I've got a lot of thinking to do."

"You don't have anything?"

"Nothing."

"Good luck, Nick."

"Thanks," I said. "I think I'm going to need it." I put the phone away and dug out my car keys. At the car, the paper on the windshield that I thought was a ticket from the young security guard, was not a ticket at all. It was a phone number. No name.

Who would have left the number? The security guard?

In the car, I took out my cell phone again and dialed the number.

"Yeah," the man on the other end said.

224

"This is Nick Tartaglia. Your phone number was left on a—"

"I know who you are," the man said.

"Gee, that makes me feel a little inadequate. You know who I am but—"

"You don't need to know who I am."

"Why don't you tell me who you are, and I'll be the judge. You're probably right, I don't need your name, but it couldn't hurt, could it?" I said. I checked my watch. It was after twelve. Scanning the area around my car, I wondered where I might be calling exactly.

"Let's say you can call me, Dick."

"As in head?"

"Don't be a wise ass, Nick. You don't want to screw around with me."

I wondered if *Dick* might be the man I was looking for, the head of the cult. Was it possible that I'd rattled the cage enough to receive personal attention from the head honcho? God that made me feel special. I needed to hear him talk a little more to try and associate an age with the voice. Did he sound like he might be black, or white? Southern accent, or could he be from Boston?

"All right, Dick. What can I do you for?"

"I know where your friend is. I know where she's being kept."

"And you know this . . . how?" I said.

"She's being kept in their church, tied to the altar."

He told me where she was without giving me a location. It sounded like a trap, a teaser. All I needed to do was figure out where the satanic church was located.

Dick was connected to the satanic group somehow, this I knew for sure.

"Is she all right?"

"She is so far. I mean, nobody's touched her. She's still wearing her skin," Dick said. I understood the threat.

"What are you trying to tell me?" I said.

"Leave this whole investigation alone."

"It's a little late for that. I'm not alone on this. There's a police department involved now. People are dying, and trying to kill themselves. If it were just me, I'd call it quits. But it's not just me. See my problem?" I said.

"Oh, I see your problem all right. I just think you don't. Let me tell you one thing and I'll make myself perfectly clear, then I have to go. I have many things that need to get done before the day is over," Dick said, sounding distracted. I'd guess he was older than thirty. White. A local fixture.

225

"Please, enlighten me," I said.

"It's too late for your friend, no matter how you look at. It's over for her. But how she spends her last few weeks can be entirely up to you. Do you see what I'm saying?"

I did, but couldn't give in that easily. I was trying to get a feel for the person I was talking to. He was crazy, I had no doubt, but in control. He sounded very familiar. I'd heard his voice before. "No. I thought you were going to make yourself perfectly clear?"

He did not sound angry when he spoke again. He talked slowly, saying, "Stop your investigation right now, or your friend will begin to die a little each day for the next month. By Halloween, your friend will be begging for death because the pain she will endure will be nothing to the peace she'll be looking forward to. What one can do to a raccoon is nothing in comparison to the torture that can be inflicted on a human. And do you want to know why? Because a human knows enough to be afraid, and fear heightens the anxiety, it increases the amount of pain felt."

There was nothing I could say. He had me. I felt like Father Paul. "How can I just stop."

"It's simple, Nick," he laughed. "Quit digging. And don't think I won't know if you've stopped or not. Because I'll know. You can't dig a hole, even if it's a small hole and not expect it to be found. Understand?"

"I do, but it's a really lousy metaphor," I said.

"Yeah, well see if you can understand this metaphor. I'll know if you call the police. If you do call the police, I'll be wearing her skin as a cape before the RPD chews their last donut and waddles their fat ass to their car. And no matter when they get here—I'll be gone. See Nick, you're not the only one with connections on the force," Dick said and hung up. Somehow Dick knew about my brother-in-law.

But was it a credible threat? It could be. Then again, it might be nothing more than a red herring. Either way, I couldn't risk calling the police. I was now being forced to do this alone.

I plugged my phone into the laptop and went to a web site for cross-reference telephone listings. I typed in the telephone number, hoping the computer would be able to provide me with an address. It was unable to. I turned off my laptop and dialed zero. The operator came on. "This is Detective Thomas Cerio of the Rochester Police department. I'm investigating a homicide and have come across a phone number here. I need an address to go with that number."

"Do you have a case number, detective?"

226

"I do," I said. I shuffled some things around on my front seat. I wanted the operator to think I was looking for the case number. "Dammit, it was here. Hold on one second." I put the phone up to my chest to muffle the sounds the operator would hear. "Dick, where's that paper you pulled off the fax? You put it on my desk? Shit, where?" Tommy was going to kill me for using his name. I got back on the phone. "Look" I said, "I can't find it. Let me give you the number and you can fax the information to my police chief, Carl Delski," I said. "Let me give you the number I need the address on and while you do that, I'll dig up the chief's fax number. How's that sound?"

"Detective, I'm also going to need a subpoena."

"I'm aware of that. Now I know I can fax that over before the end of the day, that shouldn't be a problem," I said. I knew all of this. I used to work at a phone company part time while I was in college. "Look here's the number I need an address check on," I said. I waited. I heard the operator clicking away on her keyboard. "And where is that address?"

"There isn't one. It's a payphone listing in a Chinese restaurant called The Dragon Wokery. It's in Monroe Plaza," the operator said. She asked me for Chief Delski's fax number.

"I'll get back to you on that," I said, thanked her and disconnected our call.

A payphone. Great.

I started up the car, left the campus and headed north to the Monroe Plaza. It was less than two miles away from the college. Main Street was a single lane road with a speed limit of only thirty miles an hour. Traffic, for some godforsaken reason, was heavy.

In front of me, an older woman driving a Reliant did just under the speed limit. When I could stand her cautious habit no more, I decided to take action, flashed my high beams, hoping the silver-haired driver would pull the car over. When that didn't work, I beeped the horn a few times. It became obvious she might be partially blind, the way the car exceeded the lines in the road, so perhaps she couldn't see my lights flashing. She might be partially deaf, too, which would explain why she didn't seem to hear my horn honking.

I gave in, driving at a steady twenty-seven miles an hour. I lit a cigarette.

The plaza was coming up on my left. I signaled my turn and pulled into a large, half-filled, freshly paved and yellow-line painted parking lot. I parked as close to the Dragon Wokery as possible, shut the car and ran inside.

The young Chinese man behind the counter was dressed in black slacks, a black vest and a white dress shirt. He held a single menu in his hands. He had seen me coming and was ready to seat me immediately. Behind him was a large bar with two cash registers. "One, sir?"

"Actually, do you have a pay phone in here?" I said.

"We do sir, in back." He turned and pointed to the far back corner. The restaurant was dark, but I saw a sign advertising restrooms and a pay phone. "Do you mind?"

"Help yourself, sir. Will you be eating with us today?"

"I don't think so," I said. I had reached into my pocket and removed my wallet. I pulled out a five-dollar bill, handed it to the host. He smiled and backed away.

At the threshold leading into the dining area a large gold statue of Buddha sat, blankly staring at me. I rubbed his big belly and wished for luck. As I moved through the dining area, I noticed the dark red carpeting, the mauve painted walls and three dimensional dragon art. I also noticed a table of three men and two women, all in business suits with briefcases by the legs of their chairs. Up front, by the window a heavy, lone woman dined on what looked like a Poo-Poo Platter for two.

A few men sat at a table in the center of the dining room, eating feverishly, as if their lunch break would end and they would get in trouble if they returned to work late.

Other than them, the place was empty. I still moved slowly and cautiously to the back corner of the restaurant. The sign for the bathrooms and phone dangled from two small chains clipped into the false ceiling tiles. A long, narrow hallway led me to the pay phone. No one was on it. I didn't really expect anyone to be.

I went up to the wall mounted booth, anyway. Looking for clues, I hoped to find something, but came away with nothing. Ducking into the men's room, I looked to see if my man might be hiding in here. He wasn't.

When I came out and went back to the front door, the man I'd tipped was staring at me. "I'm looking for somebody who just used that payphone, right before I got here? It was a man—but I don't know what he looks like. Did you see anybody use that phone?"

"Yes."

"Did he eat here, or did he just come in and use the phone like me?"

"He ate here. Yes."

"What did he look like?"

"Um. You, kind of," the host said.

"Me?"

"Yes. He white."

"Okay, good. Good. Was he younger than me, would you say? Older?" I said. I watched the host's face contort in confusion.

"I not sure. He have some gray hairs," he said, suddenly excited. I thought of Jeffrey Granatta. He had gray hairs. "But I not sure if he older or younger. No offense, but most white people all look same to me."

"We do, huh? I can understand that. Listen, do you mind if I talk with some of the people in here eating, ask them some of the same questions?"

"Yes. I think I mind. These busy people come here to enjoy lunch. If I let you disturb them, then they get bad taste in mouth for this fine Chinese restaurant. Okay? You want, you wait outside, talk to them when they leave." He smiled apologetically.

I clapped him on the back with understanding and slipped him another five. "Thanks for your help. I mean it, you've helped me a lot."

Leaning against the wall outside the Dragon Wokery, I waited for customers to leave. The first to come out was the heavy lady who had been dining alone, her purse slung over her shoulder. "Ma'am," I said. "Excuse me?"

She looked over her shoulder, but kept walking.

"I just wanted to ask you if you saw a man in the restaurant earlier, maybe with some gray hair? He would have eaten, then got up to make a phone call?"

She stopped. I gave her one of my cards. She looked it over, tucked it into an unzipped compartment on her purse. "Mister, a crowd of people left right before you came in. This place has an eleven to noon rush hour. The place was packed. I didn't notice anyone in particular, but I'll tell you this, almost everyone in there today, I thought, had some gray hair. That probably doesn't help?"

"Yeah," I said. "Kind of. At least now I know I won't be able to figure out who I'm looking for from anyone in this place."

"If you maybe knew what he was wearing, that might help?"

"I know, let me describe a man to you, tell me what you think?"

"Will this take long?" she said.

"I'll try to be fast. I'm sure you're busy." I described Jeffrey Granatta.

She listened carefully to the description I provided, chewed her upper lip and shook her head after a few minutes of consideration. "I don't really think that sounds familiar, but like I said, the place was really busy. People were coming and going."

"Okay," I said. "Look, thank you."

She nodded, turned and started walking away. She walked down the sidewalk, maybe headed to one of the other shops or the grocery store in the plaza.

She couldn't remember seeing Granatta. Dammit. "Oh, hey, miss," I called out, ran up along side her. "One more person, okay?"

"I really don't have time for this."

I pulled out my wallet, took out a ten dollar bill. She considered the money, didn't reach for it. "Is this really important?"

"I'm investigating the kidnapping of a college girl. She also happens to be a friend of mine. I happen to know that her life is in serious danger. The longer it takes for me to find her, the worse her chances are of surviving this ordeal," I sounded desperate. I felt that way, too.

"I don't want your money. Go ahead, give me your description."

I described Father Paul, but did not tell her the man was a priest. I wanted to hold that back for the final descriptive detail.

"I don't know. That sounds kind of familiar."

"Ma'am, the man I just described is a priest," I said.

"Yes," she shouted. "God, yes. There was a priest in there eating today. He was the man you described. You know how it is when a priest or a nun goes someplace . . . different and they stand out because of their costumes?" she said.

I don't know if calling a priest or a nun's uniform a costume was appropriate, but I knew what she meant. "Yes. And you're sure the priest I just described to you was in there eating."

"Left not ten minutes before you came in."

I felt sick. Father Paul. It didn't feel right. I was so sure he wasn't involved. Yet, I was coming to the end of the mystery. I felt excited, wanted to kiss this woman.

"Thank you, Ma'am. Really. Thank you!"

I needed to call Tommy.

Talking with Tommy, I felt nauseous. He told me there wasn't much the police could do. They wouldn't go after Father Paul of St. Anthony's Church just because a woman said a priest was dining in a Chinese restaurant. They could discreetly look into the man, and would. Tommy promised to run Father Paul through the police computers to see if anything came up. He told me he'd get back to me either way. Tommy admitted it was a lead, thin, too thin to request a subpoena for searching the church and rectory where the priest worked and lived. A judge would require sound evidence; a positive ID, prints on the phone that matched the priest's prints in the computer. Since it was a public pay phone, obtaining a clean, true set of prints would prove challenging. How many people might have used the phone since the call? If the priest didn't have a criminal record, then nothing would turn up in the computer, then prints would be useless anyway. "And Nick," Tommy said. "I don't know this priest, but I'm willing to bet he doesn't have a record."

"Yeah. He probably doesn't, I agree, but you'll still check. The guy on the phone, though his voice was muffled, sounded familiar. It was him, Tommy. He's got Eleanor."

"Like I said," Tommy had said. "We need more to go on, or a judge won't take the time to even read our request for a subpoena. But we're on it. We're going to be watching."

"I'm going to do a little more than watch," I said.

He reminded me of the threatening phone call I'd received. "Look, Nick, if this priest is the man who has Eleanor, and he told you to back off, and the same day he tells you this you show up in his church asking more questions—"

"I know what you're saying," I told Tommy. "But I can't sit here and do nothing."

"It's your call right now, but I don't think antagonizing him is good, Nick. We already know he's dangerous."

I changed the subject. "Hear anything from Eleanor's parents?"

"Driving in from Horseheads this afternoon. They're a mess. Can't blame them. First Eleanor calls them, explains that her roommate's dead, then she turns up missing. They didn't sound too thrilled about their daughter hanging out with a private investigator, either. They know she was staying with you, too?" Tommy asked.

"I didn't think so. Maybe Scar told them. She probably did, gave them my phone number or something. She likes to do shocking things, I wouldn't put it past her."

231

Chapter 29

Strong Memorial Hospital was a good distance away from Monroe. The paramedics must have felt confident about keeping Patricia Helms' alive, to risk a drive out to Henrietta. The hospital, besides being one of the best teaching schools in conjunction with the University of Rochester, was noted and often awarded for it's outstanding care units.

The thing about the hospital that drove me crazy was the parking. The front entrance was more than a quarter of a mile away from the closest parking lot. Shuttle buses ran every ten minutes, stopping at small shelters scattered every seven rows. I parked, noted my row by a giant number painted onto a light pole at the end of my row, and walked over to a shelter.

Several people waited for the next bus. It came. I climbed on last, found a seat up front and rode in silence like everyone else. The driver of the bus was a large black woman. She had on a blue uniform, a radio tuned into a country music station. Her fingers tapped the steering wheel while she drove. Her lips moved, singing silently along with Garth Brooks.

She drove past the emergency entrance where an ambulance sat, lights flashing, sirens off. Doctors and the paramedics were at the rear of the van, unloading an injured, or sick, or dying person. My stomach muscles tightened. I hated hospitals. I hated to see people suffer. More than people, I hated to see children suffer. Cancer in children—Leukemia—bothered me the most. I hated to think of kids getting chemotherapy, or spinal taps, or bone marrow transplants.

It might help them, make them better, but the thought of them suffering through painful and nauseating therapies smashed my heart and depressed me. I donated to one kind of charity, limited to those set up to help children.

Last on, first off. I thanked the driver for the safe ride and stepped off the bus. I lit a cigarette and stood with my back to the hospital entrance. The bus pulled away. I looked to the sky. It was still gray, hadn't really cleared since the rain. I missed the sun.

Someone tapped me on the shoulder. It startled me. I spun around, tense, then saw the brass.

"I'm going to have to ask you to smoke that someplace else, sir," the old security guard said. "This area near the front of the hospital is a non-smoking area."

I held up the lit end of my cigarette. "I'm outside."

"Doesn't matter, sir. Hospital owns this land, they don't want you smoking on it. I got to say, it's a little inconsiderate on your part besides. These people are sick. Many of them with cancer, or emphysema, they don't need to see you and your habit. Not to mention the safety issue," the guard said.

"I know, my health—"

"The hell with your health. I mean the people who get out of their rooms and manage to come outside, wheeling a tank of oxygen with them." He pointed to a woman holding the handle of a small green hand truck, a tank of oxygen strapped to the frame. "So put it out, or go smoke down by the main road."

He was very angry. Preaching, really.

I took one long drag off the butt, walked over to the grass, away from everybody, dropped the cigarette, crushed it under my foot, picked it up and dropped it into a Styrofoam cup of liquid sitting on a garbage can. I dropped the cup into the garbage can, gave the guard a smile, figuring I'd just saved myself a lecture on littering.

He returned a genuine smile. How could you not love the Good Samaritan? Bastard.

Just because I hated hospitals, didn't mean I was a stranger to them. I had a large family. Someone was always sick, or hurt, or dying. I spent many nights at this and many of the other Rochester hospitals, hoping, praying and waiting.

At the information counter just inside the lobby, I asked the young girl about Patricia Helms.

"She's still in the emergency room. Only family can see her, though," the girl explained, smiled. "Are you family?"

"Ah, practically," I said. The girl looked confused. Good. I used my hands while I talked. It could only assist in confusing her more. "Her mother, my mother. Then the whole thing with our siblings . . . It goes like that. You understand, of course?"

"Sure. I've got a lady we call aunt. She's not though. We've just known her forever. Do you know where emergency is? She hasn't been moved up to a room yet."

"Yeah, I know where emergency is. So, they will be admitting her?" I said.

"Oh, I don't have that information, sir. The doctor will be able to tell you more." Another big smile. I thanked her and walked away from the counter.

The gift shops were all the same. Same gifts, same blown-out prices. If I'd thought about it, I would have picked Patricia up a little something at a grocery store, or stopped off at the mall. Time was short. Karis was ordering flowers anyway.

I looked at the magazine rack, recognized many of them, had no clue what Patricia might want to look at. I decided she was a writer, grabbed the latest Grisham paperback, a couple of candy bars and paid for the gifts.

The hospital was busy. Visitors, doctors and patients moved up and down the halls. I moved quickly against the wall to avoid having my toes run over by a teenager in a wheelchair. He didn't look sick, just screwing around.

I needed to get to the far east side of the hospital. It took a special kind of talent to follow a mix of signs with arrows, and the ability to maneuver a small maze of hallways to come out in the emergency room. I could do it though, perhaps in my sleep. This fact was not at all comforting. It simply meant I spent too much time in hospitals.

At the large lobby, I knew I'd reached my destination. The waiting room, to the left, was mostly windows with a double wide door-less doorway. The lounge was filled with sofas and chairs and small round tables with untouched magazines on top. One wall was lined with an assortment of vending machines. A television hung from the ceiling showing a soap opera nobody seemed to be watching.

The room was nearly full, nobody was crying. The sound of people talking came out of the room in a low, constant murmur. I walked past the lounge to the emergency room desk. A large nurse in a clean white uniform looked at me, her eyes seemed to ask: *What do you want?* "I'm here to see Patricia Helms?"

"Are you family?"

"Yes." A flat out lie. Word tricks and hand gestures weren't going to get me by this Hun. "How is she? Have her parents been contacted?"

"They're here, in the waiting room."

"Okay. I haven't been in there yet. How's she doing?"

"She'll be all right. The pills she took were as harmful as aspirin. She'd need three times the amount she took to actually risk death. You the one got her to vomit?" The nurse asked me, her eyebrows arched. She knew I wasn't family.

"Yeah. That was me."

"Good thing. Saved her system, her stomach really, a lot of pain."

"I'm going to go and talk with the family for a minute. Anyway I can get in to see her?"

"She's been awake, talking. She's not feeling too good about herself. Pretty depressed. She won't talk about why, but they rarely do. Our staff psychiatrist is in there with her now, actually. After they talk, we'll decide if she's going to be admitted to our psyche ward. It's tough seeing kids try to throw it all away. I know life is hard for them now, but it gets better." There was no conviction in the woman's words.

"Does it?" I walked away and into the lounge. At the Pepsi machine I bought a Dr. Pepper. No one was watching me as I turned and opened the can. Taking a sip, I scanned the faces of the people around me. I was looking for a husband and wife who resembled Patricia Helms.

I thought I saw them. They sat together, held hands, silent, both staring at the wall. "Mr. and Mrs. Helms?"

They didn't look at me. From behind Mr. and Mrs. Helms, a man's voice said, "I'm Mr. Helms."

I turned. He was a good looking, young man. His hair was dark, parted down the middle, up over the ears. His blue eyes looked deeper and darker under thick eyebrows. His nose was short, rounded at the tip. His chin, strong, was marked with an uncentered cleft. He stood up, wiped his hands down the thigh of his dark dress slacks. He wore a white dress shirt, a plain black tie, dress pants and loafers.

We shook hands. "I'm Nicholas Tartaglia."

"I'm Alex Helms," Patricia's father said. "You know my daughter?"

"Yes," I said, motioned for us to sit down.

"What's going on? How do you know her? I mean, do you know what's happening? I'm at work and I get this phone call. It's the police and they tell me my baby's in the hospital. They tell me she tried to kill herself, you know? And I don't believe them. She's got everything in the world going for her, right? You know her. She's only a job away from receiving a Pulitzer in journalism. I tell the police this. They listen to me, don't say a word, then when I'm done they ask me to come down to the hospital again. So I say why, and they insist on telling me that Patricia tried to kill herself." He takes a deep breath and swallows. "I get here, I see her and dammit, the police are right. I want to yell at her, you know?" Alex starts crying now. He's sucking in deep breaths to control the sobs while he talks to me. "But she's just in this bed that looks too damn big for her, and she's in this ugly white and blue

235

flowered gown and her hair's not done and her lips look so pale. I just go to her bedside, I grab her hand and before I can say anything, she says to me, she says, *I love you, daddy*."

Alex hides his face behind his palms. "Why would she do this? Do you know?"

"I might," I said. "Would you like to take a walk?" People are watching us. No one is staring, but they're watching. It shouldn't make me uncomfortable, but it does. Alex and I are like a television set, we're keeping the others in the lounge from thinking about their own loved ones suffering in the ER.

As we passed by the front desk, I nod to Atilla the Nurse. "We'll just be outside if you need us."

She gives me a wink.

Outside, the sky has finally managed to let the sun shine through. The gray has relinquished its hold and blue skies cap the city. There is no ambulance in the drive, still we walk over to the lawn where a park bench has been set under a maple tree. We both sit.

"You mind if I smoke?" Alex said, pulled a pack of cigarettes out of his pants pocket.

"Not if you don't mind me smoking," I said, pulled out my own. We both lit up and took long satisfying drags. Held the smoke, counted to ten, exhaled. "So how is she?"

"She's doing fine, actually. Someone made her throw up, found her in the bathroom in her dorm."

"That was me."

"You? Then I have to thank you for saving my daughter's life," Alex said. He shook my hand again. He looked at me funny. I could tell he wanted to ask me again how I knew his daughter, but didn't want to insult me. Perhaps he thought our relationship was sexual.

"I'm a private investigator," I said, handed him one of my business cards from Safehouse. I was going to have to have new cards made up as soon as I came up with a catchy name for the business. (I could always give Karis that job, she was the writer, the creative one).

"A PI?"

"There's a lot to tell you and not very much time. A lot of this story you might not want to hear, you might even find unbelievable, but I'm not going to lie to you," I said. Inside the hospital I'd debated telling Mr. Helms the truth, the whole truth and nothing but the truth, as I understood it. He had a right to know. "But I'll need your permission to speak with your daughter.

They won't let me in to see her. I'm not family. All right?"

"Let's hear what you have to say before I agree. Fair enough?" He sounded like a businessman now. Wheeling. Dealing.

I started at the beginning, skipping only the supernatural parts with Darla. He didn't need to hear about my client. It would discredit me. Alex might think I'm not the sharpest knife in the drawer.

When I was done, we both sat and stared at an ambulance as it's sirens filled the air and the vehicle sped up to the front emergency room doors. The doors swooshed open. A team of doctors and nurses rushed out. The paramedics opened the back doors of the van.

Déjà vu.

I lit another cigarette, turned away from the scene. I hated hospitals. "So what do you say, Alex? Can I speak with your daughter?"

"Of course. I don't know what else to say, I don't know what to make out of all of this. If Patricia's mother were alive—oh, I don't know if that would make things any easier. It might. She died when Patricia was young, seven. Breast cancer."

"That must have been hard."

"It was. For both of us. She looks just like her mother, too."

"Then your wife was a beautiful woman."

Alex stared at me, smiled. "Thank you. I'm just confused. I mean, what do I do now? What's my next step with Patricia?"

"Maybe the doctors who talk with her will have some ideas. You probably shouldn't let her know everything we just talked about, not until she's ready to tell you. As long as you know it though, passing it on to her doctors in confidence might give them a little direction during therapy sessions," I suggested.

"You think, do you think everything will work out?" Alex stood up.

"I know that Patricia is a smart, strong girl. Personally, I think it's going to take time, but I think she'll pull through." We waited for the ambulance to pull away before we walked back into the emergency room.

Alex told the large nurse that I could see his daughter. She looked at me, her look softened. "As soon as she's done speaking with the psychiatrist, if she's not too tired, all right?"

I thanked her, led Alex back into the waiting lounge. I bought him a Diet Pepsi. We waited together. When Patricia was done with the doctors, Alex went in first to see her. He stayed in there for roughly an hour. When he came out, he looked older. The brims of his eyelids were red, swollen. "You can go in and see her," he told me. "She wants to see you."

237

I thanked him again, told him I wouldn't take too long.

Patricia's bed was in a room walled by curtains. She looked like a child in the large bed. Small. Young. Frail. Her eyes were open and she smiled a small smile when I'd knocked on the curtain and asked if she was decent.

"How are you feeling?" There was no equipment in the room with her; no IV needle in her arm. At this point they couldn't trust her. I stood beside her. She reached for my hand. Her lips and chin were stained dark, like she'd been eating black licorice. The doctors must have given her charcoal to eat. It was often given to victims who used pills to try and commit the selfish act.

"I don't even know you," she said when I took her hand. She gave mine a squeeze. She felt warm. I wondered if she had a fever. Did the nurses know she was warm? "I feel like I do though, like we've been friends for a million years. Isn't that funny?"

"Ha, ha, ha."

"I'm serious," she said. "I knew you were coming to see me the other day, I knew what about, pretty much anyway. I wanted to talk, Nick. I needed to tell someone everything that was going on. I knew I was in too deep, that I couldn't get out. My God, I was scared for my life."

"Did they tell you to try to kill yourself?" The question was blunt, forward. There was no other way to ask it. I needed to know exactly what I was dealing with. The evil power of the cult was strong, manipulative. They had told Maryjean D'Amonda to kill herself, and she had. I needed to know if they had told Patricia the same thing. I knew I was involved with a copycat Helter Skelter cult, a cloned Charlie Manson type.

"No. They would have. They didn't, but I know they would have."

"So why?"

"Because I saw no other way out, Nick. What were my options?" She was crying, used her wrists to cover her eyes, her hands were tightly balled into fists.

I touched her shoulder, left my fingers there. "The same as they are now."

She was still crying, but lowered her arms. She bit her upper lip. "What?"

"Tell me who they are, where they meet. Scar's in serious trouble. You know how dangerous the Tenth House is. Don't let them sacrifice her, Patricia. You might be the only person who can tell me where to find Scar. I need your help," I said. I felt a tightening in my own chest, like I might cry. My own situation was feeling, for the first time, hopeful.

Patricia closed her eyes.

"Patricia, please. Help me."

She opened her eyes, wiped her tears, took a deep breath. "Okay, I don't know who the high priest is—that's the truth. I've never seen his face. He wears a hooded robe. But I can tell you where they meet. I can do that, is that enough?"

I didn't trust myself to speak. I nodded.

Patricia Helms told me where the Tenth House met. "Thank you." I kissed her on the forehead, squeezed her shoulder. Bingo! Now I had the son of a bitch and I'll be damned if I didn't immediately begin to think of the best way I might kill him. "I hate to sound corny, but this means a lot to me. I know how hard it must be for you, trying to deal with all of this, but I'll help you with anything you need help with. Okay?"

"Nick. They meet tonight, at midnight."

"Tonight? How many of them are there?" I asked.

"Roughly? Maybe thirty," Patricia said. She looked tired. I could tell she wanted to sleep. Her night had been long, her day, longer. Her mind wanted to shut down and just take a vacation. Things were going to get tougher for Patricia before they got any better, the mind knew this, wanted to rest while it could.

"Patricia, how many in the cult are men?" I needed to know what I might be up against. A cult full of stoned women and I might get out of there all right. A room full of high men, and my life might be drastically changed for the worse.

"Most of them are men. Twenty, maybe, a few less, I'd guess. There aren't many girls." Her eyelids fluttered. She was going to fall asleep. I didn't have any other questions at the moment and it was a good thing, she wouldn't have been able to answer them anyway. She fell asleep.

Chapter 30

Just because I felt angry and anxious didn't mean I was suddenly foolish. I knew I would need a plan. I couldn't just go and kill Father Paul and rescue Scar. It couldn't be that simple. I needed to act fast, though. If the threat made to me on the phone held any truth, then Scar was in danger. He promised to start torturing her if I continued on with my investigation. I had to assume that the cult members were beginning to realize that I was close to finding them. They might be ready for me. I needed to be ready for them, as well.

I didn't want anything to happen to her.

I drove to Karis' house. We needed to touch base. She threw on a pot of coffee and we started talking. "It's like the splatter method I sometimes use when I write," she explained. "I know where I need to get in a story, so I write that fact down in the center of a sheet of paper. Then I just start jotting things down around that center fact, whatever I think of, relevant or not. I take the paper and start going through all the words I'd written and group them, crossing out whatever I don't want, then make an outline. It lessens the pain needed to write a complete article."

"Okay," I said. "Now we know where they meet."

"That helps," Karis said. "So it'll be safe to assume that he has Scar there."

"Sure. Why keep her anyplace else?" I held my coffee cup with both hands.

"Should you call the police?"

"I don't know. Maybe. I guess I should, but I don't think I'm going to," I said.

"Why?"

"They might not want to do things my way."

"What are you saying?" Karis said.

"I'm sorry, but I have to do what needs to be done. The police won't go for that. A licensed private investigator has rules, laws that he needs to follow just like the police. The only difference is, I don't care. This is solo. A police officer has to worry about reporting things to a boss. I am the boss. If I kill the bastard, it's because he has it coming to him. A police officer wouldn't do that." I said.

"I'm not saying I don't want the guy dead, Nick, because God knows I do. I just don't know if acting out like a vigilante is the best way to—"

"Bring justice? Sure it is. What if we get this guy, have him arrested and he's not convicted? There's a chance that could happen. A strong chance, Karis. The system fails society all the time. Defense lawyers find loop holes and if there aren't any loopholes, guess what? They make them. Happens all the time. In many cases it seems like the courts give more rights to the person being prosecuted than to the victims. The guilty walk free, Karis. If he walks, we'll never get a second chance at doing what needs to be done. Do you understand what I'm saying?" The anger in me was hot. I had talked with this man twice, both times he'd fooled me. I considered him a sick, demented man. I was reduced to one line of thought: *The world will be better off without him.*

I lit a cigarette, grabbed the ashtray off the counter by the sink. I leaned against the counter. "If you don't want to be a part of this—"

"That's not what I'm saying. I mean, just yesterday we didn't know who it was, so it was easy to think things through differently. Now that we know, it's weird."

Closure. Sometimes, looking for answers is all we have to live for. Maybe Karis doesn't want to find answers. It will end her drive. "I'm going after him, Karis. I may not kill, but if he gives me any reason, I will."

She stood up from the table, walked over to me, wrapped her arms around my waist. "I'm with you, Nick. We can do this together."

The first part of the plan was simple. We needed to find Father Paul. It would be best if the priest was alone when we found him. I would use as much force as necessary to question, and I promised Karis that he would give us answers. I had a pretty good idea where they were keeping Scar, thanks to Patricia's help. Still, I wanted that information confirmed by Father Paul.

The main priority was rescuing Scar. Once I had her and she was safe, I would take care of the priest. If I had my way, I'd send him to meet his master. I'd then pray that, while his spirit leaves his body, he gets a pitch fork up his ass.

"You call the church," I said to Karis.

241

"You want to go after him now? Today?"

"Why should we wait? They meet tonight, Patricia told me that." I had my mind made up. She needed me. I wasn't about to let her down. "We have to get to Scar as soon as possible. This man's crazy. He plans on hurting her."

"Okay. What do we do first?"

Karis picked up the phone and called the St. Anthony's rectory. She chewed on the skin around her thumbnail, her eyes darted back and forth, as if looking at everything around the room. She didn't look at me while she waited for someone to answer. I stared intently at her. She looked beautiful.

"Ah, yes, hello," Karis said. "I was hoping to speak with Father Paul?"

I leaned in closer. I desperately wanted to hear both sides of the conversation, but could only hear the things Karis said.

"He's not, huh? He hasn't been? All right. No. That's okay, no message. Do you know when he might be back? No? No, I'll just try calling tomorrow. Thank you," Karis said. She hung up.

"Well?"

"He had to go to the hospital, visit a sick person from the parish. He hasn't been back. They don't know when to expect him. I just said I'd call again tomorrow." Karis explained.

"A sick person in the hospital, huh? Patricia?"

"That's who I was thinking," Karis said.

"She could be in danger." We could have called the hospital, told them to keep an extra careful eye on Patricia, not let any priests in to see her, but they'd think we were crazy, would ignore the warning. "You call the hospital, find out how she's doing. I'm going back there. I'm going to talk with some of the doctors and nurses, and if Alex—her father—is still around, I'm going to give him an extreme warning."

"Go, Nick, go. Don't waste time telling me what you're going to do!" She had the phone book out, was flipping through the pages. "I'll call right now."

When I arrived at the hospital, I parked near the Emergency entrance. I ran in and up to the counter. A different shift of nurses staffed the area. One nurse looked up at me from her computer terminal, after a moment she stopped typing, cocked her head. "I'm here to see Patricia Helms?"

"She was just moved to a different wing, sir, not more than twenty minutes ago."

A different wing, the nurse had said, not up to a room. The psycheward. "Okay. How do I get to see her?"

"I'm not sure, sir."

"Can you tell me how I can get to the psychiatric wing?" I said. The nurse understood *then* that I was aware of Patricia's situation. She gave me a warm smile along with an easy set of directions.

The psychiatric ward seemed like a different entity set off from the rest of the hospital; the carpeting more plush, the walls freshly painted and decorated with modern surreal art, the nurses' station was behind a mahogany counter, under track lighting. Plants stood in all corners of the room. Music softly played from speakers I could not see. The sofas, provided for those who arrived early, were black leather. The coffee table had an array of current magazines on its face. Impressed? Completely.

In my head, a dull throb began. The beginning stages of an all out major headache were in the works.

"Can I help you, sir?" A young man sat behind the counter. He didn't appear to be working on anything.

"I need to speak with Patricia Helms and her doctor. It's rather urgent," I said.

"You must be Nicholas Tartaglia? Is that how you pronounce it?" he said.

"Yes. How did you know?"

"A woman just called—"

"And?"

"And she explained about a crazy priest—"

"That's how she put it?"

"No. Just paraphrasing, here. She said that a priest might be coming to see Patricia, Father Paul? And that we shouldn't let him near, that he might be a very dangerous man and extremely upset with our patient." He smiled.

"Exactly."

"No worry, then," the male nurse said. He wasn't wearing a nametag. This annoyed me.

"Why is that?"

"Only her father has been with her. She was just given a room five minutes ago."

"But she was brought up to this wing more than twenty minutes ago," I said.

243

"What can I say? This place has inefficiencies."

"I'd like to talk with Patricia's father and doctor, then. Please hurry," I urged the unmoving man

"Other lives to save?" He was mocking me, perhaps wondering if I should be a patient under his care. I wanted to smack the condescending smile off his face.

"Move it," I said fiercely, and he did.

Alex Helms turned a corner and walked up to me. We shook hands. "What's this about, Nick?"

"I'm afraid your daughter might be in trouble."

"Trouble?"

I told him what was going on, explaining the situation with Father Paul. "When we called the rectory, we were told he'd come to the hospital. They didn't know when he'd be back."

"I can tell you this, no one, except my brothers and sisters, have come to see Patricia. I must say, if a priest showed up . . ."

"You would have let him in. I know. That's why I came down here. I knew you needed to hear the warning from me, not just second hand," I said.

"I appreciate your efforts."

I glanced at my watch. "I have to go. Please pass this on to the doctor. Stress the fact that you don't want anyone, understand, no one, to get in to see your daughter. Make sure each shift of nurses and doctors knows this."

"I will be careful. I promise. But what about the police? What are they doing right now? You've called them, right?" He looked so concerned. He was terribly worried about his daughter's physical and mental health.

"I'm working with homicide. I—we—hope to have this situation cleared up right away." I had not called Tommy back. He didn't know everything, wasn't up to speed. Karis and I had discussed it. I saw no reason to pull Alex into the middle of the conversation. If I had to give a WAG, I'd say that Alex looked like the kind of man who would want justice served my way.

"Let me know what happens."

"You've got my word."

I left, back through the hallways, out to my car. I thought I'd have a ticket on my windshield, for parking in the emergency parking lot. There wasn't. I was relieved. Those bad boys were starting to add up for me. I didn't want to have a warrant out for my arrest due to unpaid parking tickets.

Chapter 31

I drove out to Monroe after leaving the hospital. Karis would be waiting for me, but I needed to pass by St. Anthony's first. Father Paul could be any-where, doing anything. What he told the secretary at the rectory did not make his word gospel.

Traffic seemed more congested. I caught every red light. The day was losing its battle. Evening was beginning to take the lead. I wasn't ready for the night. There was too much to do. I wanted to have Scar out of the cult's clutches before dark.

There was no room for error. The plan should be simple. I know where they meet. I should be able to just go in, get her and get out.

Yeah. It's that simple!

Driving past the church, I parked on the curb, just a hundred yards down the road. There had been no cars parked in the front of the church. I knew that didn't mean anything that the garage was around back, behind the rec-tory. I called Karis on the cellular phone. It rang four times before she answered. "Karis, he wasn't at the hospital. Well, he might have been, but he didn't go see Patricia."

"I sent her those flowers."

"Thanks. Hear anything?"

"No, and I don't like any of this. Nick, I think we should call the police. I really don't think we should be trying to save this girl on our own. What if something happens? What if everything goes wrong?" Karis sounded scared and upset.

"What time have you got?"

"Four-thirty, why?"

"I'll meet you at your place in a little while. I need to take care of something."

"What are you going to do?" she said. "Nick?"

I didn't want to lie. At this point, Karis sounded close to snapping. She didn't need to worry about me, too. There were no comforting words to say, so I just hung up, turned my phone off and locked it in the glove compartment.

I got out of the car, slapped at my side, felt the comfort of my gun. Wearing it all day, sometimes you forget it's there. (My father used to run around the house looking for his glasses. He was wearing them. It was too funny, no one would tell him where they were.)

The sun was playing peek-a-boo with me, slipping in and out from behind clouds every few seconds. The wind picked up, though it wasn't cold, and lifted the back of my sport coat while I walked. I smelled someone cooking a steak on a grill. My stomach growled.

Acting like I belonged, I strolled across the church parking lot, hands at my side. The rectory was dark. Perhaps the secretary was sent home early on Tenth House meeting nights. It would make sense, unless she was a part of that group, too.

In back of the rectory, the garage door was open. No car in there. What Father Paul had been working on in the garage the other day had piqued my curiosity. Perhaps the arts and crafts piece was still in there?

Walking in to take a look around, I had the odd sensation of being watched. I spun around ready for confrontation. I was alone.

The garage was meticulous. Tools hung on a peg-board wall, ladders, garden hoses, and workbenches. There was nothing to tell me what Father Paul had been working on, though I did smell paint. The A-frame loft had a lawn spreader, a store bought carton of tulip bulbs and some lawn chairs.

Under one of the workbenches I saw a cardboard box with a fitted top. I knelt and reached for the box. It was heavy, scratched across the floor as I dragged it closer. Lifting the lid, I saw it was filled with paper.

Before I could look at any of the paper, I heard a car. I covered the box, slid it back under the bench, stood up, grabbed the crossing beam of the A frame, hoisted myself up and into the loft. I lay on my belly and watched as Father Paul's car pulled up the driveway and into the garage. "Oh just . . . this is just great," I mumbled.

Farther Paul opened his door. The bastard was whistling. The tune didn't sound familiar; it had a gospel beat. It was probably a hymn sung in Sunday's mass. He must have pushed a button, or pulled a lever because his trunk popped open. He got out of the car, locked the doors and closed them. From the trunk he removed a few grocery store plastic bags, holding them by the handle in one hand. He left the garage. I waited where I was for a few more moments, making sure he didn't come back for another package.

In a way, having the good father come home, was better than not knowing where he was. There were two choices available to me now, well, three really. I could get down from the loft, go back to my car and head to Karis' house. Or I could get down from the loft, go to the rectory door, sucker punch Father Paul and tie him up. I could then head to the subbasement in the church and free Scar. I guess I could get down from the loft, go directly to the church's subbasement, free Scar and get the hell out of there before anyone knew anyone was the wiser. Decisions, decisions.

Of those three options, only one thing was common across the board. Get down from the loft. So I did that, first.

If I went directly to the church, Father Paul might see me or someone else might see me and call Father Paul. That sounded dangerous. Getting caught wouldn't help Scar and wouldn't be too healthy for yours truly either.

Father Paul was a variable. I needed to deal with him next.

After leaving the garage I went to the front of the rectory, I rang the doorbell. I had my hand in my sport coat, held my gun, ready to pull it out of the holster. I looked around, over my shoulder, still feeling eyes on me. The sensation sent a finger of ice to trace my spine. I shivered.

The wood door opened. Father Paul smiled, looked genuinely happy to see me, pushed open the screen door. "Nick, how are you?"

"Hey," I said. "You eat at the Dragon Wokery today?"

His eyes gleamed, cocking his head. "Why, yes, I did?"

His eyes lowered and saw the gun I'd drawn. His smile thinned, transformed into a grimace. "Nick, I don't . . . what's going on?"

"Give it up, Padre. I know all about you. You sadistic pig!" I backed him up with the barrel of the gun waving. "Get inside."

I closed and locked the door with one hand, the other kept the gun trained on Father Paul's belly.

"Nick—"

"Shut up. I know where she is. I'm going to get her."

"Scar?"

I didn't answer him. It was a stupid question. It was the end of the game. I wanted him to drop the charade. He wouldn't. "I'm sorry this will spoil you're meeting today. You didn't think I'd figure it all out, huh? You left way to many clues."

"Clues? Nick, for Heaven's sake," he pleaded, holding his hands up, palms facing me. I'd backed him into a small family room. There was no television set. Two sofas, one recliner. I told him to sit down. He sat on the recliner. "Nick—"

"There were only three people who knew about Darla hiring me. Darla's mother, Scar and you." Heavy emphasis on *you*. It came out in a sneer.

"Someone called my boss at Safehouse Investigations, told him a ghost was my client. Why would Darla's mother do that? She wouldn't. Scar might have, but now that she's been kidnapped, that scenario doesn't make sense.

"Then when I got your phone call—"

"Phone call? Nick—"

"Just listen, Father. This story has a couple of twists. I don't want you to get lost." I pulled the shades closed and sat on the sofa across from the shaking priest. Fear showed in his eyes. The man was terrified. I'd be lying if I told you I wasn't enjoying my job right now. I was enjoying the hell out of it. "You called me from the Chinese restaurant," I said, regaining my hold on the story.

"I did not."

"Yes. You did. I had the call traced, talked with people at the phone company and with the host at the Dragon. There's really no lying your way out of this. I'm not the only one who knows the truth," I said.

"You have your truth wrong. All wrong!"

I stood up. "I'm done with games."

"What are you going to do?" Father Paul asked.

I leveled the barrel of the gun, aiming it at his head. One shot. Clean. Crisp. I closed one eye. My finger slipped inside the trigger guard, my thumb switched off the safety. I heard my own labored breathing. My heart pounded in my ears. I watched Father close his eyes tightly, pray in loud whispers. The end had come. I've won.

"Dammit," I said. I couldn't shoot him. Quickly, I moved to stand beside him. Held the gun by the barrel, knocked the priest out with a whack on the back of the neck. His chin fell, bringing the head with it, rested on the man's chest.

He was still breathing.

I found twine in a junk drawer in a small kitchen. I tied the priest to the back of recliner. Tied his wrists together and his ankles. I left the rectory, confident that Father Paul would no longer pose as a threat. I looked at the time. Six-thirty.

Across the parking lot I began to wonder if the church doors might be locked? Should I have looked for a set of keys? It was too late now. I needed to keep moving forward. There was no time to turn back. The climax was coming. I could feel it. The anticipation and anxiety was driving me crazy. Adrenaline pumped my body.

I entered the heavy wooden doors of the sanctuary and fell to my knees as something blunt and solid slammed into the back of my head. As I dropped onto all fours, I thought the church was collapsing. Another whack, same spot, worse pain, knocked my lights out.

Chapter 32

Somebody set off a bomb. The explosion was taking place in the back of my head causing a chain reaction, blowing away brain cells, starting brain tissue ablaze. I felt the heat, the after shock, the constant breakdown and heard the vicious rumbling.

I realized my eyes were open, blinding light the cause. I closed my eyes, careful not to squeeze them shut. The pain subsided some. Slowly, I opened them again. There was still pain, discomfort, small bombs exploding, but not nearly as bad as it had been when my eyes first opened.

Though I couldn't see yet, I had a pretty good idea where I was. The church's sub-basement. In the sanctuary of the Tenth House. A prisoner, though. I would be no help to Scar.

Without much effort, I realized the desperation of the situation. My arms and legs, outstretched, were bound tightly with straps to a flat surface. I was in an upright position. I felt like the girl in a carnival on the spinning wheel. Any minute now a blindfolded knife thrower would emerge from behind curtains and the audience would wildly applaud.

When I could, I opened my eyes all the way and let the light in. After a moment my eyes adjusted, along with my head. The pain was there, but more like a steady throb now.

The room blurred, came into focus, blurred, then focused and stayed focused.

I looked out over a church, lit by candlelight. Shadows danced, coming alive. The dark wood pews lined in two rows, went six deep. The walls were cinderblock, cracked, wet and moldy.

"Nick," a whisper came from somewhere to my left. Desperate.

"Scar?"

"Nick, my God, I thought you were dead. I thought he'd killed you." Scar sounded okay. Scared, worried about me, but okay.

"How are you? Have they hurt you?"

"No. No, not yet. He promised that tonight he would. He is going to tape your eyes open and spin you on that thing. He wants you to watch them skin me." She was crying. I could hear the fear in her voice. I felt it myself, for both of us.

"It's not going to happen," I said. It was a stupid lie. It was meant to be comforting. Wasn't. Scar didn't tell me to shut up, or ask me if I was crazy. She said nothing, ignored my feigned confidence. I had to persist. "We're going to get out of here."

I was naked, I realized suddenly, and felt very vulnerable and degrading because of it. I couldn't see Scar. I imagined that she might be naked, too. "How long have I been down here?"

"A couple of hours? I don't know. I've been here so long, I have no concept of time. I don't know if it's daytime, nighttime, nothing. They come, in their stupid robes, free my arms and legs and lead me to a bathroom twice a day. Then they tie me back up on this altar," she said. I wouldn't be surprised if it scarred her for life. Years and years of therapy were in Scar's future—granting the fact that we did get out of this alive.

"What about eating?"

"They've fed me. Never much, just enough to sustain me. I'm so tired, weak. Nick, I don't want to die. I'm so afraid to die this way." She never stopped crying, but now she was sobbing, unable to control her emotion. She was nearing a breaking point. Her sanity was on a thin string. That string, I guessed, was shredding. If she snapped, it would be over for her, mentally.

I couldn't let that happen. I struggled against the straps, tried to kick my legs, move my arms. The straps only seemed to tighten their hold, cut circulation. I felt the throb in my head reach out to continue its beat in my wrists and ankles. "Okay, there has to be another way."

"What? There isn't."

I heard it then. The soft murmur of what might be a chant.

"Ah God, they're coming," Scar cried. "They're going to skin me. Nick, don't let them hurt me. Please. Please, Nick, don't let them hurt me."

"They won't. They can't, Scar. I won't let them," I said. What could I do to stop them? What did the high priest have in mind for me after he sliced up Scar, might I dare wonder? "Scar, you said I wasn't out long. If they're coming, it must be midnight."

"I told you, I have no concept of time." An apology.

A door at the back of the room opened, only one figure in a maroon colored robe entered, his face hidden under a hood. It had to be Father Paul. "Let us go. This is crazy. Let Scar go," I said. "You got me. I've got to be worth more to you than her. I'm your true adversary—you'll get more pleasure out of killing me. Let her go."

251

"A clever adversary, I'll say. Of course," he said, paused. I knew something was wrong. I'd made a mistake. "Of course, you're still in the dark as to who I am."

It's not Father Paul. That's not Father Paul standing there in the red robe. Who is it? It didn't sound a thing like Granatta. Could it be a professor?

"Have I met you? Do I know you?"

"You've seen me. Never really met me." He lifted the hood. "I can do this now, before the others arrive. The two of you are as good as dead."

I knew the face, a fleeting memory. Who was he, though? Fifty, maybe older, gray hair. The voice was familiar, but didn't help. And like a hammer, it hit me. Not the high priest's name, but where I knew him from.

He came forward, took my testicles in his hand and squeezed them. The grip couldn't be any tighter than a vise could grip. My breath caught in my lungs, my chest muscles tightened. Pain rippled in my belly. He ground them in his palm. I thought I might pass out. Could they break? I suddenly wondered. Crack?

"You don't know me?" he asked, disappointed. He let go. I began to cough. I couldn't breathe. I needed to roll myself into a ball, having my ankles and wrists tied, prevented me from finding any comfort.

"You're the handy man here at the church," I managed between coughs. "Zach."

He punched me in the gut. I thought I felt his fist hit the table behind me, the punch was that powerful. Oxygen rushed out of my lungs before getting the chance to spread air to the rest of my body. I thought I might throw up.

"I prefer Zachery."

"I won't forget, believe me," I said. My eyes were watering. Hot tears rolled down my cheeks.

Zachery grabbed the wheel I was mounted to and angled me differently in the room. I was now able to see Scar, she could see me. We exchanged looks, eyes locked, fear evident in her expressions, probably in mine, too. She was naked, spread eagle, arms outstretched on the table, bound by leather straps similar to my own. (Did Darla get Kenny's birthday gift from Zachery? He sure seemed to have bondage paraphernalia in excess, didn't he?)

"You went to lunch with Father Paul. You called me from the Chinese restaurant?" I said. The pieces, despite my pain, discomfort and suffering, all fell together now. The puzzle was complete.

"That's right. You are a tough man to shake. You don't know how delighted I was to see you snooping around the garage this evening. I had you, I knew. You'd come into the church looking for Scar. It was the way I planned it." He smiled a tooth-filled grin.

I wanted to break all his teeth. "You were listening that first night I came around and talked with Father Paul. You called Baxter at Safehouse, told him a ghost had hired me? Didn't you?"

"I still find that whole supernatural crap hard to believe, but yes. I was listening, practically followed the two of you down the back hall to Paul's office," he said. He called the priest, Paul.

I thought about what he said, finding the whole supernatural crap hard to believe and almost laughed. He worshipped the devil. What could he find hard to believe about the supernatural, then? I didn't ask him. My testicles couldn't handle the answer.

"The two of you sounded so pathetic in there, exchanging ghost stories over lemonade. I had to hold my stomach and cover my mouth and pray to Satan you wouldn't hear me laughing at you."

He regarded me, then seemed to regard his thoughts, let out a laugh in one quick, harsh blast. "Darla really came to you, hired you to find out who killed her?" Zachery was interested. I had a link to the hereafter. He didn't. Was he jealous? It sounded that way.

"Not to find out who killed her, but to stop her killer from murdering anyone else."

"I see. Darla was my first human sacrifice you know? I started small. The church was small. We did animals, mostly. Lots of them. The police don't launch an investigation over missing wild animals. We always ate the beast after. Bones are bones. We'd toss them. But, like anything, the sacrifice of animals didn't pacify us anymore. We needed something else, something greater. Darla was our first. She was our virgin, though hardly was she one herself." He chuckled, clearly amusing himself. He was trying to insult me. It was working. His casual retelling of hideous crimes and unusual punishment appalled me.

I needed a plan. This man didn't care about life, probably not even his own. He planned to kill Scar and me. I had no doubt in my mind he would try. "Zachery," I said. "You should let us go. The police *will* come for you. I've been working with them on this, you know? Scar, me . . . we're more than animals, Zach. It'd be hard to explain our disappearances. It's not a threat, the police will come."

"They may. I'm not afraid to die, or of going to prison. There will be disciples in prison," he said, smiled. The thought excited him. I could see it in his face. His words horrified me.

The dancing candlelight cast moving shadows in the room. I felt like the room had suddenly filled with supernatural shadows, all intent on watching the performance. Was Darla among the shadows? Could she intervene? Why couldn't she free Scar while I entertained Zachery?

He took a knife out of a sheath held on a rope belt tied around his robe. He reached for me with his free hand, grabbed the edge of the table and spun me. The sensation was horrible. I felt parts of me flip and flop, sore as I was, I wanted to scream. My head hurt, forcing the blood in and out of my skull only added to the pain.

I saw Zachery, in an abstract way, reach for the knife and touched the tip to my stomach. My own blood dripped onto my face when I was upside down, falling into my nostrils, onto my eyelids.

The sounds of Scar screaming echoed in my mind. Over and over she screamed. *Close your eyes,* I wanted to tell her. *Don't watch, close your eyes.*

The knife didn't hurt, there was little pain associated with the cutting he did. He wasn't jabbing me, just slicing the skin.

"I think I will kill you first, Nick," Zachery said. "Dispose of you before the others come. They understand what I've been going through. They've all been very helpful. I'm sure they would enjoy seeing you die, but I don't want to over excite them. They have Scar's death to look forward to at the end of the month. I can keep her alive until then, it will be my pleasure in doing so. But to keep both of you alive until Halloween? That sounds ludicrous. And if I can't keep you alive long enough to watch Scar die, then why keep you alive any longer than I have to?"

"Because you've always wanted to achieve a humanitarian award?"

He didn't laugh, but raised his knife instead.

"Wait, wait," I said. "I've got to ask you something. One thing, one question!"

He let me spin, but stopped with the knife, waiting for the question. He had time, I realized. It could not be midnight. Scar was right, maybe I was only out for a little while. Was this good, or bad? At this point, I had no idea. "You said something a little while back, you said this all happened the way you planned. How could you have known I'd come here? As far as you knew, I didn't even know where the cult met?" I said. Then: "Oh . . . oh, my God."

"Would you care to answer your own question?" Zachery said. He took a step back, looking amused. This whole thing was funny to him. He looked so normal, it was driving me crazy.

"Patricia Helms," I said. "She set me up."

"She did."

"The nurse at the hospital told me that for the kind of pills Patricia had taken, she would have needed three bottles full to cause any real damage." I felt so betrayed. This girl had faked a suicide, put her father through hell, all to set me up for death.

Now I had two reasons to live. I needed to save Scar and I needed to speak to Patricia's father. Alex needed to know the truth. His little girl, the devil's concubine.

Zachery stopped me from spinning, raised the blade high over his head. It reflected the candlelight in a dim ray. The shadows of the blade from the light were more prominent. It was time to die. There was no way to get out. I gave one last, futile attempt at freeing my limbs. I wanted to close my eyes, but couldn't. Everything moved in slow motion.

Scar had given up screaming. She cried and sobbed. I heard the sounds of her agony clearly. They were the only sounds I heard, next to my own heartbeat, my own breathing.

Finally, I no longer heard Scar. Zachery sucked in a lot of breath, a gasp. His eyes opened wide, his tongue stuck out of his mouth as if he were dry heaving. He came at me like a falling tree. I was able to close my eyes. Like when he'd been cutting my belly, I felt, miraculously, nothing. No pain. I thought the point would rip through my flesh, the serrated edges would burn as the blade sawed across bone. But no, there was nothing.

I heard Scar crying, again. I opened my eyes. I could not believe what I saw. Father Paul was holding a butcher's knife. Somehow he had freed himself from the chair. But his hands were still tied together. He dropped the blade, his blood covered hands covered his face. He cried into them.

Zachery was far from dead. "*You!*" he said, spitting blood. On weak legs, he stumbled forward at the priest. His shoulders hunched together, a vain attempt at relieving the pain. His hand reached over his shoulders. There was no blade in him, though it must have felt like there was.

Father Paul did not move back as Zachery came at him with the speed of a sloth.

"God forgive me," Father Paul said. "How could it be you, Zachery? How could you be the one?" The turmoil inside the priest was evident. Zachery, a friend, had betrayed him. "You are my Judas."

Zachery seemed deaf to Father Paul's words. Blood was spilling from the hole in his back, the blood red robe looked dark maroon where the blood soaked into the material.

Gathering the strength to stand, Zachery shoved the priest backwards hard enough to send him reeling. Like a crippled, hunched over old man, Zachery turned back to sneer at me. A chill ran down my spine. "This ain't over," he said. He ran forward, full of energy. He was going to escape. The door at the back of the room was open, Zachery ran out it.

"Father, you have to get me down." My words felt stale. As I spoke them, they did not sound real to my ears. My heart was hammering away. "Father Paul," I yelled. The voice was louder, still not real. Maybe because the priest was not reacting to my words, I thought I might not be speaking.

"Father, get Nick down," Scar shouted.

Father Paul stood up. He looked terrible. Blood and tears were on his face, dirt and blood on his hands. He stared at us. "I'm so sorry. I should have known. I should have known what he was up to. All these years. I should have known."

"Father," I said, feeling my old self kicking in again, my body, like a pool, filling with water. "Get me down. I have to catch him. We can't let him get away."

"It felt terrible, stabbing him." He closed his eyes, balled his hands into fists. "How can my God forgive me of that sin! How can I forgive myself!"

I hated seeing him like this. But now was not the time. "Father! Paul! Get me down right now!"

He walked towards me. "It was the worst feeling when the knife actually poked through the skin. The flesh was so much stronger than I would have imagined." Kneeling, his hands loosened the straps on my ankles. "That's good, Father," I said. I moved my legs around, tried to get the blood circulating. "Now my hands, Paul. Get the hands!"

"I felt the blade," Father Paul was still saying, "scrape across bone." He stayed on his knees and buried his face into his palms. His sobs annoyed me at this point.

My feet tapped him. "Please, Father. Let's not let him get away. Please, unfasten my wrists!"

Father Paul stood up. Clumsy fingers worked the leather straps. Once he'd freed my left hand, I kindly pushed him away. I slid down, my feet hit the floor. I loosened the strap on my right wrist. "Clothes," I mumbled. In the back of the room, on a table I saw my things. "Father, free Scar. Okay, get her free," I said. On the way to the back of the room, I picked up the priest's butcher knife. The blood on the handle was warm and sticky. I felt bile work its way up my throat and linger. It was hard to swallow.

I set the knife down, grabbed my pants and jumped into them. Looking back, I saw Father Paul setting Scar free. "Give her my shirt!"

I ran out the back door, two feet out of the subbasement, and stopped. The sudden darkness felt overwhelming. It was complete. I could see nothing. I felt around. The walls—damp, moss covered rocks—were cold. My toes tapped on the floor ahead of each step.

Stairs. I climbed them. Each step I climbed felt like an entire staircase mounted. If there had been light, I would see that I'd maybe only gone up a couple of feet. It was the darkness that left me disoriented.

At the top of the eight stairs I was confronted by a closed door. As quietly as possible I felt around for a doorknob. My hand, acting on reflex, reached behind me, swung back and forth, just in case Zachery was climbing up the stairs after me.

My lungs had a hard time working. I couldn't breathe normally. Fear and anxiety mixed with panic and apprehension. My phobia complete.

The doorknob turned in my hands. I pushed the door open. Expecting to be in the church, I came out of the room quickly.

Stepping into more darkness, I dropped to my knees.

I had just emerged from a subbasement into a basement.

Zachery would have been easy to follow in the light. I was sure a blood trail would lead me right to him. There was just no way to see where the trail might be.

If I'd only thought to grab a candle out of the sub—

I dug my hand into my pocket, grabbed my lighter (the first time I'd ever think how lucky I was to be a smoker, I'm sure). I lit it. The small flame did little to fight the prevailing darkness. However, some of my phobia subsided.

I held the tiny lighter out in front of me. Its heat warmed the little spinning wheel that caused enough friction against the flint to produce the flame. When the flame went out, spinning that hot wheel was going to burn the hell out of my thumb.

The room was full of boxes, holy statues and candles.

At a shelf rack, I grabbed a lavender colored candle, lit the wick. The candlelight lit the room better than the lighter had. I put the lighter away, held the candle out in front of me. Across the room was another staircase.

Shadows danced.

The strange sensation of being watched gripped my nervous system. My body tensed. Spinning around, I saw nothing but animated images cast by the moving flame.

On the ground I saw spots; blood spots.
They led toward the stairs. I followed them. The stairs were wooden.
There were at least ten of them. At the top of the stairs, another closed door
waited for me.

Thrusting the candle first, it fearlessly led me up to the top. I turned
back, quickly, expected again to see Zachery coming at me. He wasn't anywhere to be seen. On the wall, by the door, I saw a light switch, flipped it.
Nothing happened.

"Should have guessed," I mumbled, turned the knob, pushed the door
open. Expecting darkness, I was surprised to see the hundreds of candles lit.
I stood in the doorway, let the door swing all the way opened, and just stared
around the church. The pews were all empty, the windows all pushed open.
Candles were everywhere, a shrine.

I saw him then, in the choir balcony. A dark figure; the devil. His hands
were on the ledge, he seemed to be staring right at me. It was a challenge
that I had no clue how to react to, so I blew out my candle and dropped it.

Coming out of the doorway I walked to the center aisle, stood in front of
the altar. Chills and goosebumps broke out all over my flesh. I imagined a
skeleton-like finger of ice tracing my spine and shuddered.

Spinning around, I saw two young people kneeling, facing me, their
backs to the suspended cross dangling from the ceiling. Looking back to the
balcony, I noticed others with him.

"Holy shit," I whispered.

"Welcome to our mass, Nick." Zachary's voice boomed. He sounded
strong, revitalized, uninjured. "Welcome everyone," he said.

The doors at the east, west and south of the church opened. People came
in. Young and some not so young. They saw me, but did not stare. I could
not help but stare at them. They moved into the pews at the back of the
church. Standing, they faced their leader, the head priest. Not one of them
cast a curious glance back at me. Zachery had them trained well. I counted
maybe twenty-five of them.

One man stayed at each door. Guards. Big guards, I heard my mind
add.

I sensed the movement, without seeing it. Turning to my right, two
figures close together emerged from darkness. I raised the knife.

"Nick, no it's us!" Father Paul said, stepping into the candlelight. Scar
was in my shirt, protectively wrapped in the priest's arms. There was a
moment of silence before Father Paul gasp. "For the love of God."

"Not tonight, Paul," Zachery said. "Tonight, there is no love. Tonight, you can pray to your God all you want, but he won't hear you. He won't be able to help you. But we'll help him. You being such a good man, and all. We'll send your spirit racing up to him in heaven, Paul. Tonight, you get to meet your maker."

Father Paul swallowed hard. His fear nudged at me, I didn't need to accept it. I had enough of my own. I heard Scar trying not to sob, it only made her sobs that much louder. This was crazy. It was crazy, and yet, I could see no way out.

"Look," I said. "We don't want to impose on your religious beliefs. We'll just go and you can carry on in private."

Zachery laughed. He started to chant. He raised his hands shoulder high, palms up.

When he'd finished, the rest of the church responded in chant. They were not speaking English, as best as I could tell. The words had a Latin sound to them, though I spoke no Latin.

"What are we going to do?" Father Paul was right beside me. His hot breath tickled my neck.

"Silence!" Zachery shouted.

There was no way he could have heard father Paul's question. Not over the loud chanting. "We're going to get out, that's what," I whispered back.

Father Paul moved Scar towards me, stepping up onto his altar. He walked with confidence to his pulpit. I watched him as he flipped open his Bible. His fingers moved across the page as a guide for his eyes. He was looking for a quote from a chapter.

"Your words, from your book mean nothing, Paul."

"My words, Zach, may not. But these are not my words, this is not my book. These are God's words, Zach. His book!" Father Paul said. The microphone beside the pulpit was not on. The priest's voice carried clear and loud across the church.

Candles danced with his words. He was reclaiming his temple. Like a priest out of the movie The Exorcist, Father Paul began to read from the Bible. Spittle wet his lips. His arms moved about in the air, his finger pointed to the heavens.

I was impressed.

Scar snuggled in close, I felt her trembling.

Zachery was yelling also, in his foreign language. His disciples chanted, too. They filed out of the pews into the center aisle. The dancing candles sent shadows into a frenzy. The somber looking faces of Zachary's followers made me think of zombies. At the head of the line, Patricia Helms smiled at me. One quick question dashed through my mind, *How in the hell did she get here so quickly?*

"Patricia," I whispered. She smiled at me, as if she could hear me over the infernal chants and Bible passages being screamed out loud.

Zachery was no longer in the balcony. He'd disappeared. "Scar," I said. "You have to snap out of this. I'm going to need your help."

"I'm ready to help," she whispered. "I just can't stop crying."

"You can cry, just be ready to fight." There were twenty-eight of them. If a fight started, we were dead. The odds were against our survival.

Handing Scar the knife, I stepped up onto the altar.

The disciples had started walking toward us, very slowly. Not the men posted at the doors, though. They stayed put.

I blew out a candle on a wrought iron stand. Tried to knock it to the floor so I could use the stand like a bat and swing wildly at the zombie-like people. The candle didn't budge. I grabbed it, slid it off the long sharp shaft it sat on. The shaft kept it from being accidentally knocked off the stand. I loved it.

Now I had a sufficient weapon to at least defend myself with against the members of the Tenth House.

"Where'd he go?" Scar asked.

"I don't know." I couldn't hear him debating Father Paul's reading. "Father, grab something!"

Father Paul must have realized that Zachery was gone, too. He closed his Bible, kissed the leather bound cover, made the sign of the cross and stepped down from the pulpit.

As he blew out the candle, the back of the church burst into flames. A thunderous whoosh. The sound of crackling followed. Sparks and embers shot into the air, floated to the ground and helped spread the fire. Dark velour drapes hung where the confessional booths were. The flames shook and jumped as the fire consumed, as if being blown by a strong wind.

The flame, like fingers, seemed to be holding the balcony. The back door stood open. The guard ran from the fire to stand next to Patricia. She looked up at him, a gleam in her eye. They both turned to look at me and my entourage.

Just when I thought that Zachery had set the fire and escaped. I saw him. He was standing where the guard and Patricia had been. His arms were raised high.

Father Paul slid the candle off his stand, dropped it, picked up the stand and wielded it like a sword. "Nick, let's get the hell out of here!"

"From your mouth to God's ears," Scar said. She dropped her knife, ran onto the altar to a stand, knocked the candle to the floor before blowing out the flame. Fire caught on the carpet, raced to consume all that it could.

The heat in the church intensified. All the windows were open. The oxygen was feeding the fire. It was all a part of Zachary's plan. He was like David Koresch. He wanted us to die with him.

Father Paul had stabbed him, and he was dying. He could not go to the hospital, because he would be arrested. He said in the subbasement that he did not mind going to prison—but I'd bet the thought of going terrified him. He could only die. If he had to die, then he was taking us all with him.

"We have to get out of here," I said. Father Paul stood on my left, Scar to my right. We held the candle stands like swords, like the Three Musketeers. "He plans for all of us to die!"

"It took you that long to realize this," Scar said. Always full of sarcastic remarks!

"I have a way out!" Father Paul said.

The disciples moved slowly, but they were coming. Zachery started to walk faster toward us from the back of the church. They were almost at the altar. We'd all stepped up. Like blind baseball players we spread out, swung at them.

"What are you waiting for," I shouted. I raised my club, knocked one on the shoulder with a full home-run swing. It skidded off him as he fell and slammed into a girl's head. Blood spilled from her eye. I had no choice. They were the ones that made the decision tonight. They were here to kill me.

I caught the sight of Father Paul pulling Scar into the back room. I was alone on the altar, expressionless cult followers ready to pounce. "Wonderful."

In the back of the room, someone caught on fire. Screams more horrible than I ever could have imagined echoed, competed with the sounds of the flames eating the church. Many turned to watch as a burning human ran, mad, until he could run no more. The person fell, withered, continuing to scream.

"Help him," I shouted. "Someone, my God, help him!"

A few people were crying now. I still held my weapon, taking steps backwards.

Zachery stood in back of the group. His hood hid his face. I watched him raise one arm into the air, one finger pointed to the roof. "Get him!"

"No," I screamed, swinging like a mad man as they charged. The stand knocked several people down. The others stepped over them and came at me. I didn't have a chance.

One hand caught my swing, held onto the stand. The others grabbed it, pulling it out of my hands.

I turned and ran. I heard the pounding feet of the others behind me. I imagined the fingertips reaching for me, thought I could feel them. The hall was dark. Afraid I might stumble and fall, I did not dare run as fast as I could, or should. I crashed into an object in the hall, its corner banged my thigh, sent an exploding firecracker of pain up my leg. I grabbed the ottoman, knocked it over behind me. The effect I'd been hoping for. Someone fell. Others had to be tripping over the fallen one.

At last I entered Father Paul's office. I stopped, looked around.

"Nick, come on!" Scar and Father Paul were both shouting. They stood by the door. The outside just behind them. Sanctuary.

As I smiled, someone knocked me to the ground, began to bite my back. Screaming more in surprise than pain, although the biting hurt, I rolled over, threw my elbow into the person's belly. The bite loosened. I scrambled to get away, jumped to my feet. The girl that had bitten me was balled up, holding her belly.

I ran for the door as two more people tried to push their way into the office.

I closed the door behind me.

Running, I plunged into Scar and Father Paul. "Let's go, let's go!"

They were standing still. In front of them, Zachery stood, the butcher's knife Father Paul had stabbed him with was tightly gripped in his bloody hand. "This is where the game ends."

The door I'd closed behind us burst open. The disciples all came out of the priest's office, slowly they began to encircle us.

"Ah man," I mumbled.

"My words exactly," Father Paul said.

Scar stayed quiet as she began turning in a circle. Her eyes were wide with terror. "I want this to end, please, Nick, just make this all end."

Her request did not fall on deaf ears. I just didn't know how to respond.

Father Paul held up his hands. "This has got to stop," the priest shouted. A tremor in his voice betrayed his authority. Behind us windows exploded. The fire roared. Black clouds of smoke rolled into the star lit sky.

In the distance, the fast approaching sound of sirens could be heard.

"Screw this," I said, charging Zachery.

He was ready for me; he swung the knife. My left wrist blocked his forearm. I punched him in the gut with my right fist. My punch seemed to have little effect on him. He was moving his arm wildly, trying to slice me with the blade. His free hand reached for my face, fingertips tried to gouge my eyes. I grabbed his wrist, pulling his hand away from my face.

I felt his knee come up, hit my thigh hard, but he missed my testicles. My foot, hooked behind his knee, kicked back, knocked him off balance. We both fell to the ground. The knife dropped from his hand.

On top of him, I tried to straddle his belly. He was strong, I could feel the muscles in him working. He bucked, knocked me off. I fell near the knife. As my hand reached for it, he punched me in the arm.

His group of followers was singing. My friends must have been watching in silence. If they jumped in, tried to help me, then the others would jump in and kill the three of us, I had no doubt.

Zachery had me down, climbed onto me, used his knees to pin my arms to the ground.

Father Paul had stabbed Zachery in the back, I'd followed the blood in the basement. The man had to be hurting. Where was he getting all his strength?

I kicked up my knee and slammed it into his spine. I bucked my hips at the same time. I was hoping for my knee to connect with the knife wound. Whether I hit it or not, I was able to throw Zachery off.

Rolling over quickly, I was on all fours.

Zachery looked hurt. "Back into the church," he yelled. "Now!"

The sirens were so close. In the distance I could see the spinning lights.

"No," Scar was yelling. "Don't go back in there! Don't. Stop them, please!"

I couldn't take my eyes of Zachery. He would lunge at me if I did. Scar had to be screaming at the cult followers because they were going back into the burning church.

Zach and I were both down like dogs, eyes locked. Then, Zachery got to his feet slowly. The fight was out of him. He looked at the knife for a long minute, then his eyes looked past me. Blood oozed from his mouth, dripped in long strings of drool from his lip. In obvious pain, he started to walk towards the church.

"They're all going back into the church!" I heard Scar say.

Zachery walked confidently, pulled open the door leading to Father Paul's office. He stood in the doorway, looked at me, smiled. "I'll see you in hell, Mr. Tartaglia. All of us will be waiting for you."

"Don't hold your breath," I managed.

Four fire trucks pulled into the parking lot. The riders jumped off the moving vehicles, scrambled to get to the hydrants. Three police cars pulled into the parking lot next, two ambulances.

These people had murdered Darla, killed animals, kidnapped and planned to sacrifice Scar. I hated them. Knowing they were all in the church, waiting for the fire to consume them, began to jab at my conscience. They deserved to die, Zachery did. He was the poison. His disciples were the ones under his spell. Did they deserve to perish, too?

"Send the others out, Zach," I said. "Don't let it end like this." I walked closer to the church. Zachery pulled the door closed. I ran, grabbed the knob, tried to turn it. Locked. I heard people screaming from inside. "Zach!" I pounded the palm of my hand on the door. "Zach, send the people out!" In defeat I turned away from the church.

Scar made a run for the temple. Father Paul restrained her. "We can't save them," he said. I could barely hear him. The sound of the fire burning was deafening. The smell burned my nostrils, burned my throat.

Two firemen ran up to us. "Let's go! Come on. This building may blow up. Let's go."

"There's people in there," I yelled. "Thirty people!" I remembered the one boy who already burned up. "Twenty-nine."

The bell tower crumbled in on the church. Walls collapsed, flames ate away at everything. Soon all that would remain standing would be the skeletal remains of the church.

Father Paul had Scar by the shoulders. He was keeping her from charging the burning church again. I walked up to the both of them. Scar stopped struggling and lowered her head. Shaking, she cried and Father Paul let go of her. She ran to me, hugged me tightly. Father Paul and I stared at each other, turned and walked away while firemen rushed around us, spraying water from large hoses uselessly onto the flames.

"You know," Father Paul said, "perhaps God wanted the church to burn, to cleanse itself of the evil sins committed in that horrid temple."

"I don't doubt that one bit, Father," I said. "Not one bit."

Chapter 33

Father Paul went to the mission room and grabbed clothing for Scar. Her clothes were probably somewhere in the sanctuary, in ashes. The clothes the priest found for Scar didn't fit, two sizes too big, but were clean. Paramedics examined all three of us. I was the most seriously hurt. The cuts and bruises looked bad, but no longer seemed to hurt.

Scar gave me back my shirt. I put it on.

Scar nuzzled in close. I wrapped an arm around her. She was shivering. It was not cold out. I rubbed her shoulder.

"Nick," Father Paul started to say something, but stopped. I had the feeling he needed to tell me something. I wasn't going to force him. God can only forgive his sins. Father Paul must know this, so he has no reason to confess to me. There must be something about clearing the soul, though, to mortals, that makes life more bearable at times. "Nick, I think I always knew the Tenth House met in the subbasement of the church."

He waited for my reaction. I didn't react. "But I swear, Nick, I swear, I never knew Zachery was involved, much less that he was the high priest. Do you believe me?"

"Yes, Father Paul. I do." And I did.

An unmarked white Caprice police car pulled into the parking lot. It was Tommy's car. He got out, stared at us sitting on the back fender of an ambulance. Deanna wasn't with him. I was glad to see him. In the car with him, were a man and woman. I heard Scar say something in a whisper. I looked down at her.

"My mom and dad," she said.

There was no point in lying. I told my brother-in-law the whole truth. It was a long story. We sat on the church steps after the fire had been put out, and smoked. He let me get through the whole story before he asked any questions. When he started with the questions, I thought they might never stop. I've been through many depositions. Getting drilled by my brother-in-law was worse.

He was fuming, I could tell. Perhaps wanted to strike me, but he was also relieved that I hadn't died. My sister would be so pissed at him if I died, whether it was his fault, or not.

We stood up. "Oh," Tommy said, "one more thing."

"Yeah?"

He grabbed my shoulder, pinched my neck muscles between his hand. It hurt. The pain was almost strong enough to drive me to my knees. "Upset, Tommy?"

"The next time you impersonate an officer with the phone company, don't even think about using my name. I'll press charges. I don't care what your sister might think. Do we understand each other?"

I nodded. By this time, between some of the pain returning and coercing its way through my neck, I could no longer talk.

"Good." Tommy finally let go of my neck. He slapped me on the back.

Father Paul was talking with two police officers, giving them a statement, I imagined. There were several ambulances pulling out of the parking lot now. It did not use any siren. They were all dead. Why hurry?

Leaning against Tommy's car, mother, father and Scar held each other. No one seemed to be talking. Scar waved me over. I really didn't feel like talking to anyone, or explaining the story again. I was anxious to see Karis. She had no idea what might be going on. She had to be worried. She was probably sitting on the sofa by the phone debating whether or not to call the police.

"Hey Tommy, you got a cell phone?" He did. I called Karis, told her everything was over, that I'd be home soon and I could fill her in on all the details then. She said she'd have something for us to eat. I told her just make sure there's plenty of beer in the 'fringe, I wanted to get drunk. "I love you," I said. She said she loved me, too.

I gave Tommy back his phone and walked over to meet Scar's family.

As I got closer, I saw that Scar was no longer crying. When I stood in front of the family, Scar started crying again and hugged me. I held her, looked at her parents over her head.

Scar's mother said, "Eleanor has told us so much about you, Mister —"

"Nick," I quickly interjected. "Just call me Nick."

We finished the introductions. Scar seemed to have fallen asleep in my arms.

"I've heard most of the story from Eleanor, but I think I need to hear your version," Scar's father said. The idea came to me then. I hadn't thought of it before. As I retold the story, I imagined it in book form. Just because I wanted to write fiction, didn't mean I couldn't turn this whole ordeal into a best selling non-fiction book, right? Change the names, protect the innocent? The money from an advance could help me get situated in a new office. It was a great idea, suddenly full of inspiration, I couldn't wait to get the story written.

"All I can really say, Nick, is thank you."

"You're welcome," I said. "Sc-Eleanor is quite a girl. When she graduates, she's going to make a fine police woman."

Scar looked up. "Maybe I'll go into the private eye business. Who knows, maybe you'll need a partner."

"You'd be a better partner if you were on the police force. Then I'd have a contact. You'd help me, right? If I needed a favor every now and then?" I asked. I was serious. Having Tommy and Scar in my corner would be great in solving future cases.

"Sure would."

She kissed me. It felt like a kiss from a kid sister. I loved it this way, I think she did, too.

"I'm going home with my family. I think next semester I'll try to get into Ithaca," Scar said. "I don't want to go back to Monroe."

"Can't say I blame you. Ithaca is a fine school."

We hugged good-bye. She was crying. I wasn't sure, but I thought I might have something in my eye, perhaps an eyelash. "I'm counting on you to get in touch with me every once in a while."

"I will, Nick."

Just then an ambulance attendant told me I had to go to the hospital to get checked over. Some of the cuts were deeper that I thought. It was probably a good idea because there were spots that were beginning to hurt. I also thought it would give me a chance to wash some of the blood off me before I saw Karis.

Karis was up and waiting for me.

We sat on her sofa, drank beer and smoked cigarettes. I told Karis the story of what happened from the time I got to the hospital until the time I left the church parking lot. She, like Tommy, listened to the end, then drilled me with questions, concerns and worries. "I was so scared. I didn't know if I

267

should call the police, or what?" She was crying a little. She stood up, then took me by the hand and led me into her bedroom.

The following morning, before going down to the police station fill out an official police report, I found where the Helm's lived and drove there. I had spoken with Patricia's doctor. Apparently sometime during the night, Patricia had left the hospital. Her father had been sound asleep in a chair in her room.

When I knocked on the door, Alex answered. I could tell that he had not slept at all. The police had contacted him already. I had been able to give them Patricia's name during the preliminary statement I gave to an officer last night. She was in the church when it burned down, I had told them.

"Mr. Tartaglia." He tried to smile. It didn't work. "Nick, my God, Patricia ran away. I was right there with her, never left her side. I was so concerned, and it was all a game to her. Nothing more than a game."

"I don't know what to say, but I wanted to come and see you, to offer my condolences. It might not mean anything to you, I don't know. I just, I needed to tell you in person how sorry I am how things turned out."

I thought Alex might hate me, blame me. He hugged me and I was shocked. I hugged him back. "This is so hard," he said. "I don't know what to do, how to feel."

After our hug, he invited me in for a drink. It wasn't even ten in the morning. I had a double scotch on the rocks. It went down smooth. I looked at a photo album of Patricia with Alex. He cried. I listened. By eleven, I'd left, went down to spend the rest of the day helping the police re-open the case on Darla and close the chapter on Zachery and his Tenth House cult.

Chapter 34

A friend of Karis' was a Realtor, Matthew. He was tall, black, nicely dressed in an expensive suit. He drove us around all day on Sunday in his BMW, from one office building to the next.

We were trying to find a place for: *The Tartaglia Agency.*

Like it? Karis came up with it. I was looking for something cute, catchy. She thought simple, direct.

I had to admit, it had a certain ring to it. I liked it.

We started downtown, looking at two room offices and worked our way into the suburbs. Our last stop for the day was in Spenceport. Main Street resembled small towns in the early nineteen hundreds. The brick-faced buildings, the tiny two screen movie theater on the corner, its advertisement sign a two dimensional triangle protruding out over the sidewalk. Green streetlights with lantern tops. A post office, a mini-mart gas station, the telephone company, a hardware store, a grocery store, all in walking distance.

I loved the area, hoped the office Matthew had to show matched the atmosphere.

"Remember," Matthew said. "Location. Location. Location. People are going to feel good about coming to meet with you. Everybody loves this little town."

He parked at the corner of Main and Verona. The movie theater was directly across the street from his car, the mini-mart was kiddy corner. We got out of the car and stood on the sidewalk. I looked at the building behind me. Tan brick. It was an antique store named Reliquus with an eloquently decorated front window. Upstairs, in a smaller window I saw a red sign on white cardboard. Office Space For Rent.

"Go into the antique store." Matthew pulled open the door for us. Inside a small foyer were two doors. One led right into the store, the other had an identical sign to the one I'd seen in the second story window. Matthew used a key, unlocked and opened the door.

We took a flight of stairs up to the second level, using the handrail. We were all tired. We'd been out driving around since nine. It was just after one now. I was ready for something to eat.

There was only one door at the top of stairs, the top half was clear glass.

"Picture it, Nick," Karis said, standing in front of the door. "The Tartaglia Agency, Nicholas Tartaglia, Private Investigator. Maybe an eye for your symbol under all the writing?"

"Corny. The eye. I like the rest though."

Matthew let us discuss decorating the door for a minute, then opened the office door.

"Place hasn't been vacant all that long. Used to belong to a lawyer. Guy moved to Memphis, thought he was John Grisham, or something, wanted to write books. Everyone wants to write a book these days." He laughed.

Karis and I exchanged a knowing smile.

The office was big. All the way to the right was another door. Two other doors in the back diagonal corner. Gumwood trim, gleaming hardwood floors. A ceiling fan with a light fixture. "This was where his secretary sat," he said about the empty room. There was a window on the left wall and one in front, where the sign was. I looked at the windows, and guessed they were new, or close to it. He pointed to the two doors in the corner. "Closet, bathroom," Matthew said.

"Nice," I said. I loved it. *Stay calm.* I could tell from the squeeze Karis gave my hand, that she liked it, too.

"Back here," Matthew said, walking to the back door, his wing tips clicked and clocked on the hardwoods, the sound seemed to boom in the room. He opened the door. "Would be your office, Nick."

I went into the room. It looked very much like the front part of the office, where Karis would work; ceiling fan, light fixture, two windows, gleaming hardwoods, gumwood trim. There was a closet and a bathroom. I ran the water from the sink in the bathroom and flushed the toilet. The water pressure was good, strong.

A beeping sound filled the room. Matthew looked at his pager, a gold chain linking it from his belt to a belt loop. He glanced at the display. "I've got to run back down to the car. I left the phone there. Why don't the two of you look this place over, I'll be back in a minute. If you don't like it, let's get some lunch and press on a little longer. What do you say?"

"Sounds fine," Karis said. I just nodded. My mind was already made up. I wanted this place.

When Matthew was gone, Karis smiled. "You like it, don't you?"

"Love it."

"Me, too. I can't believe we're really doing this."

"I think we should take this one. We've looked at over fifteen places today. I don't think anything else Matthew has up his sleeve will top this one. What about you?"

"Take it."

"I will."

We hugged.

"Mom." A voice said.

Our hug broke. Darla was with us. She was nearly transparent this time. She floated. She looked like she might have been crying. Karis was crying, her fingers uselessly reaching out to touch her daughter. "Darla . . ."

"I love you, Mom. Nick, thank you for everything."

"Forget about it."

"Nick," Darla said, "In the closet, on the floor you'll find what you're looking for."

"Where are you going to go now, I mean, I'll still get to see you, won't I?" Karis asked.

"I'm going someplace better. I won't be allowed to come back," Darla said.

Karis and Darla tried to touch fingertips. Pressed palms together. Though neither could feel the other, they both looked content. I watched from a distance. From over her mother's shoulder, Darla gave me a wink, then vanished.

Karis turned and hugged me, cried into my chest. "Ah God, I miss her so much."

"I know you do," I said. "But you know she's all right."

She looked up at me. "I do. I know that, don't I? It doesn't really help, though."

"I don't imagine it does," I said, holding her tighter. I kissed her on the forehead. God how I loved this woman.

When Matthew returned, we told him we would take the office. He looked relieved and excited. We were still going to go to lunch and planned to do most of the paper work in the restaurant.

Before we left, I went to the closet. I had looked in the closet when we first entered the office. It had been empty. This time, it wasn't. On the floor was a plain white envelope. I didn't open it. I stuck it in my pocket and followed after Matthew and Karis.

At my house, alone, sitting at the table, I lit up a cigarette. It had been a long day.

In the morning, before heading downtown with Karis, I would stop in at Safehouse and say good-bye to Ned and Betty and clean out my office. Ned would try to stop me, until he found out about my own agency, hopefully then he would wish me luck and shake my hand.

I remembered the envelope, took it out of my pocket and stared at it.

Opening the flap, I found inside an instant lottery ticket.

I laughed. What the hell was this?

I pulled a quarter out of my pocket and scratched off the top half of the game, won five dollars. I laughed a little harder. Stuck the cigarette in my mouth, and concentrated on playing the bottom half.

Screaming, I jumped out of my chair, holding the ticket tight between thumb and finger. "I won ten thousand dollars!" I yelled. "Ten thousand and *five* dollars!"

It was payment for my services. Darla was paying me for my work. That little bastard, I loved her. This money I could use to buy a computer, some desks . . . really get the new office into shape.

Epilogue

It was the Monday morning after Thanksgiving, black ice was buried under six inches of snow. Where were all the plows? I drove carefully to the office, a white-knuckle grip on the steering wheel, the radio off.

Karis and I parked in back of the building, in a small lot. We left the front slots on Main Street open in the hopes of attracting clientele. Since opening, we've done pretty good. Several little jobs that kept the utilities paid, and gave us some cash in our pockets.

What I needed was a big case.

The ten thousand and five dollars I'd "won" helped to furnish the office. I had to also dip into my savings. But it was worth it. The place looked great.

Arriving safely, I parked next to Karis' car. We don't live together, in case you're wondering why we drive to work separately. We spend time with each other, spend nights at each other's house, but we are taking it slow.

I grabbed my laptop, closed and locked the doors. Walking down the sidewalk, I slipped and slid and did everything I could to keep from falling. I made it safely to the front of the building. I unlocked the door. The antique shop wouldn't open for another hour. I went in, re-locked the door and climbed up the stairs. It was freezing outside and the warmth in the hall was immediately appreciated.

I loved the way the printing on the stain glass looked. It was a pretty good feeling to see your name and company on the glass. I had new business cards made up, too.

"Good morning," I said to Karis. She smiled.

We kissed. "How was your night?" Karis asked.

"Good. I couldn't sleep. Nightmares."

"So you wrote?" Karis asked.

"All night."

"The books coming along?"

"Great."

"When can I read it?" She said.

I wasn't sure I wanted her to. There were things about Darla that might upset her. (Maybe I could lighten up the things I found out about and save some feelings. Yeah. That would work). "When it's done," I told her. "Hell. I'll let you edit it."

"Gee, what a treat."

She had her computer on, a notebook was opened in front of her. She was working on an article. That was fine by me. As it was, we had no clients to tend to. That was a rather depressing thought. I was confident, though, that business would pick up.

"Let me throw my lap-top in the office, then I'll run down to the bagel café and grab us some breakfast."

"Sounds great, Nick. I'm kind of hungry." She smiled and touched my hand. The glow was in her eyes. The glow she'd had in high school, but lost somewhere down the road. I loved that glow. I loved Karis with all my heart. I would do anything now to make sure that glow never again vanishes.

I went into my office.

A little boy, maybe seven years old, sat in the chair on the opposite side of my desk. His feet didn't reach the floor. They were crossed at the ankles. He looked up at me; big brown puppy dog eyes staring at me. He smiled. He was missing one front tooth.

Thinking that Karis forgot to tell me someone was here I smiled back. "Can I help you?"

"Who you talking to, dear," Karis called.

"The little boy in my office," I said, turning away from the boy. Karis was walking over to my door.

"Who? There's no one in your office," she said.

I pointed to the chair, the boy turned transparent. He waved at me right before he disappeared. "I need your help. I'll be back," I heard a distant voice promise. Was it the boy's voice?

Wonderful, I thought, Darla must be handing out my new business cards to spirits in never-never land.

About the Author

Phillip Tomasso III's first novel, the critically acclaimed thriller, *Mind Play*, was released February 2000. He was chosen as editor for an anthology of collected pieces entitled, *Dry Tales 2000*. Is is currently writing the script for the digitally animated sequal of RAVEN, byt Daredevil Films. Tomasso is the author of more than 30 published short stories and articles. His work has appeared in an array of magazines ranging from *Crossroads, Ascending Shadows, Bathory House, Mausoleum, Lost Worlds, Lynx Eye, Eclipse, Rochester Shorts, Lite, Bay Forest, Dogwood Tales, The Legions of Light* and *Western Digest,* to *Byline, Modern Dad* and *Intellectual Property Today.* He works full time as an Unemployment Insurance Hearing Representative for the Eastman Kodak Company. Phillip Tomasso III lives in Rochester, New York with his wife and their three children. Currently, he is tenaciously at work on the next Nicholas Tartaglia thriller.

Phillip Tomasso III would love to hear from you. If you wish to contact the author directly, please send e-mail messages to:

ptom3@hotmail.com

or visit his web site:

http://philliptomasso.go2click.com/